To Keep Our Honor Clean

Charles R. *"Chuck"* Dowling

TO KEEP OUR HONOR CLEAN
Copyright © 2002 by Charles R. Dowling

ISBN trade paperback: 0-9712525-0-5
Library Of Congress Card Number: 2002110624

This book was printed in the USA.

For inquiries or to order additional copies of this book, contact:

Gardenia Press
P. O. Box 18601
Milwaukee, WI 53218-0601 USA
1-866-861-9443 www.gardeniapress.com
books@gardeniapress.com

Dedication

To Chuck and Sharon,
Tim and Rosalie,
Erin and Bob.

Of course to Cody and Carson,
and Anna and Samantha.

And especially to Arlene.

I love you all.

Acknowledgements

...To Pat Hayes, owner of the delicatessen where I worked part time while in college, who regaled me with the moving adventures of a certain Private Patrick Hayes on the island of Iwo Jima during World War II. He planted the seed that eventually grew into my becoming a Marine.

...For Elizabeth and Bob at Gardenia Press, for giving me the opportunity to publish this novel.

...For Jill, my editor, who cleaned up a lot of my careless grammatical errors and made the book into something of which I can be proud.

...For the five-volume history, U.S. Marine Corps Operations in Korea, by Lynn Montross and Nicholas Canzona, et al, which provided most of the detail and background I required.

...For the senior Marine non-commissioned officers who guided my path through training and then filled me in on what combat was really like.

...And finally, for the many Korean War veterans I have talked with over the years, who never received credit for their sacrifices during "The Forgotten War." I hope this book lifts them a little higher in the estimation of the American people.

From the Halls of Montezuma
To the shores of Tripoli.
We fight our country's battles
In the air, on land, and sea.
First to fight for right and freedom,
And *To Keep Our Honor Clean.*
We are proud to claim the title
Of United States Marine.

– The Marines' Hymn, first verse

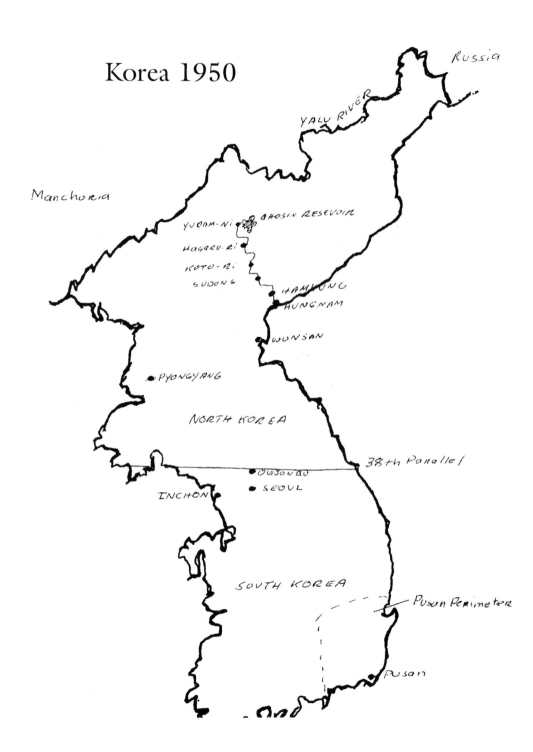

Korea 1950

1

A Question of Honor

Rain, in rampaging rivulets, raced wildly across the window while the train sped north through the driving storm. The already dim scenery was fading from view as the dreary day moved from a dismal afternoon into a dark and shiny evening. Matt sat at the window staring at the moving vista, but not really seeing it. His mind was on what lay ahead.

The old railroad car had seen better days. The green, felt covered seats were worn and some of the armrests were broken. In the center aisle, where millions of feet had trod, the dull metal floor had been rubbed shiny. Pale green paint peeled from sills and window frames. The few electric lamps that still functioned emitted a dim yellow light that flickered when the train rocked from side to side. At the end of the car, the sliding door opened and closed in rhythm with the motion of the train. The year was 1947. The war had been over for more than two years. Idly, Matt wondered why the railroad had not yet started to refurbish their equipment.

The car was less than half full. Each passenger had his own double seat. Most of the travelers were spread out, taking full advantage of the room. A few couples sat close together, their needs different from the other passengers. Matt sat alone, occupying a single seat near the rain-splattered window.

In a few hours, they would cross under the Hudson River and travel through the New York City railroad caverns to Pennsylvania Station. He would have to make his way to Grand Central Station at that point and head up the Hudson River Valley on the New York Central Railroad. His final destination — Kingmont.

Tears had filled his eyes that morning. Now they were dry. He was about to give up the life he had lived for the past three years and, the future he had dreamed of living. When he finished what he planned to do, his existence would be changed forever. From this day forward he would walk a new path, his future unknown.

As he stared at the window covered with the bobbing and weaving raindrops, he saw his reflection in the glass. His square handsome face was drawn. The confident smile that came easily to him was nowhere to be found now, replaced by something else—self-pity, fear, resolve? He noted that he looked grim, his blue eyes set deeper, his face and close-cropped hair darker. Today, the tall, sleek, athletic body seemed less athletic, less sleek, less military. He didn't look like a man of action, but more like a man with a burden.

The train proceeded on its lurching, rocking journey. Continuing to look at his somber reflection, his mind took him back to the chain of events that had led to this place and time.

* * *

Autumn in upstate New York is a special time of the year. The mantle of reds, greens, yellows and browns, the cleared fields with corn shocks and hay stacks, the pumpkins and gourds, the cool crisp air, the hint of frost, the smell of home fireplaces, the early sundown — they all create Norman Rockwell images of house and home and family.

Although this had been just such a day, the weather being wonderful and crisply fall-like, for the Flahertys, the beauty had been lost. Today they had buried Mike, beloved husband and father. He had fought a long, painful battle but the end had been inevitable.

His four sons, Matthew, Mark, Luke and John, along with their little sister Maggie sat in the living room of their comfortable old house. A late afternoon sun slanted in the through the front windows. Katie, their mother, had gone to bed, the stress of the last few days finally catching up with her. She had held up well until the end, but putting Mike into the ground had been the final step before her collapse. She was exhausted.

Mike and Katie had come a long way since they were children in New York City, fresh off the boat from Ireland with their parents. The Big War in France, when Mike had joined The Fighting 69th and had been wounded fighting the Germans, the long years lifting heavy burdens on the docks and the crushing years of the depression during the 1930s had taken their toll.

Their move to Kingmont to start a new life had worked for a while. The early 1940s, the World War II years, although one of the worst disasters in history for the world at large, became a boon for the Flahertys. They were able to buy a small farm and turn it into a happy home. Mike was able to obtain work in a defense plant near-by. Katie and their sons Matthew, Mark, Luke, and John worked the farm and the apple orchards. Together they brought in enough income to make the farm profitable.

Katie's sons were growing up strong and reliable. She was proud of them. Being a religious woman, she had named them after the four evangelists to ensure their place in heaven. Maggie, Katie's youngest, and her only daughter, was her cross to bear. Maggie was a little "slow."

* * *

Matt sat in his father's old chair. Maggie sat on the floor at his feet, playing jacks. Her hair was dark like his and she wore it in braids. Her face was pretty and although her eyes lacked a certain spark, she was obviously a loving and caring child. Luke said she looked like Margaret O'Brien. Maggie and the young actress were both eleven years old.

Since Matt had arrived home from the Naval Academy, she hadn't left his side. She seemed to sense that the torch had somehow been passed to him. He was deeply touched by her attachment. He loved his little sister with a passion even he didn't understand. He would do anything for her.

Mark sat on the sofa opposite Matt, his short, stocky frame rigid. His green eyes were fixed on his brother. He looked like a wide version of his mother except that his hair was brown. Mark was not staring at Matt as much as he was thinking things through and he did not want to shift his gaze until he finished. He looked older than seventeen.

Luke and John stood in the alcove formed by the bay window in the front of the house. They remembered the day that their father had brought that window home. A house in town was being remodeled. The workman *gave* him the window. Their father actually had to borrow a wagon and a team of horses to get it to their house. They had all laughed about it, but now, a few years later, it was a source of pride. It added just the right touch to their home.

A lamp with a colored glass shade and beaded tassels stood on a round table in the alcove. The boys stood behind it. The table was draped with a lace runner used like an antimacassar. Luke and John stared out the window. Neither wanted to speak. They seemed to need each other's presence for support. Luke, at fifteen, looked younger. Although he was tall and rangy, his face was soft. His hair was blonde, his eyes a pale blue, his face ruddy. The little peach fuzz that grew on his chin did not yet require a razor.

John was an inch or two shorter than Luke, but he had a wider chest and shoulders and chest. His face still retained a baby-faced look. He had reached the age of thirteen, but he was not yet showing any signs of physical maturity. He had his mother's auburn hair and green eyes.

"Well, I'm glad that's over." Mark broke the ice. "I love dad and I didn't want to lose him, but now that he's gone, we've got to think about moving on."

Matt looked at him a moment, his hand idly touching Maggie's hair. "You're right, Mark. Ever the practical one." A slight smile on his lip.

Mark blushed a little. "Well, it's true, isn't it? We need to discuss what comes next, don't we?" He felt he was right, but he wasn't sure of Matt's reaction.

Matt removed his hand from Maggie's tresses and ran it over his own close-cropped hair. He looked at Mark, feeling a warm familial affection for the sturdy young man. "You're right, Mark, but some of us need a little more time. It won't hurt anything to wait a few days to make decisions." He touched Maggie's head again, looked down at her and smiled. She smiled back.

Mark's way of handling his grief was to set out on a course of action, to get busy. It was the way he handled everything. Matt told him he was a little rigid, he needed to be a little more flexible. The husky young man wasn't sure what his brother meant by that. He realized however, that what Matt said was the best way for the family.

"The family?" Matt seemed to be able to hear Mark's musings. "This sure hasn't been like the Irish wakes we always heard about. Except for ourselves, we have no family."

A few of the neighbors had brought food and helped out for a few days. They were wonderful people but they were not "family." Some of Mike's pals at the plant and his friends on the police force had come by. But they were not "family," either.

"What about the insurance? We need to make a claim soon, don't we?" asked Mark, still the practical thinker.

"I'm sure we can do that two or three days from now, Chunk." Matt used his own pet name for Mark. "We don't need to rush."

"Mr. Van Scooten paid for the funeral, didn't he?" asked Luke, walking across the room and sitting on the floor by Maggie.

Mark looked at him in mild exasperation. "Yes, Luke. We don't have to worry about that, but we're still going to need the insurance money."

"Well, Mr. Van Scooten also said he would take care of us. He liked Dad and he wanted to repay Mom for all Dad did for his company."

Mark looked at Matt. Matt spoke first. "Luke, people say things sometimes and they don't follow through, especially at times like this. He probably means well but we can't depend on that."

Mark looked satisfied that Matt had backed him up.

"Besides, I'm not so sure about Mr. Van Scooten. He seems okay on the surface but there's something about him that bothers me."

"Me, too," Mark chimed in.

"I don't like the way he acts around Mom," said John, entering the conversation for the first time.

"Why? What's he done?" Luke retaliated. "He just acts like he cares for her . . . and us."

"I think he cares for her too much." John's words were harsh. "He really doesn't care for us. It's just her he wants."

"How do you know that?" asked Matt.

"I don't know." John was feeling uncomfortable. He didn't know how to express himself. Tugs of maturity were bumping against adolescence. "He just is . . . well always . . . touching her. He wants to be near her."

"He just feels sorry for her. She needs help and comfort, someone her own age," Luke continued. A stubborn look crossed his face. "Besides, I think you're jealous."

"Jealous? Why jealous?" John's face was red. "She's my mother. I'm just looking out for her."

"You always were her favorite. You don't like someone else horning in," Luke railed. John started toward him, his fists clenched.

"Hold it, Squirt!" Matt boomed. John stopped. "There'll be no fighting here. Especially on this day." Matt stood. John backed up. Luke, who had also risen to his feet, sat back down next to Maggie. Maggie looked confused. She didn't understand arguing and was worried. Matt sat down again and tousled her hair. "Don't worry, Maggie. Everything's okay."

She smiled up at him.

"I have problems with him, too," offered Mark. "There's something about him I don't trust."

"Aw, you always put people down. You don't trust anyone," said Luke defensively.

"You trust everyone. You need to become a little better judge than you are," replied Mark. He could also speak with strong words.

Matt held up his hand. He looked at each of them with a small grin on his face. "Hold it. You're both part right. We can't be too critical, but we also can't be too trusting. We'll just have to see how this plays out." Matt looked around at the group. "Also," he paused for emphasis, "we'll look at the finances tomorrow. Mom has the final say anyway. Then we'll decide, as a family, what to do next."

* * *

Mike had been buried on a Wednesday. The following Saturday, Matt was in his room packing his things for his return to the Academy. Mark, Luke, John, and Maggie had gone into to town to do some shopping. The family had spent the better part of Thursday and Friday attending to the financial details. For the most part, everything was settled.

As Matt emptied drawers and placed items into his green duffel bag, he heard music coming from somewhere in the house. Puzzled, he stopped what he was doing and listened, then went looking for the source. He didn't think it was the radio. His mother hardly ever listened to the radio and, in addition, she was the sort of person who would not participate in any sort of entertainment while she was grieving, not even radio broadcasts.

Walking down the hall, it seemed the music was coming from the living room. He wasn't sure, but it sounded like an old record that he hadn't heard in years. When he entered the room, he saw his mother, sitting in a rocking chair, with a shawl around her shoulders, her eyes closed, and a faint smile on her face. The shades had been drawn, making the room fairly dark. She was rocking gently and listening.

The lid of the old record player that she and Mike had brought from New York City when they moved to Kingmont was open and a record revolved on the turntable. The piece being played was a very old recording of *Danny Boy*, sung by John McCormick. The tone was tinny and distorted, the sounds of the accompanying instruments discordant and outdated, but the magic quality of the poetry, sung by the world's foremost Irish tenor, came through with magnificence. If the listener could somehow get past the poor quality of the recording, the wonderful sound of the man's voice was a joy.

Katie opened her eyes, looked at Matt, and broadened her smile. She said softly, "Sit down, Matt, and listen with me. This was your father's favorite piece of music. Mine, too."

Matt moved to the nearby sofa, sat down and listened in silence. The beauty of the man's voice and the sad quality of the poetry in the lyrics reached something inside him. He responded involuntarily and before the song was finished, his eyes burned and tears trickled down his cheeks. He looked at his mother. She was also crying. At that moment he felt a strong connection to her—and his father.   The tune ended.

Katie rose, went to the record player lifted the needle arm off the disk and set it in its holder. She switched the machine off, lowered the lid and returned to her rocker.

"Whenever I hear that record, I'll think of Mike." Moisture glistened on her cheeks. She wiped them with a hanky that had been rolled in her sleeve. "I know the record is so poor that it's hard to make out the words, but it's the story of a woman staying home while her lover goes off somewhere, to war, I think." A sob caught her voice and she held the small handkerchief to her nose for a moment. Regaining her control. She continued, "She pledges that she will wait for him no matter what. She tells him that she'll still be there, even if she's dead and she wants him to pray over her ... her grave. 'Say an *Ave* there for me' she says." She stopped talking, lowered her head and wept. Matt went to her and held her. Katie cried deeply and quietly for a long time.

When at last she felt she couldn't cry any longer, she gently dislodged herself from her son's arms and stood. She looked at Matt. "It really should be sung by a woman you know, but John McCormick does it so well."

"I think you needed that ... a good cry, I mean," Matt said gently.

Katie nodded. "I think so, too."

"Thank you, John McCormick," said Matt.

"Thank you, *Danny Boy*," said Katie.

2

Honor and Dishonor

Rain was descending in torrents in New York City, much as it had been when he left Annapolis. He managed to become soaked just traveling from Pennsylvania station to Grand Central station. The soaking suited his black mood. A few more hours and he would be done. His new life would then start, such as it promised to be. Earlier, he thought he had no more tears, but he had been wrong.

Mr. Van Scooten had been good to his word. He did in fact take care of them. He set up an investment trust for the boys' education and provided Katie with a monthly income. He found odd jobs for her in his home and at his factory, which didn't provide enough work to justify the generous pay he gave her, but it allowed her time to take care of Maggie, and to maintain her dignity. When she worked in his home, he somehow managed to spend time around her. She was a little surprised that a man of his stature had so much interest in the mundane workings of a household. Although he never did anything improper and there were always other people present, he did find ways to touch her, to be near her, to look at her. Katie was flattered and confused at the same time.

Matt went back to the Naval Academy and sent home what he could from his meager midshipman's pay. Mark and Luke worked part-time jobs after school and added their share to the family funds. John had a paper route. They all worked the farm when they could, including Maggie. Overall, the income was sparse but adequate.

One afternoon, near the beginning of April, six months after Mike's death, Katie was helping the Van Scooten's housekeeper prepare for the Community Chest dinner that Mr. Van Scooten was hosting at his home. They were assembling hors d'oeuvres and canapés when he came into the kitchen and beckoned to her.

"Katie, take a walk with me, please. I wish to discuss something with you." She stood up, puzzled. He seemed very formal. He had a way of always keeping her off balance. He opened the back door, ushered her through and then led the way out into the garden. She wasn't sure what he wanted, something to do with the dinner she supposed.

He was wearing a gray wool cardigan sweater over a plaid shirt and tan slacks, looking very sporty. He was handsome in an alabaster statue way. They walked for a short space to a stone bench where he sat down and patted the seat next to himself.

"Sit, please. I need to tell you something."

He appeared nervous. It was a pretty day in the garden. Although the air was cool, the sun was warm, suggesting warmer days to come. Tulips and crocus were pushing up, and the grassy areas had a new greenish tinge to them. The view of the Hudson River from this height was magnificent. Katie sat, feet together, hands in lap making sure she left a little space between them. She looked at Will expectantly.

"Kate," he fumbled a little. His thin face looked anxious. "I have something I've wanted to say to you for a while, but I was never sure when the time was right."

Katie watched him, a little puzzled. He had perspiration above his lip. She nodded to go ahead. He squirmed then took a deep breath, not looking at her but staring straight ahead. More perspiration appeared on his upper lip.

"Kate, I want . . . no, I wish to . . . ." He struggled for the right words and failed. "I want to pay court to you," he finally blurted out. Then realizing how silly that sounded, he relaxed and said, "I would like to have you for my wife." He quickly shifted his position on the bench and clarified his request. "I've wanted to ask you for months, but I didn't know when you'd be ready. I ... I want to marry you." Words ran into words. He appeared to be afraid he might lose his nerve if he stopped.

Katie sat and looked at him. All at once she became aware of how *she* looked. She wore an old print housedress and white apron. She had a small kerchief on her head to hold her hair back, sturdy, clunky shoes on her feet and no make up. She couldn't have looked worse. She pushed a strand of hair back from her face.

"Oh, I must look awful."

"Oh, no. You look beautiful."

Then, what he actually had said dawned on her. "You want to marry me? You want us to be husband and wife?" she asked, somewhat bewildered. The garden was quiet, as if even the flowers and the birds were waiting for the answer.

"Yes, Kate." He seemed to be relieved that he had been able to get that out and that she understood. "I've wanted that for some time. But, I knew I had to wait." Her eyes still reflected confusion. He took her hand and hastened to add, "Kate, don't answer yet. I know this is a shock. Maybe it's too soon. I wanted you to know of my feelings. Just give it some thought. There's no rush. We need to get to know each other."

Katie was awash with emotions. She didn't know how she felt. She needed to think.

He put down her hand and interrupted her thoughts. "Kate, I have the dinner tonight, and I have to go to Albany tomorrow, but let's take a drive on Saturday. We'll take a picnic if it's warm. We'll just get to know each other. Is that okay?"

She nodded her head, not sure why she agreed. She felt a strong need to be by herself for a while. She stood up. "Yes, we can do that," she said softly. Then, hesitantly, "I need to get back to helping Jean." She started to walk to the kitchen, with long strides, her mind whirling.

"I'll pick you up Saturday morning about ten, okay?" Van Scooten called after her.

"That will be fine," she said, turning halfway toward him as she walked. He was standing by the bench looking after her with an inscrutable look on his face. She really needed to think.

And think she did. Among many things she thought about, Katie thought back to the last time that she had had a conversation with him, before Mike died.

* * *

"How's Mike doing, Katherine?"

Katie looked up from the laundry she'd been folding. Mr. Van Scooten was standing at the screen door looking in. Tall and thin, he wore à light tan suit, white shirt, stiff collar and a blue and white bow tie. In his hands he held a white straw hat. His dark hair was parted in the middle and shined from hair oil. He exuded an essence of Eau de Cologne.

"Oh, you startled me," she said, with a touch of a brogue. The lilt of the Emerald Isle was gone from most of her speech, but when she was excited or upset, it sometimes emerged. "I didn't hear you come up."

"I'm sorry. I didn't mean to frighten you. Just passing through. I thought I'd see about Mike. We sure miss him at the factory."

Katie put down the sheet she was holding and went to the entrance-way. "Forgive me. I seem to have forgotten my manners." She unhooked the door and swung it open.

"No problem, Katherine. I stopped by unexpectedly."

"Please, come in. It's a hot day today. Would you like some lemon-ade?"

He entered the kitchen and glanced around. The door bumped shut behind him. "You've done wonders with the place, Katherine. It's a real home." He turned to her. "Yes I'd love some if you don't mind."

"Not at all. Not at all. Let me take your hat." Katie was pleased by his comment. She was proud of her house.

He handed her the Schooner and she placed it on a sideboard. She noticed he had perspiration on his upper lip and his forehead. Crossing to the icebox, she opened the top section and chipped some ice from the block in the compartment. She put it into two tall glasses and then filled them with the pale yellow fluid from the pitcher from the lower section. Electric refrigerators were becoming more popular, but Katie liked her icebox and couldn't see spending the money.

He walked around a little, looking the place over while she poured the drinks. Outside, John was playing with Maggie near the barn. Every now and then Maggie let out a squeal of delight.

"Here you are, Mr. Van Scooten. Please, have a seat."

He turned from the window and reached for the frosty glass. "Thank you, Katherine." He moved to the proffered chair and sat down. He held the glass against his forehead for a moment, feeling the coolness. "Please call me Will, if you would. We don't need to be so formal."

"Well . . ." Katie blushed a little. "It's a little hard to do that with you owning the company Mike works for, and the Bank, and you being so important and all . . ."

He laughed. "Katherine, don't let that keep us apart. We're both about the same age. We live in the same area. We're just neighbors. Since my wife died, I . . . sometimes . . . I need someone to talk to." He stopped speaking for a moment and looked at her, a little strangely, Katie thought. "I would prefer that you call me Will. May I call you Katie?" He smiled at her. Again she sensed something not quite right. He seemed unusually uncomfortable.

"As you wish . . .Will." She also felt uncomfortable.

"Great. I see we're going to get along fine."

Katie moved to sit opposite him. As she leaned over to pull the chair out, the top of her housedress fell open a little, exposing for just a second the top half of one breast. It was hard to miss the intake of his breath.

Katie realized what had happened and immediately closed her hand over the opening, blushing as she did so. "Oh, I'm sorry. This is an old dress. Apparently the top button was loose and fell off." She fumbled for words.

"Don't worry about it. Nothing to be ashamed of, just an accident." His voice was little strained. "Besides when one is as pretty as you are . . ."

Then he stopped, seemingly unsure of what to do next. She noticed the perspiration on his lip was more pronounced. He quickly took a sip of his lemonade, then started looking around the room again. Katie sat still, uncertain as to what to say. She held her hand at her dress top, keeping the garment closed.

"In any event, Katie," Van Scooten turned back to look at her again, more in control now, "how is Mike doing?"

"As well as can be expected." Katie remembered that was his original question. "He's in pain constantly. They give him something for it but it doesn't always work. I pray for him all the time. He's a good husband." Her eyes began to brim over. She wiped at them with the hanky she always kept rolled up in her sleeve. "I think it would be better if the Lord took him though. He's been such a good man. A good husband, a good father a good provider. I hate to see him suffer."

Van Scooten stood as Katie was extolling her husband's virtues. He went over to her and put his arm around her shoulder. She looked up at him in appreciation for his comfort.

"There, there, Katie. Everything will turn out all right." He held her closer. She dabbed at her eyes. Her housedress came open again. She didn't notice. He did. This time he could see the top half of both breasts. His breathing became quicker.

"Katherine, you are so beautiful. You deserve much better than this." His voice was husky now. He stroked her arm. Katie began to notice the change in him. He had seemed so solicitous, now she wasn't sure. She gently disengaged herself from him. He seemed to want to hold on, then relaxed. He turned quickly from her so she couldn't see his face. "I'm sorry, Katherine ... uh Katie. I was overcome by your grief." He stumbled through the words, still facing away. "I just wanted to hold you and comfort you."

Katie wasn't sure about his reasons, but she decided to give him the benefit of the doubt. "Thank you, mister . . . uh . . . Will. Sometimes it gets to me. I need a shoulder to cry on. You were very helpful."

"I would like to help you all I can, Katherine." He turned to face her once more. "You can always depend on me. I'm always here for you." He returned to his seat.

"That's very nice. Thank you."

They spoke about inconsequential things for a while, the war, the factory, Kingmont. It was a pleasant conversation. Then Mr. Van Scooten stood up. He came over to her and gave her a big hug. "I have to go now, Katie, but if there's anything you need, anything at all, please contact me. I'm your friend."

He was looking down at her as he held her. His eyes were darting from her face to her bodice. When he finally let her, go he turned and strode to the door quickly. She thought, a little too quickly. He spoke once more with a husky voice. "I'll stop by again in a few days to see if there's anything I can do and to see how Mike's doing then. Goodbye . . . Katie."

"Goodbye," she repeated, as he opened the door and stepped out. A moment later she heard a car start up and then pull away.

Katie was confused by the whole incident. Was he sincere or was he a lecher? She looked at her dress top again. It dawned on her that when he was holding her he could see almost her whole breast. Her temper flared. He *was* a lecher. Then reason returned. Maybe not, he *was* a man. Maybe he was sincere and he was just reacting to something he couldn't help. Men couldn't always help their reactions, particularly when it came to sex. It was how they handled it that mattered, she decided. She reasoned that Mr. Van Scooten certainly did nothing wrong. She remembered Mike liked to look at her breasts, too.

* * *

She replayed this meeting in her mind off and on for the next two days, but when Saturday came, she had not made any decisions about Mr. Van Scooten except to meet him at ten o'clock.

The ride in the country that day turned out wonderful. It led to more rides. Then they went out to an occasional dinner. Then they went out to dinner once a week. They had dinner at the Van Scooten home on a number of occasions. Will introduced her to his family and included her in his circle of acquaintances. They all accepted her with measured politeness. There was a certain "coolness" toward her. Katie was only peripherally aware of this reserve. She didn't realize she wasn't the "right class" and that she was Irish.

For her part, Katie was growing. She had worked hard all her life and had been satisfied with what she had, but now her horizons were expanding. She wouldn't have believed that such wealth existed. All the people he knew had large homes, mansions really. They all had servants. They all had big cars. They all had summer homes. They all went to Florida in the winter. It began to dawn on her that Will—she was finding it easier to call him that—Will, had all these things and that she could have them too. And Maggie could and the boys could, too. With the money Will could provide, Maggie could have the best of everything; the best schools, the best teachers, the best doctors. They would be set for life.

But, there was something about him that was different. He seemed to want her sexually. Was that bad? Didn't most marriages start that way? Romantic love first, then it grew from romantic love to real love. That's the way she and Mike had done it. With Will, it seemed different somehow. She was naive, inexperienced in matters like these. She felt ambivalent. Would she ever love Will? She didn't know. But she might. The whole thing was filled with "buts."

Up to now, she had been swept along with the wonder of it all. She hadn't been able to think logically. Now, she was beginning to think other thoughts. She began to realize how much this could mean for her daughter. The good life would be nice, but Maggie came first. He would be good for Maggie and she felt she could learn to love him. Katie finally made her decision.

In July, they agreed to marry. The wedding took place in September. Katie insisted on a Catholic wedding. The other Van Scooten's had some problems with that, but Will finally persuaded them. The whole Flaherty family was together for the occasion. Mark had joined Matt at the Naval Academy that summer and, in order to come home, he had needed special permission. Van Scooten somehow arranged that. First year midshipmen were usually little more than microbes to the academy, especially in the first few months. But, the power of Van Scooten money and high level contacts from past government contracts prevailed.

Mark and John had misgivings about the whole thing. They didn't like Van Scooten. Mark felt however, that as long as his mother was happy, he could accept the marriage. John was barely civil to his stepfather-to-be.

Matt and Luke took still different views. Luke had no problems with Van Scooten and he thought Van Scooten would be good for his mother. Matt took a wait-and-see approach. He had some misgivings but his mother seemed to be happy. And, it really was her decision.

The couple honeymooned in Jamaica and visited a few other Caribbean islands. In October, the whole family moved into the Van Scooten mansion. Luke and John had their own rooms in a separate wing of the house. Katie kept Maggie near her. Days passed and they settled into a routine.

The first hint of trouble surfaced one morning in late November. Katie came down to breakfast with a bruise on her cheek. Van Scooten had left earlier for his factory. She told Luke she had walked into a door when she went to the bathroom in the dark. Luke accepted the explanation. John wondered.

* * *

The New York Central passenger cars were in no better condition than those on the train from Baltimore. The paint was worn. The lights were dreary and they malfunctioned. The doors didn't stay shut. It was a depressing experience, but it matched Matt's mood. He looked at his watch, almost 11 p.m. He would be in Kingmont in a little more than an hour. He would have to walk. There would be no buses. He shied away from using a cab. The fewer witnesses, the better. It was still raining. He rationalized that it was only a couple of miles. He was already wet. He thought through his situation for the umpteenth time. The decision was still the same. This had to be done. His throat ached at the sadness of what his life would probably become. Honor was at stake however; the honor of the family, the honor of his mother, and his own honor. Honor had to be served. He would have it no other way. He had to keep his oath.

He also had to protect his mother—and Maggie. Perhaps most of all, he had to protect Maggie. What would happen to her if something happened to their mother? He knew that Katie shared his feelings.

* * *

Katie was delighted. It was her first Christmas in the Mansion and her whole family was going to be with her. Both Matt and Mark had been able to come home from the Academy for a few days.

The house looked magnificent. She, Maggie, and the servants had spent days festooning the halls with holly, stringing lights, decorating trees, hanging mistletoe, and cooking. There would be dozens of different types of cookies, dozens of cakes and pies, and all sorts of candies. There would be eggnog, hot buttered rum, and imported wines. On Christmas day, they would cook a turkey with all the trimmings, and the traditional Christmas goose that Will insisted on. Champagne would be served with the meal. Gifts would be exchanged in front of the large fireplace in the main room. It was to be a truly festive occasion.

When Matt and Mark arrived two days before Christmas, Mark was exhausted and after paying his respects to his mother, immediately headed for bed. Matt stayed downstairs for a while, playing with Maggie and gossiping with Luke, John, and his mother. He then asked if he could borrow a car to go into town. He wanted to shop and do a little visiting.

Luke told him that an old friend of his from high school and his father had opened a bar downtown. Jack Gannon had been Matt's best friend while they were in school, but they had drifted apart after Matt had left for the Academy. Suddenly, Matt was eager to see him again.

He stopped in a number of stores along the main street, smiling at the warmth of the season as he moved among the bustling shoppers. He bought something for each of his brothers and he bought a bunch of presents for Maggie. He bought a simple globe terrarium with African Violets for his mother. The lady in the florist shop had been very helpful. She wrapped the globe with great skill. It looked like a green basketball with a red ribbon. It was an inexpensive gift, but he knew his mother, who now had everything, loved violets and would appreciate the thought.

When Matt left the florist, he noticed that there was a music store across the street. On a whim, he crossed the thoroughfare and entered the shop. There were a dozen people moving among the bins and the aisles, mostly teenagers. The clerk, a pretty high school girl, approached him. "Can I help you?"

"Irish music? What records do you have in Irish music? Maybe some songs?" He was a little uncertain of how to ask for what he wanted.

The girl wrinkled her brow. "I'm not sure. Maybe over here." She led the way to the record bins on the far wall. As they neared them, Matt noted that the records in this area were grouped by ethnic type. He looked along the wall, Spanish, German and Irish! There *was* an Irish section.

"Thank you. I see where they are now."

"You're welcome," she said sweetly. "If you want to listen to any of them, we have cubicles in the back." She pointed to a row of small, square stalls with glass doors.

"Thanks again. I just might want to do that."

The records were organized by artist. He flipped through them. The words *Danny Boy* caught his eye. He pulled the record out. A performer named Carmel Quinn sang it. He had never heard of Carmel Quinn. He looked through the remainder of the paper covered black platters but there were no other *Danny Boy* records. He went back to Carmel Quinn and turned it over. *Galway Bay* was printed on the label on the other side. Intrigued, he took the record to the listening booth.

Halfway through the recording, he knew he had found a gem. Tears glistened at the edges of his eyes. Carmel Quinn had the most beautiful voice he had ever heard, deep and throaty, but with an astonishing range. She sang with a soft brogue. She put more feeling into every word of the sad ballad than he realized anyone could be capable of. And his mother had been right. The lyrics to *Danny Boy* were for a woman to sing. He had his special present for his mother.

When he went outside, it was beginning to snow. Just big, light flakes at this point. The air was cold. He put all the bundles in the trunk of the car, but he kept the African Violets up front. He drove to where Luke had told him Jack's place was and parked across the street. Matt didn't want to leave the flowers in the cold car so he took them with him.

Jack and his father had named the place *The Shamrock Inn*. The bar was in a storefront location on a side street. It wasn't far from the Van Scooten factory where Matt's father, Mike, had worked after Van Scooten had moved some of his operations from Poughkeepsie.

The name was spelled out in gold letters on a green background over the glass front. Neon Ballantine Beer "three ring" signs hung in the upper part of the two large windows. The glass on the windows and the door was painted a dark, opaque color from the bottom up to about eye level. The lights inside were low. At the moment Matt entered, the jukebox was playing Christmas carols.

He looked around the dim interior, trying to acclimate himself. Two men were at the bar, wearing overalls and plaid jackets. Each had a bottle of beer in front of them. They turned to look at him when he entered, then turned back to their beers. There were no booths in the bar. Chairs and tables constituted the seating arrangements. At the back a group of men had put some of the tables together, and if laughter was to be the deciding factor, they were enjoying themselves immensely.

The waiter was delivering a tray of beers to them when he looked up at Matt. It was Jack. He did a double take and then bounded over, put the tray down, and opened his arms as surged forward.

"Matt, how the hell are you? I haven't seen you in a coon's age." He wrapped Matt in a bear hug. Matt had forgotten how strong Jack was. He almost dropped the terrarium.

"Jack. Jack. It's good to see you again," he said between gasps. Jack turned him loose and held him at arm's length so he could look at him.

"God, Matt, you look great. The navy's been good to you."

"You too, Jack." He put the wrapped globe on a table.

Jack was about well over six feet with broad shoulders. He had short brown hair and blue eyes. He had been Matt's blocking back when Matt was the tailback on their high school football team. Thanks mostly to this dynamic duo, the team had been undefeated their senior year.

Matt waved his arms around. "You got your own business. That's great."

"Me and Dad. He's in the back. Want to say hello?"

"Sure. He retire from the police force?"

"Yep, last year. Bit of a disability. He got hurt in a car chase. Fine now though."

They stepped through a swinging half door behind the bar and stepped into the back room. Jack's father was putting beer bottles into a cooler. He looked up, saw Matt, and a big smile crossed his broad face. "Hey, sailor boy. How you doing?" He straightened up and stuck out a big paw. He was almost as big as his son and the handshake hurt. Matt remembered Frank Gannon as a hard, but fair, cop. He'd take his nightstick to a wayward youth's backside before he'd arrest him. Matt had felt the "stick" only once. The teenagers around Kingmont respected Officer Gannon. Very few were ever arrested. Very few caused trouble.

Frank came to the front with them so they could talk and watch the customers at the same time. They reminisced a little. Frank remembered the time he had to "paddle" Matt. They both laughed. Frank also remembered that Matt's father had come by after that and thanked him. Matt hadn't known that. He noticed, however, that right after Frank brought up the incident about Mike's visit, his face changed. It was as if he had thought of something. He continued the "old days" discussion with Matt and Jack, but there was definitely something on his mind.

After awhile, the noisy group in the back began to break up. They started to drift out of the bar in small groups, calling out Christmas greetings as they went. Frank grabbed one of them and asked him to stay a minute. The man shrugged, ordered another beer and sat back down. After the group was gone, Frank brought Matt over to meet him.

"Matt, this is Lieutenant McQuinn, *Detective Lieutenant* McQuinn. Pat, this is Matt Flaherty, Mike's son. The one who's in the Naval Academy."

A strange look crossed McQuinn's face. Matt stared at him a minute. He was in his fifties, gray, wiry hair, a little paunchy and a little puffy in the face. He wore a rumpled suit, tie askew. Matt could see the small pistol at his belt. McQuinn held out his hand.

"Happy to meet you. Mike was a great guy. I was sorry to see him go."

Matt took his hand. He remembered him from the funeral. He also noticed the lieutenant was just a little tipsy. His speech was a faintly slurred and his eyes focused properly only on an intermittent basis. Matt hadn't thought about it earlier, but apparently the whole group that had been sitting at that table had been cops.

"Pat, I think you need to tell him about . . . you know, the case you worked on and had to give up."

McQuinn looked at Frank, first with anger, then with uncertainty. "I don't know Frank. That's all past now. Why dig it up?" He glanced at Matt, showing a little hesitancy.

"Pat," Frank said, his pique showing, "I know you've been following what's been going on. You know the dangers that exist. You can't just pass it by."

McQuinn looked up at Gannon. His eyes were bleary. His thought process was slow, but what Frank was saying sank in. "Okay, Frank. I'll tell him. Mind you, don't you ever tell anyone I told him."

Frank looked satisfied. "Not from me, Pat. Not from me." He grabbed Jack and motioned him away. Jack looked at his father, puzzled. They left Pat and Matt in the back of the bar.

The lieutenant fumbled around for a moment. "Kid. I don't know where to start." He was wrestling with the effects of the alcohol while trying to form his words. Matt noticed that he shoved the almost full bottle of beer out of reach. "Let me ask you a question first."

Matt nodded.

"How well do you know Wilhelm Van Scooten?"

Old wives' tales say that a person feels a chill when someone walks over the spot where their grave is going to be. Someone must have just walked over Matt's grave. He felt himself shudder. "Why? I don't know. What do you mean?" He fumbled the words.

McQuinn's eyebrows pressed together. He persisted. "How well do you know him?"

Matt thought a moment. "Well, I guess I know him a little. He's an important man around here. He's wealthy. He does a lot in the community." He was looking at McQuinn, his eyes searching the policeman's eyes, as he spoke.

McQuinn was shaking his head. "No, I mean *really* know him. How he thinks. What his virtues are. What his *vices* are." He put a peculiar emphasis on the word vices.

Matt's emotions were unclear. He was starting to become a little frightened. He firmed his voice however. "What are you trying to say, lieutenant? Does he have problems?" He hoped he had mistaken the policeman's intent.

McQuinn laughed. "You might say that."

Matt waited, hopes sinking further.

"He's been a frequent visitor to a number of brothels in Poughkeepsie and Albany for twenty years."

Although shocked, Matt felt a need to mitigate that statement. "Hell, lieutenant, lots of guys go to whores . . . once in awhile," he added weakly.

"He always wants kinky sex. Nothing normal or straightforward," McQuinn continued.

"Some guys are like . . . ."

"And he often beats them up after." McQuinn interrupted.

That stopped Matt.

"We think he may have killed one of them, in Poughkeepsie." The words were as harsh as the reality. "She was found dead in the woods. The evidence was pretty good, but when the police tried to pursue it, they were pulled off the case. There were more important things to do than investigate dead prostitutes. Nothing ever happened. It just died. Like the girl" He smiled, a sarcastic twist to his mouth.

Matt was confused. In his world, things like this did not happen. He understood that there was evil out there and that some men were less than honorable, but Van Scooten? "You're really giving me something to think about. My head is spinning."

"So's mine, but mine's from the beer," he said, with a sardonic laugh. Then he became serious again. "Kid, I don't mean to laugh about this. There's a problem here. This is serious. You need to be warned." He stopped what he was saying and looked at Matt. He seemed to be making a decision. "Everything I've told you up to now could have been gotten by you, just by asking the right people. What I'm going to tell you now could cost me my job or worse if it got out." He looked over to the bar, where Frank was in a conversation with the two men in overalls. Jack wasn't in sight. "I'm doing this for Mike. Mike was a good guy. He helped me out once. I don't forget." He looked back at Matt, his face reflecting a sheepish smile. "You're a lot like him."

"You mean there's more?" Matt's mood was sinking still further. The compliment went right by him.

"Yeah, Kid. Much more." The detective's speech was improving, becoming less slurred. His eyes were beginning to clear. "Did you know he was married years ago?" McQuinn was back in the questioning mode.

"Yeah. She died, didn't she? Maybe fifteen, twenty years back."

"Right. In 1928. Do you remember how she died?"

"No, I guess I never knew. He just told us she died. We didn't question it. It was a long time ago." Matt's stomach was churning. He suspected where this was leading.

"She was murdered, Kid." He stopped to let that sank in. "Hell, Kid, what's your name? It's Matt, right?" he suddenly recalled. "I can't keep calling you 'Kid.' You're too old for that."

Matt sat waiting for the other shoe to drop.

"Now comes the part I risk my job for. Maybe my life." He looked around the bar. "Van Scooten killed her. I'm as sure of that as I am my own name. He had already beaten her a number of times. People saw her with cuts and bruises. They just minded their own business. She called the police once or twice, but you know how that goes. It's hard for men to believe that a man will beat his wife without a good reason, especially a big wheel. The guys at the station, they just brushed it off. She stopped calling, then one time he went too far."

Matt sat in stunned silence, his mind working. Then he asked, "How did they explain her death? If it wasn't him, who killed her?"

"A burglar," responded McQuinn with disgust, as he sat back in his chair. "There was no real evidence of a burglary. Someone broke a window and left it open. They tossed a few drawers. They took some sculptures. That's all that was missing. The story was that she surprised the burglar and he beat her to death. Bullshit. She was naked. Her nightgown was torn and thrown in a corner. There were semen stains on the floor. Did the burglar rape her? I doubt it. The autopsy showed no signs of rape, at least vaginally. It did show semen in her mouth and stomach. The room also showed signs of a struggle. She was beaten. Burglars don't take time to beat people. She had bruises where she had them before, on her face and neck." He stopped and looked at the young man, with deadly serious eyes. "Matt, she was murdered, and Van Scooten is the killer."

Matt stared at the wily cop. "You couldn't prove this? Did it ever get to court?" But then Matt stopped. He knew it hadn't. "I guess not or everyone would have known it."

"Matt, your confusion is understandable. It was all hushed up." He looked at Matt, his face darkly serious. "I was the first detective on the scene. I started the investigation, and then I was suddenly reassigned to a disappearance case. Some man had disappeared the year before. Now they needed someone to track down those clues. What happened to that investigation last year? Why didn't they assign someone last year? They said they didn't have the manpower last year, and on and on."

He stared steadily at Matt. His eyes were focused. "They just wanted me out. I'm not part of the right clique." He looked off into space. "I ran down all those clues on the missing guy. I ran all over the state. They were dead ends."

He looked back at Matt. "When I got back, the Van Scooten case was closed. They had checked the state files for similar MOs. They had put out bulletins and all that. They 'knew' it was a burglar but without any other physical evidence, they could go no further."

Matt's mind was working furiously. He realized he couldn't go back and stir up the old case again if a detective with 30 years on the job couldn't get it reopened. What he should do is put his mind to what he needed to do to protect his mother and his brothers and sister. How was he going to do all that? He'd have to think hard.

McQuinn reached over and grabbed Matt's arm. "There's one more thing, just an observation. The two women, the pro and his wife, were both slim women with sort of reddish, curly hair."

"Like my mother."

McQuinn nodded. "Matt, be careful. Don't do anything stupid." He seemed to have read Matt's mind. "I told you this so you could protect your mom. That's what Frank had in mind. You'll have to figure out how to do it. Maybe you should tell her. Don't use my name though." He looked at Matt with concern. "Frank was right to tell you about this. I've been trying to forget it for so long . . . ." He trailed off. Then he turned to Matt again. "You need to be on guard." He stood up. "I've got to go now. If I can help, I will. It's best for you though if no one knows I'm helping. If I can answer any questions, I will. Give my best to your mom. I don't know her well, but what I saw, I liked. Good luck." Lieutenant McQuinn walked, almost perfectly, across the room and out the door.

Matt sat for a while, thinking. After a few minutes, Frank came over and sat down with him. "I guess you got an earful."

Matt nodded. He was in a state of shock. He could not think clearly.

"McQuinn's a straight shooter. You can accept what he says as gospel." Frank wiped the table absently with a cloth he had in his hand. "If Jack or I can help you in any way, let us know. I don't know what I'd do in your case. Right now, I'd suppose you don't know either. All I can say is, don't do anything stupid. Think it through first. Come back to me or to Pat for help. We still got a few connections."

Matt looked at Frank in appreciation. Jack came over at that point. Matt stood up. "Well, it's getting late and I got some thinking to do. What a great Christmas this is going to be. Oh, yeah." A thought occurred to him. "The lieutenant mentioned that my dad did a favor or something for him once. Do you know what that was?"

"Sure. It goes back a few years," said Frank. "It was in Pat's uniform days. Before he made detective. Some guys jumped him in an alley. There were six of them. Mike was going by and saw the commotion. He didn't know McQuinn, but he saw that the guy getting the worst of it was a cop. He yelled out, ran down the alley, and started beating on Pat's attackers. It was touch and go for a few minutes, but then some other guys from the factory heard the noise and they pitched in. It was over in minutes. Probably saved Pat from some crippling injuries or worse."

"Thanks, Mr. Gannon. I never knew that."

"It's Frank, Matt. Frank. Mr. Gannon was my father," he said with a twinkle.

Matt left in a state of confusion. He forgot the violets. He had to go back the next day and pick them up.

Two days later, Christmas Day, he was still uncertain about what to do. The twenty-one-year-old midshipman was miserable. He had no idea how to handle this situation. He tried to put on a good face so he wouldn't spoil everyone's holiday. It was difficult, but for the most part, he was able to pull it off. He fooled his mother and Luke. Mark and John noticed something was different, but they didn't bring it up. Van Scooten also didn't seem to notice anything, but their relationship had never been more than polite and formal anyway.

His mother loved the violets but she almost broke down when she saw the record. She looked at Matt with a special sort of smile.

For the rest of the day, Matt watched Van Scooten closely for any signs of irrational behavior. There were none. Quite to the contrary, he seemed very caring and solicitous of Katie. He waited on her from time to time. He brought her little snacks and goodies from the kitchen and filled her glass when it was empty. They were even seen holding hands a few times. His mother seemed happy.

A few days after Christmas, the time came for him and Mark to return to the Academy. He was beginning to think that perhaps McQuinn was overreacting. But that just didn't seem logical to him. McQuinn was an experienced professional. Yet Matt had seen no evidence of any sort of problem. He had seen only marital bliss.

He finally made a tentative decision. He told John about the possibility of some problems. He didn't tell him everything. He told him just enough so that John would watch and keep his eyes open. John was to particularly watch for any signs of violence or beating. John remembered the bruised cheek and mentioned it to Matt. They both agreed it wasn't enough to go on yet. John was to report anything bad to Matt, however, as soon as he could, by telephone. He told John he picked him over Luke because he knew John didn't like Van Scooten and would be more conscientious about watching him. He also felt that Luke, although older, was a little too easily taken in by people.

Matt also talked again to McQuinn and told the lieutenant that John would be watching for anything unusual. If he saw anything, he would call Matt at the academy. McQuinn suggested having a uniformed patrol stop by the house on a routine basis on some technicality. The officer would be on some insignificant mission, but would ask for the lady of the house, just so he could ascertain if she was okay. This strategy would show a uniform in the area regularly. The idea was protection through prevention. Matt agreed.

Lastly, on the trip back to Annapolis, he told Mark. He told him the whole story, except for McQuinn's part in the old murder. Now Mark now knew more than John did. This was done in case something unforeseen happened to him. He had been afraid to tell Mark while they were still in Kingmont. Having one more person who was aware of the story while they were still near Van Scooten, could have jeopardized the situation. Mark was a little hurt by not being included earlier, but he finally understood. It was Mark's first contact with *need to know* exclusions. This was something he would experience many times during his career in the military.

He had agonized over whether to tell his mother or not. If Van Scooten was a wife beater, she needed to know. If on the other hand, he was not a wife beater or he had reformed, then he didn't want to interfere with her happiness or to put unnecessary suspicions into her mind. In the long view, he finally decided that the "early warning" system he had set up with John and the police would protect her from serious harm and still allow the couple to have a normal life if his fears were unwarranted.

3
Crossing the Rubicon

"Bancroft Hall. Midshipman Ransome speaking."

"This is . . . uh . . . can I speak to Midshipman Flaherty? Matthew Flaherty, please?"

"Who's calling?"

"Uh . . . John Flaherty. I'm his brother. I need to speak to him about a family matter."

"Flaherty. Roger. Wait one."

The handset was left to dangle from the wall phone as the CQ (Charge D'Quarters) went in search of Matt.

Three minutes later, Matt picked up the phone. "Midshipman Flaherty speaking, sir." The CQ hadn't told him who was on the line.

"Matt, it's John."

Matt's heart sank at the sound of John's voice. It had been almost three months since he had come back to the Academy, and there had been no problems. He had finally been able to shove the worry to the back of his mind. He was actually starting to think it was all a tempest in a teacup. "What's up, John? Trouble?"

"Yes. I think it's bad."

Acid seeped into Matt's stomach. "What do you mean 'bad?'"

"Today, I came home from school and Jean told me Mom hadn't left her room all day. Jean thought she was sick. No food. Just stayed in bed. Kept the curtains drawn, all that. I went up to see her. She was asleep. I went in the room, I would never do that but . . . well, you wanted me to watch things."

"You did right, John. What happened?"

"I opened the curtains and then I looked at her. He beat her, Matt." There was a catch in his speech, like someone holding back a sob. "One eye was closed. She had a lump on her forehead and she had a cut on her lip. I don't know what else. I saw bruises on her neck. She covered herself up and told me to leave. I left." The tinny echo from the phone couldn't hide the concern in the young voice. "Matt, he's an animal."

Matt could hear the near panic. Perhaps he had been wrong in putting the responsibility in John's hands. "John. It's okay. You did right. Did Mom go to the doctor or hospital?"

"No. She refused. She told Jean later that she fell, and she'd be okay in a day or two. I told her we ought to call the police. She got upset. She begged me not to do that and denied everything. She said they would only make a big deal out of nothing."

"Damn, that proves it, doesn't it?" Matt was thinking out loud. "Okay, but she needs to get checked out. There could be more damage."

"I'll try again, Matt, but I don't think she'll listen."

"Okay, John. Try again. Tell her you're worried she might be hurt more than she knows. You know, internal injuries or something."

"Matt. There's a little more."

Matt closed his eyes. An ache was developing behind them. What next?

"I didn't see Van Scooten this morning but Luke did. He said he had scratches on his face. Van Scooten told him he scratched himself on a wire in the closet. Luke said they looked like four fingernail scratches to him. Luke also said that he'd had breakfast with them a couple of times in the last week and they seemed to be, I don't know, cool I guess is the word. You know, to each other."

Matt remained silent, listening.

John took a deep breath then he spoke again. "Matt, I told Luke all about it. I think I need his help. He was hurt you didn't include him. He's with us now. He hates him, too."

"That's okay, John. I probably should have told him. At the time it seemed best. Tell him I'm sorry." He was coming to a decision. "John, don't say anything to anyone yet. You can tell Luke though." His thoughts rambled a little. "I'll be coming home to talk to Van Scooten. We've got to put a stop to this now. I'm going to have it out with him. I don't know what I'll say, but I'll find something. That's the last time he'll lay a hand on her."

"We can sure use you, but can you get away? Will they let you go?"

"I'll get away, John. It may take me a few days, but I'll be there."

* * *

It took almost a week.

He had to convince his commanding officer that he needed emergency leave for family problems. Trying to provide enough information, while not revealing too much, was difficult. His mother was hurt. He was the oldest. He had to be there. He shuttled back and forth between the Chaplain's office and his CO for three days. Finally, he received the leave. The paperwork took another day.

He decided not to wait for a train. He hitchhiked. Getting to the George Washington Bridge wasn't too difficult but getting upstate took a while. The State Police picked him up. They had to verify his story. That took the better part of a day. He finally arrived in Kingmont at two o'clock in the morning, six days after John's phone call.

* * *

Matt entered the house through the kitchen door. It was the only key he had. The house was dark, everyone asleep. He was quiet, not wanting to wake anyone. He walked cautiously through the hall to the main stairway, the intention being to catch a few hours sleep and confront Van Scooten in the morning. He was about to turn left toward the wing where Luke and John's rooms were when he heard a noise coming from somewhere upstairs. He thought it was a woman's voice, a cry for help. Was it his overworked imagination? He stopped and listened a little longer, straining for any sound, but heard nothing. Perhaps his imagination was working overtime.

He turned back to continue down the hall toward the other wing when he heard the sound again. It was someone crying out, a woman's voice. He was sure this time. He turned and ran up the stairs. Trying to be as silent as possible. He headed down the hall toward their bedroom deliberately, placing one foot down before lifting the other. When he arrived at the door, he could hear distinct words.

Van Scooten was yelling, "Suck you bitch. Suck. You're not sucking hard enough. Suck or I'll beat the shit out of you."

Another voice, muffled, a woman's voice crying, pleading. "Please, Will, I'm doing what I can."

"No you're not. Suck harder. That's the only thing that works." There was the sound of a slap, then a whimper.

Matt's face was white. He had heard enough. He tried the handle. It was locked. He backed up and launched himself at the door. The flimsy frame gave way on the first impact. Splinters flew and the door snapped open, partially clinging to the broken wooden casing as it banged against the wall. Matt tumbled into the room.

What he saw fulfilled his darkest visions. Van Scooten sat on the edge of the bed, naked from the waist down. Katie, totally naked, was on her knees with her head in his crotch. She had just released his penis from her mouth. He had his right hand tangled in her hair. He had been pulling her hair in order to hold her head in place.

Matt was angry enough when he crashed through the door. Now he became a madman. That was his mother being abused!

He was across the room before either Van Scooten or his mother could move. He brushed her aside roughly and landed on Van Scooten. Van Scooten fell back on the bed in surprise, releasing Katie's hair. Matt grabbed him by his shirtfront and pulled him up and then with all the strength he could muster in his young, athletic, body he smashed a fist right into Van Scooten's nose. Bone and cartilage crackled with the blow. Blood spurted.

Matt yelled, "Bastard."

Van Scooten fell back onto the bed completely stunned. Matt grabbed his shirtfront again and hit him flush in the face once more, yelling "bastard" again as he did so. More blood flew. More bone crackled.

He hit him a third time, again flush in the face, and then holding him by the shirt with one hand, he lifted him up by the other. Van Scooten's face resembled a bloody piece of meat. He was somewhere between terror and unconsciousness. Blood poured down his chin and onto his neck. Matt pushed his face into Van Scooten's mangled countenance and screamed at him. "That's my mother, you bastard, not some slut. That's a woman, not an animal." Spit flew from his lips into Van Scooten's bulging eyes

Matt reared back from his hapless victim's face, and slammed his fist into his stomach. Van Scooten whooshed as he lost his air. Matt picked him up, one hand on his shirt and one on his crotch and twirled him around over his head. Then, with a grunt, he threw him across the room, his fingernails cutting into Van Scooten's scrotum as he released his hold. He was yelling "bastard," over and over. The shirt tore in the process and the thin Poltroon landed in a grotesque lump near a corner.

By this time Katie was attempting to stop her wildly flailing son. She had her arms wrapped around his body from the rear. She tried to wrap her legs around his legs to slow him as he was straining to reach the unconscious Van Scooten. She had never seen him like this. Matt was in a blind rage. She would have thought he would be satiated at this point, but he seemed to need to punish his victim even more for his atrocities.

Somehow, through the red haze of his lost temper, though, her efforts to control him had an effect. Before he reached the fallen wife beater, the bizarre nature of his situation began to sink in. His *mother* was holding him. She was actually wrapped around him and she was *naked*. He stopped. He stood for a second catching his breath. Some additional measure of control returned. Then he relaxed. He turned his head and spoke to her softly.

"It's okay, Mom. I'm done."

They both relaxed.

"Let's get some clothes for you."

Katie released him, and at that point, realized she was naked. She turned quickly to find cover. Matt had already picked up a blanket and was wrapping it around her. She looked at him with tears flowing. They were tears of embarrassment, gratitude and fear. "Oh, Matt. I'm so sorry you had to see this. He's really not a bad man. It's just sometimes he loses control."

"He's a bastard," growled Matt through clenched teeth, looking back at the pile of beaten humanity in the corner. "Men don't beat women. He's a coward and . . . ."

"No, Matt, no he's not." She interrupted and then stopped. She couldn't defend him any more. "Matt, it's only when the . . . rage hits him."

"What rage? He's an animal. He's a spoiled brat who got older. He was never disciplined. He never learned to control himself. Men, real men, don't beat women. They don't force sex on women, even their wives. Real men have honor. They don't let rages take them over like that. He's an animal in heat. Human beings control those urges. Animals don't."

He stopped talking, his anger somewhat reduced. Katie turned and looked at her husband. He was still unconscious. "He's okay, isn't he?"

"I don't know. It wouldn't bother me if he was dead."

"Oh, don't say that, Matt. That would be murder." She went over to Van Scooten. He was still breathing, although the gasps coming through the blood and mangled nose sounded terrible. "He's hurt bad, Matt. What are we going to do?"

Matt walked over. Knelt down and raised Van Scooten's head. He moaned and started to open his eyes.

"He'll make it, Mom. He's not hurt real bad. Broken nose maybe. He won't look as pretty." He dropped Van Scooten's head back on the floor without any attempt to be gentle. "But what about you? You look kind of beat up to me."

Katie had bruises, cuts and scratches in a number of places on her face, arms and neck. There was still a red hand imprint on her cheek where he had slapped her. Matt couldn't see beneath the blanket.

Katie went over to her firstborn and embraced him. She held him tight. Matt put his arms around her. "I'm okay. These will heal." She touched her face as she buried it into his chest. "I can't go to a doctor. He'll want to know how it happened. You can't hide things from a doctor. In a week or two, these will be gone." She was touching bruises on her arm.

"Maybe you should still go to a doctor, even if he does figure out what happened."

"Matt. No. No. I don't want the scandal. We can't do that." She was pleading. We have to think of Maggie. She could lose everything."

* * *

Neither Van Scooten nor Katie went to a doctor that night. When Van Scooten came around, he wanted to call the police but Matt dropped a few hints about Van Scooten's past and he backed off. The first wife was not mentioned, just the prostitutes. Van Scooten grudgingly agreed to accept the beating. His nose *was* broken, his wrist was sprained, and his lips and face were cut in a number of places. His groin ached. Walking was torture for him. Later, after thinking it through, they decided they needed medical care after all. They concocted a story to cover both of their injuries, about the brakes failing on their car and banging their faces into the dashboard and some sharp glass when they hit a wall. Then they went to a doctor.

* * *

Matt slammed the door of Van Scooten's study. He walked over to the desk where the injured husband sat waiting. Van Scooten's hand trembled slightly as he touched the white bandage that covered his nose. His other arm was in a sling. He followed Matt's movements warily. Matt pulled a chair up to the side of the fine cherry-wood piece of furniture, swung his leg over the back of the seat, and straddled it as he sat. He brushed some papers, which had been on the desk, onto the floor. He leaned forward across the corner and glared at Van Scooten, his young, athletic body rigid, his handsome face now contorted with malice.

"I need to leave soon but I need to *discuss* a few things with you first." It was difficult for him to speak civilly. He set his jaw firmly. "Over the last couple of days I've spoken to my mother quite as bit." His eyes told the trembling Van Scooten that Matt was barely restraining himself. "She has agreed to stay with you in this house," he shook his head, "though for what reason, I can't fathom. I don't think you will be sharing a bedroom, but that's up to her." Matt's eyes flashed real contempt. "Note shithead, I said that's up to *her*." Van Scooten flinched. "And, by the way, just so you know who's in charge here, let me tell you what I know about your background."

He smirked when he thought about the impact his words might have.

"If anything happens to her again, in addition to the personal beating you'll get from me—a rematch of our bedroom tussle—" He waited a minute for the reaction and smiled as Van Scooten visibly shuddered, "all the following information will find it's way into the newspapers, police department and wherever else I can put it."

Van Scooten swallowed.

"You have gone to prostitutes in the past. I also suspect you might still be doing that. You had a reputation of beating them. A prostitute you were once involved with was battered and killed. Your first wife died under mysterious circumstances. She also had been beaten. You have as of this point, beaten your present wife at least two times. There is some evidence of a third time." He looked at his prey intently. "Is all this clear?"

Van Scooten nodded, perspiration staining the facial bandages. The room was not warm.

"Good. Now let me tell you what I think of someone like you." He looked him over from side to side. "You are an animal."

Van Scooten winced, his tongue licking his cut lips. He had always thought of himself as a gentleman. If he were in Europe, he would be a nobleman.

"You are a man without a shred of decency. You have no honor whatsoever. You beat women. Men don't beat women. You can't be any baser than that unless you beat children, too. You were probably raised as a spoiled brat and, although you hide it as an adult, you are still a spoiled brat. I'll bet you were never told 'no.'"

"I do all sorts of charity work. I have taken care of your family . . . ." He had summoned up enough courage to defend himself a little.

"Don't give me that shit," Matt roared. Van Scooten winced again. "You had some kind of an ulterior motive for all of that. Maybe you just wanted to make it with my mother. I don't know."

He looked at the wretch before him with contempt. Then, seemingly, he relaxed. "But I have to try to understand." He spoke with mock gentility. "Lots of marriages start with sex." His eyes sharpened their focus. "They don't get to this point, however." He went back on the attack. "What you do is to use your money, your position, your power, and all that shit to get your way, and I repeat what I said before. You are an animal. You have no honor. You raise money for charity to enhance your standing in the community. That's good for business. Maybe there's nothing wrong with that, but *admit* the reason. Don't use it like a shield. It's business."

Van Scooten wasn't sure where this was going. Matt interrupted his speech and stared at him for a moment.

"I'm rambling." He was barely controlling himself. "My anger gets to me sometimes. In case my message hasn't gotten through to you though, let me reinforce what I have said." He took a breath. He wanted to be clear with his message. "I consider you less than human. The only way to deal with non humans is with force. So I use force."

He leaned close to Van Scooten's face again. Van Scooten backed off a little. His bowels surged, fear still showing.

"If you ever hit my mother again, I will kill you. I hope I am making myself clear. Do you understand what I am saying?"

Van Scooten nodded.

"If you ever force her to do anything she doesn't want to do, I will kill you. Understand?"

He nodded again.

"If my mother or any member of my family is ever cut off from any money or inheritance they have coming, I will also kill you." He looked at the thin man he so hated. "Am I clear?"

Van Scooten swallowed and nodded.

Matt stood up and started to walk to the door. He turned back to the wretch he had been browbeating. "You might want to consider professional help for your . . . uh . . . *cravings*." He smiled, again, in contempt. "I don't mean a whore, I mean a doctor."

Then he looked at him in pity. "But what you really need is to just become a man. Men develop some discipline. You don't have any discipline. That's why you are so despicable. You are not sick. You just don't have one shred of maturity or control in you. You are a spoiled brat, who has grown up and become dangerous." He turned to the door, opened it and then turned back. "Remember my oath to you about the consequences to you for any," he smiled maliciously, "bad actions on your part . . . *any* bad action." He looked for the last time at Van Scooten. "I keep my oaths."

* * *

Matt went back to the Academy and the situation quieted. For a time, Will and Katie lived apart. But after a little more time they reconciled and started living together again. None of the boys were happy about that. All she would tell them was, "Things will be better. Maggie will be better off." It was their mother's choice. They made sure of that. All in all, circumstances appeared to be greatly improved. Both Matt and Mark were able to come home for only a short time that summer. Matt had to take a class of first year midshipmen though initial training. Mark had to go on a training cruise. Luke and John were keeping a watch on the situation, but things stayed calm.

Then the phone call in October broke the bubble.

* * *

Matt was now walking in the rain from the railroad station to the house. It had rained hard here, too. In addition to the soaked streets, there were a lot of leaves and small branches down. Footing was precarious in spots. The sky was overcast, so little light from the moon or stars filtered through. The streetlights reflecting on the wet streets created a black and glistening world.

He couldn't get the phone call out of his mind. Luke and John had put Maggie on the phone. She was to tell Matt exactly what she heard.

"I heard Mommy scream. She said 'you're hurting me.' Then he said some things I couldn't hear. Then I heard a slap. Like when Angela slapped me at school. I heard Mommy cry. I couldn't open the door." She was crying a little. Luke urged her on.

"I know it's hard, Maggie, but you've got to tell Matt what he said." Maggie wiped her eyes.

"It was funny. I don't know what it means. They didn't have anything to eat in their room."

"Go ahead and tell him any way, honey." Matt was puzzled by the food comment. "He said, 'Suck harder, you bitch. Suck harder. It's not working. Suck harder."

A chill coursed through Matt's body. The same words. Maggie could not have made them up. He had to protect his mother. He had to protect Maggie.

Now Matt was at the house. No lights were on. It was dark just like the last time. He reached inside his jacket. He had his return ticket to New

York City. He had some cash. He would wait until just before dawn, so he could arrive back in town just in time to catch the six a.m. train.

Time passed, and then he bowed his neck and strode purposefully across the lawn. Matt went inside, again through the kitchen door. He was sad and a little worried. His new life was about to start. Where it would take him, he knew not, but the die was about to be cast, the Rubicon was about to be crossed.

* * *

When Luke and John came down for breakfast later that morning, they found an envelope on the kitchen table. It was addressed to all of them, and written in Matt's strong, firm, writing style. Luke opened it. John read over his shoulder.

Dear Mark, Luke and John.

I have taken care of Mom's problem for her. We'll all be better off this way. You won't see me for a while. Don't worry about me, though. I'll be fine. Don't try to find me. You won't be able to. When the time is right, I'll get in touch with you.

Mark, finish the job I couldn't do. Get your Bars. The Marine Corps needs good officers like you. You've also got to lead the family now.

Luke, go to school. Get your degree. There will be plenty of money for you. Don't worry about that. You should be a writer or an actor. Go where your talent takes you.

John, stay out of trouble. Don't let the usual teenage crap steer you wrong. Be a man. You were great during these troubles. So was Luke. It's a shame all this had to happen at this time in your lives but that's life. You should be stronger for it.

All of you, take care of Maggie. She needs special love and special schools. See that she gets them both.

Last but not least take care of Mom. She's a really special person. She needs you all more than ever now.

Good luck. I Love You All.
Matt.

Although the paper was now dry, there was a small rumpled spot near the bottom that looked like it might have held a drop of water. A tear perhaps?

4
La Legion Estranger

Le Nord, or Northeastern France as it is known in English, was a study in contrasts. Beaches, mud flats, cliffs and two major seaports all lay within a few miles of each other. One of the seaports was Dunkirk, *Dunkerque* in French. The word probably derived from early Celtic words, which meant *church in the field or meadow*.

The port itself was a bustling, but dirty, harbor. Its chief claim to fame was that it was only 35 miles across the English Channel, the *Sleeve* as the French call it, from England. This area is the closest point that England comes to the Continent. Frequent ferries crossed the straight from Dover to Dunkirk and to Pas d' Calais, the other port.

Another reason for its more recent renown was that it was the route taken off the mainland for over 300,000 English, French and Polish Soldiers as they fled the onrushing Wehrmacht in the early part of World War II. The word Dunkirk had become synonymous with retreat.

In late 1947, it also was also the home for a busy recruiting and processing facility of the French Foreign Legion, third only to Marseilles and Paris in its recruiting numbers. Many Scandinavian, Russian, Polish, and English Legionnaires had come into the Legion through this facility, as well as recruits from the Russian occupied lands of Latvia, Estonia, and Lithuania. The Legion post was precisely the reason Matt Farrell, formerly Matt Flaherty, was there.

He had arrived late in the day via the ferry from England. He had entered England by crossing the Canadian border in Vermont, working on a freighter to earn passage to Ireland, and then another ferry to the British Isle. While in England he had worked some odd jobs to acclimate himself to his new surroundings. As he suspected, few questions had been asked of people willing to work.

The day was gray and the mist rolling in off the North Sea was dropping a cold and clammy blanket on the coastal area. In an effort to orient himself, Matt walked along the wooden boardwalk slowly, his coat collar turned up against the chill. The quays were lined with fishing vessels of all sizes, the vista one of ropes, halyards and masts in a confused riot of vertical and horizontal lines. The dock area itself was composed of a collection of fish stalls, vegetable stands and bars that catered to seamen. The buildings across a cobbled walkway from the docks presented a line of clapboard shacks, half-timbered houses, and stone block structures. As Matt walked, he looked at each stand and into each bar. There was activity here and there among the stands as fishermen and merchants haggled over the day's catch, but overall the area was quiet.

At one point he passed a statue of a man known as Jean Bart, a pirate who had sailed from this port in the Seventeenth century. He wasn't sure if his high school French still served him, but the inscription on the base of the statue seemed to say that Bart was buried in the church. Up to this point, no church had been in evidence. He looked around and had almost decided there wasn't any when he spotted a spire, almost hidden in the mist, off in the distance.

A shudder coursed his body. It was involuntary. He had gotten wet coming over on the ferry and the moisture was now seeping through his clothes. His plain wool jacket had kept him dry for a while but finally his flannel shirt had started wicking the dampness from the jacket to his body. His brown corduroy pants and work boots were damp, but not wet enough yet to be a problem. His flat cap, which snapped down in the front, kept the drifting mist from his head and eyes. He had bought it in Ireland just before he left. It was a popular style there. In a small bag he carried over his shoulder, he also had a cable-knit sweater, another flannel shirt, and a change of underwear and socks, along with his toilet kit. The street along the quay ended. The dock continued on, but there were no more buildings. He had to make a decision. He probably would wait until tomorrow to present himself at the Legion post, but before it got any darker, he wanted to know where it was. The cold and wet were also pushing him to find shelter soon. His choices were limited. He decided to walk up and down a few of the side streets before he gave up. In an effort to create some body heat, he picked up his pace. It worked, to a degree. At least his shivering subsided.

The wet streets were constructed from cobblestones. They were worn and slick and had probably been here for ages. Most of the buildings along the way had two stories, shops and businesses on the first floor, dwellings on the second. Half-timbered fronts, sharp gabled roofs, and a jumble of chimneys were the architectural standards.

Luck was with him. As he came down the second street, he saw the

Tricolor flying from a pole fastened to a wall. When he neared the building, he saw the sign over the door in small gold letters, *La Legion Estranger*. He grunted in satisfaction.

There was a picture in one window of a battle scene. It showed Legionnaires fighting Mexican banditos in front of a hacienda. The other window had a stylized picture of a legionnaire, clad in a blue coat and white kepi, rifle in hand, beckoning the observer to follow. Sand dunes and date palms dotted the background. The French words on the poster apparently spoke of adventure. Matt was satisfied. Now it was time to dry out.

On the wharf earlier, he had noticed that the fishermen and seamen did not frequent one of the bars. It seemed to attract younger more military types, a probable Legion hangout. He headed for that establishment.

When he entered, there were only a few men in the bar, all sitting at tables near the back. The place was unremarkable, no windows, dirty wooden floor, dim lights, and stained walls. The tables and chairs were rickety, the tables mostly just square sheets of wood on spindly legs. The chairs were blocks of wood on equally fragile supports. A small stove, centrally located, gave off very little heat.

He took a seat at a table near the front and waited. After a few minutes no one had come to serve him so, he decided this must be a place where you get your own. He rose and walked to a counter on the side of the room. A gnarled, thin man with one arm stood behind the counter. He wore a patch over one eye. In his best French Matt asked, "Cognac, sil vous plait?"

The man looked him, turned, and through spaces left by missing teeth, he spat on the floor. "No Cognac. Calvados?" He held up a small, odd shaped bottle. It looked like brandy.
Matt nodded his head. He just wanted something alcoholic and warming. He didn't care what it tasted like. Somewhere in the recesses of his brain he recalled having heard of Calvados, but he couldn't bring the information forward.

"Oui, Calvados, sil vous plait."

The tall man poured a generous portion in a brandy glass. Matt handed him a one-pound English note.

The man looked at the note and then spat on the floor again. Apparently he didn't like English money. He yanked out a drawer in the counter, however, and rummaged around. He finally pulled out a handful of coins and threw them on the bar, counted out an amount satisfactory to him and shoved them across to Matt. It was a substantial pile. Matt had no idea what the Calvados cost, but apparently it was cheap and an English pound was a great deal more than enough. Matt picked up the coins and filled his pocket with the weighty load. He took the glass back to his table, sat down and took a sip of the drink.

To his pleasant surprise, it was strong and warming, just what he wanted. The warmth spread through his upper body pleasantly. It also tasted like apples. Then he remembered. Calvados was apple brandy. He leaned back a little, opened his jacket, and continued to absorb the welcoming warmth of the sweet drink. Taking some of the coins from his pocket and spreading them out on the sticky, stained table, he looked them over trying to make some sense of their value.

The young American looked quite a bit different now than when he had left Kingmont. His hair had grown long and it would curl over his shirt collar soon. His beard and sideburns had grown thick and full, thereby changing his appearance substantially. Baggy clothes hid his athletic body. The transformation had taken his image from neat and clean-shaven, to messy and hairy. The man who fled Kingmont a month ago would be hard to recognize.

He took another sip of his drink and again felt the warmth. He gave up on the coins and shoved them back in his pocket. He looked around at the other men in the bar. They seemed to be drinking some kind of a dark beer with a small head on it. Some of them were looking at him, a few with hostility. He wasn't one of *them* he supposed. Matt looked away, trying to strike a non confrontational pose, but also one that did not display fear.

The men he could see were a mean-looking group. They all had short military haircuts, scars and tattoos. They were not wearing uniforms, but it was apparent some of their shirts and pants had been part of a uniform at one time. Their clothes were, for the most part, khaki in color. No one took any overt action toward him, but it was evident he wasn't welcome. One of them went to the barkeeper and said something to him. They both looked at Matt. Matt decided he'd probably gotten his last drink from this bar.

The hostility bothered Matt. He'd wanted to try to meet a few Legionnaires to get a feel for things in the Legion, but it didn't look like that was going to happen

As he sat sipping his Calvados, trying to determine his next move, the door opened and a big blond man with wide shoulders entered the room. He had a smile on his face and his voice boomed. He went over to the barman, slapped him on the back, almost knocking him over in the process, and said something to him in French. The barman reached under the bar and pulled out a bottle of what looked like brandy. He gave it to the big man.

The man grabbed the bottle, pulled the cork with his teeth and took a swig. He then went over to a table with three or four of the other men. They made room for him. He sat down with a bang and offered the bottle around. They all took a drink and passed it back to him. They were smiling, all talking at once, in French, of course. Matt had no idea what the conversation was about.

After a few minutes of laughter and conversation, one of the men tapped the big man on the arm and pointed to Matt. The big man had been sitting with his back to the young American. Now he turned around. He eyed the Matt for a moment, in a curious but not unfriendly way, and turned back to his group. After a few more words, he stood up, passed his bottle around again, joking and laughing as he did so. Then he collected his bottle, nodded to the group, turned and approached Matt's table.

He said something in French to Matt. Matt didn't understand.

"Pardon, non parlais Francais," he replied.

"Ah . . . an American. I asked you if I could join you at your table," he said with a big grin and only the hint of an accent.

Matt was surprised. "Sure . . . sure. Sit down. You're welcome." Matt half stood, drawing a chair out as he did so.

The big man sat by swinging his leg over the back of the chair and then straddling the seat. He took off his jacket and threw it over the back. "My name is Jacques." He held out his hand. "Jacques Lescoulie."

"Matt Flaher . . . uh, Matt Farrell." He grabbed Jacques hand. The grip was firm. "Glad to meet you."

"Same with me, Mr. . . . Farrell, you said?"

"Call me Matt."

"Matt it is."

He looked at Matt for a minute. Then he looked at Matt's glass, which was half empty. "What is that you are drinking?"

"Calvados, I think he said," replied Matt, nodding toward the one-armed man.

"Calvados! A woman's drink," he said with a laugh. "Here, have a man's drink." He slid his bottle over.

Matt took a small taste, not knowing what to expect. It was brandy. Good brandy too, he thought. "Thank you, that's quite good."

"It should be. It's Cognac."

"Cognac. I see." He smiled with a sardonic twist. "Your friend behind the bar told me he had no cognac." Matt glared at the one-armed man. The barkeeper looked at Matt, turned and spat on the floor, and then looked back at him.

"That's just old Patou. He keeps the good stuff for us. He protects us Legionnaires." He looked back at his friend. "He's an old Legionnaire himself. Besides, he probably has more Calvados than he has Cognac and, well . . . business is business." He turned to old Patou and rattled off something in French. Patou smiled. The smile was mostly toothless. He reached under the counter and took out another bottle and brought it over to the table. He placed the bottle between them and went back to the counter. Matt noticed that he limped. Matt also noticed the bottle said Cognac on it.

Lescoulie saw Matt looking at Patou. "Very few people around here know Patou's real name. He wants it that way. We call him Patou because he spits. You know the sound you make when you spit. 'Patou.'" He laughed as he said it.

Matt laughed, too. People were strange.

Some of the other men asked Jacques a few questions. Matt couldn't grasp what they were saying. He heard a few words, Anglais and American among them, but he could not piece them together. Lescoulie enlightened him. "They thought you were English, mon ami. They don't like the English. I told them you are American. Americans are okay. Not good mind you. Just okay." He laughed again.

It could have been his imagination, but Matt could actually feel less hostility emanating from the group. "Why don't they like the English?"

Lescoulie shrugged. "Why does anyone not like another? There are many reasons. In Dunkirk, they see them all the time. They both get drunk. They fight when they get drunk. They fight over women. They fight over honor. They remember past slights, hurts from the bad times during the last war. There are many reasons."

"I hadn't realized . . . ."

"Of course not. How would you know?" He took another draft from his bottle and slid it over to Matt. Matt picked it up and took another swallow. A little bigger one this time.

Matt looked at Lescoulie as he took his mouthful. The Frenchman was, for want of another word, big. Six foot three or four at least. He had wide shoulders and a long neck. He was tan to his close-cropped scalp. He was white from that point on. The result of wearing a cap, probably a kepi, while working in the sun. What little hair existed was blond. His eyebrows and eyelashes were almost white, his eyes, a very light blue. He had a scar on his cheek. His narrow waist along with the broad shoulders gave his upper body a triangular look. He wore dark trousers and a short sleeved khaki shirt. A wide leather belt with a big buckle kept his shirt tucked in. It was a short tan jacket that he had thrown over the back of his chair earlier. Tattoos showed on his massive arms. From where Matt sat, the tattoos were indecipherable.

"Now, Mr. American, enough about us, tell me why are you here. And why are you dressed like an Englishman."

Matt was a little startled by the directness of the question. But he decided he liked this big Frenchman so he thought he'd respond positively. Besides he might be able to bring the conversation around to the things *he* wanted to talk about. "Well, as you probably can guess, I came here looking to join the Legion."

"Ah, another candidate for the Legion of the Damned, the Legion of Lost Souls." Jacques leaned back in his chair and smiled. The wooden frame creaked under his weight. "And why would you want to do that? A tragic affair of the heart? A misunderstanding with another that turned into something more than a simple misunderstanding? A place to hide? Another life that looks too bleak to endure?"

Matt looked at him sharply. He thought the Legion asked few questions. "Something like that. But I think you are too nosy." Anger rose in his voice.

Lescoulie looked at him a moment.

"The new Legionnaire has a temper." Then he said more solicitously. "Of course I ask too much. That is one of my failings. But my heart is in the right place. You look like a man who has prospects. I don't want to see you make a mistake."

He leaned forward, his arms on the table. Matt could see the tattoos now. The one on his left biceps was a picture of a rippling French flag, the Tricolor. The one on his right biceps had three words bunched together — *Egalatere, Liberataire, Fraternitie*. On the back of the fingers on his right hand, in crude letters, was spelled out *Marche ou! Creve*. Matt understood the flag and the French motto, *Equality, Liberty, Fraternity*, but the hand tattoo stumped him.

"Mon ami," the Frenchman looked Matt in the eyes with a serious expression, "sometimes men come to the Legion for the wrong reasons. What I am telling you is no different than what the officer in charge will tell you when you meet him. They try to warn people off. He may leave out a few details however. I will tell you all."

He smiled at Matt, took a swig from his bottle, and continued. "Many Englishmen and Americans have read books. *Beau Geste* maybe or *Under Two Flags*. They have seen movies, eh?"

Matt reddened. He had read both. He had seen both movies.

Jacques noted the reddened face. "I strike home, eh? Well these stories are romantic. They tell some of the story, but not all."

"Jacques, I have read the books and seen the movies. I've also seen real life. I think I can separate the romance from the real world."

"Perhaps, mon ami, perhaps. But let me go on."

Matt nodded.

"In the books. They describe a hard life. They don't hide that, although they don't go far enough. That is part of the romance. The romantic joins the Legion knowing it will be hard. He would be disappointed if it were not. He often needs the hardship to, how do you say it, expiate himself from guilt or to forget his other life. Hardship is not the problem. It is something else."

Matt reached out and took another drink from Lescoulie's bottle. Others had entered the bar, passing into the back. Some nodded to the big man.

"But having said that, let me get into the hardship a little first before I go to my main point." He took a drink. "In the Legion, we only eat two meals a day, both are soup, with a little meat and some bread. Sometimes we get some fruit or some vegetables, but not too often. The first meal isn't served until near noontime. Americans are used to a breakfast. As trivial as this sounds, this is hard to adjust to."

Matt thought it didn't sound too bad.

"Legionnaires don't wear socks. We wax our feet to protect against blisters. It doesn't work too well. Our boots don't fit, yet we have to march. We live by marching. We march thirty or forty miles a day, with eighty-pound packs. The Legion is proud of its marching tradition. It has saved many a Legionnaire from death, but it is hard. Legionaries have the worst feet in the world. They are always bleeding. They always have sores and blisters. They have corns and warts. They suffer in quiet misery. Incidentally, the Legion does nothing about this ongoing problem."

He held out his right hand. "These words, *Marche ou! Creve*, they mean *March or Die*." He looked directly at Matt. "The Legionnaire doesn't take breaks. When he is not soldiering, he is building. Hot sun? Rain? No matter. He soldiers or he works, and works hard. No other choices."

Matt felt he could handle that. The life he had intended to pursue in the Marine Corps wouldn't have had much less hardship than the Legion. In some ways, it might have been worse. He felt prepared.

"In the Legion we have something called *Le Crapudine*. It is a form of punishment. It was outlawed years ago but …well, some sergeants don't remember that it was outlawed, and in the Legion, the sergeant is God. Even the officers don't interfere with them. It doesn't take a court martial for the soldier to be awarded *Le Crapudine* either. It comes at the whim of the sergeant. No crime is necessary."

Matt thought about the power of drill instructors and gunnery sergeants in the Marine Corps. The Legion seemed to be a little worse, but the NCOs in the Marine Corps were a tough bunch, too. "What is this Crapudine thing? How does it work?" he asked. "It sounds like a shitter to me, an outhouse."

The big man laughed. "It is hardly that, mon ami." Then he became serious again. "It is a torture. A man is tied up in a kneeling position with his hands behind him. His arms are tied as flat to his body as possible and with as much strain on his shoulder joints as the ropes can inflict. His head is bent back by a rope, which is also tied to his feet. His feet and legs are tied together. It is a totally unnatural position for the human body to be left in, but the soldier is then left in that position, often for days. The pain is excruciating. One can't move. To shift an arm pulls a shoulder joint out. Moving a leg tightens the rope around the neck, not enough to cause strangulation but enough to cause some loss of air. Moving the head cuts off circulation in the legs. Rolling onto your side causes all the ropes to tighten, creating more pain. You fear sleep. You might fall over. But you crave sleep as a way to escape the pain. I know of a man who ended up paralyzed because he was left too long. I heard of another who lost his mind. It is a barbaric process."

"What is the purpose of something like that." Matt asked with disgust.

"Discipline. Revenge. Sadism. Take your pick. Those who use it say it is for discipline. I don't accept that. I don't believe you maim a soldier to discipline him. Just as floggings on the old sailing ships did not discipline sailors. Once a man has been flogged or has been given *Le Crapudine* he is no longer a good soldier or sailor. Those who use it, enjoy it. That's why they use it. They are pigs. It is still used and it is still a part of the Legion. The officers look the other way."

Matt's innards contracted at the mental picture.

"There is more, mon ami. There is the stealing."

"Stealing. Who steals from who?"

"The troops. They steal from each other. You have to always be on guard. You can't keep any money unless you keep it on your body. And even that doesn't always work. Personal clothes disappear all the time. Most Legionnaires have only uniforms and other Legion issued clothes and equipment and even that gets stolen. It is almost a game. You have to steal back again, just to keep even."

Matt nodded. This tended to explain why most of the Legionnaires he had seen wore leftover uniform parts. "I find that terrible. How can men live in close quarters and not be able to trust each other? How can men fight together if they can't trust each other?"

"Somehow it still works. It is a Legion tradition to die for each other. They will not leave a wounded comrade, but they still steal from him. There is more. Often men form cliques, usually among national groups like Germans, or Italians, or Swedes. *They* do not steal from each other. They will protect each other. These groups usually work, but sometimes . . . ." Lescoulie related more of the trials and tribulations of a Legionnaire and then little by little he slowed down. Finally he stopped.

They sat for a while without talking. Matt was letting it all sink in. The room had filled up. Every table was taken. The customers all appeared to be Legionnaires. They all seemed to be drinking beer and they all seemed to be smoking. The room was filled with a blue haze worthy of a sea borne fog.

After a little time Lescoulie looked back at Matt. "Then there is something called *Le Cafard*, the cockroach."

"*Le cafard*? What's that?" Matt asked, not sure he wanted to know.

"It is a mental illness. It afflicts Legionnaires all over the world. It is a real problem for the Legion. Boredom, inactivity, and persecution cause it, persecution by sergeants and other legionnaires. Sometimes the troops take a dislike to someone. They will persecute him. He has no friends. They all steal from him. He can't sleep at night. He is, I think the word is, *ostracized*. Then there is the tedium of the same routine, the same food, and the same surroundings, no relief from work, from marching or from the weather. And tell me, mon ami, what is worse, 115 degrees in the desert or 115 degrees in the jungle?"

He looked at Matt seriously. Matt was silent.

"Men go mad. They plot to mutiny. They think everyone is after them. They attack NCOs. They attack officers. They desert. In combat, they join the enemy. In foreign countries they go native."

Matt just listened. He had no answer for that.

Lescoulie let that sit for a moment, then he asked abruptly, "Matt. Is that short for Matthew?"

"Uh . . . yes, it is." Matt frowned. He was still trying to keep things to himself, thus the hesitation.

"Matthew, I am getting hungry. I know where we can get some good food cheap. Would you care to join me? I'll buy. We might even be able to find some female companions, if you so desire."

Matt wasn't sure he wanted any female companionship, especially the type that a Foreign Legionnaire might have available, but he did want to eat, his head was a little light from the alcohol, and he also wanted to hear more about the Legion.

"Sure . . . okay with me, but I'll buy. You've been providing the cognac. I'll buy the dinner."

"You have enough money, mon ami?"

"I have enough. Not a lot, but enough. Besides, I pay my debts, my big friend."

"You are a fine man, Matthew, too good for the Legion, but a fine man. Let us go. I have much more to tell you."

* * *

They walked up one of the streets, moving away from the dock area. Jacques regaled him with more Legion stories as they went. The cobblestones ended and the street became a dirt road. They walked for about fifteen minutes more, the seaport town falling away behind them. Topping a rise, they descended to a fork in the road with a few buildings facing the junction. One was an old thatched roof farmhouse that had been converted into an inn. The attached barn was now living quarters. They had arrived at their destination.

Jacques barreled his way into the thatch-roofed building like he did everything else — with gusto. He grabbed a buxom woman who had her back to the door, lifted her up, and swung her around. He planted a big kiss on her lips. She almost dropped the tray she was carrying. She squealed with delight.

"Lescoulie . . . Lescoulie . . . ," she blurted out and then ran off a string of French words which Matt felt sure were not all in dictionaries. Jacques laughed and kissed her again. This time she wrapped her arms around him and kissed him back.

He broke away from her and turned to introduce Matt. He described Matt as "an about to be reprieved condemned American." She laughed. He introduced her as Marcy.

"American, eh? Bon. You join the Legion?"

Matt noticed that her ample breasts surged upward and were pushed half out of her white peasant blouse.

Before he could answer Jacques boomed, "Not if I can help it."

Marcy let Jacques go, somewhat regretfully it seemed, and grabbed Matt and hugged him. She was soft all over. She smelled like cold cream and cooking and perfume. Some erotic thoughts surfaced. He shoved them back. She released him and looked at Jacques.

"He has hard muscles. His body is hard." She looked coquettishly at Jacques. "Is he hard all over?"

Jacques roared his glee. Matt reddened.

The bantering went on for another minute. Then when Jacques

finally made it clear to Marcy that they had come to eat, as well as to see her, she sat them at a table near the fire. Although the sun had set, for most Frenchmen, it was too early to dine. There were only a few other people in the restaurant. Matt noticed that when Marcy sat Jacques down she made sure her large breasts were in his face. She also gave him a little extra tug on the napkin as she placed it on his lap and smoothed it. He smiled appreciatively. Matt didn't get any such intimate attention from Marcy, but when the various courses were served, Marcy's helper, a pretty dark-haired girl, introduced as Colette, served *him* and she found ways to touch him quite often during the whole process, albeit just on the hands and arms. She also wore a low-cut peasant blouse and she also smiled a lot.

The meal was outstanding. They had steamed oysters for an appetizer, followed up by a rabbit stew cooked in a red wine sauce with leeks and small boiled potatoes. A tasty local red wine washed it all down. Dessert was a caramel pudding.

They lingered over dinner but did not discuss the Legion. Marcy and Colette were extremely attentive. Matt felt himself warming to the pretty Colette, even though they couldn't understand each other's words. People had been arriving all during the meal so that when they finished the restaurant was almost full. They told Marcy they needed a place to talk but they didn't want to take up her tables. She gave Jacques the key to her house, which was next door. She also gave them a bottle of wine. There was an inherent promise in Marcy's last statement as they left. "We'll see you both a little later," she had said, giggling.

The air was cool outside. They decided to walk a little before they went to Marcy's house. Matt in particular wanted to shake off the effects of the brandy, the wine, and the big meal. Without making a conscious decision, they did not head back to the shore but walked inland, at a slow pace, feet crunching on the dirt road.

"Well, mon ami, what do you think of Marcy? She is something, is she not? And Colette? Eh? I think she likes you."

Matt blushed. It was dark enough so Jacques couldn't see it. "She's very pretty. You think she likes me? I wouldn't want to take advantage of her. I'm just passing through."

"Oh, mon ami. This is France. Vive la France. If she likes you, it will not matter. She will think only of today. She will understand. If she doesn't like you, she will not see you again. There is no *taking advantage*. You are too, how is it said . . . sensitive. But then, maybe I am not fair. You have things on your mind. You have big decisions to make."

Reluctantly, the comment brought him back to his problems. He began wrestling with a number of thoughts but before he could speak Jacques started talking. "Let me tell you about the Legion and my time in it. Perhaps you will understand what I say when I say this is not for you."

"Before you start let me ask a question." Something had been bothering him. "You seem to put the Legion down yet you are a Legionnaire. Why do you do that? If you don't like the Legion why don't you leave?"

Lescoulie stopped walking. Matt stopped too. The big Frenchman turned to Matt. "I don't dislike the Legion. There are many things I like about the Legion. It has been my home for five years. I will always be proud that I was a Legionnaire. I would not trade my time in the Legion. What I am saying is that it isn't right for you. It is also not right for me either . . . right now. I *am* getting out. Perhaps I did not tell you. I thought you knew."

Matt just looked at him in confusion.

Lescoulie thought a minute. "Perhaps when I was talking about it in the bar or with Marcy I was speaking French and you did not hear. I didn't realize . . . . I am sorry. This is my last day. Five years ago today I joined the Legion. My enlistment is up. Now I am leaving."

Matt was a little unsettled. Then it sank in. He had found a friend and then was going to lose him. "Jacques, I didn't know. I don't know what to say."

"Mon ami, don't be sorry for me. I will be fine. Let me tell you what I was going to tell you. You will understand better."

They were now out of sight of the inn. Broken clouds scudded across the indigo sky. The moon was just out of sight. A wind blew and the air was a little cooler than earlier.

"The ways of God . . . yes, I believe in God," Matt had looked at him sharply, "are mysterious. He has a plan for us all." He looked straight ahead as they walked. "I joined the Legion in 1942. I was sixteen. Yes, sixteen." He had seen a puzzled look in Matt's eyes. "The Legion needed men. I was almost as big as I am now. They had no problems with my age. Voila, here I am. I trained some in Morocco and Algiers and then I was assigned to the 13th DBLE, the Demi-Brigade Legion Estranger. Before I joined them, the 13th DBLE had been trained to fight the Russians in Denmark. They were going to help the Germans. Then the Germans invaded Norway so they went to fight the Germans. They came back to France. Germany attacked France. France surrendered and we were German allies again. This was a terrible time to be in the Legion. We didn't know what side we were on.

"Some units supported capitulation and Vichy France. Others wanted to resist. A large number of Legionnaires were German. The Legion has had large numbers of Germans for many years. Germany had just invaded and taken over France. There were still many people who thought we should have fought them, but there were also those who said we should just go along with Germany and not ruin our country. The Germans who were in the Legion had the same problem.

"The Legion offered them a choice. They could stay in the Legion and do the Legion's bidding. That might mean fighting Germans. Or they could leave and go back to Germany, to join their Fatherland's army. Most stayed in the Legion, but a lot of them were repatriated to the German army. Some stayed in Algiers and worked in labor battalions. They didn't want to fight against Germans, but they also did not want to fight for Hitler and the Nazis. There were some German Jews in this group.

"To add to the confusion, there were Legion units that did not come over to the Allied side at all. Their commanders felt that the French Government was now pro-German so they should be pro-German also. This created a situation where Legionnaires might have to fight Legionnaires."

"Shit, that's an impossible situation," Matt stated incredulously. His mind boggled at the information he was receiving. "How did you fit in all this?"

"When I joined, I was too new. I went along with almost anything. I wanted to fight for my country. We had been invaded. It was my duty to fight back. In 1942, there was no French Army to join. My country had given in, but I didn't feel I should give in. I didn't hear about the Resistance until later, but I still would have joined the Legion. It wasn't until I finished my training that I found out about all the switching back and forth. I almost quit. Deserted. Then my sergeant told me the 13th DBLE would fight the Germans. They would fight for the Allies. So I stayed. Charles DeGaulle led the 13th. He had smuggled the unit out of England after the debacle here at Dunkirk. And brought it back to Africa. That is where I joined the Brigade."

Matt was fascinated.

"We fought, behind the lines at a place called Bir Hakeem in Syria. We harassed Rommel. We cut off his supplies. We messed up his communications. There were less than a thousand of us but we performed well. He sent a whole regiment after us. The regiment had a lot of Legionnaires in it. They did not want to fight with us. They just went through the motions. We were a real problem for Rommel. We evaded his soldiers. We fought a guerilla type of war. He was still able to win at Tobruck shortly after Bir Hakeem, but eventually he lost at El Alemein, in no small part because of our efforts."

"You've seen a lot of action haven't you?"

"Yes, Matt," he said soberly. "And I saw a lot more. After Africa, we went into Italy and helped in the drive north. We also fought in France, in the Alsace area. Along the way, many of the Germans who had been Legionnaires came back, but we also added a lot of French and others to our rolls. When the Allies landed at Normandy, we attacked from the southern part of France to help out. We were the first Allied unit into Paris. We fought later in the war also, when the Allies pushed into Germany."

"This is all something to be proud of. While I was in high school and . . . ," he almost said the Academy, "uh college, you were actually fighting for . . . for freedom. I envy you."

"Merci, but that is only the background. There is more. Besides, I did not participate in all those battles. Only some of them."

They stopped a minute and then turned around and started to walk back. It was getting colder.

"Fighting in Africa, and in Italy and later in France was good. This is what I expected. This is what I *signed on for*, as Americans say. I knew very little about the turmoil that went on before, except what I told you. When the war ended it all came out. I was very upset."

"I can see why."

"Even though we put our country before everything else, our government did not appreciate us. We had not done what they wanted. Although we had helped to save the country, we had disobeyed them. They had surrendered. We had not surrendered. We were the pariahs."

"Jesus Christ, what a short-sighted view."

"What happened next is the worst. They cleaned out the officer corps. They retired most of them, but they also court-martialed and executed some. They left very few experienced people. They thought the Legion was too strong. We stood as examples of resistance to their perfidy. They did not like that.

"We always were able to get the best officers graduating from St. Cyr, our West Point. This was usually the top five or six men in their class. Now it is no longer. You hear about the heroism and the fighting heart of the Legion. It was as much due to the officer corps as it was to the men. Now the top officers are assigned elsewhere. We get the bottom of each class."

They walked. Matt listened, thinking.

"There are other things." He took on the air of a college professor. "Colonies are revolting. They want to rule themselves. The age of colonization is over. But France will not allow that. The Legion will have to fight those people. This will happen in Africa. It will happen in French Indo China. The Legion's next wars will be putting innocent people down, people who want only to be free. We won't be fighting invading armies or oppressors. We will be the oppressors. I don't want to fight that kind of war."

He was lost in his dissertation. "There is already trouble brewing over Algiers. There are Legion officers who think we should give Algiers freedom. There are those who want to keep the colony. They need to keep their *Empire*. Remember, Napoleon was still revered and he had been an Emperor."

Matt was absorbing it all. The picture he was getting disturbed him.

"Matt, there is still more."

They stopped a minute. They were nearing the intersection with the inn and Marcy's house. Music and chatter still emerged from the restaurant. "Are you ready to become a member of the Legion of the Damned?"

Matt was puzzled by the question. "You mean, am I ready to join the Legion?"

"No. I mean are you ready to join the Legion of the Damned?"

Matt stood on the road and looked at the big Frenchman quizzically.

"The Damned, Matt . . . the Damned. Do you know why they call us the Legion of the Damned? The Lost Souls?" His voice had risen. "Do you know why Legionnaires fight so well?"

Matt shook his head.

"When you enter the Legion, you enter to die. You are already dead. The place and time of your demise has not been determined yet, but you are dead. Men join the Legion to die. They want their death to have a meaning, but they expect to die. Normal human beings fear death. Legionnaires do not. They are already dead.

"We revel in the heroism of Camerone, when five survivors fixed bayonets and charged two thousand Mexican troops rather than surrender. We applaud battles fought and lost when there should have been no fight at all. Many times, we are put into impossible positions and we lose. Sometimes we win, but not usually. The Legion has lost as many battles as it has won. The Legion has been involved in more battles where there have been no survivors, than any army in the world. Losing is not a problem. Dying well, bringing your wounded back, saving your honor. These are the important things. Those are laudable feats, but they should only come about when absolutely necessary.

"In other armies, a soldier knows he is risking his life. He knows he might die. But he goes in to combat expecting to win. That is the difference."

Matt struggled with this. He had never thought about anything like this before. He was beginning to doubt his decision.

Lescoulie continued with enthusiasm, "The Legion is the right place for the poor of the world, where the new life is a step up from their old life. It is the right place for men who have been displaced from their homelands. It is a place for those who want more opportunity than they can get in their own country. It is the place for dispossessed and unemployed men. After the Spanish Civil war, those who fought for the loyalists flooded the Legion. After the First World War, the Germans came in. The Germans are now coming back and so are people fleeing from Communism in Poland, Russia and the Balkan countries. The Legion will give them a home and they will do its bidding in gratitude."

He stopped and took a breath. He looked at Matt in the moonlight. "It is not the place to hide, Matt. There will be no glory, no romantic life . . . or death. There will be only ignominy. It is not the place for me anymore. It is not the place for you."

Matt looked at him steadily. "I don't know, Jacques. You've given me a lot to think about. I don't know."

"Well," Jacques shrugged. He put his arm around Matt. "Let's go into Marcy's house, open this gift of wine, and let the whole thing settle. We'll wait for the girls to come. Then we can forget everything for a while."

They walked toward the door. "You really think Colette will come?"

"Trust me, mon ami. Trust me."

* * *

A few hours later, the fire they had made was at its romantic peak with low flames and glowing embers. The cottage was a warm, cozy place. The furniture was overstuffed and comfortable. The lighting was low. The rooms were small, but friendly. They had found some records and they had the windup record player ready to go. The wine was gone, but Jacques had brought his brandy. They had not discussed the Legion the whole time. They were sitting in two easy chairs half asleep. In a drowsy voice, Matt asked a question. "Now that you're out of the Legion, what are you going to do?"

"I have a few matters to attend to in Paris, then I'm off to America." Jacques answered, also sleepily.

Matt sat up. Sleep almost gone. "America?"

"Yes, your home country. My country, too."

"How's that?" Matt was wide-awake now.

"My mother lives in New Orleans. She is American. I lived there, too, for a number of years, when I was small. My father is French. He comes from the Loire Valley area. That's where I was born. The northern part, near Normandy. I'm sorry to say he was killed in the war. Fighting at the Maginot line. He was too old to be fighting, but he did. Hah, I was too young to be fighting, but I did, too."

"I'm sorry to hear about your father. I didn't know your mother was American. You have dual citizenship?"

"Yes, I do."

"Well, I'll be hornswoggled." He remembered a movie where Andy Devine used that expression. It seemed ideal for situations like this. "What are you going to do in the U.S.?"

"Well I think I'll do a little sightseeing, visit an old girlfriend or two, and then I just might join the Marine Corps."

Matt sat – frozen in place. The room was silent. He had just received the second big jolt in less than a minute. He did not move a muscle for a full thirty seconds.

Finally Jacques asked him, "Are you all right, mon ami?"

"Yeah . . . I'm, uh, fine." He didn't trust himself to say much more.

The door opened and Marcy and Colette tumbled in — all fun and games. Serious conversation stopped. They had brought more wine and some cheese. Within minutes both of them had gone into a bedroom and shed their working clothes and were now wearing kimonos. Colette's looked a little big on her. It was probably Marcy's. There didn't appear to be anything but bare skin under either of the wraps. They drank some wine, ate a little cheese, listened to French love songs and laughed a lot. Jacques and Marcy sat in one of the chairs. Little by little, Jacques clothes came off and he became more and more wrapped up inside the kimono with Marcy.

Matt didn't speak French and Colette didn't speak English, but that didn't create any problems. After sitting and listening to the music for a few minutes, they rose to dance. Colette's gown worked its way open. They finished the dance with Matt inside the kimono with Colette. These robes were great, thought Matt, caught up in the sheer sensual pleasure of the moment. A few more turns around the floor and they were totally wrapped up together. As they walked with their arms around each other toward the small bedroom in back, the kimono fell off. Jacques and Marcy were already gone.

* * *

Matt stood with Jacques at the bus stop. According to the posted schedule the bus was due anytime. The day was cloudy and misty, still cool, but the damp was beginning to burn off. Matt wore his sweater under his jacket. Lescoulie wore his jacket. Matt had his small bag. The big Frenchman had a small backpack.

They had roused themselves early so Jacques could make the bus. The girls were still sleeping. The two "warriors" had headaches.

"Here's the money you left on the table." Jacques handed him a couple of one-pound notes.

Matt was surprised. "I left that for the dinner. I said I would pay for it. No one ever asked for any money. I thought I would just leave it."

"Oh, my naVve friend. I took care of the dinner. If they had seen this money, they would have been angry. They would have assumed you were paying for their services. They would have been insulted. They are not *ladies of the evening*. They are friends. Marcy is an old and good friend. We have done many things for each other. Colette is Marcy's friend and apparently yours, too." His eyes twinkled. "We want to treat them right."

Matt was crushed. He had almost made a monstrous gaff. He had a lot to learn. "Jacques, I'm sorry. I didn't realize. The last thing in the world I would do is hurt them. That was a wonderful night. I feel like a fool."

"No harm, mon ami. I have come to your rescue . . . again."
Matt caught the *again* but he wanted to clear up something first. "I said I would pay for the meal. You said you paid for it, therefore, this money is yours."

Jacques face was wreathed in a big smile. "Mon ami, you *are* a man of honor. I accept your money." With that, he shoved the bills into his pocket and looked up the street to see if he could see the bus coming. The street was empty.

They were silent for a while. Then Matt spoke. "Jacques you've got me totally confused about what to do next. Things just don't look the same as they did a few days ago. I feel a mixture of disappointment and relief. It's very confusing."

"I hope so, Matt, for your sake." His face was serious. "It really is none of my business what you do. But I like you and I think you are making a mistake. I can be very practical, but I also can be emotional. I have an emotion, a need, which cries out for me to keep you from a mistake. It frustrates me. It will be a waste."

Matt looked at him steadily. He was only twenty-one years old and he was forced to make some big decisions. What should he do next?

A little more time passed. The bus was still not in view. Lescoulie broke the silence. "Matt, come to Paris with me. Don't make the decision yet. If you still want to join the Legion you can do it there. Nothing will be lost. I have a place to stay in Paris, actually an old girl friend . . . ." He looked a little sheepishly at Matt. "She has some room. We can both stay there. We can talk some more."

Matt looked at his big friend. This was something to grasp at. He didn't ponder long. "That would give me more time, wouldn't it?"

He was working the idea around in his mind. "Okay ... okay." He looked around at the buildings on the street corner. "Where do I get a ticket? What does it cost?"

"You get the ticket on the bus. It's just a few francs."

5
Marche ou Creve¹

Jacques slept on the bus. Matt dozed a little but he had too much on his mind to fall asleep.

Among other things, he was thinking about Colette. He had been a virgin. She was his first. He wondered if she knew. He fantasized about her, lived the evening over. It had been so sweet, so wonderful. The Church taught that what they had done was wrong, however. It was a mortal sin. Sex was only for marriage. He had never had a problem resisting temptation before. He'd dated girls, but he had never gotten close to any of them. The most he had ever done was a little kissing. There didn't seem to be time to do more. Some of his friends had gone to prostitutes, but he had no interest in that. He was going to save himself for his future wife. He knew he shouldn't have done it with Colette, but it was so, *nice*. How could that be wrong?

Then he remembered Van Scooten. That animal had done a lot worse than have sex, a lot worse. His soul was really damned because of that. He had died in sin. Wasn't it Hamlet who wanted to kill the king while he was committing incestuous sin in bed with Hamlet's mother so the king's soul would go to hell? Matt's scruples pushed to the forefront. He'd have to find a way to get to confession. Maybe in Paris. They must have english-speaking priests there.

He started to question his decision-making ability. Had he and his mother made the right choice? Would self-defense or a justifiable homicide defense have worked? Should they have faced the music?

The Van Scootens had lots of money. They could have fought that. Didn't McQuinn tell him how they "quashed" the investigation of the first wife's death? How would it look? Self defense? Hardly. It would look like a young, athletic stepson, out for revenge or jealous retribution. Even a journeyman lawyer would be able to show that —and the Van Scooten's had crack lawyers.

Justifiable homicide? Matt didn't even know if that was a legitimate defense or something from the movies. He agonized — again. He wasn't sure if they had made the right decision or not, but it looked like they would have to live with it.

The scenery floated by. Plowed fields, farmhouses and cattle dominated the view. Here and there, however, there was a rusted and burned out tank or a tumble of rocks that had been a building. In one small corner of a rock walled farm was a classic picture. It was a single plastered wall with a window frame in it. The rest of the building was a pile of rubble. The war had passed through here in the not too distant past.

Now the question of joining the Legion crept back into his mind. Had that been a bad choice? Based on Jacques portrayal, it looked like it. Why had he decided to join the Legion? He had to get out of the country. He had to let things cool down. Okay, but why the Legion? He felt he was a soldier. He wanted to continue to be a soldier. What better way? No, there was more. Jacques had been right. It was the romance of it all.

He *had* read *Beau Geste*. Beau Geste had fled to the Foreign Legion with the fake *Blue Water*, an imitation of a diamond of great value. His aunt had been forced to sell the real diamond. He stole the fake to protect her. He was protecting the family's honor. Matt had also fled to the Legion to protect the family's honor. That was the nut of it.

Okay, so that was true. Now what? Should he still join the Legion? If he did, how would things come out? Was the big Frenchman right? Was the Legion as mixed up as he said? He thought Jacques was probably right. If he joined the Legion and he had to fight, would he be risking his life for a cause he couldn't believe in or maybe worse, no cause at all? If he didn't join what would he do then? He had to make his next decision the right one.

* * *

Paris was magnificent. The City of Lights. The Eiffel Tower. The Arc d' Triumph. The Champs Elysee. The museums. The huge public buildings. The River Seine. The ornate bridges. Notre Dame. The small neighborhoods with fine restaurants. The good wine. Paris was a joy.

After they had settled into his friend's apartment, Jacques took him on a little tour. The apartment was near the place where the Bastille had been. The actual prison had been demolished some time ago. A plaza occupied the spot now. The neighborhood was shabby and run down, but the third floor apartment was neat and comfortable. There were three rooms. One had a bed, one was an art studio, and the other doubled as a kitchen-living room. There was cot in the studio and a couch in the main room. The view, through French doors that opened onto a small balcony, was of bustling streets with vegetable stands and outdoor cafés. Cecile, Jacques friend, would not be there for a day or two.

After the neighborhood tour they went to a small restaurant down one of the side streets. Of course the restaurant people knew Jacques. It was cool, but they still sat outside. They ate steak tartar, a large salad, fresh bread, and red wine. Matt had never eaten raw meat before. Properly seasoned, it was quite good. They split the bill. Matt's money was running a little low but he didn't want to tell his friend. There was no discussion of Matt's future yet. Matt still had some thinking to do.

The next day, Jacques went off to take care of a few things he had to do in Paris. Matt strolled the streets near the apartment. He had a café latte and a croissant at one of the cafes. The café latte reminded him of the half and half his mother drank. Her half-and-half was milk and tea. He walked along the River Seine. It was mid-December. The trees were bare and the day was gray but there was still a beauty about the city which mere grayness couldn't suborn. He looked across the river at Notre Dame Cathedral. He remembered that Notre Dame was on an Island as were a number of the French government buildings. What was it called? Oh. Yes, the Isle de France.

The thought of the government brought him back to his predicament. It was becoming more and more evident as to what his decision should be. He should not join the Legion. But what would he do? Was it was time to bring Jacques in on the whole story? He didn't want to burden him with his problems, but he seemed to want to help, and the Lord knew, Matt needed help. Jacques returned to the apartment early in the afternoon. Matt was waiting for him. When Matt told him he would not join the Legion and that he needed help as to what to do next, the big Frenchman said. "Bon. That's good. It's good that you are not throwing your life away and it's good you asked for my help. I want to help. I . . . like you. I'm honored you would ask for my help."

Matt was buoyed by the response. He fought back tears. "Thank you, for your understanding."

Jacques waved off the thanks. "I haven't helped you yet. It might not be good help." He laughed. "You can thank me later, if deserved."

They were sitting on the sofa, which was in a window alcove. "If I am going to help, my friend, I'm afraid I am going to need information." He raised his almost white eyebrows, quizzically.

Matt nodded. He thought for a minute and then like wine from an ewer, he poured it out. He told him the complete story, describing the beatings and degradation of his mother, Van Scooten's problems with his first wife and the subsequent murder, his obsession with prostitutes, and the frustration of the police. Matt told Jacques what he had done when he caught Van Scooten in the act. He told him what Maggie heard and about the last night when had gone home.

He told him about his brothers and what they were like, about Maggie and her cross. He described his father and the life his family had built. He told him about the Naval Academy. He held nothing back. At the end he was crying. And so was Jacques.

The afternoon wore on. Darkness crept into the room. Matt was wrung out. He leaned back and closed his eyes. He had done it. He had put himself in the hands of another.

Jacques said nothing at first, absorbing what he had heard. He rose from the sofa, turned on a light and went to a cupboard. He took out a bottle of wine and opened it. The room was quiet except for the squeak of the corkscrew, the pop of the cork, and the clink of glasses. He poured two servings, handed one to Matt and sat down on a kitchen chair. He didn't look at Matt. In a few moments he turned and appraised the American. Matt thought he looked as serious as he had seen the big man in the short time he had known him. He wondered if now that Jacques had the whole story, he might regret his offer to help.

He needn't have worried. "Let me make a few observations," Jacques stated. He looked away again as his mind worked. "You did what was right. I would hope I would have the courage to do the same thing. The man was a beast. He deserved to die . . . horribly, I might add." He said this with a smile. "The honor of the family must be upheld." He stood and walked a little. "I cannot judge whether, 'facing the music,' as you put it, was the best choice, or fleeing was the better choice. You chose to flee to protect the family so that seems to be the best option. I cannot fault you for it.

"You almost made a bad choice about the Legion, but then," he shrugged, "you knew no better. Now you do. So what do you do next? Obviously you can't go back or . . . ," he paused, his mind working, "or can you?" Gradually, his expression was changing. "You were going to be an officer in the Marines, correct?"

Matt nodded, not sure where this was going.

"By the way, I was very glad to hear you almost became an officer.

It confirms what I thought. You are a man of great talent."

Matt smiled. He was grateful for the comment but he wanted Jacques to go on.

"You were going to join the Legion. Right?" He didn't wait for Matt's affirmation. "Your place in life appears to be a military one."

Matt agreed. That's all he ever wanted to do but . . . .

"Mon ami, why don't you pursue a career in your Marine Corps, under an assumed identity?" Matt sat up. "Wait, hear me out." He was responding to Matt's look of incredulity. "I can help you with that. I have connections. People I know. If the details can be worked out, is this something that appeals?"

"Of course . . . ," Matt stumbled, "but it's . . . impossible. How could it be done? I don't want to get my hopes up."

"Matthew, Matthew. Have faith in me. It can work," Jacques cajoled with that big confident smile Matt was getting to know so well. "It will work. I can promise you that."

Matt was caught up in Lescoulie's enthusiasm. He still had his doubts, but he wanted to explore it further. It was the first time he had felt any hope in weeks — a month.

They discussed it a little more, then started to put the plan into operation. The first step was to contact a few of the people Jacques knew.

He was looking through phone directories and writing down numbers when Cecile came in. She was a striking woman, tall and thin. Statuesque would be a good word to describe her. Almost as tall as Matt, she had short dark hair and a thin pointed face. The bright red lipstick she wore was a wonderful accent to her creamy white skin. She walked with a fluid grace. She had been a fashion model and it showed in her carriage. Now she was pursuing a career in design and was having some success. She had just returned from a show in Belgium where she had managed to exhibit some of her designs. They had been well received. She was ecstatic when she saw Jacques and she rushed into his arms.

This man sure had a way with women, thought Matt, with a smile.

The evening passed without any thought given to their plans. Cecile had insisted on cooking a dinner for them and they agreed. They helped her with the shopping and with cooking the meal. They had a good time, but understandably, Matt was a little impatient. The next day Cecile took off again for a few days. She and Jacques had shared the bedroom. Matt slept on the cot. Right after she left, Jacques and Matt started on their project.

They had to change Matt's identity. After a great deal of discussion they decided Matt would have a background similar to Jacques'. He left home in 1942 at age sixteen to join the Foreign Legion. He had wanted to fight but the U.S. Armed forces wouldn't take him at that time. He was to have come from Fall River, Massachusetts. This was so that he could cover his slight New York accent but still not be from New York. Matt had noticed that a midshipman he knew at the academy from Fall River had a cross between what Matt would call a Boston accent and a New York accent. He and Jacques would have met while going through basic training in Algiers and naturally gravitated toward each other.

They would have participated in all the same campaigns together so Jacques could provide the right background. Now their enlistments were up and they were coming back to the U.S. They would join the Marine Corps. The Corps would be glad to get two good physical specimens with combat experience.

They went next to a doctor Jacques knew. He had been a Legion doctor. He was now retired. Jacques had saved his life. In the past, apparently, he had also helped others who needed a new identity. They agreed that Matt would have to endure some minor surgery. He had a scar cut into his forehead. It was made to look like a fragment wound. He had his hands burned with acid to remove fingerprints. Other parts of his hands and his palms were burned also, so as not to look like it was simply finger print removal. The pain had been intense. The story would be that while in Italy, he burned his hands removing a comrade from a burning vehicle. He would get a small medal for that. The doctor would provide a certificate that said that field surgeons had treated Matt when the burns first occurred back in 1944, but that he recently had some scar tissue removed which explained the relatively new medical work. Surgery done in the field is not always the best.

The next soiree was to a forger who provided discharge papers, a commendation to go with the medal, a birth certificate from Fall River, and a French passport. He would not have a U.S. passport because he had left the country secretly five years before. Besides, he was only sixteen at the time. He wouldn't have known about such things.

They also went to a tattoo place and Matt had two tattoos needled into his arms. He had a Tricolor put on his left arm and a motto *Legio Patria Nostra*, The Legion is My Country, on the right. Matt never thought he'd see the day he'd wear a tattoo.

Jacques drilled him in the French language and information on the Legion and their part in it. He was only able to spend a few days with Matt, however. He had to leave for New Orleans. The final part of the plan was that Matt was going to join him when his wounds healed.

When Jacques left, Matt's hands were still wrapped in bandages. Matt stayed with Cecile. She continued his education in French. He had to know French as well as someone who had spent five years in the Legion.

When his hands had healed somewhat, Cecile was able to get him some work driving a truck for one of the dress designers. It was easy work, and it brought in a few Francs. The whole healing period took seven weeks. When he left, he took what money he needed from his savings and left the rest for Cecile. She protested, but he hid it in her dresser. She didn't find it until after he had left.

On his last night in Paris, he took her out to dinner. They had a pleasant evening. They rode the metro to a neighborhood near the Eiffel tower. Cecile knew a small but good, restaurant there. Matt had veal kidneys for the first time in his life. They were excellent. They walked part of the way back, taking in the lights and the atmosphere of Paris at night. It was too cold to walk the entire way, so they hopped a bus for the last part. When they reached the apartment, Cecile opened a bottle of wine and then she took off her shoes and sat next to him on the sofa, legs curled under. They talked for a long time.

Cecile seemed intrigued by Matt. After some time had passed, she surprised him by asking him why he had never made any overtures to her. After all, they had lived in the same apartment for almost two months and they seemed to enjoy each other's company.

He was puzzled by the question. He told her she was an eminently desirable woman, but she was Jacques' friend. He would not do anything to hurt Jacques. Tears came to her eyes. She held her hand out and stroked his cheek. She kissed him lightly and told him he was an honorable man. She admired him for that. The conversation did wonders for his self-esteem.

When he left Paris, he went back to Dunkirk. Before he left the city, he sent a letter to his mother.

Dear Mom:

Just a note to let you know I'm well. I will be leaving for Germany when I mail this, so I won't be able to write again for a while.

(This was a code he had hastily worked up with her on that last night. It was telling her he was coming back to the U.S., but he was not coming back to Kingmont. They didn't know whether the police had some way of reading her mail, but just in case.)

I think of you often and I know we are doing the right thing. It's funny, since dad died when I do think about you, I also think about Danny Boy. It may sound like superstition, but I truly believe that people in families, connect somehow on a mystical level. Danny Boy could be a link for us. I have no trouble believing that. I also believe that anytime the words or the tune comes into your mind, it's probably me thinking about you, too.

Say hello to Mark, Luke, John, and Maggie. I miss you all.

Love, Matt

He figured he could get work on a boat going back to the U.S. easier in Dunkirk than the other ports. Besides, if he had to wait a few days for a ship, he thought he could find ways to pass the time there pleasantly.

Colette was ecstatic when he showed up. She was also pleased with his newfound grasp of French. She was also concerned about his hands and his scar, but she did not ask any questions. In addition to their other pursuits, they were able to talk about many things. It took three days for the right ship to come in. They were three very sweet days.

Three weeks later he was in New Orleans and a few days after that, he and Jacques were at the Marine recruiting station downtown. Two and a half weeks later, they were stepping off the train at Parris Island to the bark of a drill instructor and a whole new life.

6

And Then There Were Three

Boot camp was tougher than either of them had anticipated. With his time at the Academy and Jacques' combat experience, they thought Parris Island would not be the test that it turned out to be. They *did* welcome the physical side of the training, although they fell into bed each night exhausted. They understood this as the conditioning phase. What bothered them the most was the seemingly needless harassment and the petty nitpicking by the DIs. They saw no purpose to this. Matt thought back to his academy days. There had been some of that there too. It seemed some people didn't see the line between pushing someone to his limit, and just plain harassment. They resolved to accept the pressure, however, and to try and emerge as good a Marine as they could be. They sometimes had the impression, because of whom they were, they were being singled out for a little extra harassment. They probably were.

The early part of the recruit training was designed to tear down the newly arrived recruit, to make him one of the herd, to strip the civilian out of him. At the same time, his body was being subjected to more physical development than the average person would ever experience. Once the recruit was at the bottom, the rebuilding process could begin.

The recruits made conditioning hikes. They ran the confidence course. They did calisthenics. Again the intent was to condition the individual's body and mind. They learned drill, the emphasis on the individual movements. They learned to take care of their gear, their living space, themselves. They learned the history of the Corps. They actually took physical abuse. All geared toward the stripping process.

When the rebuilding phase started, they worked as a squad or a platoon. The team was now important. Before, when they had run a conditioning hike, with pack, cartridge belt, helmet, and rifle, each man had to think of how he could get through. The same was true with the obstacle course and other physical venues.

Now he had to think of how he could help to make sure that his squad at first, and subsequently his platoon got through. After they had done that, then they had to learn together how to get the unit through as fast as possible.

The same emphasis was applied to the drill fields, log carries, tugs of war, scores on tests, the rifle range etc. The emphasis was on duty to your buddy, your platoon, the Corps, competitiveness, and the system. Teamwork and physical skills were stressed. A whole scoring system to determine the honor platoon was put into place. It stressed teamwork, but there were still some individual accomplishments that could add to a platoon's score.

As expected, Matt and Jacques had done well. On the rifle range, Matt had shot a 246 out of 250, but Jacques had shot a 247. Both scores qualified for expert. Matt had done better than Jacques on the knowledge testing and housekeeping parts of the training, thus prompting Jacques to call Matt "the maid." They both finished first or second in all the physical tests, Matt besting Jacques on the events that required quickness, Jacques winning those that emphasized strength.

There was a bit of a hiatus from training near the end of the training schedule, as their whole platoon had to stand mess duty. This meant working in the galleys most of each day, serving, cleaning, and peeling for the other recruits. Each platoon took turns. While a platoon was on mess duty, other training was held in abeyance but physical conditioning still continued. Matt and Jacques accepted mess duty with forbearance. It was a necessary part of getting the work done and a way of humbling the proud Marines a little. It's hard to feel like a warrior when you are up to your elbows in slop.

The final event for platoon score in the honor platoon competition was to be the pugil stick bouts. Each platoon was to determine a champion and that man faced off against the other platoon's champions.

The pugil stick is a 2-inch by 2-inch piece of wood, four feet long, with padded bags on each end. It is designed to simulate a rifle with a bayonet attached. The Marine holds the stick at port arms, (in front, at an angle across his body), and uses it to poke or butt his opponent. Each pugilist wears a football helmet with a face bar, shoulder pads, and a padded groin protector with a steel jock. With a sardonic curl of the lip, the Marines call it a diaper. Padded gloves, similar to those worn by hockey players, complete the equipment.

The scoring system awarded one point for each jab or butt stroke that landed on the body, two points for head strokes, and three points for a knockdown. Fifteen points was a winning score.

Earlier in training, they had worked with the real thing – a rifle with the bayonet. They had learned all the proper strokes and parries, but they had not actually struck each other. Now, they could put their training to the test. The pugil stick contests were the highlights of boot camp.

Each of the platoons chose their own champion through competition. In Matt and Jacques their platoon, the DIs, sensing the superior abilities of the two men, seeded them so that the two men would not compete against each other unless they made it to the platoon finals. The arrangement worked.

Matt circled to his left. Jacques followed his movement. They were inside a ring of howling recruits. Some cheered for Matt, some for Jacques. Both men had stripped to the waist. The sweat trickled down Matt's face, stinging his eyes. It was hard to see with an oversized helmet on and a bar across his face. But his opponent had the same handicap.

Jacques did a quick shuffle of his feet, getting Matt's attention.

"Ah, you are awake in there, mon ami. I just thought I would check," boomed the Frenchman with a sly smile.

"Look to yourself, you big shitbird. You'll get yours soon enough," Matt spat back, smiling.

"Ooh, the 'maid' is testy today." With that statement, he made a lunge at Matt with the point of the stick. Matt reacted quickly and parried the thrust. Continuing in one motion he moved inside the parried thrust and smacked Jacques on the helmet with the point of his stick.

"Two for Farrell," barked Sergeant Sibley, who was the referee.

"The 'maid' has a sting," said Jacques as he moved in closer to Matt.

Matt saw his chance, so he faked a thrust with the point, catching Jacques' stick in the process and knocking it aside. He swung his stick like a right cross and caught Jacques on the right side of the helmet causing him to stumble.

"Two more for Farrell. That's four," shouted the referee.

Lescoulie became a little more serious and made some cautious moves. Matt parried easily. A few minutes went by with parries and thrusts, but no scores. The hot Carolina sun beat down. Then Jacques did a double shuffle with his feet causing Matt to lean in the wrong direction for a split second. He didn't know what hit him. He suddenly found himself on the ground. His helmet was turned. He was looking out the ear hole.

"That's three for Lescoulie," said Sibley, barely holding back a laugh. "The score is now four to three." The group of spectators howled at the spectacle of Matt with his helmet on sideways.

Matt brushed himself off, straightened his headgear and stared at the big Frenchman. He loved that man, but right now all he could think about was beating him. He became sharply focused. He embarked on a strategy of quick moves, thrusting and parrying, attacking from the edges. He did not want to get into a situation where he could be hit like that again. His plan worked.

He danced around Jacques, never letting his opponent get set. At first, he scored a single point here and a single point there, but he didn't get hit hard. Jacques figured out what he was doing and when Matt reached to get one of his touch points, he ducked and came up under Matt's guard. He hit Matt with a good blow to the chin and staggered him, but Matt didn't go down. At that point Jacques took the lead nine to eight. Matt grimly continued bobbing and weaving and with his sudden strikes he built up his lead again, this time to Thirteen to ten. Jacques, not to be outdone, was able to rally at this point and score a touch point. And then, he put Matt down again. Now the score was fourteen to thirteen in favor of Jacques.

Matt came off the dirt like a wildcat. He seemed to come at the Frenchman from all directions at once. The only thing Jacques could do was fight off the blows and wait for Matt to tire. Matt didn't tire. In fact he seemed energized by every blow. He finally ended the match by scoring the fourteenth and fifteenth points with vertical butt strokes to the chin. Jacques had been falling back and had partially blocked the stroke by crashing his stick onto Matt's hand, but the force of Matt's swing was too strong. The blow went through and hit Jacques squarely on the chin. The group cheered and jumped up and down. It had been a good fight. The combatants were spent. Jacques moved over to Matt and threw his arms around him.

"Good fight, mon ami. You are too quick for me. I salute you." He held out his hand.

Matt took his glove off. When he grasped Jacques hand, he felt a twinge of pain. He looked at his hand and for the first time he realized he had been hit there. There was a red mark across the knuckles and some swelling had started.

"Those were some blows you hit me with. I saw stars a couple of times," replied Matt graciously.

"You did look funny, sitting on the ground with your helmet turned around."

They both laughed. Matt looked at his hand again. That blow must have been a powerful collision. It went right through the glove. Well, nicks and bruises were a part of life. Nothing to worry about.

The finals between the platoons were to be held the next day. There were three platoons going through training. The other two platoon champions had already fought. Matt had to face the remaining champion. He hoped the injured hand wouldn't hinder him.

The next morning the DI noticed that Matt's hand had swelled considerably and it was turning blue. He sent him to sick bay. The diagnosis was two fractured fingers. They decided a cast would be of no value, so they just wrapped the hand and gave him some pills for the pain and to reduce swelling. No more pugil sticks for Matt though. Jacques would have to take his place. Matt was a little miffed. He wanted to compete, but the doctor said no.

The physical parts of the training were completed and Matt would not have to miss anything important. He was deflated but he was also glad Jacques would represent them. Jacques was a one tough hombre.

The arena for the final match was an area near the confidence course. The ground was sandy and there were bleachers facing the *pit,* as the DIs called it. Matt and Jacques' platoon had arrived first and commandeered all the best seats. The other platoon jogged up in formation a minute or two later. There was a little pushing and shoving for better positions, but the DI's barked them under control. There were 150 recruits between the two platoons and another 30 or 40 Marines wandered over to watch the show.

Matt stood on the side, helping Jacques don his protective gear. They looked across at the other platoon's champion. He was an extremely well built Negro. They were surprised. There weren't many Negroes in the Marine Corps. There were none in their platoon. Some of the cooks in the mess hall were Negroes, but that was it.

Matt commented quietly to Jacques, "The DI in that platoon is a real redneck. If this guy is his champion he must be outstanding."

Jacques wasn't sure what a redneck was but he understood what Matt was trying to say to him. "Later you will have to tell me what a redneck is. In any event, my opponent won't be any tougher than you, mon ami. And I almost beat you."

"Well I hope you learned from that shithead. I beat you because I was quicker and you spent too much time trying to knock me down instead of scoring points."

"Matthew . . . Matthew . . . . You beat me because you got mad and attacked like a devil. I couldn't defend against that."

"Whatever" Matt cut short what he was going to say. The referee was motioning Jacques over.

Jacques looked at his opponent while the referee checked their equipment The Negro was a large man although a little shorter than Jacques. He was well muscled. His muscles had definition. They were sharp-edged. There was no fat at all on his body. His upper body, like Jacques, had a triangular shape – wide shoulders, narrow waist.

His skin was dark, very dark. Ebony would be a word that fit the man perfectly. Through the front of his helmet, Jacques could see white eyes showing against the blue-black skin. The man's eyes were fixed into a stare. They looked right at Jacques as if trying to penetrate him. Most people's eyes are partially covered by lids. The entire pupil was not visible unless they were surprised. Not so this man. This man's normal eye position was perfectly centered all the time.

The referee finished his inspection of the two men. He was satisfied and bid the combatants to begin. Immediately they both went into a crouch and circled to their left, a few steps at a time. They also edged closer to each other. Jacques threw the first punch, a short jab. The black man leaned back. The jab missed. The Negro made the next move and lunged quickly at Jacques. Jacques parried and stepped inside the jab to score the first points with a poke to the head. His platoon cheered. Score one for Matt. Jacques had learned that move from him.

They circled a few more times when Jacques' opponent suddenly rushed him. Instinctively he fell back. The black man moved inside and hit his chin with a vertical butt stroke. Tie score.

Matt had done that to Jacques too. But he hadn't learned from *that*. He'd better stay more alert. Jacques remembered his double shuffle had worked on Matt. He tried it again and he was satisfied to see his opponent sitting on the ground staring at him.

If it was possible, the Negro's face grew darker. His eyes became more intense. He jumped off the ground and attacked Jacques with fury. Jacques fell back defensively, then he forced himself to stop and hold his ground. He took a hit and then gave one. He took another blow and then knocked the man off balance causing him to stumble. The man came back at him again, though, his eyes even wilder with aggression. The Frenchman kept parrying, but the Black man was wearing him down. Finally Jacques took a blow on the side of the head that floored him.

While on the ground he called out, "Score? What's the score?"

The referee, a different sergeant than before, yelled. "You're losing eleven to nine."

Lescoulie rose slowly, keeping his eyes on the other Marine. He circled slowly to his left recovering his breath and composure as he did so. He thought he would try Matt's technique for awhile. He fought conservatively, a jab here, a poke there. He scored a few points. When he felt he had gained his strength again, he launched another attack preceded by the double shuffle. The Negro was waiting for that move. With a quick side step he parried the attack and knocked Jacques down for the second time. It was now Jacques' turn to see red. He came off the ground with a roar. He surprised his opponent. The Marine parried the first blow, but Jacques was inside his guard and he planted the point hard into his gut. He went down with a whoosh of escaping air.

"Got you that time you, shit head," he yelled at his fallen opponent. Then he looked at the referee. "Score?"

"Fourteen to Fourteen."

The black man didn't get up right away. He just sat on the ground gasping for air. Jacques went over to him. "Are you hurt, man? Can you continue?"

The Negro looked at Jacques. "I need my breath. It is coming."

"Looks like you won, son," said the referee.

"No," said Jacques. "He can still get up. I don't win by default."

The referee looked over at the fallen Marine. He *was* getting up. "Okay, Frenchy, you asked for it. Go get him."

They circled again slowly. Jacques was conservative again. He didn't want to underestimate his opponent. Suddenly the black man rushed him. Jacques fell back parrying. He saw an opportunity and lunged. The man was not there. Jacques was suddenly sick. He knew he had been beaten. The blow was light. It hit his helmet on the left side, but it was a definite hit. The Negro had won.

The black man's platoon cheered. He took off his helmet and moved so he could look into Jacques face. His eyes showed deference. "You are a warrior. Man. I respect you."

His shaved head glistened with sweat. Little tendrils of steam drifted into the air. He smiled at Jacques and put his hand out. It was difficult, but Jacques took his hand and smiled back. He took off his helmet. "You are a warrior too, my good man. I salute your prowess. What is your name?"

"Spears. Ivan Spears. What is yours?"

"Lescoulie. Jacques Lescoulie."

"Ah . . . you are one of the foreign legionnaires I heard about. I am honored to have bested you. But, I would not have won if you had not given me a second chance."

There was trace of an accent in his speech. Jacques couldn't place it. "Every man deserves a fair chance. You knew how to use it."

"I hope, my big friend, that if you face a real enemy you will not be as generous with him as you were with me," he said with a faint smile, his eyes in their stare mode.

"If you were an enemy and if you were still alive when we reached the point we reached, I assure you, you would have been killed by the stroke into your belly or by the head smash that would have immediately followed it."

The black man stared into Jacques' eyes a moment. He grinned. "I believe you."

Matt approached. Spears looked him. "Is this the other legionnaire?"

Matt spoke first. "Yes, I am. Who are you?" he asked, smiling.

Spears gave him his name and then the confab was over. Spears' DI grabbed the black Marine by the neck and pushed him toward the platoon. "Okay, Spears. Get your ass over with your platoon. You're still a fucking boot. You ain't got time for lollygagging." Other DI's moved toward Matt and Jacques.

Spears smiled slightly, nodded his head to Matt and Jacques and then trotted away from the pit.

When he was gone, and they were stumbling back to their platoon, Matt turned to Lescoulie and asked, "Did you pick up any kind of an accent from him?"

"Yes I thought it sounded slightly English, but I wasn't sure. I guess I didn't hear enough."

"That's what I heard, too. He's got some eyes, doesn't he?" Matt commented. "Maybe he comes from the Caribbean. Some of those people speak with a British accent, although most of them have some sort of a lilt to their speech which I didn't catch with him."

"I agree, mon ami. I don't think he's from the Caribbean. He sure is a fine specimen of a warrior though, isn't he?"

"He sure is." At that moment, their DI grabbed them roughly and along with a few well-chosen words, sent them off stumbling toward their barracks.

Boot camp ended three days later with a parade. The three platoons were bedecked for the first time with their green uniforms and shooting medals. They wore the flat overseas cap with the small, bronze, globe and anchor on the side. Those who had made private first class wore their red trimmed stripe proudly.

At ten hundred on the final day, in typical military fashion the troops had been standing on the parade field for two hours, the last hour at attention. In order to be sure the troops were ready at ten hundred, the depot commander had ordered them on the field by oh nine thirty. To make sure they made that deadline, the company, from which the three platoons derived ordered them out for an oh nine hundred muster. The DIs had them ready at oh eight hundred.

At ten hundred exactly, the command staff marched into the review position between two guidons on the drill field. The staff included the recruit depot commander his staff, and visiting dignitaries. They posted themselves in a small boxlike formation, facing the troops, in front of the bleachers that had been set up for the family and friends of the graduating Marines. There were several hundred such guests, all in a gala mood.

At ten-o-one, the Parris Island Base band marched onto the field, and began to play Souza marches. They wore their greens and carried their instruments and red and gold music packets strung over their shoulders. They entertained the gathering with precision marching and by playing rousing tunes — *The Washington Post March* (the monkey wrapped his tail around the flagpole), and *Semper Fidelis*. The bandmaster, a tall master sergeant, twirled his large baton in a series of complicated maneuvers, displaying, flare, skill and precision. He also used the long staff to signal commands to his musicians.

After a few minutes of music and more precision marching, the band formed up on one side of the parade field and dropped into a drumbeat mode. The parade adjutant stepped forward from the assembled troops and informed the commanding officer that the parade was formed. The commander told the adjutant to proceed. The adjutant spun on his heels and boomed.

"Pass in review."

The drill instructors took over and commanded,

"Right shoulder! Arms!"

There were sharp, precise *cracks* of hands against wood as the recruits executed the maneuver.

"Right! Face!"

Three hundred men moved a precision quarter turn to the right.

"Forward!" The adjutant went up on his toes as he boomed the command "March!"

Left feet stepped out gingerly at first. There was a great deal of moaning as troops who had stood at attention for more than an hour forced their rebellious knees and legs to move. The initial steps were awkward, but within a few stumbling seconds they were a precision team again.

The band moved out from their stationary position and led the troops. As they passed the review stand. They played *The Marines' Hymn*. The marchers moved in behind them, executing the column lefts and rights necessary to position themselves to pass the reviewing stand. Most of the observers, particularly the "old salts," had lumps in their throats. This is what it meant to succeed, to endure. This was what it meant to be a Marine. *The Marines' Hymn* was a moving piece of music, in which they all took pride.

The colors came next. The command staff saluted and then the platoons of proud new Marines marched by, each group executing severe *Eyes Right*, as they passed in review.

One by one the platoons returned to their prior positions. When they were all assembled again, the final command was given. "Dismissed!"

Three hundred hats flew in the air. And then there was a scramble. Unlike the cadets in the service academies who no longer needed their Academy hats, the Marines had to find theirs again. It was still part of their uniform.

Most of the new Marines had family or friends at the graduation. The assemblage broke into small groups as proud parents, grandparents and brothers and sisters crowded around their hero. There was a great deal of laughter. Many of them would go to lunch or dinner at a restaurant for their first good meal in months. There would be parties at some of the hotels.

Matt and Jacques had no one to honor them. While the others celebrated, they went back to their barracks and retrieved their gear. They already had their orders so they were free to go.

The next stop in their career would be infantry training at Camp Lejeune, North Carolina. They had three days to get there. They looked around at what had been their home for three months. They had learned and endured on this place, but there was nothing to keep them here now. They decided to leave right away. They would check in early and they would take liberty in Jacksonville North Carolina rather than in South Carolina. They could also down a few brews in town as they waited for the train.

Ivan Spears walked slowly away from the smiling happy people at the reviewing stand. He also had no well wishers to help him celebrate. He was glad the initial training was over. He had found it taxing, but not overly so. He decided growing up in the African bush had prepared him well for a life such as this. He was looking forward to the infantry training. He too was leaving right away for Camp Lejeune.

Their train arrived late in the day. Matt and Jacques reached the station just before it rolled in. They'd had enough beer to make them happy, but not enough to impair their capabilities. Spears was already there. They boarded together. Matt, noticing the black Marine, invited

Spears to sit with them. The passenger cars on this train were old, vintage railroad. The seat backs could be swung from the back of the seat to the front so the two seats could face each other. The trio quickly swung theirs around.

A few other Marines were also on the train but Matt or Jacques didn't know any of them. They talked with Spears about inconsequential things for a while and then Matt asked about his name.

"Spears is not my real name. My real name is complicated. It is an African name. I took Spears because it sounds like a warrior's name."

"You're correct, it does," agreed Jacques. The mention of Africa prompted him to ask, "I have some familiarity with some African languages. Perhaps I would recognize your real name."

"The name of my clan is Cestwayo."

"Cestwayo." Jacques repeated his brow furrowed as he tried to pull something from his memory. Then he smiled in satisfaction. "Zulu."

"You are correct my big friend. It is Zulu."

"Zulu," said Matt to himself. Images and legends about one of the fiercest military armies of all time flooded his mind. That probably explains the accent. "Is your first name a . . . taken name, too?"

"Partially. I have a tribal name. Ib-ano. Ivan was close. Also, isn't there someone called Ivan the Terrible?" He asked with a little twinkle in his dark eyes.

Matt laughed. "You bet, but he was no warrior. He was a mad dictator."

"That is close enough," Ivan said with, what was as near to a smile as he seemed capable.

The train was rattling along, swaying from side to side as it passed through the coastal lowland scenery. Jacques had been thinking. "Ivan, I seem to remember a famous Cestwayo fighting against the English in the late nineteenth century.

"You are very smart, Jacques, if I may call you that."

"You can call me anything, mon ami. We are 'buddies' I think the Americans call it."

"Thank you, my friends." He looked at Matt to include him, too. Then he turned back to Jacques. "The Cestwayo you refer to was my great-grandfather. He beat the English at Isandilwana. He had only spears and brave warriors. The English had guns and cannons, but we still won. It was a great victory."

"What happened after that?" asked Matt.

"We couldn't stem the tide. Eventually, the English brought in more and more troops. We ended up negotiating a treaty with them. We really had no choice. It was that or many years of bloodshed. They were not hard to live with. They left us alone as long as we didn't try to extend our kingdom. Things have been peaceful for many years. We are now cattle breeders and farmers. The warrior ways are gone."

There was something sad in the way he said that. He looked out the window for a few moments. The three were silent.

Then he turned back. "For me, I desire something else. I could stay there and be rich by our standards, but I hear the call. I see too many weak-willed people around me. I see bad people, people without honor. I have problems accepting that. I also feel the need to compete against an opponent, to test myself. If I stayed there I would have to suppress that or I would get in trouble. Either way is bad."

"We can understand that, eh, Jacques." Matt turned to his friend to get his agreement. Jacques nodded. "We feel somewhat the same." He looked back at Ivan. "You speak excellent English. Did you attend an English school?"

"Missionaries, my friend. We had American and English missionaries at churches near us. My father insisted I go to one or the other. I went to both. So did my brothers. I have twenty-seven brothers."

Matt looked up, startled. "What? Twenty-seven brothers."

"And eighteen sisters, although my people don't count them. I keep track of them because I learned some Christian ways. Women are important, too. Incidentally, my father had eight wives when I last saw him."

Matt shook his head. He decided that he was a long way from understanding Ivan's culture, but Ivan looked like a good Marine, and that was the only way Matt was going to judge him.

"How did you hear about the Marine Corps?" Lescoulie asked.

He looked at Jacques with the wide-eyed stare for a second and then said, "I was in Johannesburg. I saw some Marines wearing dress blues at the embassy. I asked who they were. I talked to one of the officers. He was kind enough to give me some pamphlets and some books. One was called *Guadalcanal Diary*. Another was about Carlson's Raiders. I read them many times. I was, as some of you say . . . hooked."

They laughed. Both Matt and Jacques understood the power of books in creating desire.

The rest of the trip revolved around a discussion of their backgrounds. Matt's story and his fake history passed muster admirably. A bond was developing. Ivan seemed to like them and they liked him.

Infantry training is just that. The graduate recruits had earned the title of Marine. Now they needed to learn *how* to be Marines. They assembled and disassembled every weapon the individual Marine used.

They also fired them all. That included M-1 rifles, BARs (Browning Automatic Rifles), Carbines (a small automatic rifle), sub-machine guns, and 45 caliber pistols. They worked with crew served weapons such as 30-caliber light and heavy machine guns and mortars. They learned small unit tactics and how they fitted in with large unit tactics. They learned how to use supporting arms like artillery, naval gunfire, air strikes and mortars. They worked with tanks, landing craft, and rocket launchers. They worked with grenades, satchel charges and other explosives. They were introduced to flamethrowers. They used radios and land telephones.

At the end of four weeks they had either used or at least been introduced to everything a Marine infantryman would need. From this point on Marine training would vary. Marines would be assigned to different specialties to meet the needs of the Corps: communications, armor, supply, and others. But this infantry training was a basic principle of the Corps. It was provided so that, regardless of what a man's specialty was, in a pinch, any Marine could become an infantryman and be able to help the cause. The value of this doctrine had been proven many times over.

Matt, Jacques, and Ivan sweated out their orders. They hoped to stay together. When the orders finally came through they were elated. They were all going to California. They were to report to the Fifth Marine Regiment at Camp Pendleton. They were authorized leave time, but they opted not to take it and to report as soon as they could. They reasoned that they would save the leave for a better time. Besides, they were anxious to get started on their warriors' life.

7

In Another Part of the Forest

Meanwhile, back at Kingmont.

The party was getting out of hand. The parking area in the picnic grove was filled with teenagers admiring the latest hotrod innovations. Amidst the roar of "souped up" engines, John and some of his drag race buddies had been arguing with some teens from across the river about who had the fastest 'rod. Some of the partygoers had brought beer, resulting in arguments that got louder and more vehement. Being only sixteen, John wasn't much of a drinker. As a matter of fact, the only time he did drink was at these drag competitions. Somewhere in the back of his head it nagged at him that these "meets" were getting out of hand, but he shrugged it off. He had three beers that night and he felt he could take on anyone, in a fight, or in a drag race, or whatever. Some of the girls, naïve young bobbysoxers, who had fawned over the "rodders" earlier, drifted away as some pushing and shoving took place and the party became rougher. Others, of a less genteel stripe, stayed close, looking for forbidden thrills. There might be a fight. There might be blood.

Near midnight, John and a skinny teen named Barry decided they needed to settle the drag race issue. If there were to be a fight, it would have to wait. Everyone piled out of the picnic area and ran for their cars. John had a street 'rod that he and a few of his friends had built from a 1937 Plymouth. It was a classic two-seater with a rumble seat. It had been modified to go over 100 miles per hour. Even if it wasn't the fastest 'rod around, it made the most noise. The car had no muffler, only a straight pipe.

Barry had a 1940 Ford coupe with a pre WWII engine that had been souped up. It had never been let all out, but Barry felt it would also do more than 100 miles per hour. His hotrod boasted a deep-toned Hollywood muffler.

The party moved, en masse, from the picnic area to the darkened and deserted business district of the town. The two "chariots" lined up abreast on Grand Street, engines rumbling. Grand Street was the widest street in town. The original city planners had designed this to be the main street, but for some inexplicable reason, the commercial business-es had never located along this street the way they had on the other streets. At present, there were only a few run down stores and unoccu-pied buildings on the thoroughfare. Grand Street was a long straight-away, making it a favorite drag strip of the teenagers.

Both racers pumped the gas pedals, creating bigger and better roaring sounds and fueling their adrenaline. The two drivers looked at each other, defiance in their eyes. Someone raised a handkerchief and then dropped it. The racers were off with a scream of spinning tires, burning rubber and clouds of smoke. Barry was leaning over his wheel, his head almost against the windshield, "pushing" his rig with his body. John was tucked into the left corner of his, chin tight to his chest directly behind his wheel, guiding his "bomb." They roared down the street, both cars fish-tailing as tires fought to gain traction. Buildings, parked cars, stop signs, light poles, and trees all flashed by in a blur of muted color. They were a half-mile into their drag before either dropped into third gear. Within seconds, both boys were pushing the magical 100 mph mark, twisting and roaring in a magnificent display of all out driving.

Suddenly a line of headlights turned on directly in their path. The lights were still a distance away, but they all were on high-beam. They were spread across the street and aimed right at the windshields of the two hot-rodders. The brilliance blinded the young racers and they immediately began to brake, skidding and spinning as they did. It took time and control to bring their vehicles down from high speed with safety. Again rubber burned, brakes locked, cars fish-tailed.

As they managed to bring their cars back to a reasonable speed and to look for a way out, for the first time, they noticed flashing red lights behind them. They were boxed in. The police had been waiting for them.

Barry did a "wheely" and spun around. He was going to try to make a run for a side street but the red lights were too close. John had already decided that. He braked hard and came to a stop a few feet short of the bright headlights in his path. Another of the police cars pulled up behind him and pinned his vehicle. A tall uniformed policeman came from behind the lights and walked up the car. As if the high beam headlights weren't enough, he shone a flashlight in John's face.

"Get out," he ordered, with no preliminaries. There was no smile or politeness on the policeman's face. Other policemen were moving around the two cars.

John boosted himself out of his seat, and swung his legs over the door. He dropped to a standing position, not sure what to do next. He couldn't see Barry's car in the glare.

The policeman shoved him back against his car and made him put his hands on his head. He patted him down from head to foot. Satisfied, he told him to put his arms down. John figured the cuffs would come next. His anger at being stopped began to wane. Shortly other thoughts crept into his mind. How would he explain this to his mother, or worse, to Mark, especially the cuffs?

But, there were no cuffs. The policeman grabbed John by his arm, forcing his hand into John's armpit and started walking him off the street and into a little park that was on the side of the road. His grip was tight and it hurt. The Policeman held John's arm high enough so that he had to stumble as he walked. John's thoughts focused. This was one strong cop. But, he had his pride. He would not complain about the pain.

After they were out of the lights and into the park, a figure stepped out from the shadows of a large chestnut tree. It was too dark to pick out details and John's eyes had been exposed to bright lights, but he was able to determine that it was a middle-aged man, wearing a topcoat and a fedora. Probably a plainclothes cop, he thought. There were other figures still under the chestnut tree, but John was not able to make them out.

"I'll take him, Ed. See if Bob needs any help with the other one," the plainclothes man ordered.

"Okay, lieutenant. You need any help, let me know."

"I won't need any help, Ed. Thanks."

Ed released John and left them to see about Barry. The man wearing the coat turned to his new charge. John was standing in front of him massaging his arm where the policeman had held him. The man moved closer to John, looked in his eyes, and shook his head.

"Well, Mr. Flaherty, it seems you've gotten yourself into a bit of trouble, wouldn't you say?"

John didn't answer.

"You should answer your elders, John."

John did not respond.

The man shook his head again. "Playing tough, huh? Well, let's see what we have here."

John's eyes were adjusting. He now recognized the older man as the lieutenant who had led the investigation into Van Scooten's death.

John's best memory of him was that behind the hard-nosed police demeanor he projected, there seemed to be a basic fairness about him. John couldn't have expressed it that way but that was the impression he had. The lieutenant had been very nice to John's mother. His name came to him after a moment … McQuinn. The lieutenant was flipping through a small notebook.

"First. You were driving a car, am I not correct, John?"

"Yes, sir," John spoke his first words.

"Is it nighttime, John?"

"Yes, sir," John was puzzled.

"Is your driver's license a junior driving license, John?"

Now he knew where this was going. "Yes, sir."

"If I'm not mistaken, people with junior driver's licenses are not allowed to drive after dark. Is that the way you understand the law, John?"

He had a sinking feeling. "Yes, sir."

"Good. That's settled. Now let's see." He looked at his notebook again. "What's the drinking age in New York John?"

John just looked uncomfortable.

"You do understand the drinking age in New York is eighteen, don't you, John?"

"Yes, sir"

"How old are you, John?"

"Sixteen, sir."

"Have you been drinking, John?"

John mumbled his response.

"I didn't hear you, John. Have you been drinking?"

"Just a couple . . . sir."

"I see. So even though eighteen, the legal drinking age in New York, is the lowest in the United States, you couldn't even wait to get to that legal age."

"Yes, sir . . . uh no, sir."

McQuinn turned another page in his notebook. He had a pencil in his hand. He tapped the point on his front teeth. "I spoke to Officer Watson, the policeman who walked you over here, and he says he figures you were driving close to one hundred miles an hour when we turned all the lights on."

John looked straight ahead.

"He figures that might be a little hard to prove in court but he knows he can establish at least eighty miles an hour. John, do you know what the speed limit on Grand Street is?"

"No, sir."

"John, it's a city street. What's the maximum speed on any city street in Kingmont?"

"Uh … thirty-five?"

"Yes, John, thirty-five."

"Well I talked some more with Officer Watson. He's ready to accept seventy as the speed you were going. Wasn't that nice of him?"

John hadn't seen McQuinn talk to the other policeman. But he was getting the message. John was beginning to feel trapped.

"Yes, sir"

"John, how much is seventy less thirty-five?"

"Thirty-five," John whispered.

"How tidy. Let's sum it all up," his voice changed. He was now all business.

"Driving at night on a junior license, drinking under eighteen, and driving double the speed limit. Does that sum it up for you?"

John was miserable. He said. "Yes, sir."

McQuinn walked around for a moment then turned to John.

"Mr. Flaherty, I owe your father from long ago. And I feel some responsibility for your brother and his problems. I also think your mother is one of the finest women I know. So, in order not to embarrass them any, but also to give you the punishment you deserve, I decree . . . doesn't that sound great?" He smiled at the now miserable youth. "In any event, I decree that you are going to receive the following punishment."

He cleared his throat. "Twenty-five lashes on the bare rear end with a leather strap and forfeiture of your right to drive for two months."

John looked at him incredulously.

"I . . . I . . . don't—"

A voice boomed out of the darkness. "Take it, John. Take it."

John looked into the dark, but he couldn't see who it was, though the voice was familiar. He looked around miserably.

"The alternative is . . . court . . . something on your record . . . embarrassment for your mother and your brothers . . . a family . . . uh, let's say scandal. What say you, John?" McQuinn arched his eyebrows.

He looked around desperately for some way out. He could run. They'd catch him though. He could refuse and take the court. But he was in the wrong. They'd convict him. Finally, he looked at McQuinn and nodded. He agreed.

"There's one more thing, John."

John looked at McQuinn with annoyance. He was changing the deal.

But McQuinn was adamant. "I want your word. There'll be no more drinking until you're legal."

John breathed a sigh of relief. "I agree."

"Okay, John. Drop your drawers and lean over the stump there." Someone from the dark came forward with a strap.

John did as he was told.

Nothing in his whole young life had hurt as much as that strapping. He never wanted to go through that again. He did not cry out, however, until he had only two or three strokes to go. Even then they were more like whimpers than cries.

When it was over, he pulled up his trousers. McQuinn handed the strap back into the shadows. The strap left welts and plenty of red skin, but no wounds. McQuinn said to him, "John, you took your punishment like a man. Your father and your brothers would be proud."

He held his hand out, palm up. "I will keep your license in my desk drawer. Two months from today, let's see, that will be November 30, you come and see me and I'll give it back to you. Fair?"

John handed him the license with shaking hands. "Yes, sir."

"Remember, John, you gave me your word about the drinking. If you break your word, we'll meet back here for another session with the strap. Okay?"

"Yes, sir."

"You can go now, Mr. Flaherty. You'll have to walk. I have your license, besides its dark now and you can't drive after dark." He smiled at the chastened young man. "I also figure you might not want to sit down for a while." He said the last with a smile. "One of the boys will bring your car over in the morning. Get a good night's rest."

John walked toward town, limping slightly, and touching his rear end gingerly.

McQuinn turned toward the tree. Two men walked out, Frank and Jack Gannon. Frank had the leather belt. "Not the same 'tool' I used with Matt years ago, but it works just as well." he said.

"That's all he needs. He's a good kid. He just needs a little direction. Matt or Mike would have done the same thing," said McQuinn. "Do you think we should tell Mark about this?"

"Naw. Mark has his own problems. Besides it wouldn't be fair to the kid. He took the strapping as an *alternative* to that."

"You're right. We'll let it lie."

They walked to where they had their cars parked. Most of the police cruisers had gone. The other teenagers were nowhere in sight. The street was quiet again.

"How's Katie doing, Pat? I don't hear much since all that trouble died down."

"From what I can see, she's doing real good. At first, the Van Scootens were going to disown her, but Mark got some attorney from New York City to handle her case. I think Mark told me he was the father of one of his classmates at the Naval Academy. In any event, she came away with a bundle."

"She didn't get the mansion though, right?"

"That's about all she didn't get, Frank. She was Van Scooten's wife. She owned everything with him jointly. She didn't want the business or the big house, so she got a cash settlement. I heard it was more than a million dollars."

Frank whistled. "She deserves it."

"No argument here. Oh, also," he remembered something else. "She gets an income from the profits of the business."

"Sounds like that city lawyer did a good job," said Jack Gannon.

"It also helped having a police lieutenant tell him about Van Scooten's history so that he could tell the Van Scooten's attorney." Frank Gannon prodded.

"That's *the doctrine of continuous circulation* in operation."

"The what?"

"What goes around, comes around."

The elder Gannon laughed again. They stopped at McQuinn's car. McQuinn wrestled the keys out of his pocket.

"She's really fixed up the old farm," Jack contributed. "She added more rooms and bought more land around it. She seems to have a going thing there. I was out there a couple of months ago, when Mark came home. They want to make it a working farm. Some cousin of Katie's and his wife have come over from Ireland. He seems to know about farms."

"Know anything about the little girl, what's her name . . . Maggie?" asked Frank.

McQuinn scratched his jaw. "Katie keeps her at home mostly. She has some teachers come in to help her. She goes to a special school in Albany, too. I don't know much about her. She'd a pretty little thing. It's a real shame."

"Makes you wonder sometimes, about God and all."

McQuinn looked at Gannon oddly.

Gannon noted the look. "No, I mean why does God let those kinds of things happen to good people while the world's bastards get away with everything. Shouldn't he reward people like Katie and her family . . . ?"

"Where were you when the nuns taught religion? God's ways are not for us to question. He has a divine plan. We won't know what it is until we die."

"Yeah, I know. Somehow it doesn't seem right though."

McQuinn opened the door of his car and got in. Jack had wandered off. For some reason Frank wanted to talk some more. He leaned on the open door and looked down at McQuinn.

"Did you find anything funny about the way Van Scooten died Pat?"

"Why? You know something?"

"No, it's just . . . well, weren't there some questions, some loose ends?"

"What are you driving at Frank?"

"He was stabbed by a knife, right Pat? Isn't that what killed him?"

McQuinn saw where he was headed. "Yeah, he was killed by a knife. Stabbed five times. It was in the paper."

"You figure Matt did it, right?"

"He left the note. He took off. That sure looks guilty to me. Don't get me wrong Frank, Van Scooten 'needed killing,' as they say in Texas, but everything sure points to Matt having done it. Hell, if he stayed around he might have been able get off. All he needed to show to a jury was what Van Scooten did to her. It looks like Matt stabbed him to me."

"Except for one thing."

"What's that?"

"It ain't Matt's style. I figure Matt would have beat him to death not stabbed him."

McQuinn sagged a little. "Frank, that has nagged at me, too. But everything points to Matt. Maybe he just lost his temper and grabbed what he could. It's all over now. If Matt is ever found, maybe he can enlighten us. I need to go."

Frank backed off and let him close the door. McQuinn rolled the window down.

"Frank, I appreciate your help tonight. The best we can do for that family is to make sure those boys come out right. Luke seems to be okay but we need to keep an eye on this young hellion. If we get to talk to Matt, maybe we can help him, too, but right now we just got to let it be."

Gannon nodded. He really did understand.

McQuinn had started the car. He was putting it into gear.

"One more thing, Pat."

McQuinn looked at him in exasperation. He loved Gannon, but sometimes . . . . "What?"

"It's 1948. Neither the Yankees nor the Brooklyn Dodgers are in the World Series. We still have to bet. Who you taking? The Boston Braves or the Cleveland Indians?"

McQuinn almost hit him as he jammed the accelerator down and sped away.

In "Another part of the forest . . . ."

Rosalind was finishing his/her epilogue.

"I charge you, O women, for the love you bear to men, to like as much of this play as pleases you: And I charge you, O men for the love you bear to women, as I perceive by your simpering, none of you hates them, that between you and the woman the play may please. If I were a woman, I would kiss as many of you as had beards that pleased me, complexions that liked me and breaths that I defied not: And, I am sure as many good beards, or good faces, or sweet breaths, will, for my kind offer, when I make curtsy, bid me farewell."

With skirts whirling Rosalind left the stage.

The ovation was enormous as the entire audience in the compact theatre came to their feet, clapping and stomping. The small building shook. When the curtain was raised for a final bow, the noise increased. As the actors came on stage to receive their accolades, it grew still louder and when Rosalind stepped out, the only appropriate word would have been, deafening.

Curtain call followed curtain call for a full ten minutes. Finally, after it seemed the din would never end, the energy of the audience waned and the curtain stayed down. The show was over. The actors filed off the stage and went down the stairs to the cramped quarters in the basement where they could leave Shakespeare's medieval Europe, change from their costumes, remove their make-up, and return to the world of modern day 1949.

Luke sat in a cramped corner, taking off his grease paint. He had already removed the wig and the skirts. People crowded around him congratulating him, slapping his back and sharing in his success. For his part, he was trying to disassociate himself from the part as quickly as possible. He had been enthralled with the idea of being a man and playing Rosalind. As a result, he had volunteered for the part. Then, he'd had second thoughts. The director, Walter Carlson, head of the English department, had told him he was just right for the role. According to Mr. Carlson he had the movements and grace to play a woman, but he still came through as masculine enough that the audience would be able accept him as a man. The audience needed to be able to see that all was not as it seemed on the surface. They could join with the characters and take the situations . . . *as you like it*.

Within the madcap switches of sex, and the changes of costumes by

Rosalind and the other characters in *As You Like It*, having a man play a woman who disguises herself as a man and then back to a woman, was a stroke of genius. Everyone thought the idea was wonderful before the show was staged. Now that the performance was over, their ingenuity and creativity had been rewarded.

Luke was pleased with the reception he received. He liked acting and this was his first starring role, but he still had his worries. He did not want anyone thinking he was . . . well . . . a fairy. Many theatre people didn't have problems with that way of life, and Luke himself thought it was up to the individual, but he wanted no part of it for himself. He had been brought up in a masculine family, and he wanted to stay masculine.

He had also wondered about Mr. Carlson, but he had seen nothing untoward and he really did know his Shakespeare and his drama. Well, in any event he had done it. It was over. He was glad he did it. It was now back to reality.

Luke's first year in college was winding down. He was doing well. He had been able to juggle cross-country running, indoor track, and the drama club and still maintain a B+ average. This summer he was going to work in a summer stock theatre in Stockbridge, Massachusetts. He wanted to perform in as many plays and shows as possible and then see about going on to Broadway or someplace else to act after graduation. He thought he had a gift. Even Matt had said he had a gift. It was what Luke wanted to do in life.

When summer came, Luke met Taylor Essex. Taylor was also working at Stockbridge. She wanted to be a stage designer, not an actress, and she was there to make sets, costumes and stage props. Her interest in acting was marginal. She did play some walk-on parts, however, just as some of the actors built sets. Summer stock tended to be a democratic experience.

She was a year older than Luke was, and she had already completed a two-year technical college. In the fall she planned to attend an art school in New York City.

Taylor was tall and very slim. Her shoulders sloped, her breasts were small, her waist was tiny, and her hips were narrow. At one point, Luke had wondered how, if she got pregnant, she would handle childbirth. For her part, Taylor had no intention of ever becoming pregnant. She had shoulder length, wispy, medium blonde hair. Her eyes were a very pale blue and had a dreamy quality. She was lovely in a faint gossamer fashion. Luke was enthralled by her exotic beauty.

When she first met Luke, she wasn't sure she liked him. He was attractive in a gangly way. His wavy blonde hair hung continually in his face and he had developed a "brush-it-back" habit that she found endearing. She loved his sense of humor and his nonchalant laid-back manner. She had a problem with his background, though. His family seemed to have money, but he came from Irish stock. She'd always been taught that the Irish were okay people, they made good servants, but not to get involved with them. The Irish weren't high enough on the social scale.

In spite of that, as the summer moved along, she found herself seeking him out more and more. A large number of the other actors seemed to be caught up in their own excellence, but Luke was not into self-adulation. As a matter of fact, although he seemed to be a romantic, she was also finding him to be a very down-to-earth person. When she found out he was interested in poetry she forgot all her reservations. He had written his own poetry and he could actually recite Elizabeth Barrett Browning's poems by heart. And Poe! He knew almost every poem Edgar Allen Poe had written.

The company at Stockbridge operated as a repertory company and they staged a different play each week. Performances were at night, with a matinee on Sunday, for this week's play and then they rehearsed and built sets during the day for the next week's play. By necessity, those with large parts one week played minor parts the next. It was a wonderful way for actors to learn their craft.

One night, a few weeks after the start of the season, the group was doing a night of one-act plays by Eugene O'Neil and Boothe Tarkenton. Two of the three actors in one of the plays were hurt in an accident two hours before the opening curtain. The company scrambled. The show had to go on. They considered many options. Finally, Luke volunteered to do some Browning and Poe poetry readings instead of the ill-fated play. They all agreed, reluctantly, to go ahead with it.

The evening opened up with a Tarkenton play, *The Trysting Place*. The second play was *The Long Journey Home* by O'Neil. Luke came on last. The first two plays were well received.

When Luke walked in front of the lights for the third segment, he was in costume. He wore a dark wig with collar-length hair, a drooping, black moustache, and a black mid-nineteenth-century, tailed suit with a ruffled shirt and a poorly knotted black bow tie. He strode to the center of the performing area. The stage was empty except for a high stool that sat in the middle of a spotlight.

"Ladies and Gentlemen, we have had a small tragedy today. Two of our players were hurt and they will not be able to go on." The audience turned to each other. There was a low buzz of confusion. "As a result we will not be able to put on the scheduled play. In its place, I will do some recitations of works by Edgar Allen Poe and Elizabeth Barrett Browning. I hope you approve."

There was a little shuffling in the audience. People looked around. Some were agitated. There was a scattering of applause, then quiet. The spotlight dimmed and when it came up again, Poe was sitting on the stool. There was a pedestal behind him with a white bust of the Roman orator, Pallas.

"Once upon a midnight dreary,
while I pondered weak and weary,
Over many a quaint and curious volume of forgotten lore . . . ."

Luke recited *The Raven* from start to finish. He cried out at the right places. He wept at the right places. He whispered for the lost Lenore. He grieved for his lost love. Tears glistened on cheeks, and the audience was moved. When he finished, they stood and applauded.

Next he recited *Ulalume*, building the onomatopoetic sounds of doom and gloom and ghouls into scary little vignettes.

"It was hard by the dim lake of Auber,
in the misty mid-region of Weir.
It was down by the dank tarn of Auber,
in the ghoul haunted woodland of Wier."

His voice rose to shouts and fell to whispers as he told the tale of despair. His face turned to the light as tears tumbled again from his closed eyes. The picture of the man on the stool, the tears, the words of a grieving man, all created an image of great loss, of despair.

The audience was silent when he finished the poem. They were loathe to break the spell he had created. Then, they burst into applause that lasted a full minute. Tears filled many an eye. Luke sat for another minute looking at them, and then he stood.

For his next selection he chose *The Bells*.

The Bells — the poem that relates a story of a life. He was soft when he told of the silver bells and their joyous melody of childhood. He was bold when he told of the wedding bells. He was rancorous when he told of the brazen bells. He was somber when he spoke of the iron bells of dying. He increased the speed of his words and the volume of his voice with each quatrain. Each stanza was spoken at a faster pace than the last. As he approached the ending, the words were pouring out in a torrent and were being shouted at the top of his range. He roared through the last line at breakneck speed, and then stopped with a jerk . . . finished.

He bowed his head.

Silence. There was no sound for ten or fifteen seconds then the applause started. Slowly at first, then louder, then an enormous crescendo. The audience loved it.

Luke paused. He looked at the mass of people and smiled. He was ecstatic with the reception he was getting. He walked over to the edge of the stage and sat down, his legs dangling from the raised platform. He was as close as he could get to the audience without leaving the performing area. He looked down. Taylor was sitting in the first row, directly in front of him. He looked at her as he spoke to the assemblage.

"If you will bear with me, I would like to dedicate the next poem to a special friend who is sitting here in front of me."

A number of heads turned as people looked to see to whom he was referring. Taylor blushed.

"I hope you all will like it. It is my favorite poem."

Luke gathered himself for a moment, looked out at the audience, and then spoke.

"It was many and many a year ago,
in a kingdom by the sea,
That a maiden lived whom you may know,
by the name of Annabel Lee."

A large part of the audience applauded. They knew *that* poem.

Luke continued the tragic story of the lost love while keeping his eyes closed. When he recited the last verse, he opened his eyes and looked at Taylor.

"For the moon never beams, without bringing me dreams
Of the beautiful Annabel Lee.
And the stars never rise, but I feel the bright eyes
Of the beautiful Annabel Lee;
And so all the night-tide, I lie down by the side
Of my darling . . . my darling . . . my life and my bride
In the sepulchre there by the sea . . .
In her tomb by the sounding sea."

Tears wet his cheeks again. Tears ran down Taylor's face. The audience was crying. As happened earlier, at first there was silence. Then the people began to roar and burst into applause. The applause grew. They stood up and called for more. They chanted for more

He had intended to do Browning at this point, but they wanted more Poe. He obliged them. He recited Poe for another half-hour. The original plan for a half-hour segment of poetry ran past an hour.

The next day the word spread. The playhouse was filled for the rest of the week. Luke was not quite able to reach the level of performance he had reached that first night, but his effort was till superb.

And Taylor? That did it. She was his. They became inseparable.

The Bible says, "time and time wait for no man," one of many truisms in the Good Book. Autumn came, and so did the end of summer stock. Although they had been intimate a number of times, Luke and Taylor never lived together during the summer. Most of their tender moments took place in the countryside during picnics or long walks. The separate male-female dormitories made real intimacy difficult.

Taylor moved to New York City and started her classes at the art school. Luke, after a visit home, went on to Cortland for his second year of college. Parting had been a bittersweet experience. They agreed to write every day. They also agreed that they would also meet in the city during Luke's Christmas break from school.

In still "another part of the forest . . . ."

It was late in the fourth quarter. Mark was lined up across from a big lineman. The lineman looked at him menacingly. He was missing two front teeth. His uniform consisted of a black shirt with gold stripes on the sleeve, tan football pants, and a gold helmet with a black stripe. To Mark's left front was a smaller player, similarly dressed, who was split off the line a short distance. Mark decided that as a linebacker, it was his job to cover the smaller player so he slid over to a spot in front of him.

Mark's uniform was similar to the West Point uniform except where West Point wore black, Annapolis color was navy blue.

With the war having been over more than four years, the service academies were not the football powerhouses they had once been, but the Army-Navy game was still a small war. This year's game held true to form. Injuries had been mounting on both sides throughout the afternoon.

Mark was not a starter on the team. He was too small to be a lineman, not quick enough to be a back, and not tall enough to be an end or a quarterback. He was a "tweener." As a result he played on kicking teams and as a backup player at a number of positions. Due to injuries to starters, he was now filling in at a linebacker slot.

The game had been like a bell clapper, a ding-dong affair. First one team had the lead, then the other. The score at this point, was 24 to 23 in favor of Navy. Though the high number of points seemed to indicate a wide-open offense, exactly the opposite was true. Each team had scored only one touchdown. The remainder of the points had been accumulated by a combination of field goals and safeties

The day was dark, with rain or snow in the air. What the precipitation would actually be, would depend on the temperature. Either was a possibility. This *was* the last weekend in November.

The stands were full, as they always were when Navy played Army. The site was Philadelphia, a mutually agreed upon neutral site. The stone grandstands, the mass of uniforms, the gray coats of the crowd, and the overcast sky created a chilly, drab picture. The screaming, swaying, roaring and foot stomping were the only upbeat, sensual part of the experience, but that was more than enough to stir the blood. The quarterback for Army was calling signals. He was stationed behind the middle of the line, with his hands under the center. Both of the teams had switched from the old direct snap formations to the new "T" formation.

Mark could barely hear the quarterback over the din. He felt a real need to do something important. He had played off and on during the year, and he had played well enough. He had never made a difference though. Now his team needed him. Injuries had depleted the squad. He had to step up. Beating Army was uppermost in his and a few other substitute's minds. They had to hold.

Mark looked across at the player he had shifted to cover. He was set in a three-point stance, crouched, one hand on the ground the other tucked into his chest. He was slender, not big like most football players. He wore a low number, like a quarterback. Mark had not seen him in the game before. He was probably a pass receiver. Mark would bump him when he came off the line. The safety would pick him up.

The hand on the ground was his right hand. Mark noted almost absently that the skin on his wrist showed a white band. He probably wore a watch when he was outdoors.

Mark's subconscious worked on that white band. Somehow it was important. Why? The quarterback continued his count and then the ball was snapped. The lines came together in a crash, leather against leather. As Mark set himself to hit him, the player did not come forward. He stepped back and started moving to his left, behind his line.

Suddenly it all came together for Mark. The man was left-handed. He wore his watch on his right wrist. He was going to throw a pass, a left-handed pass. They had a trick play. The passer would swing from the right side of his line to the left side, receive a pitch or a handoff, continue further to the left and look down field for a receiver. His receiver might even be the quarterback.

Defenses did not anticipate pass plays from an end going to the left. It was an unnatural throw unless the passer was left-handed. Defenses also left quarterbacks alone once they had handed off. They could drift down field, free to catch a pass. This play had more than one deceptive element in it.

As soon as the possibility of a left-handed pass dawned on Mark, he charged after the player. He chased him across the field as fast as he could go. He saw him receive the ball from the quarterback, then keep going. Mark put his head down and pushed himself to the limit. The man was fast. Mark strained to catch up. The images came to him in slow motion. He saw people going down as they were blocked. He saw players running down field. Someone lurched at him to block him. He hit the man a glancing blow and continued toward his goal.

Mark's target was slowing. He was looking down field. He seemed to be zeroing in on a receiver. He slowed more. His left arm began to come up but Mark was gaining. Would he be on time? The player's arm drew back. Mark wanted to be another step closer, but he couldn't wait. It was all or nothing. He launched himself into the air. The player's arm came forward. Mark was off the ground in flight as he stretched himself to the furthest possible point he could reach.

His fingertips *touched* the ball. It wasn't a block or a slap down but it knocked the ball off its track a little, and it went tumbling end over end. An Army player grabbed for it and missed. The ball landed on the ground. The play was over.

Mark ended his flight through the air by landing on the cadet. They went to the turf in a tangle. He bounded up in time to see the pigskin bouncing crazily across the field. He had succeeded. He was ecstatic. He turned to the fallen cadet and held out his hand to pull him up. The cadet accepted. When he was on his feet, he said. "Good play, 'swabbie.' My man was open. That was a touchdown."

"Not today, Dogface." He turned to head back to his huddle, pride in his accomplishment. He looked back. "Thanks for the compliment."

The cadet nodded as he trotted off the field.

Navy held on and won 24-23. Mark was a hero in the locker room. One of the coaches confirmed what the cadet had told him. The Army quarterback was all by himself on the ten-yard line when Matt had tipped the pass.

With the end of football season, Mark decided to put a little more time into his studies. He was also on the wrestling team, but he gave that up. He had done fairly well, there but he was not one of the top wrestlers at the level of competition he faced, so he saw no point in continuing. His time at the academy was drawing to a close. He was becoming more conscious of his future.

Being a naval midshipman was teaching him about engineering, naval tactics and ship handling. But he was going to be a Marine officer and he wanted to learn more land tactics and amphibious warfare. The academy offered little in those fields. He decided, with typical Mark Flaherty pluck, to teach himself. The Marine liaison officer supplied him with a list of books. He bought a dozen of them and began his self-education. When his time at the academy was done, he would be ready for the Marine Corps.

8
Honor, Dishonor and Maturity

Rory and Helene had made a real difference since they had arrived. If it weren't for them, life would have much more difficult for Katie. Oh, she still would have had her money from the Van Scooten settlement and her comfort was assured, but in the two years since the couple moved in, her estate had grown. At Rory's urging, she had bought acres and acres of grassy land around the farm and some prime apple orchards nearby. They grazed Holstein milk cows on the grassland and sold the milk to a nearby dairy cooperative. The apple crop was a real bonus. She used that money to pay for everything on the farm, including the money she gave her cousins.

Katie had expanded the farmhouse into a thirteen-room home. She worked hard to maintain the old farmhouse flavor, including the bay window. It was more room than she needed but she felt she wanted it. It was good to be able to do things just because you wanted to. She wished Mike could have with her.

Rory had written to her from Ireland when he heard of Van Scooten's death. He needed to get out of the Emerald Isle, something to do with the IRA, and he offered to come over for a few years with his wife and help Katie get on her feet in return for asylum. Katie had never met him but he was the son of one of her cousins, so he was real family.

His stay blossomed into a lot more than protection. Rory understood land and farming. Helene understood milk cows and homemaking. Katie, at the urging of Mark, gave Rory and Helene some of the land for their own. They built a small house on it. They would probably stay more than a few years.

Katie walked down the path to the front gate to get the mail. The dust that Rory and Helene's pickup had stirred when they headed into town still hung in the air. They had to buy farm supplies and groceries.

The early spring day showed signs that winter was losing its grip. She remembered another early spring day with — she shoved the thought aside with a shudder. She wrapped her light coat around her, the chill coming more for the memories than the cold.

She reached the mailbox; a typical curved roof loaf rural mailbox, and opened the flap in the front. There were fifteen or sixteen envelopes and fliers in the box. She took them out and started to walk back to the house. As she walked she flipped through the envelopes. A bill. Another bill. A circular, the feed store had its semiannual sale of flower bulbs. Something from the bank, the monthly statement she guessed. More fliers. More bills, and a few letters. One of the letters caught her interest. It was from Mark. The envelope was thicker and heavier than his normal letter and it intrigued her.

She went into the house, the screen door banging behind her. She decided to leave the outer door open for a while to let some fresh air in. She walked back to the kitchen, laid the letters on the table, Mark's on top, and turned water on for tea. She exchanged her topcoat for sweater.

In a few minutes the water was hot and Katie poured it into a cup. The tea leaves went into her silver tea strainer, which was placed into the water to brew. She went to the refrigerator to get some cream. She liked cream in her tea. Drinking tea straight had never appealed to her. Sometimes she used a little sugar. Today however was a no sugar day.

After the tea had brewed the mandated five minutes, Katie took the strainer out and added the cream. She stirred the hot liquid for a moment. Except for Mark's letter, the mail was pushed to the back of the table. She used a kitchen knife to open the envelope. Inside was another envelope with the words *Mom-Confidential* written on it.

Curious she opened the second envelope. It contained four pages written in Mark's concise but jerky style.

March 10, 1950

Dear Mom:

I've got some good news for you. I think I've found Matt. I decided to write rather than phone because the only phone available to me is a wall phone in the hall of the barracks. It's not very private.

In any event let me tell you the story.

Yesterday, we had a big inspection. I was one of the inspecting officers. This is all part of the leadership training. Fourth classmen inspect first classmen, etc. When I went into one room, I noticed a picture in the midshipmen's locker. It was a picture of six Marines all wearing boxing trunks, strap shirts with USMC on the front and boxing gloves. Three of the men were kneeling down. The other three were standing behind them.

I don't know why, but I looked a little closer at the picture and I saw MATT.

Let me go back a minute. The man who has the picture is an ex-enlisted man. Every year some of the middies that go through here are from the enlisted ranks in the Navy and the Marines. They score high on tests, and so on, to get in. In any event, he is one of the people in the picture. He's kneeling down in the front. One of the other two guys in the front is a Mexican guy, he's dark. The other is light haired.

In the back, one of the guys is a Negro, one is a tall husky blonde guy and the other is, I'm sure, Matt. His head is shaved. He looks huskier than I remember, and he has some tattoos and a small mustache, but there's no mistaking him.

Remember how we always said, except for hair color, Matt and John look just alike. Well, remember when John got that buzz haircut last year and it looked like he had shaved his head. He looked just like Matt does in this picture.

But there's more. I asked the guy, casual like, about the picture. He told me he had been on the Camp Pendleton Boxing team. He said they boxed all over California against other base teams. They never lost a match. Sometimes one of them would lose a bout, but as a team they never lost.

I asked who the other guys were. He said the guy next to him was Humberto Duran, Hubie was his nickname. He came from L.A. A tough city kid. The other guy next to him was from Indiana or something. I don't remember his name. The Negro in the back row was a real African. He was a Zulu. And, the other two guys were ex-Foreign Legionnaires. The big guy was a Frenchman, but the other one was an American who had gone over to fight in the war before he was old enough to enlist here.

Mom, remember the post card from Paris. He must have been there setting up the Foreign Legion thing when he sent that. He told you in code he was coming back to the U.S.

But it gets better. I asked the guy about the names of the other guys. I was still trying to make it look like just conversation. He didn't seem suspicious. He told me the Zulu's name was Spears. Great name for a Zulu huh? The big guy was Jacques Lescouter or something and the other guy was Matt Farrell.

I could have kissed him.

Mom. Matt Farrell. Matt Flaherty. It's a natural. He's changed his identity, but he only changed his name a little.

In any event I thought you'd want to know as soon as possible. Sorry I couldn't call.

I don't know what I can do at this point about this, probably nothing. But when I get out of here maybe I can look him up. It may have to wait until I get out of Basic Officer School at Quantico though, now that I think about it a little, that's another six months after I graduate from here. Oh well, I'll do what I can. I have mixed emotions. I want to see him real bad but I don't want to blow his cover.

I hope everything's going okay at home. Say hello to Maggie, Rory, Helene and John for me. I guess you don't see too much of Luke lately, but you tell me he calls a lot, so I guess that's good. Say hello to him, too. Give Maggie a big special hug for me. You told me she's doing real well in school in your last letter. That makes me feel real good.

You'll probably want to tell the boys about this letter. They'll be glad to hear about Matt. Make sure they know to keep it secret though.

I'll either call or write again soon.

Take care, I love you, Mom.

Mark.

Katie read the letter again. Then she put it down and stared at the wall. She was sure it was Matt. Mark didn't jump to conclusions. If he said it was Matt, it was Matt. A burden had been lifted. She knew where Matt was. The guilt feelings about that horrible night were still there however.

Pat McQuinn and Frank Gannon were sitting on one of the picnic tables in the park at the end of Grand Street. It was late in the day. The air was cool, but in March the air was almost always cool, especially late in the day.

"You think he'll come?" asked Gannon.

"Yeah, he'll come. He knows he has to come if I send for him," replied McQuinn.

"That fight was a pretty big fight. Some of the boys got hurt. Apparently the guys from Reinburg are a rough crew."

"Our guys hurt them, too. The chief over there called me on it. Some of them ended up in the hospital for a few days."

"How did you find out John was involved? He wasn't one of the ones our guys arrested."

"His jalopy was seen. He was there. Some of the Reinburg guys described him, too." McQuinn laughed as he recalled the questioning.

"They said that one of the Kingmont guys was a mad man. They called him a "whirling dervish." They said he was everywhere. He's responsible for a lot of the injuries."

"Did he use anything? Clubs? Billys?"

"No, apparently not. Just feet and hands."

"How did he get away? You said he wasn't there when your guys showed up. Where was he?"

McQuinn laughed again. "Some of the Reinburg guys tried to get away. He went after them in his jalopy. My guys showed up right after that. Hell, they might have passed him on the way without knowing it."

Off in the distance they heard a rumble and a screech of tires. They both turned and looked down the street. A stripped down Ford with no windshield and no motor hood was flying up the avenue. It came to a stop at the curb, opposite where they sat, with a squeal and a lurch. John shinnied himself up from the driver's seat and jumped out. He walked over to them head high and with a *what the hell do you want with me* look on his face.

McQuinn smiled. He slid off the table and walked up to John. It was amazing how much he looked like Matt. Different hair, but everything else was the same. He held out his hand.

Gannon walked a little distance away.

"Good to see you again, John. How's your mother?"

John was thrown off balance by the pleasantry. He thought McQuinn would rant at him. He didn't expect a civil greeting. "Uh . . . she's fine . . . . The whole family's fine . . . uh, lieutenant."

"Good, glad to hear that. I really think a lot of your mother, John. She's one of the finest people I know. How are things working out with her cousins? From where I sit, it looks like they're all doing well."

McQuinn noticed how much John had grown since the whipping. He was a full sized man now, broad-shouldered, narrow-waisted, mature looking.

"Yeah. They're doing fine, too." John was waiting for the axe to fall.

"Good. And Luke and Mark? They okay?"

"Uh, yeah. Mark's finishing up at Navy. Luke is in New York. He's trying to make it as an actor." John chided himself for being so chummy. McQuinn wanted him about the fight. Why didn't he get to it?

"Tough job. Trying to break into acting. He should have stayed in college. You're going to college next year aren't you?"

"I think so. I've applied to a couple. I'm waiting to hear," John mumbled the last. He wasn't about to tell McQuinn that he really did not want to go to college.

"Good. Good. We need to talk a little more about that, but I don't have the time now."

John stiffened. Here it comes.

"Oh, one more thing."

What now? John thought

"If you ever hear from Matt, tell him to call me. I know he's a wanted man and I have to try to bring him in, but I also think I can help him. It isn't just a killing thing. It's not simply a murder. I know there's more to it than that." He looked at John seriously. "If he ever calls you. Tell him to call me. Okay? I Owe Mike, your father, and I owe Matt. I'm on your side. I have the law to uphold, but I'm on your side. Okay?"

John mumbled an okay.

"Now John, tell me about the fight."

Just like that John was taken off guard again. "Uh . . . fight?"

"Yes, John, the fight."

"I . . . uh . . . don't . . . ."

"John, you were there. Don't play games with me. You know what fight. Now tell me about it."

"Well, lieutenant . . . uh . . . we were just protecting out turf." At first he spoke with reservation, trying to give only what he had to. "The guys from Reinburg came here. We didn't go there."

"I know that, John. The fight was here. It would be hard for you to have a fight here unless they came here." McQuinn replied with thinly veiled impatience.

"Well, yeah, but they came here for no good reason. They just wanted to mess with us."

"So a bunch of guys drove twenty miles from Reinburg, to . . . uh . . . mess with you for no good reason. Do I have that correct?"

"Uh . . . yeah."

McQuinn reached over to the end of the table he had been sitting on and picked up a leather strap. "Remember this, John?"

John looked at the strap. He remembered. He took a step back. "I won't let you use that this time, lieutenant. That's okay for a kid but I'm not a kid any more." He stated this quite clearly, looking into McQuinn's eyes as he said it.

McQuinn looked at him with a paternal smile. "You are correct, John. That's for youngsters who need a lesson. I would never think to use that it on an adult."

He looked at John seriously. "I have two thoughts about that, though. What you did the other night, the gang fight, shows me that you are still a child."

John bristled.

"Also," McQuinn went on "the fact that you won't own up to any wrongdoing also shows me that you haven't grown up yet."

"McQuinn" John had never called him that before. "I don't know what your problem is, but your always messing in my life and I don't like it. I . . . ."

McQuinn straightened up. "Back off, lad." His voice became firm. "You committed a crime. I could arrest you. I could put handcuffs on you right now and put you in jail. If you resist, I can use whatever force is necessary to bring you in. You could be in a heap of trouble."

John pulled back a little, but he looked at McQuinn defiantly.

"You don't appreciate what is being done for you, John. What do you suppose Mark's reaction would be if you were arrested? What do you suppose Matt's reaction would be if he were around? What about your father, God rest his soul? And most important of all, what about your mother?"

John saw that he was beaten. The last vestiges of rebellion seeped out of him. He looked at McQuinn in surrender. "You don't fight fair, lieutenant. You know I wouldn't hurt my mother and I sure don't want to get Matt or Mark down on me. That's dirty pool you just played."

"What's the alternative?"

John looked at him without speaking for a few moments. Then he asked, "What do you want to know? I won't rat on anyone."

"Okay, John. You're no stoolie. Just tell me what happened."

John settled himself a little, walked over to the picnic table and sat down on the table itself. Frank had been sitting on the bench the whole time, not saying anything. It was now almost dark. The light of a distant street lamp was their only illumination.

"Last fall, a bunch of us went up to Reinburg to go to the county fair. We had three or four carloads of guys and girls, mostly guys, but there were a few girls. We spent all day. We had a good time. That night one of the Reinburg guys tried to pick up one of our girls. She told him to shove off. He kept coming on to her. I told him to back off. He wouldn't so I . . . uh, hit him."

"You threw the first punch?"

"Yeah, but he was pretty belligerent. Ask any of the other guys. That was the only way to stop him."

"Did it stop him?"

"Temporarily. He chickened out of a real fight. He went back to get his guys. They came to see us. By this time, we had gotten all our guys together, but there was more of them than us. We had a little scuffle, nothing too serious, just a few cuts and bruises. The cops broke it up. We left after that."

"That's all? What caused the fight the other day?"

"Just a culmination of things. It's a long story."

"Try me. I have patience."

John looked at him with a little trepidation, but he continued. "Well … a week or two later, the guy who came on to the girl, came down. He had found out where she lived and he tried to see her again. She told him to buzz off, again. He's really a creep, but he wouldn't go. He and one of his friends hung around all day. She called me. I came over and we convinced him to clear out. I had brought two other guys. We messed them up a little. They left. A few weeks later they caught one of our guys alone in Poughkeepsie. How they knew he was there, I don't know. They kicked the shit out of him."

McQuinn and Gannon were taking this all in.

John looked at them before he continued. "One thing led to another. We stiffed a few of their guys. They ambushed a few of ours. Finally we decided to settle it all once and for all."

"And that was the reason for the fight the other night?"

"Yes, sir" He looked down.

"Has the matter been settled? Did you come to an agreement not to fight any more?"

"Uh . . . I don't know. There was no agreement, but I don't think our guys want any more. It seems to be getting out of hand." He gave out a short laugh. "Your cops scared a number of guys on both sides." He thought a moment. "I don't know about the Reinburg guys, though. Will they stop?"

"We'll work that out. I know the police chief in Reinburg. He'll keep the lid on there."

No one said anything for a while. Then John said cautiously, looking at the strap, "Was there anything else, lieutenant?"

McQuinn smiled. "I think I have the picture, John. It's all bravado shit, isn't it?" He stepped away from the table, then turned back. "A bunch of young studs with nothing better to do than to prove their manhood. And you, Mr. Flaherty, appear to be one of the worst."

John looked at the ground. "What happens next?" he asked.

"Well, it seems like all that happened was some cuts and bruises and assorted other small injuries. Maybe you guys can sue each other, I don't know. But nothing real bad has happened." He looked at John seriously. " It could have, though. Someone could have been hurt bad or worse, killed. This shit has to stop."

He walked around a little as he thought. Then he turned to John. "If I let you go, then I have to let everyone go. I can do that, but I want a promise from you."

"What's that?"

"This whole thing is over, no more fights. The Reinburg guys stay in Reinburg, I'll take care of that. The Kingmont guys stay in Kingmont. Okay?"

"Yes, sir. I think I can convince our guys if you can convince their guys." He brightened a little.

"A deal." McQuinn smiled as he noticed how John still tried to keep a little bargaining edge.

"No strap?"

"No strap."

John looked relieved. He did not want a strapping. He would have fought that, but he also didn't want to have to fight McQuinn to prevent it.

McQuinn continued. "No strap . . . unless . . . ."

John's face fell. What now? "Unless what?" he asked with anger.

"Were you drinking the night of the fight?"

A smile crossed John's face. He knew what McQuinn was getting at. "Yes, sir, I was." He said defiantly. "I had two beers."

McQuinn looked at him with sadness. "You made a promise to me two years ago, John . . . ."

John looked at him in triumph. "My promise was not to drink until I was legal."

Now it was McQuinn who understood where John was going. He stopped John in mid-sentence. "Your birthday is Saint Patrick's day, isn't it, the day of the fight? I should have remembered that. You're eighteen now."

"Yes, sir, I am. Those were the first beers since that night of the strapping."

Pat McQuinn looked at John with a mixture of frustration, pride, admiration, anger and love. The boy was going to become a fine man. Hell, he was almost there.

"John, if we can keep you in one piece until you get a little maturity, your going to be all right. Get out of here."

John spun around, ran to his jalopy, and sped off to a cacophony of bangs, rumbles, and squeals. After he was gone and the noise was just a distant clatter, Frank Gannon said to McQuinn, "He didn't even thank you."

"He did fine, Frank. He did fine. Hell, I'd love to have a son like that."

Mrs. Giangrasso had worked in the rectory for more than twenty years. When she first came to this country from Italy she couldn't speak a word of English. She and her new husband moved from the New York City to Kingmont right after they were married. He had gone to work in a factory in Poughkeepsie. She had stayed home.

She was not an attractive woman. She was short and tended to be a little overweight. She had dark hair that grayed early and a few moles on her face. Some of her front teeth had been repaired with gold, which showed on the edges. Her eyes were dark and intelligent and she also smiled a lot. She was a happy person.

One Sunday when she went to Mass at Saint Dominic's, the pastor, Father Rafferty, had announced that he needed a new housekeeper. Mrs. Giangrasso still didn't speak much English, but she knew the word "housekeeper." After Mass she went next door to the rectory and applied. In her village in Italy, the priest's housekeeper was an honored calling.

Father Rafferty took a liking to Mrs. Giangrasso immediately. He could speak a little Italian. He told her she reminded him of the housekeeper his group had in Rome when he attended the American College. She started the job a few days later.

The work was easy enough. She had to make his meals, keep the kitchen, do the linens and answer the door. Not much more than she did at home. Father Rafferty was able to communicate with her quite well. Over the years, he taught her to speak English. She also learned to read and write fairly well in her new language. She could speak and read the language adequately but when she wrote, she tended to write phonetically. She wrote many words as they sounded, rather than, as they should be spelled. Bright would be "brite." Weight would come out "wait."

She was well liked by most of the parishioners, and the children of the parish thought she was wonderful. She became Mrs. G to most of them. Some of the children thought the "g" in Mrs. G stood for Grandmother. Over the years she had had three children of her own, all girls. They fitted in quite well with the rest of the parish children.

When Mrs. Giangrasso first started her job, the church had a secretary who worked part time to take care of some of the clerical duties. Eventually, this lady moved out of town. Father Rafferty decided to try and handle these duties himself with the help of Mrs. Giangrasso. He felt she that if he could do some of the work, she could do the rest. He would pay her a little more for her clerical help, but not as much as a part time person would expect to be paid. This was not a wealthy parish. Economies had to be found.

He bought a book on typing for her and he made sure she set aside some time every day to work on it. Mrs. G became quite good on the typewriter.

"Mrs. G, I forgot to tell you yesterday, but I need you to do something for me while I go to Poughkeepsie today." Father Rafferty was scraping up the last of his eggs from his plate. Mrs. G was buttering a piece of toast for him. She looked up.

"John Flaherty will stop by later to pick up baptismal certificates for himself and his brother Luke. I put the file on my desk and I signed the forms and embossed them but they need to be filled out. You know, name, address etc. I won't be around to see him or to finish the forms."

She put the plate with the piece of toast on it in front of him. "Certainly, Father. Do you know what time he'll be here?"

"Uh . . . no. Sometime this morning, he said."

"All right. I'll get to it right after I do the dishes."

"That'll be fine."

A little later Father Rafferty left for Poughkeepsie and Mrs. G cleaned up the kitchen and went into the office. She saw the file on his desk. She picked it up and carried it to her desk. The certificates were in the file. She sat down at her typewriter and put one of the certificates behind the roller. She snapped the bar closed over it.

She thought about the Flaherty boys. They were a fine group of boys. She had been shocked like everyone else by the murder of Wilhelm Van Scooten, but somehow she found it hard to find, what was his name, — oh yes, Matthew — at fault. In Italy, sometimes people needed to be killed. Maybe here, too. Van Scooten was a bum. She suddenly realized what she had just said to herself. She quickly made the sign of the cross and said three "mea culpas."

She looked back at her typewriter. "Let's see which one is John. Oh he's the one with the jalopy. Light hair, a good-looking boy. He would be right for Maria. I think she's only a year or two younger than him." She looked at the file. Yes, he was eighteen. Maria was seventeen. He would be perfect. She smiled as she typed.

Mrs. G had never given any thought to how Flaherty was spelled. She did not look into the file for the name, only the address and the appropriate dates. She had known them for years. She just typed the name the way it sounded to her. Flar-a-ty, Flaraty. In any event even if she had looked closer she would have thought it was a misspelling. In her mind the correct spelling, Flaherty, should be pronounced Flay-her-ty not Flar-a-ty.

A little later in the morning, John picked up the baptismal certificates. Mrs. G had put them in an envelope. John took a quick look, saw that there were two certificates, thanked her and ran back to his car.

When he left, she stared after him. He was *very* good-looking. Maybe he would be better for Theresa. She was younger but she was prettier than Maria was. She closed the door and went back to the office fantasizing as she went.

She sat down at the desk to tidy it up, and then she remembered she had to call the florist about the Easter flowers for next Sunday. She reached for the phone. "I wonder what he needs the baptismal certificates for."

After the hectic season of summer stock and whirlwind romance, Luke had gone back to college and Taylor had left for art school in New York City. Luke had tried to make a go of college but his heart wasn't in it. He had his taste of the theatre and he found it much more attractive than college classes. In addition, Mr. Carlson had left the school and the drama department had almost ceased to exist. The students were putting on a review that fall, but that was not real theatre. He didn't want to participate. Besides, he wanted to be with Taylor.

He stuck it out until Christmas break and then he took off to the New York City to spend his vacation with her. He had decided that he would also look around for work in the New York theatre while he was there.

Taylor had a cellar apartment in Greenwich Village, the Bohemian center of New York City. It was downstairs from the street level. The window in the living room was eye high and the view from that window was of feet and legs as people walked by. It was fun to watch the passing parade from that viewpoint.

Two homosexual men, who proclaimed themselves as married, occupied the apartment on one side of hers. Two gay women, who always seemed to be in the nude, lived in the apartment on the other side. Their walls were also adorned with a large number of photos and paintings of nude women.   Luke had problems living next to the homosexual men. He tried not to judge people, but the proximity of something he found distasteful was a little unsettling. He found that living next door to two homosexual women, however, to be stimulating. The fact that one or the other would often come to the door totally unclothed was a definite benefit — they were both attractive women.

Taylor was glad to see him. She had thrown herself into her schoolwork for the last three months and she needed the break. When Luke arrived, they had set out "paint the town red." They took the subway up town to Times Square and they walked along the street looking at all the tacky shops and the huge movie theatres. They strolled over to Fifth Avenue and went window shopping at the pricey stores. They visited St Patrick's Cathedral and the Cathedral of St. John the Divine. They stopped at Rockefeller Center and watched the skaters. They visited the

Empire State Building and took the elevator to the top. They went to Macy's and Gimbel's and compared prices.

They laughed a lot. One evening they had dinner at a Chinese restaurant on Times Square. It was on the second floor. Customers had a choice of tables in front of windows that either looked out at Times Square or looked directly at the moving headline news strip that ran around the Times Building. They intended to do Central Park one other afternoon, but it snowed that day.

On another day, they went to Battery Park on the southern tip of Manhattan. They also took a ferry to Staten Island. They went out to the Statue of Liberty. One night, they went to a place in Greenwich Village known as The Village Barn. It was a unique nightclub. The Barn was in the basement of an apartment building and it ran the whole length of the structure. The motif was hillbilly-country. The inside was decorated with red barns, barn doors, haystacks, and pictures of sheep and cows and horses.

The waiters all wore checked shirts, bib overalls, and straw hats. The waitresses wore wide black-and-white polka dot skirts, low cut white peasant blouses and milkmaid caps. The entertainment was, yodeling, country singing, hobbyhorse racing, and hog calling. To find a place like this anyplace in New York City was surprising enough. To find it in Bohemian Greenwich Village was unbelievable. The place was packed every night.

They decided to spend Christmas together. They both called home and told their families. They spent the day at a local coffeehouse with a disparate group of Bohemians with no place to go. John came down after Christmas and spent a few days with them. They took him to a number of the city sights. New Year's Eve was spent with their neighbors. The two men were circumspect in their behavior. The two women wore clothes. When 1950 rolled around, Taylor went back to school. Luke began to look for acting work.

He had learned of a number of tryouts but he didn't know how to go about auditioning. The parts were all in new plays, so he couldn't read the work and decide what part to read for. He was so ignorant that he showed up for tryouts for a new play called *Green Pastures*. It called for an all Negro cast.

He did manage to obtain a walk-on part as a spear-carrier for an opera. They needed tall men. His job was to stand on stage twice a night for about ten minutes each time. He was in a line with other spear-carriers. The opera only played for a week, then he was out of work again.

He waited on tables for a while at a coffeehouse around the corner but the pay was low and tips from the type of people who frequented these restaurants were almost nonexistent.

It was during this time that Taylor began to grow a little distant from him. He couldn't put his finger on it, but he knew that something was going on. They made love occasionally and it was physically quite satisfactory but there was a lack of warmth, and the frequency of their lovemaking was waning.

He wondered if she was losing respect for him because he wasn't able to get an acting job. He speculated about whether her school was too stressful. He tried to initiate discussions about the matter her, but she just denied anything was different. In the absence of any other information, he decided he needed to get a job to get her respect back. The acting would have to take a backseat for a while.

He looked at clerical jobs in the want ads and went to interview for them. One was near the school Taylor attended.

The interview went well. The company was clearinghouse for stock certificates. He would deliver certificates to locations around the City and do simple clerical work. They liked Luke and offered him the job. He was pleased. He went to see Taylor and share his good news. She had told him her classes were mostly hands on, practical application sessions, and there was little formal classroom type instruction. He reasoned he would be able to see her and not have to interrupt a class.

After climbing the brownstone steps, he breezed into the building looking for the office. The first floor had studios on each side of the hall. He didn't see an office. He walked down the hall looking into each studio. At one, he looked through the small window in the door. He could see people in front of easels with canvases. Interesting. He opened the door and saw a small group of students sitting around a dais, painting a nude. It was a mixed group of men and women. The model had her back to the door. She turned toward him. It was Taylor.

He was stunned. He thought she was going to school here, to learn, to practice. Instead she was modeling and *in the nude*. He turned and walked out quickly. He didn't know whether she had seen him or not.

Luke didn't know what to do next. He walked around for a while and then went back to the school. They had to discuss this. When he returned, the session had ended. He went from room to room, and found her sitting in the employee's lounge. She was now fully dressed, sitting at a table with a cup off coffee in front of her. There was a plump, but pretty, young blonde woman sitting across from her. She was wearing a silky, flowered kimono. Apparently she was also a model. Later he found out her name was Margot. When Taylor saw Luke, she went to him and threw her arms around him. She had been crying.

"Oh, Luke, I should have told you. I didn't want to hurt you. I didn't know if you'd understand. I pay my tuition by doing this," she babbled it out all at once.

"You should have told me." He was hurt. " I'd understand. We should discuss this. Can you go now?"

"Yes, I can leave. Just let me check out."

They went back to the apartment and they discussed the situation. Taylor was contrite, but she became a little huffy when he tried to get her to stop posing. He backed off. She told him she would continue to pose, but she would discuss everything with him from now on. That seemed to settle it. That night the lovemaking was good.

Luke started his new job and after a few days decided he hated it. He stayed with it however, because he couldn't get anything else that paid as well, while allowing him free time to look for acting jobs. He went to a more few auditions over the next month, but nothing materialized. Taylor was warm and cuddly for a week or two, but then she became distant again. She denied the coolness when Luke brought it up so there was no discussion as she had promised.

Luke was becoming more and more disillusioned with his life. Time drifted along slowly for him. It was time with no purpose. Love had cooled. Work wasn't forthcoming.

Then the doorbell rang. When he opened the door, Margot was standing there.

"Can I come in?"

Luke was surprised. "Sure, come on in. I have to leave in a bit, but you're welcome to stay and wait. I don't know when . . . ."

She shook her head. "I came to see you, not Taylor. She won't be home for a while." She walked in, unbuttoning her coat as she went.

"Uh . . . okay . . . uh, how can I help you?" He was a little confused. Especially since when she took her coat off, he could see she was wearing a transparent white blouse with nothing underneath. She also appeared to have lost some weight.

She turned to him and stepped close, pressing against his body. Her eyes were searching his. She seemed a little nervous. "When I saw you at the school, I knew you were the kind of man I wanted."

"Wait a minute. What's going on here?" Luke stepped back. He was flustered by the boldness.

Margot stepped forward, again pressing against him. "Your girlfriend is making it with my boyfriend." She giggled but there was pain in her eyes. "So . . . I thought, if you're game, we'd . . . I'd . . . sort of . . . return the favor." She started to put her arms around him. He backed off again.

"Wait. I don't know what you're talking about. You're pretty and all that, but I don't make it with just anyone." He had found himself responding to her, but he was still confused. Then he heard what she had just said. "What's this boyfriend thing?"

Margot stopped her pursuit for a moment. Doubt showed on her cherubic face. She looked at Luke. "You don't know, do you?" She studied his face closer. "She's been able to bamboozle you just as she did me." A harder edge crept into her speech. "Well, let me tell you. You have one bitch for a girlfriend." Her eyes flamed, her nostrils flared. "Right now, she's shacking up with Broadbeck, the guy that runs the school. He's the one who talked her into posing nude so he could get his jollies. Now he's putting it to her. He did that with me, too. I fell for the line. I thought he was a good guy. Now I know different, and women like 'miss society babe' are just as bad." She was really angry now.

Luke's mind was in turmoil. Taylor was having an affair? Luke sat down hard. He had to think. Margot came over to him and sat on the arm of the chair. Even in his mental turmoil he could feel the appeal of this woman. "Look, honey. I didn't know you didn't know. I was kinda clumsy wasn't I?" She had her emotions under control. She looked at Luke with empathy. "I thought I could get back at her by making out with her man." She thought a moment. "But I guess that doesn't work. You and I are the ones getting hurt."

She stepped away from him. Sitting there, he really was cute. She sighed. "It's not good if we do things just for revenge." She suddenly became coquettish again, as another thought occurred to her . . . . "Unless you find me attractive . . . I . . . I think you're real cute."

Luke had to laugh in spite of himself. "Margot, you are very attractive. Any other time, I would snap that invitation up before you could blink, but right now . . . I . . . I . . . ."

"Yeah I know . . . Luke. Can I call you Luke?"

He nodded. "Sure."

"You're a one-woman kind of guy, aren't you?"

He looked at her and nodded again. "I guess so." His mind was wrestling with many thoughts.

"Your lady, Miss Essex, is not a one-man woman." She looked at him again, then sighed. "I think you need time to think this through. I'm sorry I had to be the one to drop the bombshell."

"Yes, I need time to think."

Taylor and Luke had a real "discussion" that evening. Sparks flew. Taylor told Luke in no uncertain terms that he was cute and fun sometimes, but she was not going to be tied down to him. She wanted to be with other men and experience other ways of life. If he couldn't share her with others, then he could leave.

Luke was at a loss. Share her? Where was honor? Where was commitment? He understood that their relationship was only a romantic one at this point, but he thought there was still some form of commitment between them. Not marriage yet, but still ... something. Maybe he was naïve, but he thought if they didn't want to commit to each other any longer, it would be a thing they would decide together.

His face grew sullen. He had not experienced anything like this before. People did not do these sorts of things to each other. Then it began to sink in. Some people did. Some people did not operate from an honorable base. They did things on the sly. They lied. They were cowards. They did not face up to duties and responsibilities. They were not truthful and open. They were not clean with each other.

Luke wrestled with the situation. Obviously, he was young and naïve. This was the real world, but why did it have to be this way? Why weren't people honest? Where was honor?

He finally looked at the situation squarely. He decided that although it hurt, he was glad it had surfaced now and not at some point where it would have hurt a lot more. The problem now was, what was he to do next?

Two weeks later, Luke was sitting in the living room watching the feet and legs of New Yorkers going by. It was no longer fun. He had made a few decisions. He had quit his job. He had packed his possessions into a small bag. He was leaving. He wasn't sure what to do next, but he had to leave. That was certain. Taylor had gone to the Bahamas with Broadbeck. He would probably go back to Kingmont until he got his mind in order again. He needed time to adjust.

The doorbell rang. Luke was irritated. What now?

He got up from the couch. He remembered the last time the bell had rung when he wasn't expecting it. He crossed the room and opened the door.

John was standing there. "Hey brother, got a room for the night?" He walked in carrying a suitcase.

Luke was speechless. The last person he expected to see was his brother. "John, What the heck? What are you doing here?"

John looked around. "You alone?"

"Yeah . . . uh . . . I was just leaving."

John saw the bag next to the sofa. "You mean leaving? As in leaving?" he asked with raised brows.

"Uh . . . right. I was leaving — for good. Probably going back to Kingmont."

John's tongue cluck clucked, as he digested that. Then he said, "I don't know if I came at a bad time or a good time. I need some place to stay for a few days so that makes it a bad time but the fact that you're . . . uh . . . leaving makes the thing I wanted to talk to you about easier."

Luke was confused. "John, you aren't making sense. What do you want to talk about? This is not a good time for me."

"I can see that . . . uh . . . you and Taylor are no longer a couple, right? You don't know where to go next right? I show up wanting to move in. One more complication you don't need, right?"

"I guess I wouldn't put it so blunt but, yeah. You're right."

John was suddenly sympathetic. "Why don't we go somewhere and get a beer or something and talk. I don't think this is a good place for you right now. If you broke up with Taylor, I don't want to stay here any longer than you do." He stopped talking. Then he said with a twinkle, "Hey I almost forgot. If I stayed here, I might get to see the nude sisters. Hell, you go and do your thing. I'll stay here."

Luke laughed in spite of himself. "Yeah, let's go. You forget those two are homos. All you'd get is a look and nothing more. You got any money?"

"Yeah, I got a little." He looked at Luke with mock seriousness. "You never can tell about women. Somebody like me may be able to turn them around." He said this with all the wisdom of an eighteen-year-old. Abruptly he asked, "Where's a good place to get a beer? You know I'm legal now."

"Right around the corner."

When Luke closed the door of the downstairs apartment in Greenwich Village, he wasn't aware of it, but he was leaving a period of his life behind for good. The world was about to become a different place for him, a very different place.

John's idea, the thing he wanted to talk to Luke about, was a lulu. John was going to join the Marine Corps, and he wanted Luke to go with him. When John had left Kingmont he didn't know how, or even, if, he could persuade Luke, but he was going to take his shot. The fact that Luke was breaking up with Taylor made it easier. He had been to the recruiter in Poughkeepsie and worked out all the details. The recruiter had wanted John to sign right away but John told him he might be able to get his brother to join, too.

The next group would be leaving for boot camp on May 15. Today was May 2. They could take their physicals in New York, at Church Street. All their processing would be done in a few days. The recruiter had even arranged to put them up a few days if they needed it. John was anxious to go. Luke was also anxious but in a different way.

"God, John, it's a big decision. I have never given any thought to the Marine Corps for myself. It seemed right for Matt and for Mark, and I can even see you as a Marine, but me? I have to digest that."

They were seated at table on the sidewalk outside a bar called Tally's. All the tables had umbrellas that said "Cinzano" on them in green and black letters. The weather was warm. They each had a beer.

"What else are you going to do?" John sipped on his Ballantine. "I don't mean you can't do something else, but what do you want to do? Go back to College?"

Luke played with his Ballantine, making swirls with the wet ring on the table.

"Yeah, I could do that, but I really don't want to."

"You could try to make it as an actor."

"You know it's funny. I burned with the desire to be an actor a few months ago. Now that thought does nothing for me. I don't have the slightest desire to act right at this minute." He thought for a moment, looking at, but not seeing the activity of a city street. John sipped more of his beer. "I'm lost. I don't really know what to do next."

"I'm offering a solution, Luke. You know it doesn't have to be forever. Enlistments are for four years. You'll be older then, but still young enough to make a new life. You'd have a better fix on what you really want. You'd also have some good leadership training under your belt."

Luke was squirming. He was finding it harder to resist. "What got you thinking on this? Except when we were kids, I don't remember you wanting to be a Marine?"

"I never said much, but the idea always has appealed to me. I saw what Matt and Mark went through to become an officer though, and I don't want that. I don't think I could take that bullshit but something like boot camp . . . . I know it going to be tough, but I can do it. And then, I'd be a member of the best. Hell Luke. I've also got a quick temper. You know that. For some reason, I see a need to fight more than other people do. I should be in a place where I can fight. You've been gone for awhile. I've been doing some reading. I think I got what writers call, 'warrior spirit.'"

Luke absorbed all that. He didn't know if he had warrior spirit, but he knew he had staying power. He could run for miles and miles. He didn't think he'd fear boot camp or anything they could throw at him, and the part about being in the best appealed to his romantic soul. He was leaning. "What about Mom? Did you tell her?"

"Yeah, she's okay with it. She knows there's not much around Kingmont for us. The Marine Corps looks like a good place for me, keep me out of trouble, at least for a while. She worries that there might be a war, but I told her it's only been a few years since the last one. Nobody wants a new war now. You'll have to talk to her about your choice, though. I told her I'd be seeing you, but that's all."

Luke nodded. He was thinking. "What about the paperwork? Do we need birth certificates or anything?"

"The recruiter told me we could use baptismal certificates. I've already got those. Mom couldn't find the birth certificates. It would take too long to get new ones." He reached into his suitcase and pulled out the envelope. Luke glanced at it. John put it back in his bag.

"You had it all figured out, didn't you? You even figured I'd go along, right?" There was a touch of irritation in his voice.

"That was just in case, Luke. Just in case." John looked hurt. "If you say no, no harm is done."

The irritation disappeared. Luke smiled. He looked around at the cars, the people walking by, and the buildings. He was trying to let his subconscious mind tell him what to do.

"When I get out of boot camp, I plan to try and find Matt. Maybe we can all be together again."

Luke looked at John. That was the thought that finally made his decision for him.

9

Another Kind of Honor

On June 25, 1950, at 0400 in the morning, amidst a thundering artillery barrage that lit the night sky along the entire length of the border, seven NKPA (North Korean People's Army), infantry divisions and an armored (tank) division crossed the 38th parallel and invaded South Korea. Two other divisions waited at the border, in reserve. As they swarmed across the countryside in overwhelming numbers, the NKPA attacked in multiple spearheads, seizing numerous towns and villages simultaneously. The poorly trained and poorly equipped army of the Republic of Korea (ROK), was swept aside like so many shrubs before a flood.

Many of the small towns and cities along the border fell the first day. Seoul fell two days later. The Government was hastily moved south to Taejon, the day before the fall of the capitol city. At the end of four days, the entire northern part of South Korea was in Communist hands.

The incursion happened with such speed that few people had time to keep pace with the onslaught. The South Korean troops, which were, in reality, just a police force with no armor, very few artillery pieces, barely a dozen aircraft and only small personal, weapons, were no match for the seasoned, Soviet-trained Army.

"Who are you?" the small slim man sitting behind the desk asked him.

"My name is Kevin P. Canavan," he replied.

The man at the desk nodded at the soldier behind Canavan. The soldier slammed him in the back with the butt of his rifle. Canavan stumbled forward a step, gasping at the pain of the blow.

"Who are you?" the man asked again.

"I don't know what you want. I told you my name is . . . ."

Another nod, another blow between the shoulder blades. Canavan cried out as he struggled not to fall, a task made more difficult because of his tied hands.

"You have already told me your name. I want to know who you are."

The man sitting at the desk wore the uniform of the North Korean Peoples Army, a heavy brown tunic over matching pants. There was red star on his collar.

Kevin Canavan, hatless, stood before him wearing a dirty white linen shirt over dirty white pants. Canavan was also a small, slim man. "I don't know how to answer you. What is it you want besides my name?"

"You are not Korean. You are American. Who are you?"

"I am not an American. I am Irish."

"Americans? Irish? You're all mongrels. You are American."

"But my papers. They'll tell you I am Irish."

"Papers can be forged. Americans are great thieves. America is an immoral country. Everyone is a criminal. I would not trust your papers." He looked at his prisoner with contempt. "What papers are you talking about?"

"My passport. My identity papers." Canavan spoke with a raspy voice. Then he coughed. He tasted blood. "I gave them to the soldiers when they first entered the town. They demanded them." He trembled, reliving the earlier events, tanks, machine guns, artillery explosions, and maybe the worst of all, the marauding soldiers.

"I know of no papers. If you had any, which I doubt, they are gone now. I am not with the Army. I am the Political Commissar." He looked at his prisoner to ascertain the impact of that statement on him. Canavan just blinked.

"I repeat. Who are you? Why are you here? You are not Korean. Are you a spy? Were you sent here to spy on us?"

Canavan looked down in frustration. Trucks and tanks rumbled by outside the hut. A woman screamed. Occasionally, he heard bursts of automatic weapon fire. He wondered about that. There were no enemies in the area for the soldiers to be shooting at. They must be killing more civilians.

He looked up. "I am a priest. I came . . . ."

"You don't look like a priest. You do not have a shaved head. Why is your head not shaved?" the colonel asked with a sneer.

"Buddhist priests shave their heads. Catholic priests do not."

"Catholic? What is Catholic?"

Kevin was unnerved by the question. Did he really want to know? "We believe in Jesus Christ . . . ."

"Christ . . . oh yes, you are a Christian." The Commissar's face lit up. "I see, son of a carpenter. Killed by the Romans. Let's see . . . Martin Luther, John Calvin, and Henry the Eighth. They are Christians?"

"Yes, they are." Canavan answered the pain in his back subsiding. He felt he needed to add, "But they belong to a different part of Christianity. Have you heard of the pope?"

Another nod, another blow. Canavan went to his knees.

"You insult me, priest." He spouted in anger. "Of course, I've heard of the pope. He is the biggest capitalist of all. All the stolen art and statues and jewels while people starve. "

The colonel stopped his tirade. He was pensive for a moment.

Canavan rose to a standing position. The pain came back.

"How is it you are all Christians but you call yourselves by different names?"

This was a question that had bothered Father Canavan too. "Well . . ," he answered between jabs of pain. The last blow felt like it had loosened something inside his chest. "We all believe that Jesus Christ was the Savior promised in the Bible, but we disagree as to some of the other parts of our beliefs."

"It doesn't sound like much of a religion. You can't all be right. Someone has to be right and someone wrong. Your leaders, your Popes, they have been using religion to subjugate people for centuries. How many people have been killed fighting for your God? It is a sham."

The commissar stood up and paced slowly behind his desk.

"And your Bible. A book of stories and legends passed down by word-of-mouth for centuries and then written down. How reliable can that be? He turned to Canavan. "Religion is irrelevant, anyway. There is no God. You have wasted your life on a myth, just as the Buddhist freaks do."

Under other circumstances, Father Canavan would have loved to debate this man, but this was not the time.

The commissar looked at him with disgust. "Nothing you have said changes my opinion ... priest," he spat the word with apparent disgust. "You are still a spy. You are a spy for a corrupt capitalistic system that drains the lifeblood from the people so that the rich fat, cats of Wall Street . . . ." He looked at the shivering priest with a sneer. "And the pope, can get richer."

Father Canavan thought about the injustice of these statements. For five years, he had lived in a hut with dogs and chickens and lice and disease. He slept on the bare ground. He ate plain rice. He worked in the fields. The only thing he owned was his shirt and his pants. "I own nothing, colonel. I represent no fat cats. I am a humble man of God, who has taken vows, a vow of poverty, a vow of chastity. I teach people. I help people. I nurse people."

The colonel nodded again. Another smash to the back. Again Canavan went to the ground, this time onto his face. Tears coursed down his sunken cheeks.

"You insult me again . . . what is your name . . . Canavan? What is chastity? Does that mean celibacy? That's the biggest lie of all. You expect me to believe you have no sex life?" He looked at the Priest incredulously. "You've probably been fornicating with all the women in the village." Then he laughed, his face reflecting his lasciviousness. "And maybe with the men, or boys too, eh?"

He looked away and stopped speaking for a moment then he looked back at his victim. "And you expect me to believe you have no money. How do you get by? How do you eat? Where do you sleep? You are a liar."

The priest struggled to stand again. He succeeded, barely. "The people . . . ," he hissed through a pain-molded grimace, "the people help."

The colonel's body became rigid, his face crimson.

"You . . . you capitalistic dog. You take food from the mouths of these oppressed people? You suck the life from people who have noth-ing." He leaned forward his face a jumble of threatening emotions. "You . . . you . . . ," he sputtered in frustration," you are here to suck blood and then you will return home for your reward." He stepped back. "For this you will die. You are the most despicable person alive."

Now Father Canavan understood that he was going to be killed. He had suspected it earlier, but now he knew it. The thought of dying did not really bother him. The specter of martyrdom was something that all missionary priests lived with. It was a sure and direct way into heaven. To die while doing the Lords work was a noble ideal. A great honor. He would not have sought out the ordeal, but now that it presented itself, he welcomed it.

But this was not the martyrdom he imagined. This was not Joan of Arc dying to ensure that a Catholic king was crowned. This was not Saint Stephan being stoned for his beliefs. This was not the Christians in the coliseum, dying rather than worship false Gods. This was not — heroic.

He was going to be killed because this man believed he was a spy for cor-rupt capitalists. He was going to die because this colonel thought he was rich. He was being killed for all the wrong reasons. He was not going to die because he believed in God. He was going to die because he believed in Wall Street. More tears ran down his face. He looked up — to God — for help.

The colonel had regained control of himself. Canavan saw him unbuckle his holster cover and take out his revolver. He slowly walked around behind the priest. He nodded to the soldier. The soldier butted him again. He fell to the ground. The soldier grabbed him by the hair and pulled him to a kneeling position.

Father Canavan felt the cold nose of the revolver against the back of his head. He heard the click as the hammer cocked. He felt a little pressure as the finger closed on the trigger and the barrel leaned into him

His thoughts raced. He was dismayed. He was not going to be a martyr. This was a senseless death.

Then he felt God's presence. He felt calm. He smiled. The hammer came forward. Like Christ on the cross, Father Canavan's last words were, "Father, forgive them, they know not what they do."

Another kind of honor.

The North Korean Peoples Army (NKPA) had been trained and equipped by the Soviet Union and more than half the troops had fought as part of the Chinese Communist armies that drove Chang Kai Chek from China. They boasted a large contingent of Soviet T-34 tanks, heavy artillery, and jet aircraft.

The only United States forces in the Far East that could respond were in Japan or on island bases in the Pacific. No provisions had been made in advance to handle crises such as this. No contingency plans were in place. It was to the credit of the United States and the United Nations, however, that they were able to make any sort of response, as quickly as they did.

On June 27, the Security Council of the UN asked member nations to support South Korea in its time of need. On July 29, Truman appointed General Douglas MacArthur to head the U.S. forces, and subsequently the UN forces. He also authorized troops to be sent, and the waters around Korea to be blockaded. The Air Force was given permission to attack military targets.

The mission was to stem the tide and push the North Koreans back over the border. After much soul-searching and analysis, the decision was made that, given the small number of troops available, and the lack of supplies, at this point, a delaying action was the only strategy that made sense. As a result the United States Army began feeding troops into Korea on a piecemeal basis. The first American units to see action were occupation troops from Japan, a portion of the 24th Infantry Division. They arrived on July 2, and were engaged in combat on July 4, Independence Day in America. Under-strength, under-equipped, and under-trained, they to put up a spirited defense, but fell quickly.

More troops from the 24th arrived on July 7, along with advance elements of the 25th Infantry Division. By July 15, the 25th was at "full" strength, full strength meaning the approved post-war strength, about two-thirds normal size. A few days later, the 1st Cavalry arrived, but without their tanks. The Red onslaught continued. The soldiers fought valiantly, but the huge, well-equipped army they faced was overpowering. It was only five years after the end of World War II. With our military commitments in Europe and the drastic downsizing that had taken place, we just did not have the ability to handle incursions of this magnitude.

On July 2nd the Marines were authorized to send a regimental combat team with supporting Air. The 5th Marine Regiment and MAG 33 (Marine Air Group) formed the team, which was, dubbed the First Provisional Marine Brigade. The Army commanders at Pusan would later call it *The Fire Brigade*. The Brigade was needed for immediate action, but it was also to be part of a full Marine Division which would be put together for later action in Korea.

"Hey, Jacques. Did you hear? All leaves have been cancelled. Everyone has to get back to base. We're getting ready to go." Matt caught up with his buddy, as he walked by the company office.

The tall Frenchman stopped. "Well, mon ami, at last it comes. Korea?" he asked, his face a mixture of joy and intensity. "I was wondering if that little foray by the Communists would drag us in."

"Yep. Korea. And, according to Top (First Sergeant) we got to move out in five or six days."

"That is so fast. I wonder if we can do it. The whole regiment?"

"That's what he says. And the air wing."

"Merde, we have our work cut out for us, don't we? How are we going to do it?"

"I don't know. They're having an officer meeting in a little while. I guess we'll get the word after that. Excited?"

"Excited? Yes, I guess I am. I would like to know more about it. But, I guess all comes to he who waits. Nes pas?"

"I guess. We'll find out shortly." A thought occurred to Matt. "What about Ivan? He won't get the word. He's out in the hills."

"If he doesn't get the word, there's nothing they can do to him. He has leave. He's legal, right?" asked Lescoulie. "He'll come back when he comes back, and if we're still here he goes. If not, he goes with the next group, right?"

"Yeah, but he'd want to go with us, wouldn't he? We're his only friends. Besides if we get into a fight, I want him with me."

"Excellent point, my faux legionnaire." His mind studied the problem as they walked. "What do you suggest we do?"

"I don't know. We could talk to the Top. He knows his way around."

Ten minutes later, they were standing in front of First Sergeant Wilbur Gottchalk's desk. The Company office was in turmoil. Clerks were scurrying about like so many mice. Boxes were being filled. Files were put into portable containers. People were rushing madly around the curved roof Quonset hut

The first thing Matt and Jacques had to do was explain to the first sergeant that Ivan did not usually go to town or visit someplace in the area, when he went on leave or liberty. The First Sergeant listened. He liked Farrell and Lescoulie. He gave them a lot of slack. They were telling him that Ivan often spent his free time going out in the field and just living with nature. Usually, he traipsed out to remote recesses of Camp Pendleton, and was probably there now.

"When did he leave?" asked the veteran NCO.

"Yesterday," answered Matt.

"How much leave did he take?" Gottchalk could have looked it up, but it was quicker to ask Matt.

"A week. Seven days. He was going to lose it if he didn't use it."

"We'll be gone when he gets back," said the Sergeant, thinking. "You guys know where he goes?" An idea had occurred to him.

"We know the area," replied Lescoulie and Farrell almost simultaneously.

"Good," he decided quickly. "Go check out one of the company jeeps. Take it up there and get him back."

Matt and Jacques smiled. It was what they had hoped for.

The Top looked at his watch. "Get back by 1700 with or without him. We got work to do. You got it?"

"We got it, Top. Uh, do we need any orders to get the jeep."

"Naw, I'll call down. Get a radio, too. It might come in handy."

Forty-five minutes later, at about noon, Matt and Jacques were bouncing along on the dirt road in Rio Glorious canyon.

"Do you really know where he goes?" asked Lescoulie.

"Like I said to Top, and you said it, too, I know *the area*. He could be anywhere up here, but I have heard him talk about Las Pulgas. There are some rocky outcrops there. I think they remind him of home."

"That's a long way out. It will take us an hour or more to reach it."

"Yeah, I know. " Matt stepped down a little harder on the accelerator. "We gotta keep an eye on the time."

They bounced along for another ten minutes without speaking. They were eyeballing the terrain for any signs of Ivan, although they knew they were probably still far from him. There were no units training today. Normally, they would have seen hundreds of green clad men running, crawling, and walking around the small hills. Apparently they had all been pulled back in to get ready to leave.

Matt absorbed it all as they rode. Everything was so familiar. A number of trails led off the road to well-used training areas. That one to their right, that went to the combat village. They had been out there just a few weeks ago, attacking buildings, practicing squad tactics in a built-up area. Often, flamethrowers and explosives were used in this type of exercise, but that day was practice to develop facility in team tactics using only small arms and grenades. They had rocket teams with them, but had to simulate their activities. No spare ammunition was available.

A road, just a little past that village, led to the tank training area. Last month, they had worked with tanks, developing and practicing tank/infantry teamwork. Coordination and teamwork were a necessity to use tanks properly. The tank could be a devastating weapon, particularly against enemy infantry and bunkers, but it was vulnerable. Visibility was limited from inside a tank, especially when the tank was "buttoned up." The Infantry provided the "eyes" for the tank, spotting targets and antitank teams. The infantry protected the metal monsters. The tank in turn was a bodyguard for the troops and, with its cannon and 50-caliber machine gun fire, cleared the way for thinly clad human beings. It would be safe to say the ground pounders loved their tanks, but that love was returned by the metal jockeys. Matt remembered a long ago biology class where they called this type of relationship symbiotic.

"He really is different, isn't he?" Matt asked as he drove deeper into the back regions of the training areas. "Most guys go on leave, they go sightseeing, or hunting for girls, or they go home. Well I guess it would be hard for him to go home, or to visit someone. Not Ivan. He takes a small rucksack and goes out into the boondocks."

"What else does he have to do?" asked the Frenchman.

Matt thought a little. "True. When he went with us on liberty, he felt out of place. He doesn't drink. He doesn't go to movies. He doesn't dance. The white girls didn't want anything to do with him and he doesn't seem to want to have anything to do with them either." Matt scanned some of his memories. "He likes to walk."

"And swim. Remember, one of the things he liked was the beach," replied Jacques.

"Yeah I forgot that. He likes the beach. If he's not up here, he might be at the beach."

Matt slowed to take a sharp turn in the road. Some recent rains had washed away part of the gravel surface. Rains didn't come often in this part of California but when they did they were often gully washers.

Off to the left were buildings, now shut and locked, which identified the start of the live firing areas. Most of their training was done without ammunition. Here, however, individual Marines were able to fire their weapons in combat-like situations. The company had worked on this course about three months ago. A little further along they went by the "Torture Track," a series of hills that grew increasingly steeper and higher as they moved away from the road. They were conditioning hills, used to build up endurance. A Marine was no use to anyone if he was "too pooped to pop" when he reached the place of the final attack. Matt could recall a number of times when he had climbed and re-climbed those hills, often leaving his last meal along the way. "Maybe he feels out of place in a white world," offered Matt.

"Perhaps," said Jacques, "but many soldiers in the Legion were also from other places and even some other races. We had black and Chinese legionnaires. I'm sure they were lonely, but they didn't act like he does. I don't think that is his problem."

They twisted through narrow cuts in the canyon. Before long, they would emerge into a bigger canyon. They had left the area used for most of the training. The area from now on was more rugged and less frequented.

"He went to LA with some of the Negroes last fall didn't he?" asked Jacques. "I seem to recall he didn't care for that either."

"Yeah. He said they treated him as if he was a foreigner."

"I guess you could foresee that. He's different than the American Negroes."

"You know, I think that's what his real problem is. His culture is too different. We'd have the same problems if we ended up in South Africa among his people. And I think the American Negroes would have the same culture differences."

The terrain changed as they drove from dry grassland and smooth hills to tumble down scree and rocky outcrops. The temperature rose.

Matt pulled the jeep off the dirt road and stopped. They stretched and walked around to get the kinks out. They removed their blouses and took a swig of water from their canteens.

"What did he take with him this time? Did you see him go?"

"Yeah, I saw him go," replied Matt. "We went over to the commissary together the day before. He bought some vegetables, cheese and bread. I think he bought sardines too. He doesn't eat much meat."

"Did he take any clothes or blankets?"

"I think he had his poncho. He likes to live under the stars. He doesn't need much."

"I guess not. And, he walks all the way, too. One of the lieutenants offered him a ride one time. He refused."

They stretched a little more then they climbed back into the jeep and started off. Matt had the map out Jacques was driving. "Are we near the area you thought he might be staying in . . . ."

"We can't be too far. We came out here when we were running patrols during an exercise last year. He told me he liked this area. You were there when we did that patrolling."

"If you say so. I don't remember it." Jacques said, looking around.

The driving was slow. The road was narrow and covered with loose rock. They continued for about two miles without speaking. They were looking for any sign of his presence.

"Have you noticed anything different in his behavior lately? I mean *more* different, if there is such a word, and just lately?" asked Jacques.

Matt thought a little about that. "I guess I do see some different things. He seems quieter. Maybe it's because boxing is over. He really liked boxing. He used to babble on and on about that. You know how he talks. It's all serious and direct but still rapid fire."

Lescoulie laughed. It was a perfect description of Ivan, serious and direct but still talkative. "How long has it been since the season ended? Two months?"

"About that."

"Yeah, it's been about that long. I bet that's it. He's bored or something."

Jacques muscled the jeep around a big rock and entered a small valley. They stopped to get their bearings. While Matt studied the map, Jacques looked around. High on a ledge to their right he saw something white. It stood out against the drab rock formation.

"Look. Up there." Jacques was pointing toward the ledge. "A white cloth or something."

Matt squinted. Then he saw it. "Let's check it out."

Jacques put the jeep in gear and they bumped across the rocky plain toward the base of the hill where they had seen the cloth. They stopped and looked up. It appeared to be a T-shirt hung on a bush. Jacques honked the horn a few times.

"That's got to be his place."

Nothing.

He honked a few more times.

Still nothing.

Matt called. No response. "Where do you suppose he is?"

"Let's climb up and get a look at his perch."

They climbed up the face of the hill with some difficulty. In places, the rock was all scree, which made climbing difficult. They eventually reached the perch, breathing heavily.

Ivan was not there. His rucksack was there, along with his T-shirt. There had been a small fire, but the ashes were now cold. Then they heard their jeep horn. They looked down. Ivan was sitting in the jeep, shirtless. A big, for him, smile on his face.

"Got you," he said in a loud voice. "I heard you coming for the last two or three miles. You don't make good scouts."

"We were *trying* to find you, dipshit. We purposely made noise so you'd come to us," Lescoulie yelled.

"Why did you come? Did you miss me?" he asked mischievously. Then a concerned look crossed his face.

"I still have leave, don't I?"

"Not anymore. All leaves have been canceled, " said Matt. "We're going to Korea."

"Korea?" Ivan looked up at them. "To fight?"

"It looks that way. North Korea invaded South Korea. We're going over to help out."

Ivan bounded out of the jeep and banged the hood with his hand. He looked up at them again, again with a smile. It was the biggest smile they had seen him wear in the two years they had known him.

"Wonderful. Let's go. Will you bring down my shirt and my pack?"

"We should make you come up to get them because of your insults," yelled Jacques with a scowl. Matt was already starting down with the shirt and pack.

Just before Ivan put his shirt on Matt glanced at his chest and shoulders. He marveled, as he had in the past, at the man's physique. His pectorals were carved. His belly was a ladder. His shoulders were knots of muscle. His arms showed ridges of power. There was not a gram of fat anywhere. A sculptor could not have created a better body. In Paris, Matt had seen sculptures done by Michelangelo that were all muscles and hard knots. This man had the same kind of body. He shook his head and looked at Jacques. Apparently Jacques had been thinking along the same lines.

The ride back to the barracks took almost two hours. Ivan babbled happily all the way. They had discovered Ivan's problem. He *was* bored. He wanted to fight. They had forgotten. He was a warrior.

"Six days? We've got six days to mount out? And add a whole bunch of new people, too? I can't believe it."

"Well we're supposed to be the 'Force in Readiness.'"

"Yeah, I know our reason for existence is to be ready, but this is ridiculous. They mothball most of our weapons, cut us back to two platoons in a company, instead of three, eliminate one whole company per battalion, cut back on the training budget and then when they need us, we have to get ready in six days?"

"Welcome to the post-war world. We are part of the 'peace dividend.'"

Similar conversations were taking place throughout Camp Pendleton as the orders to embark for Korea came through. The Corps had been operating in what amounted to cadre status for the last few years.

The Marine Corps operated under a pyramidal structure, three divisions and three air wings. Each division has three regiments, each with three battalions, three companies in a battalion, three platoons in a company and so on. In 1950, there were only two divisions active, the First and the Second. Each division had only two regiments. Each regiment had three battalions, but each battalion had only two companies. At the time of the activation, each of the companies had two platoons, but a third platoon had been added for this operation. The air wings were in a similar condition, in effect operating at two thirds of normal strength.

Lieutenant Collins was about to hold a platoon meeting. He had just come from a battalion meeting where a great number of changes were outlined. He had a fistful of notes. Sergeant Wingo was at his side. The platoon assembled under the shade of a big pine tree behind the barracks, in a semi circle, with the lieutenant in the middle.

When the group settled down, he spoke. "Confusion seems to be the order of the day. Battalion is often confused, but this is worse than normal."

There was a ripple of laughter.

"I think I have the gist of what's going, on however." He fumbled through his papers looking for the right ones, and then continued, "We're in the process of getting some new people."

He looked around. "Some of you are already here." He noted one sergeant in particular. "We have to integrate these people into the platoon. At the same time, we are moving people out of the platoon. The company is adding a third platoon so it has to be staffed."

He looked around again and wiped a bead of perspiration from his eyebrow. July was a hot time in Southern California. "The new platoon will mostly be made up of new people. Not necessarily new to the Corps but new to the Fifth Marines. Some will be right from boot camp though. Most of the NCOs in the new platoon will be moved from existing units, like ours. Which brings me to some good news and some bad news. We're losing some of our NCOs but we're promoting some of you to take their places."

He looked around again and smiled. Sergeant Wingo handed him additional papers. He went down the list of men being transferred and then the promotions. Five men were transferred. Five men were to be promoted, two from corporal to sergeant, three from PFC to corporal. Matt and Jacques were two of the new corporals.

There were words of congratulations to those promoted. A few expressed regret about the loss of some of their buddies to other units. The lieutenant went on to talk of how the platoon would be reshuffled. Matt and Jacques would lead fire teams in the first squad. Ivan would be in Matt's fire team.

Matt and Jacques looked at each other quizzically. What happened to Ivan? They'd all been in the Fifth Marines two years. They thought of themselves as equal in ability. Why hadn't Ivan been promoted? They looked at Ivan. He appeared to be unconcerned.

After the meeting, Matt asked to speak to the lieutenant. Collins ushered him into his cubicle in the Company office. Sergeant Wingo was there, too. The earlier madhouse of activity had not abated.

"Sir, I appreciate the promotion but I have a question."

The lieutenant looked at him. "You want to know what happened to Spears, right?"

Matt hadn't expected that response. "Yes, sir," he replied hesitantly.

Collins looked at Wingo. The young officer was sandy-haired and ruddy in complexion. He was tall and thin. He had been an enlisted man in World War II.

"Where are you from, Matt? Or should I say *Corporal* Farrell?" He smiled.

Matt smiled faintly at the mention of the new rank. In response he almost said New York. Instead he said, "Massachusetts, Fall River, right on the Rhode Island border, sir" He wondered about the question.

"I figured you for a New Englander. I'm from Chicago. Never been to New England." He paused and looked at Matt. "You've also seen a lot with the Foreign Legion and all but I bet you haven't seen too much prejudice have you?"

"There was some of that in the Legion, but it was not officially accepted." Jacques had filled him in on those sorts of details during one of their training sessions back in France.

"Well it's not officially accepted in the Marine Corps either, but it exists." He leaned toward Matt. "Spears is one of the finest Marines I have ever seen. I'd promote him in a minute, but it's not that easy."

Matt looked at him blankly. He knew where the lieutenant was going, but he wanted him to say it.

"A large number of the men in this platoon . . . hell in any platoon, are from the south. They're good Marines, too, but some of them are still fighting the Civil War. They are just getting used to the idea of having Negroes in the barracks with them and using the same heads and eating with them. They are just not ready yet to have Negro bosses."

He stood up, walked around the desk. He sat down on the corner.

"Matt, maybe in a few months, a year, and we'll be able to put them in charge of white troops, but I don't think it will work now. Maybe what's more important, the brass doesn't think it will work now, either."

Sergeant Wingo spoke up for the first time. He was a Texan. "When we go into combat and these guys see that there's no difference, we can make changes. But it would only cause trouble now. Hell, I'm from the south and I grew up thinking nothin' but bad about 'Nigras,' as we called them, but I can see the need for change. Most of the others will, too. There's bad 'Nigras' and there's good 'Nigras.' Just like there's white trash and there's good whites. We'll take care of Spears when the time comes."

Matt wasn't too keen on this logic. There were Negroes going through Annapolis and West Point. What would these guys think if they had a Negro platoon leader, a Negro officer? He realized, though, that there was little he could do.

"I suspected that's the way it was. Thanks for being straight with me. I don't know how to explain it to him, though."

"I expect he understands," said Collins.

When Jacques and Matt did discuss it with Ivan, he *seemed* to understand. He showed no outward sign that a problem existed. "We are still together?"

"Yes. You are in my fire team. The first team. Jacques has the second fire team."

"Still the First Squad?"

"Yep. First Squad, First Platoon, George Company, 3rd Battalion, Fifth Marines."

"Okay. I can wait." He stared straight ahead with that no eyelid stare of his. "I still get to fight."

"You still get to fight, Ivan." Matt looked at Jacques. They were taking it worse than he was.

More and more Marines poured into Camp Pendleton every hour. They came by train, by car, by bus, by taxi, and a few even walked in. Many men, who had left the Corps at the end of the war, came back when they heard about the build up. Civilian life hadn't turned out the way they had thought it would. The units started to fill in, not to their authorized strength, but to a higher percentage than the downsizing had allowed.

Supplies came in from the giant supply depot at Barstow. Tanks, artillery pieces, mortars, machine guns, rifles, carbines, pistols, and BARs, all came out of their preservative Cosmoline and were trucked and trained down to the regiment. Ammunition, medical supplies, rations, clothing and other combat necessities emerged as the awakening war machine shook off its long sleep.

The last day before they were to leave was the most hectic. Working parties from all over the base were loading trucks and driving them down to the docks at San Diego. Matt's squad was working in a warehouse with a squad from the rocket section. They were loading boxes of records and office supplies, desks, filing cabinets, and other pieces of office furniture into a five-ton truck.

"What are we going to do, hit them with a desk? Throw a typewriter at them? What the fuck kind of combat gear is this?"

Another box of paper was tossed onto the truck.

"The only way you're going to get generals over there is to give them some papers to shuffle. It's all part of the job." Two Marines lifted a desk up to the tailgate.

"I hope you're right. I also hope there's somebody somewhere in this lash up loading guns and bullets and bombs and stuff, too."

The supply sergeant came by. "Stop your bitching assholes. Just get the gear loaded. It will all get there."

While Matt and his crew loaded their truck, they heard singing emanating from the back of the warehouse. Spears looked at Matt with raised eyebrows. Matt shrugged in response. They both looked to the back. Four Marines were loading a palette that the forklift would load onto a truck. They were singing in perfect harmony.

"Oh, give me a June night, the moonlight and you."

They sounded good. Not as good as the Andrews Sisters, but still pretty good. Jacques looked at Matt. "Is that the same song the Andrews Sisters did a few years ago?"

"I think so. Sounds pretty good. I wonder who they are."

"Back to work shitheads. We'll turn the music off if it distracts you."

Scrooge the supply sergeant was back.

"Tell them to sing a fast tune and then we'll work faster," said Matt." Smiling and tossing boxes as he spoke.

The singers must have heard him. When they finished *June Night*, they rolled into a spirited version of *Drinking Rum and Coca-Cola*. Everyone in the warehouse picked it up and started singing. By the time they got to *Boogie Woogie Bugle Boy*, the building was rocking and the supplies were flying. Even old Scrooge was smiling.

Finally, the trucks were loaded. The loaders took a break while the full trucks pulled out and more empty trucks pulled in. During the lull, Matt, Jacques and Ivan walked over to the singing group to meet them. They were four of the Marines from the rocket squad.

"You guys sound real good. You been doing that long?"

"Couple months. Just since the squad was formed," answered one, a tall rangy, redhead.

"You should make records," offered Jacques.

"We're not that good. Besides, we just imitate."

A pack of Lucky Strikes was passed around. "It still sounds good. Do you do anything besides the Andrews Sisters tunes?" asked Matt.

The tall redhead looked at the others and they all laughed. "I guess you haven't heard about us."

Spears looked at them with that bulls-eye stare. "What should we have heard?"

The redhead looked at Ivan, not sure what to make of him. Then he spoke, "It's our name. We're called The Andrews Sisters."

"The Andrews Sisters?" asked Matt.

The redhead looked at the others then back to Matt. He explained. He had the air of a patient teacher going over material one more time.

"My name is Buddy McAndrew. This here is Ole Anderson," he pointed to a big blond Marine. We call him Andy. The guy behind me is Andy Hankins, whose real name is Andrew and this guy is Angelo Marsucci." He pointed to short, wiry Marine and a stocky, dark-complexioned Marine, respectively. With the exception of Angie, we all got Andrew in our names and Angelo is close enough. So they call us The Andrews Sisters."

They shook hands all around.

"What a crazy thing," said Matt. "But why do you sing?"

Anderson spoke up. He had a slight Swedish accent. "When we realized we had this Andrews thing, we just thought it would be fun to put everyone on. We didn't realize it would sound good."

"Yeah, now we're stuck with it. Everybody wants us to sing," said Hankins with a distinct hillbilly twang.

"We don't really mind," said Marsucci. "Its better than bitching." Marsucci's accent was a little hard to pick up. Maybe Cleveland or Pittsburgh? Matt wasn't sure.

The new trucks arrived and the squads got back to work. In a few minutes, the warehouse was rocking again, this time to the tune of *Shoo Shoo, Baby.*

Six days later the Marines and the Navy had met their deadline. The First Provisional Brigade left port late in the afternoon and headed for Korea via Japan.

10

They Answered the Call

"What's wrong with the helmet covers?"

"Nothing."

"Why do we have to remove them?"

"Orders."

"Whose orders?"

"Don't know. Just orders."

"Where did you get your orders?"

"From the lieutenant."

"What did he say?"

"He said to tell the platoon sergeant to collect all the helmet covers and turn them in when you got your new leggings."

Sergeant Wingo thought that over for a minute and then asked the messenger, a company runner, "Did he give you any sort of a reason?"

"No, Sergeant." Then he looked at the platoon sergeant again. Wingo was looking at him threateningly.

The messenger coughed. "Well maybe he did."

Wingo waited as the runner looked around. The look in the private's eyes said he was about to impart some wonderful and delicious piece of gossip.

"I heard the CO, Lieutenant Gruene, tell Lieutenant Collins that some asshole doesn't want the enemy to know the Marines have landed so they're trying to make us look like Doggies."

"Bullshit. No Marine officer would say that." Then he thought a little about it. They were, at least for this phase of the operation, under the command of an Army general. The Marine general, General Craig was their immediate CG, but he reported to an Army general.

"Could it be possible that some chickenshit Army Officer actually issued an order like that?" Wingo shook his head ruefully. "I never have liked working with the Army. They are just too screwed up for me."

The long line of troops snaked in and out of stockpiles, loading up. They already had most of their personal gear, but they needed to receive their personal ammunition and the ammunition they would need for the crew served weapons. They also loaded up on hand grenades and rations. Many of them, toting boxes and bags, looked like overloaded Christmas shoppers, albeit with deadly presents.

When the units neared the end of the supply lines they had to turn in their helmet covers and receive their leggings.

Lieutenant Collins, the First Platoon leader and Lieutenant Wrobleski, the artillery forward observer who had been assigned to the company, were watching as Collins' platoon was making the swap.

"Do you really think someone issued an order for Marines not to wear their helmet covers, in order to hide us?" asked Collins

"I wouldn't put it past them. If you think the Marine Corps can be chickenshit you ought to work with an Army outfit sometime."

"But, that just bugs the hell out of me. Those helmet covers are part of us. They're a badge of honor. They're like a trademark. Marines wear helmet covers, soldiers don't. Besides, they're better at camouflage than a plain steel pot. Those pots sometimes reflect sunlight." More thoughts occurred to Collins. "With our covers we can even change colors to match the season. Green leaves on one side, brown leaves on the other."

"Hey, Tom. You're preaching to the choir. I didn't issue the order."

"Yeah, I know," he stepped down from his "soapbox." "But it just pisses me off."

He looked out over the troops as they dropped the covers into a pile and picked up their yellow leggings from another pile. They already had leggings but they were being issued new ones that were a yellow colored canvas instead of the faded tan they presently wore. He speculated that perhaps, issuing the yellow leggings was some Marine staff officer's way of protesting the helmet cover ban. The Marines would still stand out.

"I wonder why the Marine Corps doesn't use high boots like the Army does, mon ami. Do you know?" Jacques was kneeling down lacing up his new leggings.

"No, I don't. It would make more sense than to wear these boon dockers, and then have to wear leggings to keep out the sand and dirt and shit from inside the shoes." Matt stood up as he finished lacing his. He looked at Jacques legs. "They do look good, however. And we have to have something that makes us look like Marines now that they took away out helmet covers."

"You are correct as usual, my faux legionnaire. They do look good and we do need something to set us apart. What would a legionnaire be without his kepi? Remember in the last war, legionnaires threw away helmets to wear their traditional kepi."

"Yes, you are correct," Matt agreed, remembering something he had never known.

"One thing *you* were correct about, my friend, is the comfort of the boon dockers. The American boot is superior to the French boot and it is easier on the feet if you wear socks. I don't know if I will ever get used to having my first meal before noon however."

The battlefield that General Walton Walker, Eighth Army commander, had to deal with was a fluid battlefield. It was like trying to play chess on a shifting, moving chessboard. In addition to the chess pieces moving, the black and red squares also moved.

The maps behind him showed various aspects of the Korean peninsula. To some of the assembled group Korea looked a lot like the state of Florida without the panhandle.

A curved red line highlighted the lower right corner of the landmass. If it had been a map of Florida, the enclosed section would have been the greater Miami area.

General Walker pointed to the curving red line. "This is it. Gentlemen, this line, The Pusan Perimeter, our friends in the press call it, is as far as we go. I'm tired of being pushed around. We haven't had enough troops, enough time, enough supplies, enough training and enough of anything. We still don't, but I'm not running any more."

About a dozen of the senior military officer in Korea were at the meeting. This was the first time they had all been together since the war started.

"There will be no more trading space for time. I am ordering all units to stand. To the death if necessary, but to stand. We will not lose more equipment or ground."

The assembled officers exchanged approving, but questioning looks.

He noted the looks. "You are probably thinking, what's different now than a week ago? Aren't you? Why can we do this now?" He smiled. "Well, without considering the fact that we *have* to hold, let me tick off a few things."

He held his hand up and began pointing to his fingers. "One — the enemy's supply lines should be stretched to their limit. He's hundreds of miles from his base. Two — we have fallen back to where we are not spread so thin. We can have a little bit of defense in depth, a reserve if you will. And thirdly — " He smiled down at General Craig, the Marine commander. "We now have the Marines."

General Craig blushed and nodded at the compliment. Some of the Army officers looked at each other.

"In case you have forgotten," Walker had noted the exchanges. "The Marines are an assault force." He let that sink in. "We are going into an attack mode. They will join us when we strike back."

Commotion ensued. Questions began to fly. "About, fucking, time," Said one veteran officer under his breath.

The plans were laid. The 25th Division, The Army's 5th Regimental Combat Team and the First Provisional Marine Brigade would all jump off from positions around Masan on August 7 to take the fight to the NKPA. Their objectives would be Chinju and then Sachon. This was an auspicious date for the Marines. On August 7 in 1942 the First Marine Division had landed on Guadalcanal, launching the first American ground attack in the Pacific War.

The 25th Division would attack northern part of the area. The 5th RCT would handle the middle part of the zone and the Marines would constitute the southern force or the left flank. Decisive battles would soon be fought. The tide would soon be turned.

General Pang, in Marine parlance, was "squared away." The major general, commander of the 6th Division of the North Korean Peoples Army, stood before a large gathering of his officers and NCOs, looking like a recruiting poster. His otherwise drab brown uniform was tailored and pressed. His boots gleamed. The pips of rank that shone on his shoulder boards, along with the red star of communism on his high collar, were the only dabs of color, but they added just the right touch to the otherwise bland garb, to create a sophisticated appearance. He stood on a platform, legs spread, hands on hips. He wore a smile on his broad face. He was soaking up the admiration and the enthusiasm of the assemblage.

"You have performed wonderfully. I am honored to be your leader."

The mass of soldiers cheered in appreciation.

"We have swept across the Korean countryside like a tsunami surging from the sea. We have come down from the north like the north wind, chilling and killing our enemies."

They roared again, hands raised in celebration.

"No one has stood before us, not the South Korean puppets nor the American lap dogs. We have swarmed over them all."

Another roar of approval reverberated. The windows in the old warehouse shook with the sound. He dropped his hands from his hips and walked to one side. All eyes followed him. He smiled again and spoke with less volume.

"The Americans are a myth. They were a proud Army during the big war with Japan, but they have become soft. They have no stomach for this battle. We have pushed them back day after day. Sometimes, they are just overrun by us but sometimes they just run away by themselves. They are perfect examples of the results of a decadent society and the gross injustices and evil morality of capitalism."

He nodded to the political officer, Colonel Chee, in the first row. The colonel's face was impassive.

"They tried to resist in a few places, but our brave soldiers crushed them anyway. We have taken many prisoners. The sign of a bad army is how many of their soldiers are taken as prisoners." The colonel raised his voice and enunciated clearly. "They are a bad army."

The warehouse erupted in another demonstration of high emotion.

General Pang walked back to the center of the platform as he waited for the noise to subside. When he spoke again, he spoke in a normal tone. "We ourselves have fought the entire length of the Korean Peninsula and won every battle. We are about to make the final push to drive the invaders out of the last corner of *our* land. As an added bonus we are joined by the 83rd Motorcycle Regiment, another elite People's Army force."

He nodded to the commander of the regiment. Colonel Dak To, who sat next to Colonel Chee. The colonel nodded back and smiled.

"They will give us much increased firepower and mobility for our last surge." The general paused as he looked out at the tightly packed group in front of him. His eyes glistened as he thought about what was to come. He strode to the edge of the platform and spoke again.

"Comrades, the enemy is demoralized. The task given to us is the liberation of Masan and Chinju and the annihilation of the remnants of the enemy. We have liberated Mokpu, Kwangju, and Yosu and have thereby accelerated the liberation of all Korea. However, the liberation of Chinju and Masan means the final battle to cut off the windpipe of the enemy."

The hall was quiet. Attention was undivided as they watched their leader.

"This glorious task has fallen to our division!" He looked around again. "Men of the 6th Division, let us annihilate the enemy and distinguish ourselves."

They jumped to their feet and exploded with enthusiasm.

"I was beginning to think we'd never get untracked and get

moving," Matt said to no one in particular.

"The docks . . . and the holding areas, were they not crazy?" responded Jacques.

"And the train ride to Changwon, wasn't that great?" asked a disgusted Matt. "There were plenty of seats, but how can you sit on a bench where the back and the seat form right angles? There's no way — and they're too narrow to lie down."

Matt was digging a foxhole as he spoke. Ivan was helping him. Jacques was a few feet away also digging a hole. His scout was helping him. They were working shirtless and sweat covered their glistening bodies. Matt didn't know what the temperature was, but he thought it must have been close to 100 degrees. They were consuming large quantities of water.

George Company was arranged in an undulating line, their mission to block a few of the approaches to the road leading from Masan to Chindong-ni. How Company was blocking the other approaches. The First Platoon was set up on a small knoll at the base of the Hill 99, which housed the rest of the Company. The two companies had been placed in their positions in order to form the base for launching the regiment's attack in the morning. They did not anticipate any action this evening, but they were always prepared.

"The rice paddies, they smell," offered Ivan in typical directness.

"They sure do," said Matt, looking at the paddies that he could see. "I read where they use human and animal shit for fertilizer." He wiped sweat from his brow with a dirty hand. "I also read that they don't waste anything. Not even shit. The Koreans are some of the best people in the world at wringing the benefit from everything."

"I am glad I don't have to live that way," said Ivan, a little pompously.

Matt laughed. "Me too."

"The people," said Jacques, "the refugees —" He had been only half listening to the conversation as he dug. "Did you ever see such a dispirited group of people? They looked like they had been walking for days."

"They probably have. Whenever war hits, those people get it the worst ... you know the local people, the ones just trying to get along."

"They are probably fleeing the enemy. If we find out where they came from we will know where the enemy is." Ivan spoke with practical wisdom.

"By George, I think you're right," said Matt. "I wonder if the intelligence guys know that."

He winked at Jacques. Then he looked at Ivan. He had second thoughts. That was actually a very astute statement. He wondered if the intelligence people *had* figured that out.

Matt stopped digging a minute and looked at the hole. He took a drink from his canteen. He stood in the center of the hole and looked out at the valley in front of him. Ivan also stopped. He did not like to dig.

"I guess it's deep enough. We just need to widen it some. Put a little more muscle into it, Spears. It's your side that needs the work."

Ivan looked at him. "Zulu princes do not do this work."

"Well Marine privates do. Dig in, turkey."

Spears looked at him with his wide-eyed look and a hint of a grin and then went back to digging.

"I hope we don't have any more phantom enemy attacks like we did at Changwon," said Jacques, tossing some dirt in front of his hole. He stopped to wipe his forehead. "I'd like to be able to get some sleep tonight. If we jump off tomorrow, I want to be rested."

"I guess that shit happens sometimes. We've got a lot of new troops," replied Matt.

"Yes, it does. In the Legion, too." He looked at Matt between scoops of dirt. "Remember how at Bir Hakeem we had the same problem."

Matt knew the reference was for him. He nodded.

"At night, fear is prevalent. You are not used to being near an enemy and being deprived of your sight at the same time. You don't know what to expect. The rocks . . . they move. The bushes . . . they hide the enemy. Sounds are magnified. You hear invisible bolts sliding home, ghostly words being spoken, accouterments creaking. You don't take chances. You shoot."

Matt added, "It was better the second night. Only a few rounds went off. Lieutenant Collins said that a couple of the company commanders had a 'character building experience' with the colonel about that. Our CO wasn't one of them. Gruene has his head on straight."

Jacques laughed. "A 'character building experience', eh? That is an interesting turn of phrase. You still don't pronounce Gruene's name correctly though. It's more like Green. The actual pronunciation in German is something like 'gruerne' The 'ue' is pronounced like it had an 'r' in it."

"He says Green is okay though. He doesn't mind Green," replied Matt.

"C'est la vie."

"First Lieutenant Lonnie Gruene . . . 'Green' . . . from Fredericksburg Texas. I had a classmate at . . . ," he caught himself "school, who was from Fredericksburg. It's in the hill country of Texas.

I think Admiral Nimitz came from there too."

Jacques nodded. He didn't know who Nimitz was, but he had a question. "Speaking of hills, I wonder if this whole area has hills. If we have to fight the enemy in this heat and on these hills, it will be very hard."

"I would imagine it's all like this."

"Then I am worried. We spent all that time on the boat. We lost our conditioning. We also have to face the heat. We have no time to condition ourselves to the loss of fluids and to understand the need for water management. In the desert we conditioned our bodies, but it takes time. If we have to fight the NKPA soon, our bodies may not be ready."

"I hear what you're saying, but I guess we can't do much about it. The gooks should have the same problem though, shouldn't they?"

"Perhaps not. They live in Korea and they have been fighting, moving, working in this heat for a month or more. They may already be conditioned."

Matt shook his head. He hoped he'd be ready when the time came.

The news came in a little after midnight. Lieutenant Collins and his platoon were to pull out of the line, pick up a machine gun squad, proceed for a few miles and relieve an Army Company on a hill, called Yaban-San, or Hill 342.

Collins reaction was to be expected. "I appreciate that Marines are good fighting men, but honestly, Lonnie, to expect a platoon to relieve a company is stretching it a little."

"Your protest is duly noted," said Gruene. He looked at Collins with concern. "I made the same argument and so did the battalion commander and I'm sure the regimental commander did, too. An order is an order."

"But why just a platoon? Why not a company?"

"I don't know. The word is that this hill is very important to us, especially now that we're going to start our assault. This company has been up there for some time blocking the approaches to Masan. The company is depleted. Attrition has taken its toll. They need to be replaced and all that can be spared is one platoon. They're also part of the 5th RCT and they need to get back to their unit so they can participate in the assault. When the rest of the regiment finally moves up, there will be more help available for us, but right now . . . ." He finished with a shrug.

Collins looked at Gruene. The matter was decided. "Well I guess I better get going." He turned to leave.

Gruene grabbed him by the arm. "Tom, be careful up there. You'll do a good job, but take care . . . ." He trailed off lamely.

"We'll get it done, Skipper."

"Leave it to the Army to get us screwed up" said Gil Totten, the BAR (Browning Automatic Rifle) man in Matt's fire team. "The fucking battalion CP is so far behind the front that they have to use guides to get to the front and then the guides don't know the way."

"And we got to do the whole thing in the dark — a real fuck up," griped his assistant.

When the platoon had arrived at the battalion CP, they were surprised that they were still a half-mile away from the company on the hill. Collins experience was that Marine battalion CPs were never more than a few hundred yards away from the front lines. They were forced to wait for a guide.

They had been climbing toward the crest of Hill 342 for an hour when the soldier realized he had taken a wrong turn. They'd had to back track and go up another draw. They knew they were getting closer to their objective was when a few enemy artillery shells landed nearby. Needless to say, the Marines were developing a real dislike for certain Army units.

As the column of fifty-two men wound around the hills on what appeared to be nothing more than a goat track, they took their first casualties. Two of the men in the second squad were hit. The wounds were painful, but not serious. The platoon stopped and took cover. The guide suspected that the fire they received, coming from their right, had been "friendly" fire.

"Chalk another one up for the Army," said Totten.

Collins made the decision to wait for daylight to continue. Understandable at the time, this turned out to be an unfortunate choice.

When day dawned, they stared at the face of Hill 342, a precipitous mass looming above them. They used the radio to make sure the friendly troops in the area knew they were coming through, then they started their climb. Apparently nobody had contacted the Army units the night before to advise them. They would have been sitting ducks.

They made good progress at first, but just as the steepest part of the climb faced them, the sun and the heat rose to greet them also. The temperature soared above 100 degrees and the sun beat down with a vehement belligerence. Canteens emptied quickly. It was 0800 and they were only halfway up when, for most of them, the last of the water was gone. Regardless, they toiled on, waterless, sweat-drenched and parched. The lack of sleep also began to take its toll, as energy waned.

In many places, the trail was composed of loose rock and sand, which added to the misery, causing men to slip and fall backward. They had to pick themselves up and climb back over territory they had already traversed. The line of troops was becoming longer and longer as the intervals between men increased.

NCOs cuffed and pushed men to continue, but even they started to feel the pressure of the heat. They were still a hundred yards below the crest when some of the Marines began to suffer from various forms of heat stroke or heat exhaustion. Some lost consciousness. With each passing minute the toll became worse. Those who didn't faint, stood on the side of the trail doubled over, retching violently. If the enemy had attacked them at that point most of the platoon would have been helpless.

Collins called a halt. About half the platoon had been affected. Collins, Wingo, Matt, Jacques, Ivan, and a few others were still able to function. They provided what shade they could for the stricken and then sat down themselves. Other than a few sips of water, stubbornly husbanded in canteens by some of the veteran troops, there was no water.

After a brief rest, Collins decided to go on alone to make contact with the Army company commander. He left Wingo and the other NCOs to push the platoon up. Within a half hour he had made contact. Within another hour the majority of the platoon was just below the crest of the hill. They had left the worst cases along the trail, with the intention of going back for them later.

As they made the final part of their climb, the enemy had peppered them with sniper fire. They took a few more casualties. When all the men who were still effective reached the top, Collins had thirty-seven men he could count on. The heat on the top of the hill also was intense.

He met with Captain Slocum, the Army commander, and Slocum gave him an overview of the situation. As they spoke a disturbance started to the left of their position. At first, it was a few shots, followed by a few grenade blasts. Then a four or five grenade blasts. Then men yelling and more shots were fired. Slocum and Collins crept up to the crest and peered over. Fifteen or twenty Reds had swarmed into one of the company positions. They were firing in all directions. The Soldiers were falling back, some actually fleeing. The line was about to cave in. There were other Reds down the slope, advancing toward the breech.

Before Slocum or Collins could react to the situation, the decision was made for them. A group of six or seven Marines led by a howling black man flashed by them and roared toward the battle. The group was composed of Spears, Matt, Jacques and a few others.

As they neared the position, Ivan launched himself into the air and dove into the stunned North Koreans with a horrifying scream. He knocked five of them down when he landed in their midst. It is arguable which frightened them the most — the scream or the sight of this mad man flying through the air. In any event, the tactic worked. They all stopped. When the rest of the group plowed into them, seconds later, they were at a disadvantage. The communists had lost their momentum. They were on the defensive.

Ivan scrambled to his feet immediately slashing with his bayonet. He disemboweled one Red and decapitated another. Matt ran his bayonet into one of the NKPA soldiers, but was forced to drop his rifle and attack another Red with his bare hands when he couldn't dislodge his weapon. Jacques crushed the head of one of the red soldiers in front of him, and then he saw Matt's plight.

He rammed the butt of his rifle down on the head of the man Matt was fighting, crushing his head also. The man fell to the ground. Jacques yelled out, "You owe me one, Matthew." Then he was on to engage a new enemy.

Action swirled around them. Matt saw a rifle on the ground and grabbed it. He looked up in time to see a Red soldier trying to bring his burp gun up to fire at him. Matt ran at him as hard as he could and barreled into the soldier just as he fired. The bullets snapped past Matt's ear, the noise temporarily deafening him. Matt landed on top of the Red, knocking him breathless. He bounced up and sank the bayonet into his throat. He was trying to be careful not to get the blade stuck this time. It pulled free easily.

Matt spun around and went to a knee. He had no idea whose weapon he had or if it had any rounds in it. He couldn't take the time to check. Out of the corner of his eye, he saw one of the men in his fire team, Womack, shoot a Red soldier at point blank range and then stab at another.

He saw Ivan about fifteen feet away from him. He was standing on top of five or six dead enemy soldiers. He had two Reds by the throat and was slowly squeezing the life out of one while he held the other in a terrified state of stasis. He finally dropped the one he had been squeezing and wrapped his arm around the neck of the other broke his neck.

Matt quickly scanned the rest of the area. There were no Reds standing. He looked around. Bodies were strewn everywhere, most of them the enemy. There were a few dead soldiers. He saw no dead Marines. Apparently the fight was over. Jacques was walking toward him.

"Are you okay, mon ami?"

"I'm okay, Jacques."

He looked to Ivan.

"You okay, Ivan?"

"No. I need more enemy." He stared at Matt with a perfectly serious face.

Matt suddenly remembered that there were other Reds climbing up toward the breech. What happened to them?

He ran to the edge and looked over. There was no sign of anyone. Apparently, they had fallen back. Behind him, the soldiers who had held the position originally were filtering back. The expressions on their faces were a mix of guilt and admiration. Some looked at Ivan in awe.

Collins and Slocum came forward. "Well, Ivan, Farrell, Lescoulie." Collins looked from one to the other in admiration. "That was quite a show. You guys okay?"

"I think so. How's everybody else?"

"I lost a couple of my men, but I doesn't look like we lost any Marines," said Slocum.

"No, I don't think we did. The rest of the guys in your squad fought well, too. You got some good people," said Collins.

After taking stock, they determined that three soldiers had been killed and seven wounded. One Marine had been wounded, but not seriously. The other three Marines who had participated were all members of the First squad, the one that Matt, Ivan and Jacques belonged to.

After discussing the overall situation Collins, and Slocum decided to mix the Marines with the Army troops in order to shore up morale. The soldiers were a depressed lot. They had been there for days and their only experience had been, intense sun, impossible heat, rationed water and dwindling numbers. The infusion of the Marines boosted spirits. Neither group wanted to appear to be less a warrior than the other.

One other bright spot surfaced. The soldiers had been able to get some water up the hill over the last few days, and although the supply was still tight, they were able to share a little with the Marines.

The holes the soldiers had dug, kept the troops safe from long-distance shooting. They were fine once into them, but it was dangerous getting in or out The Platoon took casualties just trying to move around and improve their positions. Collins decided if he had been in command, he would not have put their fighting holes out in the open like they were. He would have used the reverse slope.

He also wondered how he would handle things when Captain Slocum received the word his company could withdraw. Setting up properly with his depleted platoon would be a problem. As it turned out, that was a moot point. Within an hour of the Marines' arrival, the "word" was radioed to the Army company to stay put. The "word" had changed. Long live the "word," thought Collins, with some sarcasm.

Matt slid down a small slope into the depression that Collins was using for a CP. Two shots cracked over his head just before he hit bottom. He came to a stop at Collins feet. The lieutenant looked up quickly. He had been studying a diagram of their position that Slocum had given to him.

"What's up, Farrell? Problems?"

Sergeant Wingo was at the side of the depression. He had been retching just a moment ago. Now he was shivering. The heat and dehydration had gotten to him, too.

"Yes, sir. I'd like to take my men down and try to bring up some of the guys we left behind."

Collins started to shake his head.

"Listen, please, sir. We've got to do it. Two of our BAR men are back down there. Our squad leader never got up and two men from the third fire team are missing. We don't have a squad."

Collins was wavering.

"I'll take Spears and Womack. Lescoulie can be in charge until we get back. I don't know why, but Spears and I handle the heat better than others and we need those other guys."

Collins looked at him and made his decision

"Okay, Farrell. We need all the help we can get. Tell Lescoulie he's in charge and Farrell . . . ."

"Sir?"

"We need you back here. Get any troops you can, but get back here pronto. Half-hour tops. Okay?"

"Roger, lieutenant. On the way." Matt looked at his watch. "Half hour."

Matt slithered back to the top of the crest. "Weenie. Ivan."

Two heads popped up.

"Get your asses up here. We got a job to do."

They started to scramble out of their holes.

"Jacques."

Lescoulie looked up.

"Take the squad over. We're going to go back and see if we can get some of our guys back." Jacques looked at Matt, a little wistfully, then nodded. "Take care, Matt."

"Roger, that."

He slipped back over the crest. Within seconds, Ivan and Womack joined him, sliding on their rear ends as they did so. As expected, rifle shots pursued them.

They descended the path slowly. Large sections of the route were open to fire from the front.   After a few minutes they came across Totten, Matt's BAR man. He was dead, curled up into a fetal position. Matt guessed he had been shot while he was retching. A tear formed in Matt's eye. He didn't know Totten well, but he had been a Marine doing his job. That was a shitty way to die. Matt took the BAR and handed it to Womack.

"You are now the Team's BAR man Weenie"

A little further down, they found a group of three Marines huddled together for protection. They were emotionally spent. Ivan pulled them apart. Matt yelled at them. Ivan kicked one. Finally they began to show signs of awareness. They looked terrible, as so did everyone on the hill.

"What the hell is this? You guys are Marines," Matt roared. "I know it's tough, but that's what you get paid for. What kind of wimps are you? If you give into this shit, what will happen when you're under attack? Get your shit together, crapheads. Let's get it moving." He was holding one by the shirtfront and another by the collar.

The Marines looked around cautiously. One reached down for his weapon. The others followed.

"Weenie, get them going up the hill. Get them near the top then come back down. Be careful."

"Roger, Matt. See you in a bit. Let's go, crapheads." He stepped off heading back up the hill. After a moment's hesitation, the others followed.

"That kid, Womack, he's going to be all right. Where'd he get the name 'Weenie,' though?"

"He said he got in boot camp," replied Ivan with what passed for a smile. "His buddies said he had small fingers and small toes so he must have a small weenie. The name seems to have followed him."

"I got to remember not to call him that anymore. He's no weenie"

They inched their way further down and they found two more dead Marines. One of them was Sergeant Millman, their squad leader. As they were checking Millman and the other Marine, something caught Matt's eye. From here he had an excellent view of the valley. About 1000 yards in front of him were a large number of enemy troops, forming lines. It looked like they were getting ready to advance on the hill.

As if to confirm Matt's suspicions, mortars were launched from behind the enemy line. They fell short, but it was only be a matter of time before the Reds improved their aim.

They had to get back. Matt was sure Collins was not aware of this approach. He stood up. Then suddenly Ivan motioned him down. He sank to a knee quickly.

"What's up?"

"Someone's coming."

Within a few seconds, two Marines crept around a rock formation. They had been climbing up the hill. One was the other missing BAR man, Rico Duran. Matt grabbed them in delight. They were exhausted and dehydrated, but they were able to move. He filled them in on the situation, and then they all took off for the top.

Collins had *not* been aware of the enemy buildup on the side of the hill, nor was Slocum. Collins called in artillery on the mortars. The first round was well short, but he remembered his FO (forward observer) training and after a few more rounds he had them bracketed and called for a full barrage. Bingo. The mortars stopped. Collins had the artillery shift fire to reach the advancing infantry. It only took one round to get the range. Then, after ascertaining that the artillery batteries had proximity fuses, he called in a full barrage. Proximity fuses detonate the artillery round in the air, as it nears the ground. The attacking enemy walked right into five minutes of carefully timed airbursts, which threw shrapnel in all directions. The attack was instantly broken up.

No sooner had the smoke cleared from the artillery barrage on the side of the hill, however, than the enemy launched an attack at the front. They came in waves preceded by mortar fire. Distances are difficult to judge in hilly country, so once again the mortars fell short of the U.S. positions. The NKPA had another tough problem to overcome. They had to climb and attack at the same time. But they were brave men and they came forward along the rocky upslope with determination.

When the first lines were about three hundred feet away, the Marines started shooting. The first to fire was the machine gun, then the BARs, and then the riflemen. Brown clad warriors went down in rows. The whole first line was almost gone. The second line quickly replaced them.

Some of the Army troops joined in and fired with the Marines. Matt was firing as fast as he could find targets. When he stopped to load another clip, he noticed that two of the soldiers to his right were just watching in fascination. They were not shooting.

"Hey!" he yelled over the noise. "Start shooting you shitheads. We need all the help we can get."

They quickly grabbed their rifles and set up at the front of their hole, looking back at Matt with uncertainty.

"Goddamn it, shoot. What gives with you guys?" he yelled in fury. Something clicked in their heads. Matt's voice? The situation? But they turned. And then, still with some hesitation, they both started shooting.

Although the NKPA was being slaughtered, there were enough of them to keep the pressure on. A few even worked their way near the top and started to throw grenades into the more forward holes. Lescoulie and his men fought a three-minute bayonet battle with about five or six enemy and won. No casualties. The small battle had tumbled all over the front of the foxholes. Jacques himself cracked two heads with his rifle butt and gutted another with his bayonet. Two other Red soldiers made the mistake of crawling into Ivan's hole. He literally picked them up and smashed their heads together so hard that actual cracks could be seen in the cranial bones that showed through the split skin.

Someone at battalion was using *his* head and called for air support. A short while after the artillery barrage on the side of the hill was over, two Corsairs, gull winged, fighter planes, had come on station. By patching through Battalion to the air net, Collins was able to direct some air strikes against a third build up of troops, also in front of the company's position. After the two planes made three passes with rockets and napalm, the enemy broke and ran. The Reds who had almost gotten to the top of the hill also fled. The combined company of soldiers and Marines stood up and cheered.

The defense of Hill 342 had been a success. Shortly after the battle an observation plane, swung over the hill and dropped some five-gallon water cans. Most split open, but enough landed safely to stave off the worst of the dehydration problems. Work parties were organized to go back down the hill and bring up water. They also picked up stragglers as they went.

Late in the day, Collins received word that a full Marine company would relieve them and the Army unit in the morning. They had done their job, the first of the Fire Brigade's rescues.

That evening they posted a fifty-percent alert, with listening posts in front. Captain Slocum wasn't sure about the listening posts but he went along with Collins. He thought they would fall asleep and they would be sacrificed. Collins felt that men rarely fall asleep when they were twenty or thirty yards in front of their lines at night.

They also reorganized their positions, set up firing lanes, dug holes for supplemental missions and in general improved their defensive set up. Collins was amazed at the small number of troops Slocum had left. His best guess was sixty. He had started out with almost two hundred. He had no officers. Sergeants were running his platoons. He felt sorry for him.

The Marine platoon had lost twelve men. Seven were killed, three were wounded, and two were serious heatstroke cases. Collins had to rearrange his squads. Matt was put in charge of the First squad. Spears took over Matt's fire team. Lescoulie and Wilson kept their teams. A few troops were added from other squads to fill them out.

When it became too dark to see, Slocum and Collins held an officer and NCO meeting. A canteen of water was passed around, the first "luxury" of the day. They talked about the next morning. Both Slocum and Collins felt that the Communists had taken a real pasting, but they were doubtful that the battle was over. The NCO's agreed. They also agreed to keep the fifty-percent alert all night.

The problem of some troops not firing came up. Matt was still steaming about that.

"Look, I can see a guy being scared. Shit, I was scared, too. But when you' re being attacked, where the hell is your head? You've got to shoot back. I thought everyone had the instinct to protect themselves."

"Corporal." It was Captain Slocum, "These men were sitting in Geisha houses two or three weeks ago. They haven't fired a weapon in years. Some have never seen infantry training. Those that had some infantry training — well that was years ago. They don't train like rifle-men anymore. They stood guard, manned working parties, did KP, and all that. They aren't real soldiers."

He leaned back on his elbows. He had been sitting up. His face was drawn and haggard. His eyes glinted with tears and reflected the sparse light provided by the stars. "We all want to do our job. We want to do our duty. We just weren't prepared. Perhaps it's not an excuse but it is a reason."

Matt didn't know what to say.

Slocum continued. "Needless to say, I was glad you were here today. I think you saved us. You gave us some backbone. That fight you put up at the left corner was just marvelous. I've never seen anything like that. And the rest of the Marines, no hesitation about shooting. That's won-derful. I saw some of my men who didn't shoot at first, start to shoot when they saw how effective your men were. I think they had given up. Your Corsairs didn't hurt either," he finished with a smile. "That is a magnificent weapon you Marines have."

Collins smiled, too. "The artillery didn't hurt either."

"Correct, lieutenant. We had artillery a few days ago, but they moved yesterday to support other missions. Earlier, I had to send my mortars down the hill because they were drawing too much fire. We had nothing but our rifles and ARs, you call them BARs, and machine guns."

Both Collins and Matt wondered about pulling the mortars out because they were receiving fire. That didn't sound too smart to them. Why not just keep moving them to protect them. That was better than removing them.

They were all quiet for a while. Slocum had been thinking a little more. "Corporal, I remember reading once that, at the battle of Gettysburg, in the Civil War, after the fighting was over, they found loaded but unfired weapons all over the battlefield. It seems to be a phenomenon that happens to untried troops. My guess is that what goes through the soldiers mind is that maybe if he doesn't shoot at anyone, they won't shoot at him."

Matt mulled that over. "You could be right, sir." Then he added, "But if I ever saw any of my men doing that, I'd kick their butts."

Dawn broke with a bang, or rather an explosion. A hand grenade tumbled into a squad position in the center of the line. Within moments, enemy troops were pouring over the ramparts onto the Army troops. Apparently, the Reds had crawled up to the lines during the night and waited for dawn to launch the attack. Collins wondered what happened to the men on the listening posts. Perhaps Slocum had been right.

Matt crawled forward to look over the front of his hole. In the dim light, he saw NKPA troops crawling and skulking fifty yards down the hill. He called back to Collins asking for artillery. Collins started to put the call through.

Matt watched the battle and decided they were going to need help. There were too many gooks for the soldiers to handle. He called back again to Collins and volunteered his squad to help them.

"No way, Farrell. You're needed where you are, "replied the young lieutenant. "They're going to have to make it themselves." At that point, a group of screaming Americans came from the other side of the hill and descended on the swirling battle. The group was a mixture of Marines and soldiers. Captain Slocum led it. After a few minutes of furious hand to hand battling, they threw the North Koreans out of the hole. They had stemmed the tide.

Shortly after Slocum's battle, the artillery rounds started to land. Collins moved down into Matt's position and using the radio, proceeded to walk the 105 millimeter airbursts all over the front of the hill. By now there was enough light that the rest of the troops could fire effectively too.

The combined arms were too much. The Reds fell back down the hill again.

During the rest of the day, the Americans on the hill heard a great deal of shooting as Dog Company fought their way up the slope to relieve them. It had not been easy. They had taken casualties and they also had heat exhaustion problems. Finally, by the middle of the afternoon Dog Company reached the crest and relieved the embattled bastion. Collin's platoon and Captain Slocum's company tumbled down the hill exhausted but happy. The Marines had stood their first test and passed.

The intelligence people estimated enemy casualties at more than 400 while trying to take Hill 342. The enemy wanted that hill badly but the cost had been too high.

11

A Bittersweet Romance

Six and a half workdays each week was taking its toll. Mark was exhausted, not so much physically, but mentally. In addition, although he wasn't aware of it yet, on the last day of this week his psyche would also receive a jolt.

The officer's basic course, commonly called Basic School, would normally run five days a week for between twenty to thirty weeks, depending on the needs of the Marine Corps. Due to the outbreak of the Korean War, the course had been shortened to twelve weeks. This shortening had been accomplished by cutting out a few subjects, trimming some others, increasing the work day to sixteen hours, and increasing the work week to six and a half days. Except for the eight hours a day allocated for sleep and four hours on Sunday for church services, the young lieutenants literally spent all their time working.

Basic school was the Marine Corps' answer to the "ninety day wonder" criticism leveled at officer training programs. Marine officers were commissioned through ROTC programs, PLC (Platoon Leaders Class) programs, OCS programs and from the service academies, but they still had to complete this next level of training, before being let loose on the Corps itself. The system created a better-trained junior officer than other systems.

The syllabus at basic school provided for weapons training and qualification, schooling and practice in platoon and company-sized tactics, communications training, working with tanks and explosives, amphibious warfare training, and other military subjects. The training was designed to provide practice and familiarity with these subjects on a personal level and how to use them from a command and leadership position.

The normal procedure for most subjects was to start with some form of classroom instruction, then go to the field to put the information and principles learned into action. The lieutenants took turns filling actual billets, both during these training exercises and during the routine administrative parts of the day. Each week, one of the lieutenants served as company commander while others assumed posts as platoon leaders, squad leaders, fire team leaders etc. The next week a new slate of leaders took over. The system provided for a great deal of hands on, leadership training.

Traditions had developed over time that augmented the normal leadership preparation. One of these traditions was soon to wrap Mark in its odious coils. It was known as the dreaded "Asshole of the Week" award, granted in each Company to the Officer who had screwed up the worst, while in a command billet during that week. In addition to the embarrassment of being singled out by your peers for your ineptitude, was the award itself. The "trophy" was a roll of toilet paper. The recipient had to keep it on his person for the whole next week, no matter what else he was involved in.

Mark's command billet during this week had been as a fire team leader. This is a corporal's job in real life. Mark had already been a platoon leader and a squad Leader during other weeks so, on the surface, Mark should have had no problems handling the duty. He only had three people to supervise. Supervising peers however was a completely different situation than supervising subordinates.

The company had been working on map reading interpretation and compass exercises most of the week. The culmination of the training was a night compass exercise. Each fire team was given an azimuth and the distance to a set point. The point was usually in the woods. At the point was a small container of some sort, more often than not, an old machine gun ammunition box. On the container was a number. The team had to record the number. In the container was a new azimuth and distance to a new point. The team then had to follow the new trail to the new point, record that number, pick up a new azimuth and distance, and march off again. Each fire team had five points to find and record.

The troops used a lensatic compass. It had a luminous floating compass pointer and was designed to be used day or night. It had a bezel that clicked, so that you could change settings in the dark without actually seeing the azimuth numbers.

Each lieutenant had measured his pace against a 100-yard marker so he knew how many paces he normally took to walk 100 yards.

Completing the exercise with all five-marker numbers correct was the ideal. Having four correct was acceptable. Anything less was considered failing. There were many fire teams moving through the woods, their trails crossing other teams, from time to time. Multiple teams used the same numbered containers.

From the time Mark's team shot their first azimuth and stepped off for their first marker, there had been a problem. They had agreed that they would take turns being the front or point man. They would switch as they reached each marker. In addition to the fact that this gave each man some practice counting off his paces and keeping the team on an accurate compass heading, it also had the practical benefit of keeping a fresh man in front as they waded through brush, limbs, brambles, streams, and mud.

Lieutenant Dombrowski had drawn the first leg. He immediately stepped off on a 275-degree heading and plunged into the woods. The problem was that he had read the instructions wrong. The heading was supposed to be 257 degrees. He had inverted two numbers. The others should have checked his reading, but they didn't. He had finished first in all the written tests on map reading and compass work. They accepted his leadership by dint of his supposed knowledge. The team plunged in after him unaware of the error.

The marker was supposed to be 250 yards along the azimuth. When they thought they had traveled 250 yards, they started to look for the box. Not finding it, they broadened their search. Dombrowski found a box about 30 yards further along.

"Those stupid shits can't keep a good pace." Dombrowski stated. "This box is at least 20 or 30 yards further than what they've written down."

"It sure looks that way," said Mark. Looking around. He thought they had paced it off correctly, too. Maybe going through that small swamp had changed their pace a little. He shrugged it off. "Let's get the numbers and move onto the next marker. Who's up?"

"I am," said Gibson, a voice in the dark. "What's the new azimuth and distance?"

Mark shined his penlight on it.

"45 degrees and 425 yards."

"Okay, let's go," said Gibson. They all strode off on a 45-degree reading.

To no one's surprise the next box was at exactly 425 yards and the azimuth and pacing were accurate. They copied the number and they took off again with Fiore in the lead. Mark took the next leg and then Dombrowski again. They finished their trek in about an hour and were at the registration desk about fifteen minutes after that. The desk was housed in a pyramidal tent. The instructor, a captain, compared their readings to the chart for their team under the glaring, hissing light of a Coleman lantern. When he finished his check, he looked up and informed them they had failed. In fact, they didn't get one number right.

Stunned would have been a mild word to describe the reaction of the team.

"Not one?"

"We found five boxes. We've got five numbers. How can they all be wrong? That's not possible is it? I mean to have all five wrong and yet to have found them where they were supposed to be?" asked Dombrowski. "That can't happen."

The captain held up the paper they had brought in and the correct chart. "Look for yourselves."

They huddled around the field desk. The captain was correct.

"Damn, that's just plain impossible. The chart has got to be wrong."

"It's not, lieutenant. Another platoon used it last week. No problems."

"We couldn't have been that far wrong," said Gibson

"Unless . . . ," Mark had been thinking, "we got the first one wrong and then found another marker and we went off on that track."

"That's got to be it," Gibson interrupted, the light dawning almost at the same time that Mark announced his theory. "Remember we didn't find the first marker where we thought it should be."

"Ski, what azimuth did you use?" asked Mark

Dombrowski fished around in his pocket and pulled out the starting paper they were given. "275 degrees. It's right here." Then he stopped and looked at it again. "It says 257 degrees."

Ski's face changed to a dull gray. He began to feel guilty. He looked up from the paper into Mark's eyes. "I don't think I used 257. I remember using 275. I screwed it up."

They walked back to their starting point and shot a 257-degree azimuth. The line was different than the one they had run. It was now obvious what had happened.

"Right. That's what the problem was," said Mark.

"I feel terrible. I screwed the whole thing up right from the get-go. We flunked because of me."

"No way, Jose," said Mark. "Yeah you got it wrong, but what kind of leaders are we? We didn't check did we? We screwed up, too."

The others nodded. Fiore put his hand reassuringly on Dombrowski's back.

"Thanks, guys but I still know I did it."

"We still got four right though, didn't we?" asked Gibson. "Let's go back and see that captain."

Their efforts were to no avail. The captain sympathized, but wrong was wrong. The team went back to the barracks, thoroughly demoralized.

The company stood at ease waiting to be released. It was now Friday afternoon. For the first time in months they would actually get a full weekend off. They didn't have to return until 0600 on Monday. The training was completed except for the "five day war" they would fight next week. The "war" was a field exercise that the company would conduct against "aggressors" that would be provided by the Marine Corps Schools demonstration troops. They would live in the field, draw up objectives and plans, call in support weapons, attack enemies and defend positions. It would put the cap on all the training. At the end of next week, they would receive their assignments. Ninety per cent of them would be heading for Korea.

The last piece of business to attend to before the fall out command was given, was the bestowing of the AHW award. The captain/Instructor for their company was reading the citation. Last weeks "winner" was standing next to him, fingering the bedraggled "trophy" and anxiously waiting to pass it on.

"For conspicuous ineptitude well below the standards of the Marine Corps and for performance well beneath the abilities of even the lowliest private, the Asshole of the Week award is hereby granted."

The captain looked up and then continued.

"The leader in line for the award stood head and shoulders below his peers as he led his four-man fire team to the ignominious score of zero during the night compass march. No other team accomplished this figure, so the award is truly one of a kind and in keeping with our lowest traditions. In addition, most recipients of the award are usually serving as company commanders or platoon commanders when they create the circumstances, which earns *them* the award. Up to now, no one in as low a position as a fire team leader has ever won the award."

The captain looked up from his paper.

"Would Lieutenant Mark Flaherty, from the Third Platoon, please come forward?"

Mark sat in the back seat of the 1946 Ford as the car sped along U.S. Route 301, heading south. Lieutenant Marlon Waterhouse, from Norfolk Virginia drove. His nickname was Spike. Lieutenant Val Dulay, from Saint Louis, sat in the front passenger seat. Spike and Val were engaged in a lively conversation. Mark sagged into the seat cushions lost in his own misery.

They were about halfway to Virginia Beach. They still had two hours of driving before they arrived at the beach house. Shortly, they would turn off Route 301 and head east. Route 301 would continue in a southerly direction, carrying the Northerners from the metropolitan areas of New York, Philadelphia and Washington toward the Carolinas, Georgia and ultimately Florida.

This part of U.S. 301 had two lanes heading in each direction divided by a grassy median. It was the best part of the road. When they turned off 301, their pace would slow while traveling on country roads.

"Hey Mark, that was a real downer, getting the AHW," Spike said, looking at Mark's eyes in the rear view mirror, "but don't let it screw up your weekend."

"Come on, buddy. It's only a symbolic thing. It doesn't change your standing or anything," said Dulay. "Besides Spike has us all fixed up with a couple of honeys for the weekend. We're coming here to forget our troubles for a few days."

Mark was struggling to determine why he felt so down. The award was an embarrassment. He had to walk in front of all his peers and receive their jeers and catcalls, but somehow it hurt more than that. He couldn't put his finger on it but there was something else.

He shook his head to clear it and then sat up a little straighter. "You're right, Val. I don't know why it bothers me so much. Maybe I'm just tired. Hey, Spike," he leaned forward a little so Spike could hear him a better. "Tell me again who this girl is that your girl friend picked out for me." He was making an effort to shake himself from his gloom.

Spike smiled. He looked again into the mirror, catching Mark's eyes.

"Her name is Madeline Precourt. Shirley calls her Maddy. She comes from Norfolk. Her father is in the Navy. Maddy says she's smart, but quiet. She says she's also cute. I don't know why she figured she'd fit with you, but woman have their own way of setting things up."

Mark ignored the gentle dig. "What does she do? Is she still in school or does she work?"

"She teaches with Shirley. They're all school teachers." He looked at Dulay. "Yours, too."

"And you said they got a house on the beach."

"Correction. They rented a house on the beach for a week. It's right on the water. From what Shirley says, you can fall out of bed, take three steps, and you're in the surf. The girls got there this afternoon. Shirley said she'd get the food. We have to stop and get the beer." He looked at Dulay. They had gone over this before. Dulay smiled. They liked Mark but sometimes he was too serious. Spike looked down at the odometer and then at his watch. "We should be there by 8:30 or 9:00."

It was a little after 7:00."

Mark hadn't been sure about whether to join in when this weekend was first broached. He wanted to get this whole school thing behind him so he could get on with just being a real Marine officer. As the time neared, he still had hesitated about this jaunt, but anything was better than hanging around the Base. He'd been doing that for three months.

As he thought about it more, his mood brightened. It might be fun. Even if the thing with the girl didn't work out, he could still swim and body surf. He was sure there would be good crab shacks and oyster bars in the area, too.

"You know what mine's like?" asked Dulay.

"Not really. Shirley calls her Sunny, like in Sunshine. I don't think that's her real name, but Shirley says she's a real upbeat person. She's supposed to be pretty, too."

"I'm glad Shirley didn't say she had a nice personality. That's a code word among women for ugly." Dulay replied, laughing.

"What's the sleeping arrangement?" Mark asked, bringing up a matter that was on both his and Val's minds.

"Hey guys. I don't know." Spike looked from one to the other with a smile. "That's going to be up to you. I think Shirley and I will probably share a bed, but . . . well what you do . . . ."

He looked at them again, shook his head and smiled. He didn't finish the sentence. "Shirley says there're beds and couches and a hammock. It'll work out. If I know my Shirley, she will have thought of everything. You know what I mean?"

They both nodded in the early evening light. Mark kept thinking in worse case terms. He could sleep on the floor if he had to. No problem.

Spike pulled the car into a small shopping plaza. There was a Piggly Wiggly store and a few other shops in one long building. Mark went into the package store to get the beer. Spike remembered something. Although Shirley planned get the food, he knew, she would never spend the money to get good steaks, So Val and Spike went into the grocery store to get the meat and chips. When they came out, Mark was emerging from the package store with a couple of cases of Pabst Blue Ribbon beer. He was muttering irritably.

"They actually asked for ID. I've been drinking beer since eighteen and they asked *me* for ID. I should have walked out."

"Hey, man. Drinking here is twenty-one. They check if you look close to twenty-one. Some of these counties don't have beer at all. They're dry counties. I know where the right places are though. That's why we stopped here."

"Still, I don't like to be checked. I *know* I look more than twenty-one."

Spike and Val shrugged. They all climbed into the car and took off. "Only fifteen minutes now," said Spike.

The house *was* right on the water. It was a square, one-story, weathered, gray shingled building, with a covered porch in the front. The "front" of oceanside properties was the part of the building that faced the water. The water was literally a few feet from the porch at high tide.

The "boys" pulled into the driveway, and parked behind an old Plymouth sedan. Mark couldn't place the year but it was definitely pre-war. The back screen door banged open and a tall, long-legged redhead emerged with a shriek. She ran over to the car and grabbed Spike in a bear hug as he stepped out of his vehicle. She wrapped herself around him and they spun around in a bout of silliness. It took a full thirty seconds, but at last she released him and stepped back. Mark had his first real look at her.

She was tall. Almost as tall as Spike and he was almost six feet. She had strawberry blonde hair and a white complexion. Her eyes, he thought, were green. She was wearing a flowered halter-top and white shorts. She had sandals on her feet. The halter was tight against her ample breasts. Her shorts were very short. They were not the Bermuda style shorts that he was most familiar with. She was quite a sexy lady, Mark decided.

Spike introduced them. She studied Mark and then Val and then nodded. Mark had the impression that she felt her decisions had been vindicated.

They carried the groceries and bags up the steps that led to the kitchen. Once inside, they dropped their burdens and walked to the living room. The other two "girls" were sitting on chairs. They both stood up when the Marines entered.

"Mark and Val, this is Maddy and Sunny." She took the shortest route in making introductions.

For a second Mark wasn't sure which was which. Then he remembered how Shirley had said it. She had gone from left to right. Maddy was the small dark haired girl. Sunny was the blonde, sort of pleasingly, plump one.

He walked over to Maddy, held his hand out and said with a smile, "Pleased to meet you."

She took his hand. Her hand was small and soft. "Very nice to meet you, Mr . . . . Flaherty. I hope I pronounced it right," she replied with a confident smile.

"Uh, yes . . . perfect, but my name is Mark. Your name is Madeline. I understand they call you Maddy, though."

"That's fine. Everyone calls me Maddy."

He turned to Sunny and shook her hand, too. Sunny kept looking at Val. She nodded to Mark once and then turned her eyes back to her date. Maddy had turned and walked to a sofa. She sat down. She seemed to be bidding him to follow her, so he did.

She really was quite pretty. She had dark, wavy shoulder length hair, blue eyes and very red lips. The eyes were her best feature. They were small and sensitive but also open and inviting. She was small, maybe five feet one or two, and slight. Her skin was white, like fine china. She sat on the sofa in a ladylike way with feet together and hands in lap.

She wore a white, sleeveless blouse that buttoned in front. The buttons went up to her neck. The blouse was tucked into a pair of red Bermuda shorts with a gold belt. She wore white tennis shoes and no socks.

Sunny was just that — sunny. She bubbled and bounced and giggled. She wore cut off jeans and a faded, sleeveless sweatshirt. Her feet were bare. The immediate impression was that she was a soft, cuddly tomboy. She intrigued Val.

Spike took command as soon as the introductions were done. "Flaherty, get the fire going. The grill is on the porch. Dulay get some beers out for everyone and get the rest iced down. Shirley, you and I get to do the salads. Maddy, you and Sunny get the table set up."

They all looked at him in feigned shock. Sunny gave him a mock salute. Then they went to do his bidding. Shirley called him Hitler.

Mark found the grill and the charcoal. Someone had left small pieces of wood and newspaper in a bin. He arranged the paper and the wood so it would ignite quickly then he piled the jagged black chunks of charcoal on top. A match from the kitchen got the process started. Boy Scout training pays off, thought Mark. He smiled to himself.

He stood back from the grill and looked out toward the water. It was somewhere between low and high tides. He wasn't sure whether it was coming in or going out. The night was balmy.

There was a movement on his left. The screen door swung open and Maddy emerged with two beers. She walked over to him and held one of the cans out. Mark could hear Shirley and Sunny laughing inside the cottage.

"Thank you. I need this." He put the can to his lips and took a long draught. Whoever had opened the can had done it properly. There were two triangular holes in the lid. One to drink from and one for air to circulate.

Maddy looked up at him and said simply, "You're welcome."

"You opened the can the right way. Lots of women don't know how to do that." He said, a little awkwardly. He chided himself for not saying something more interesting.

But Maddy laughed. "My father is a beer drinker. I've been opening his beers for a long time."

Mark smiled. She had her way of putting him at ease. "Your father is in the Navy, I hear?"

"Yes. He's a lieutenant, supply officer. He's at the naval base in Norfolk."

Mark wondered about the rank. Someone old enough to have a twenty-one or twenty-two-year-old daughter should be higher than a lieutenant. Perhaps he was a former enlisted man.

"Care to walk along the beach?" she asked sweetly. "You have to wait a while for the coals to heat up don't you?"

"Sure, let's go. The fire needs at least thirty or forty minutes"

Mark took off his boat shoes and rolled his pants up to his knee. Maddy took off her tennis shoes. They stepped off the porch onto the sand. It was still warm from the sun in some places but cool in others. The surf was gentle, mostly small rollers. It was warm.

They strolled at the edge of the water, letting the waves curl over their feet and then recede. The moon moved in and out of the few clouds flowing by, alternately lighting and darkening the sand. Conversation was difficult at first, but as they talked more about their own lives and backgrounds they became more and more at ease with each other. Other walkers passed them, going in both directions. They started to feel comfortable.

Almost an hour had passed before they went back. Spike and Val were already putting the steaks on the fire when they climbed the porch steps.

"Where the hell were you two?" asked Spike in mock anger. "The fire's been ready for ten minutes and you people are out lollygagging around." Then he laughed. Shirley gave him a push. Everyone laughed.

The dinner was fun. Steak and paper plates don't go well together, however. They ended up eating the steaks by holding them in their hands and biting into the meat, caveman style. The salads were good. The beer flowed. Jokes flew. The bathroom was visited frequently. Time passed pleasantly. When the meal was finished and cleaned up, Mark and Maddy took another walk on the beach. They weren't sure what the others did.

When they came back to the cottage, the place was dark. Mark looked at his watch. It was two a.m.

"Wow I didn't think it was that late."

"Neither did I. But it was fun, Mark. I enjoyed it."

Mark liked it when she used his name. "So did I Maddy. I really enjoyed it. I … like talking to you . . . getting to know you."

She looked up into his eyes. The moonlight, reflecting off her white complexion, turned her face into a haunting picture of beauty. Mark knew he would always have that picture in his mind when he thought of her.

He wasn't sure what to do next. Maddy solved the problem. She reached up to pull his head lower and she kissed him on the cheek.

"Thank you, for a wonderful evening. We should have a good time tomorrow, too."

With that she walked into the cottage and disappeared into one of the two bedrooms in the back. Mark stood looking after her for a moment. Then he went into the cottage. The other bedroom door was closed, presumably Shirley and Spike's room. There was no sign of Val or Sunny. Mark lay down on the sofa and reviewed the evening. It had been very pleasant. After awhile, he drifted off to sleep.

Dawn came with a cacophony of cries and squawks from the gulls as they tussled with each other over choice tidbits that had been washed up on the beach during the night. Amidst the fluttering, diving, and swooping of the gulls, sanderlings and other small water birds, raced in and out on spindly legs, thereby avoiding the wave surges, and picked still other morsels from the wet sand.

Mark opened his eyes. The room was flooded with the early morning sun. He looked around. Val was asleep on the other soda. The house was quiet. He rose, visited the bathroom, put his swim trunks on, and noiselessly went out onto the beach.

The early sun felt good. He did some jumping jacks to warm his muscles up and then went down to the water. On first impact, it was cold. But he adjusted quickly. He swam out about twenty-five yards and then turned so that he was swimming parallel to the beach. He swam for 10 minutes, heading to the south and then turned around and swam back. When he came out of the water, Maddy was sitting on the sand where he had left his towel.

"Good morning. You're up early." She stated, looking just as pretty as she had last night.

"Well, so are you, miss early bird," he bantered back, smiling.

She was wearing a dark blue one-piece bathing suit that clung to her slim body. It had lacy white trim on the bodice and at the leg openings. Two small spaghetti straps went over her shoulders to hold the suit up. She was small breasted, but they were in perfect harmony with the rest of her petite body. Mark also noticed that she had perfectly shaped legs.

She stood up as he approached her. "I wish I had come out a little earlier. We could have swum together."

"I didn't want to wake anyone. Besides, if you'd like, I'll go back in with you."

"You're not tired, after your laps?"

She had been watching, thought Mark. "Not really, besides I enjoy the water and I enjoy you." Mark wondered where he had gotten the nerve to say something like that.

Maddy's eyes lit up. "You really are sweet. Shall we go?"

"Yes, ma'am. I'm ready."

Maddy reached down and picked up a white bathing cap. It took her a moment to tuck all her hair under the cap. They walked into the water together.

Maddy was a strong swimmer. Mark had the feeling she could outlast him if long distance swimming was involved. They swam for twenty minutes and then sat on the sand to dry off. When she took the cap off, her hair fell almost perfectly into place.

Maddy touched the side of his trunks. "We're color coordinated."

Mark looked down. He was wearing dark blue boxer style trunks with a thin white stripe. She was correct. Their swimwear matched perfectly.

When they went up to the cottage, the others were up and making breakfast. Spike was the bacon-and-egg chef. Shirley made pancakes. After breakfast, they all spent the morning on the beach. Shirley had a suitcase size "portable" radio that she brought with her. They listened to a country and western station most of the time. The sun was strong and after a while they all began to get red. So they spent the afternoon in the cottage and on the porch. There was beer, and laughter, and word games. There was also some napping and quiet.

At sundown, they went to an all-you-can-eat-for-five-bucks crab shack and drank beer, ate oysters and cracked crabs. Later they went to the amusement park at Virginia Beach. They rode the rides. Matt and Maddy rode the roller coaster ten times. They also threw baseballs, tossed hoops, bet on races, broke balloons — all the things you can waste money on at an amusement park.

When they arrived back at the cottage, it was past midnight. No one was ready for sleep yet. They went for walks on the beach, each couple taking a different direction. Shirley and Spike went north, Matt and Maddy went south. Val and Sunny went into the dunes.

Matt wasn't sure if the day's activity had made them too tired to talk or if there was some other cause, but they had been walking for about five minutes and neither had said a word. They were holding hands, so he didn't think he had done anything wrong. He finally asked.

"A penny for your thoughts?" Not original, but to the point.

She smiled gently. "I was just thinking about how wonderful this whole day was, and last night, too."

"It really has been great, hasn't it? We still have all day tomorrow, too." He moved closer to her and put his arm around her. She put her arm around his waist.

"When do you have to leave?" She looked up into his face, searching his eyes. He loved it when she looked at him like that.

"Well we have to be back by 0600 . . . uh, 6 a.m. It takes about four hours to drive. I guess we can stay until midnight or a little after."

"Won't you get any sleep?"

"Aw, we don't worry about that. We find ways."

They walked for a few minutes longer, silently, then Maddy asked. "You'll be going to Korea, won't you?"

"I don't know for sure, but ninety per cent of us are going to Korea, so the chances are pretty good I'll go. I'll find out next week."

Maddy looked sad. They walked a little further. Then Maddy stopped and disengaged herself from his arm. She faced him and took both his hands into hers. She looked up at him. Tears glistened in her eyes. "Mark, I've really started to like you. You are a wonderful guy. I don't want anything to happen to you."

Mark was embarrassed. "Maddy . . . I . . . like you a lot too. This weekend has meant so much to me. I've never met anyone like you."

She curled herself into his arms and held him. He wrapped his big arms around her and hugged her. She was crying. When she turned her face up to him, he started to kiss her tears. Then he kissed her lips. She curled her arms up until they were around his neck. They clung to each other for a long time, locked in a bittersweet kiss.

Eventually they parted. Arm in arm, they retraced their path to the cottage. When they arrived, the others were not in sight. They sat on the porch swing and just held each other. The only sound was the rumble of the surf and an occasional sob from Maddy. They sat that way all night, sometimes dozing, sometimes kissing, and sometimes rocking. They felt connected to each other. Matt supposed that if he had tried, Maddy would have been receptive to a sexual advance, but it didn't seem right to him, so he didn't venture down that road. He wanted her very much, but the time wasn't right.

Maddy wasn't sure if it was the lightening sky or the boisterous cries of the gulls that awoke her, but shortly after sunrise she became aware of her surroundings again. They were still on the porch swing. She was curled up and tucked alongside Mark's body. His large arms completely encircled her. His grip was relaxed. He was still asleep.

She turned her head and looked at him. She was glad he didn't awaken as she turned. She wanted to look at him without him knowing it.

He did not have movie actor looks, but he was handsome in a big, sturdy way. He really was a big man, not so much tall, but overall big. He seemed very steady and confident. It was a quiet confidence, not a boastful kind of bravado. He had told her about his family. It seemed a lot like her family. He had been brought up right by good parents the same as she had. He was an officer, the same as her father, but he had gone to the academy. Her father had come up through the ranks. He had three brothers, two of whom were also Marines. He didn't seem to want to talk about the other brother. If she remembered right, he was the oldest brother. He had told her about Maggie. Maddy felt badly for Maggie.

She continued to examine his face. His mouth was slightly open and he snored faintly. She wondered about this attraction she was feeling for him. She had always thought that she would end up with someone who looked like Tyrone Power or Alan Ladd. Mark certainly didn't fit that mold. But there was something . . . . The words she had used in her mind abruptly impacted on her. "She would end up with someone . . . ." She was thinking about him as "someone to end up with."

She thought more about that idea. Why not "end up" with some-one like him? Everything seemed right with him. But then, she had another thought. They had only known each other one day. How could she be thinking this way about someone she had just met? And what about this Korea thing? He might not come back. Still the other men and boys she had known, did not create the emotions in her this man did. He seemed perfect.

He stirred a little, shifting his position. She pulled back so he could move better. He opened his eyes, stared at her for a second, and then smiled. "I was dreaming I had lost you. I'm so relieved to find out it was just a dream."

With that statement she was convinced. This was the man she wanted. She burst into tears.

"Hey . . . hey . . . ? What's wrong? It was just a dream."

"You wouldn't understand," she said between sobs.

Later they went for a swim. This time, they did more holding and cuddling than swimming.

Spike and Shirley served another big breakfast and as on the day before, they spent the morning on the beach. Mark and Maddy stayed within "touching" range of each other all day. Spike and Val had decided they wanted to leave by about nine o'clock that evening. They wanted to return to Quantico in time to get some of their gear ready for the "war" and also to catch a few hours sleep. Mark had to go along.

Before he left, Mark told Maddy he would call her when he found out where he was going. They also agreed to meet next weekend if he could get away. It might be the last time before he shipped out.

Leaving Maddy that night was the single hardest thing he had ever done in his young life.

12

The Fire Brigade

Battlefields are messy. It's not simply the physical litter, the destroyed vehicles, blasted trees, charred earth and downed buildings, but often the maps and unit placements were equally disorganized. Straight lines, behind which enemies usually massed before they faced off, sometimes did not exist.

For instance, while the First Platoon of George Company was having its baptism of fire on Hill 342, the rest of the regiment had not been idle. All along the line of departure — the point from which the push would be launched against the NKPA – other units were readying themselves to attack. Generally speaking the line of attack would be to the west. Before the assault could be launched however some pesky details had to be taken care of. For one, intermittent mortar and rifle fire coming from a hill that was actually behind them, an untenable position. It was harassing the regimental command post. "H," Company had to be dispatched to silence the enemy units. The mission was finally accomplished, but it took the better part of a day.

The Marines then had to hold certain positions to protect their flanks as they went into their advance. The enemy wanted to hold those places too. And, as if that wasn't annoying enough, the Marines kept running into groups of enemy troops who seemed to be trying to get to the same ground they were trying to get to.

The Army units to the north were running into similar problems. As a result, the first two days of fighting throughout the whole theatre, were actually battles fought in and around the edges of the unit's line of departure. These battles were being fought just to clear the way so the assault troops could move forward and attack. Small units, such as platoons, and in some cases whole companies, were attacking right, left, and sometimes to the rear simultaneously. The Eleventh Marines, an artillery regiment, had batteries firing north, south, and west at the same time. In addition, armed combat patrols would clear a valley and move on, only to find Communist units filtering back into the area when they left. It took a while before General Craig's staff could figure out what was happening. Finally the answer dawned on them.

They were attacking the attacker. Both sides were attacking at the same time. Usually when one side attacked the other, one unit was in a defensive position. Normal fear and confusion aside, in those situations, the battle becomes much easier to prosecute. Assaulting attackers was unusual and created disorientation. It was like watching a football game where both teams had a ball and both were trying to score.

Once the planners understood what was happening they launched a number of efforts to clear the attackers from the departure area. Within two days, the Marines cleared the starting points, and then the brigade began to move toward its objective, the town of Sachon, fifty miles away.

Since they had advanced into South Korea the NKPA had not encountered any real resistance to their efforts. They had been able to brush aside or roll over any opposition they had met. Now, in these battles, in and around the southwestern part of the Pusan perimeter, they were denied any forward progress. They had been stopped for the first time.

Along the way to Sachon, the brigade's first objective was the town of Kosong. They set out on August 10, lead by a reconnaissance platoon and three tanks, George and How Companies following immediately behind. The North Koreans contested the movement sporadically but the Marines were able to brush them off with little difficulty. Lieutenant Gruene was wounded in one battle, a shoulder wound. He refused to be evacuated, calling the injury a "Hollywood" wound.

As they moved toward Kosong, the two companies developed a high level of teamwork and momentum. One would attack and then hold. The other would pass through them and continue the attack. A little further along the first company would pass the second as *they* rested, and then still later, they would repeat the maneuver. This "leap frogging" kept constant pressure on the enemy, while providing opportunities for rest and re-supply for the Marines.

When How Company reached the outskirts of Kosong they called for artillery. After a fifteen-minute barrage, the company pushed into the town, tossing aside sporadic resistance as they did. They noted movement to the west, but couldn't immediately determine what the activity meant, so they pushed on with their mission, which was to secure the town.

George Company followed down the same road behind How

Company. Just before Kosong they swung to the south, blasted through the northern suburbs and prepared to attack a hill where spotters had noted some enemy troops. Before they actually launched their infantry attack, they called in artillery and air strikes. In a marvelous display of combined arms, the air and artillery, for all intents and purposes, blew the top off the hill. When George Company reached the crest, they found a moonscape of devastation and dead bodies. There had been over 100 defenders on the mound. There were no survivors.

The battalion paused for a moment to regroup before continuing. Matt, Jacques, and Ivan were leading their troops down from the slope when they spotted a dust cloud moving away down the road toward Sachon. The cloud was extensive, indicating a large number of motorized vehicles in transit. Apparently, the fighting on the hill had flushed them out. The enemy was running! This was good. But, they were mechanized. The Marines weren't. The enemy would escape. That was not good.

Then, Matt and his people heard a drone of engines behind them. The noise grew in volume. They turned toward the sound and they saw a flight of planes approaching. The drone increased. Along with the rest of the Marines, they stopped to watch. It was a very large flight, at least 25 or 30 planes flying in echelons. The gull like wings identified them immediately. They were Marine Corsairs, the workhorse of Marine aviation in World War II. The cavalry had arrived.

The planes began to peel off and move into attack formation. Their flight path would bring them right over the ground pounders. They had noticed the dust cloud and like wolves spotting their prey they were positioning themselves to swoop in on it.

The roar was deafening as the "Bent Wing Widow Makers" screamed overhead, just a few feet off the ground. They swept down on the motor vehicle column strafing as they went. They flew the entire length of the line of vehicles, twenty-five planes, one after another, pouring fire into the hapless convoy. Vehicles crashed into vehicles. Some ran off the road or exploded. Others just stopped. The lead vehicles and the end vehicles had been destroyed in place. The convoy could not proceed forward or backward. They were sitting ducks. Troops fled on foot. Many didn't make it.

"Son of a bitch," said Matt, without realizing he had spoken.

"Sacre Bleu, that's an inferno," exclaimed Jacques.

Ivan just stared, his eyes wider than normal.

The Corsairs turned and re-formed and made a second pass, now using rockets and cannon fire. When they finished with this run, they made another strafing run concentrating on individual targets. At last, having exhausted most of their ammunition, they left to return to their carrier. Moments later, another flight of Corsairs showed up, the flight of planes that had peppered the hill that George Company had attacked earlier. They still had ordnance left so they dumped it on the convoy. When they left, a flight of Air Force F-51 Mustangs arrived to finish the slaughter.

The battalion was at the scene of the devastation an hour later. It was a junkyard filled with burning, smoking vehicles. They counted forty destroyed trucks and jeeps and a large number of motorcycles, the last remnants of The NKPA's 83d Motorcycle Regiment. They also counted over 100 dead. The few wounded were dazed and disoriented. They confiscated a number of Soviet-made vehicles that were still in working order. Among them were jeeps with Ford engines, left over from the World War II lend lease programs that supplied aid to the Russians. Matt, Ivan, Jacques, and a few of the other Marines, had a field day riding around on a few of the still intact motorcycles, before the order came to move on and leave everything behind. They did so, reluctantly.

The brigade was now in high gear. They reorganized and set off again. The terrain was favorable for tanks, so they placed them in front to clear the way. Overhead a flight of Corsairs floated, waiting to be called. The enemy seemed to be demoralized. This was the time to consolidate the gains.

General Craig called a halt, however. They were a day's march from Sachon. He ordered them to dig in and get some rest. He also wanted to be sure they had not moved faster than the 5th RCT, which should have been a few miles away on their right. He didn't want any gaps. The night passed quietly. The next day, he determined the Army regiment was in the correct place. Satisfied, Craig ordered his Marines to attack Sachon.

However, the "word" was changed. In the world of the Marines the "word" was always changing. Long live the "word," often was the sarcastic cry of the frustrated sea soldier.

The next day, word came through to the Marines, to send a reinforced battalion back to Chindong-ni, to be used to protect the MSR (Main Supply Route) and to counterattack and take back a few artillery pieces the enemy had captured. Begrudgingly, the order was accepted and the 3rd battalion was selected. They left at midmorning. The rest of the brigade jumped off without them to attack Sachon.

True to form, confusion was the byword. When the 3rd Battalion arrived at the designated point, their guides, who were to show the battalion where to go, didn't show up. The battalion commander took it upon himself and sent his two companies out to take the high ground overlooking the MSR. When the Army general arrived, he was pleased with the initiative of the Marines. The next day they moved closer to the captured artillery pieces, fighting a few skirmishes along the way. But at the last minute, the "word" was changed again. A battalion from the 5th RCT would relieve the Marines and the 3rd battalion would go into Division Reserve.

Their compatriots back at Sachon experienced a similar happenstance. While they were involved in a battle just outside the town, they also received the "word" to pull back. The Sachon offensive was put on hold.

Disengaging from an enemy, while actually fighting a battle is a dangerous undertaking, sometimes more risky than the actual attack. The Marines lost people during that disengagement that probably would not have been lost if they had continued their assault. They did disengage, however, and by the end of the day they were also moving back to division reserve. The day was August 15.

13

The Corner is Turned

John stood in front of the mirror in the barracks head, gingerly touching different parts of his body. He was clad in white under shorts and shower shoes. Every once in a while he would wince.

Luke was leaning against the sink next to him shaking his head. A low murmur of voices came from the squad bay as the platoon prepared for the morning inspection.

"You've got to be the thickest mick in the Corps. When are you going to learn you can't sass DIs and get away with it? This *is* the Marine Corps, you know. The sergeants run this place."

"Tillis is an asshole," was the reply, as John found another spot that hurt. This one was near his belly button.

"I don't care if he's the biggest asshole in the world. He's still a DI. You can't talk back to him."

"He's an asshole. He's also a coward."

Luke threw up his hands. "He's not a coward. He got the other DIs to help him because he can't risk losing a fight. How would it look if a boot beat *him* up?"

John looked at him with a crooked smile. "He'd look worse than I do. I wouldn't only beat him in the body." He leaned forward to look at another spot, this time on his side. "Besides, you're right. I would have beat him."

"Where would the Corps be if the DIs had to fight everyone? They have to do it like they did." He looked closer at John's bruises. "Besides, I'm sure they beat you only on the body so they wouldn't leave any obvious marks."

John continued to probe his torso. Then he looked up. The only mark on his face was a cut lip. That must have happened when he tried to charge one of the other DIs. They had butted heads.

The three DIs had systematically pummeled him for about ten

minutes. They seemed to know what they were doing. The blows were designed to inflict great pain, but with minimal damage.

"You know they could have run you up for a court martial," Luke said after a period of silence.

"For calling him a shithead? I doubt it."

"John, that's disrespect. That's a court martial offense. If you add it to the other things you've said, they've got a pattern of disrespect. That's even worse. They handled it like men, not by running to one of the officers and making a complaint. It's no different than the way McQuinn handled you."

John was still angry. "Tillis is an asshole. McQuinn was a man. I'll take McQuinn any time."

Luke sighed. John was incorrigible. "John, we've only got a couple of weeks left and then we're out of here. You've just got to hang in that long."

John knew Luke was right. It was just that he did not suffer fools easily. The anger subsided. He looked at Luke and smiled. "I hear you, Luke. I guess my temper gets the best of me at times. And I hate it when I have to kowtow to someone who isn't good enough to wipe my ass, or your ass either for that matter."

Luke smiled. "That's the real problem isn't it? It's pride."

If anyone else had said that, John would have hit him. He took that from Luke. Despite their spats when they were younger, they were now inseparable. Luke was special. John smiled at him. "Luke, you're still too much of a lover. You need to become more of a fighter." He ran some water from the tap and dabbed it on his lip. Then another thought occurred to him. He shut off the water and turned to face his brother. "You're handling boot camp okay though, aren't you?"

"Yeah, I guess I am. The bullshit just rolls off my back. The military subject courses are easy. The physical side is okay. I have problems with parts of the "O" course. Weak upper arm strength, I suppose. But I can run all day. All that cross-country running back in school I guess, and . . . ."

John turned away from the mirror and grinned at Luke's verbosity. You give Luke an opening and he knew how to use it. "I wonder why we got such a loser for a DI? The other DIs don't seem to be losers," John interrupted.

Luke didn't object to being interrupted. He said, "I don't know. Remember Volkner, the guy we came down on the train with? He told me he hates his DI, too."

"Yeah well, everybody 'hates' their DI, but the other guys, all respect them."

"Volkner says, that no one in his platoon respects him either."

John chewed on that for a minute. "Maybe all the good ones are in Korea. That makes some sense. They need good people to fight the war."

"Maybe. In any event, are you going to control yourself until we get out of here?"

He looked at Luke with fondness. "Yeah, Lukie." He punched him in the arm. "You can stop being the mother hen. I'll watch myself."

The next morning, Gunnery Sergeant Tillis rousted the platoon a half hour early so they could run the obstacle course. They had a big inspection later in the morning, so falling out to run the obstacle course a few hours before was quite unusual. John knew it was done just for him. In John's mind, Tillis reasoned that John would hurt terribly this morning and that the obstacle course would be a nightmare for him. He also figured that Tillis wanted to get the platoon mad at him. Tillis wanted them to know who was responsible for this extra punishment.

John looked at Tillis with a mixture of hate and determination as the platoon trotted by him on the way to the course. He then proceeded to run the course in the best time anyone in the platoon had run it that year. In fact, the time approached a course record.

When he jumped down from the rope at the end and turned to go back to the assembly, area he passed Tillis. His eyes bored right through Tillis' eyes. His body hurt so much he almost buckled, but he was able to smile and his face was filled with smug satisfaction. Tillis turned away. The DI knew that somehow he was beaten. John Flaherty had taken all he could give him and asked for more.

Two weeks later they graduated and left Parris Island. Three weeks after that, they finished infantry training at Camp Lejeune in North Carolina. They had five days leave before heading to their first duty station. The duty station was actually a troop train in New York City that would take them to San Diego for further transport to Korea. They were going into a replacement draft for the Fifth Marines.

When the brothers arrived back in Kingmont, the family welcomed them with joy. Mark had arrived a few days earlier. He was only going to stay a day or two. He had told the family he had a friend in Virginia whom he wanted to spend some time with before he left for Korea. He was also going to the Fifth Marines.

Katie quickly arranged a big party. She invited all their old school mates. She and Helene and Maggie spent a whole day preparing food and drink. The three Marines sat around and rested and exchanged "war" stories. Luke commented to John that although Mark was their brother, he was still an officer and he felt a little odd being informal with him. John told him he was brainwashed.

While together, they determined that none of them had the time to do anything about searching for Matt. They also figured that with the war and all, their task would be even more difficult. When the picture had been taken of Matt and his friends, Matt was in the Fifth Marines. The chances were that he was still in the regiment and before long they would all be in the Fifth. They just might bump into him.

The party was held the second night they were home. It was a great fun. It was a joy to renew old acquaintances. The food and booze flowed freely. Songs were sung, jokes were told and old memories were rehashed. When the party was over, they all slept wherever they had been sitting or laying when the urge to sleep came over them.

The next day Katie shooed all but Maggie and her boys away and then spent the day just reveling in their presence. They talked about Matt and what he had done. Mark and John were both of the opinion that Matt should have stayed and faced the charges. Luke wasn't so sure. Katie said that what Matt did was right. They would understand some day.

Maggie had grown a lot. She was almost a young lady now. She was also pretty. It broke their hearts to know that she was "not right." She had shown a lot of progress in her schooling. She could read a little now, but she was still very childlike. They all loved her dearly.

They talked about Mark's new girlfriend. He was a little shy about it. Katie wanted to know why he hadn't brought her to Kingmont. He told her he had just met her and that didn't seem appropriate yet. She chided him by saying he couldn't bring her home, but he could use some of his precious leave time to go and see her. A mother's logic, how could a son answer that? Mark just looked at her with a sheepish grin. She finally laughed and assured him she understood.

The day passed too quickly for Katie. When Mark left for Virginia that night, she cried. She had held up well until then, but she couldn't hold her feelings in forever. She sat down in a chair in the living room and sobbed. Luke was the one who went to her first. He put his arms around her and hugged her. She cried for a long time. Maggie went to her and sat in her lap with her arms around her. John didn't know what to do. He finally sat at Katie's feet, just to be near her and to touch her.

After a while she began to talk. Just little phrases at first, then longer ones.

"I worry so. The war … what kind of a war is it? People die in wars. What if you all get killed? I've got four sons. Surely they won't send you all to the same place."

Luke looked at John. They were all in the Fifth Marines. They all *could* end up in the same place.

"Mom?" It was John.

"Yes," Katie answered between sobs.

"Remember the story about the Sullivan brothers. They all went down with the same ship in the war?"

Katie looked at Luke, not sure why he was telling her this. "Yes, there were five of them. That's what I'm afraid of."

"Mom, they passed a rule or something after that, remember? Brothers couldn't be sent into combat together."

Katie looked at John. There was flicker of hope in hers eyes. "Yes, I do remember. Was that a law?"

Luke spoke up. "No, Mom, I don't think it's a law, but it was an order from the president. They won't disobey that." He looked at John.

John looked at Luke, happy for the support. "When we get to Korea, they'll put us all in different units. They don't want that to happen again. Besides, I don't think this war will last too long. These gooks just surprised us. As soon as we get all our sh . . . uh, stuff together, we'll drive them out. Maybe a month or two, that's all."

Luke wondered where John was getting all this "wisdom," but he nodded quickly to let his mother know he agreed.

Katie looked from one to the other. What they said made sense. She wasn't totally convinced but she did feel better. She had seen only gloom to this point. Now she saw hope.

The rest of the evening was happier. Katie brought out scrapbooks with old pictures of the family and they had a quiet time reminiscing and laughing about the old days.

Katie didn't seem to know that they all were in the Fifth Marines. Or if she knew, perhaps she didn't realize the Fifth Marine Regiment was a relatively small unit, only around five thousand. So the chances of them all seeing action together was high. Luke and John didn't have the heart to explain this to her. It also didn't occur to any of them, that as far as the Marine Corps was concerned, the Corps didn't have four Flaherty brothers on their records. They had one Farrell, one Flaherty and two Flaratys. The Sullivan rule wouldn't apply.

The next day John and Luke drove around town looking for old buddies that hadn't been at the party. They found a few.

A day later, Luke told his mother he wanted to leave a day early so he could visit his old friends in New York City. She didn't understand. She thought he had no friends in the city any more and that was one of the reasons he joined the Marine Corps. He said, lamely that he had a few things to take care of. Katie cried when *he* left also.

John stayed until the last minute. He and Luke had agreed to meet at Brooklyn Navy Yard, which was the reporting place for the train to California. On his last day home John drove around town by himself. When he had driven around with Luke the day before, he had experienced strange feelings about Kingmont. He wanted to go back and explore those feelings.

As he drove from place to place, the old feelings came back, but he decided they didn't mean anything. His old haunts no longer held anything for him. The fairground, the race track, the picnic area he used to frequent — nothing. They also appeared smaller than he remembered. It was August. He had left in May. Even though it had only been three or four months, everything was different. His old friends who had come to the party were also different. He enjoyed seeing them but it was as if they belonged to a different time. They seemed younger, still adolescent. The things they were interested in no longer held any attraction for John.

He drove out Grand Street, not really sure why he did, other than it was one of the places he used to frequent for his drag races. When he reached the end of the street he looked to his right and saw the park with the picnic tables and stone benches. He got out of the car and walked into the park. He was exploring his feelings about what had happened there in the past. It was as if he was drawn to the spot against his will. As if preordained, sitting on one of the benches was a middle-aged man. He was wearing a bright print, short-sleeved shirt, which he wore outside of his dark trousers. He was smoking a cigarette.

"Hello, John. Good to see you again." It was Lieutenant McQuinn.

"Hello, lieutenant." He hesitated a moment and then stuck out his hand. "It's good to see you again, too."

The lieutenant stood up and took John's hand. He looked a little older to John but he still looked good. John noticed he wore his service revolver on his hip, under his shirt. Apparently, hiding the piece was the reason for wearing the shirt untucked.

"I heard you were home. Mark and Luke, too I understand. It's too bad Matt can't come home also, to complete the family so to speak." It still rankled McQuinn that Matt hadn't come to him when the troubles had occurred.

"I guess he feels he can't, lieutenant. You can understand that."

"I suppose," he said with out much conviction. "How's the Marine Corps treating you, John?"

"Okay, I guess. Boot camp wasn't as hard as I figured. I was a little disappointed. They got some asshole DIs. That kind of surprised me. Sometimes they treat you like an idiot —" He stopped. Why was he spewing this out to McQuinn? He didn't even talk like this with Luke.

McQuinn smiled. He sat back down on the bench. "Take a load off, John. Have a seat"

John sat facing the policeman. The day was warm, typical for August. The sun was bright, but the trees provided shade for the two men as they talked.

"You been driving around looking at your old haunts?"

"Yeah, I have." McQuinn seemed to know everything.

"Things look different to you?"

"Yeah, they do." How does he know that?

"Happens to a lot of people when they leave home and come back later."

"I wouldn't have thought it would happen so fast. I've only been gone a few months."

"It can happen in a short period of time. It's happened to me one time when I left and came back. Besides, you just went through a big event in your life. That changes a lot of things, especially you."

"Yeah. You're right. I hadn't realized that."

"You're going to Korea, aren't you?"

"Yeah. I leave tomorrow."

"Knowing that's out there can change you too."

"I hadn't really thought about it."

"It's all got to do with maturity, growing up and all that."

John had never understood what adults meant when they talked about having maturity. He always felt maturity was all about having a hairy chest, shaving, or a deep voice and muscles and all that. Understanding was beginning to dawn. They were really talking something else — about awareness, understanding, responsibility, and control of emotions. The light was dawning. "Yeah. Yeah. I see that." He felt like he was being reinvented.

They sat for a few minutes longer, not talking. John absorbed all these feelings and all this information. Then he stood up.

McQuinn also stood. John held out his hand. "I need to go now. I need to spend some time with my mother. The things you just said ... about maturity and all that. I never understood that before. You've really given me a lot to think about. I want to . . . thank you . . . and also thank you for what . . . you did in the past."

John couldn't believe he was saying that.

McQuinn took his hand. His eyes glistened a little. "You had it in you to respond properly. All I did was help to bring it out. But thanks for the thanks. It's always good to hear that you did the right thing."

"Right now, I can appreciate that. Good-bye, lieutenant. I'll see you down the road. Thanks again for everything." John walked to his car and drove off.

McQuinn watched a minute and then felt an overpowering urge to blow his nose and wipe his eyes.

Luke walked slowly past the outdoor restaurant where he and John had made the decision to join the Corps. It still had tables with green and white "Cinzano" umbrellas. The traffic was noisy and fast paced. Luke didn't remember it that way when he had lived nearby.

The day was warm. The ride down from Kingmont to Grand Central Station was uneventful. The subway to Greenwich Village had been a hot ride, however. He felt his clothes sticking to him. He was glad he had found a locker to check his sea bag so he didn't have to carry it all over town.

He passed The Village Barn and the little coffee shop where he had worked as a waiter. The Barn looked the same. The placards outside promoted new country western acts, but other than that he saw no change. At first, he didn't feel that the coffeehouse had changed either, but then he looked a little closer. The place seemed grubbier than he remembered. The people also looked unkempt. Was that how he had looked?

Earlier, he had stopped by the school where Taylor had been a student and employee. Apparently she no longer attended. The woman he spoke to, did not recall her name, but she had only been there a few months herself. He asked about Margot. The lady knew her. She had moved to Los Angeles. She gave him Margot's address. He stuck it into his pocket, thanked her and left.

As he neared the basement apartment, he felt himself becoming a bit apprehensive. He really didn't know why he had come back to the city or what he would say if he saw Taylor, but some need was drawing him. It was strange, though, how many things looked different to him now. Maybe those that were more familiar to him seemed the most different. He guessed that the reason he felt this way was because *he* had changed.

This thought sent his mind down another road. He was trying to figure out how he had changed. For one thing he felt more confident. He had always been confident in his ability to speak, to perform on a stage and to carry on a dialogue with others. But now he felt more confident in his decision making and his ability to analyze, his ability to influence others, his practical side. Could the Marine Corps have done that, or was it just maturity?

The steps down to the apartment were on his right. He stopped and looked. Even they looked different, smaller somehow. He descended the stairs and pushed the door open into the little foyer. The door on the right led into the apartment that had been occupied by the two gay women. He looked at the nameplate. Wanda Jones and Marcia Colson. Same names.

The nameplate on Taylor's apartment was blank. He knocked on the door. No answer. He knocked again, then rang the bell. He heard a faint "bing bong." There was still no answer. He was about to leave, half-disappointed, half-relieved, when the door of the other apartment opened slightly. Wanda looked out at him, puzzled. Then awareness crossed her pretty face.

"Luke. Luke, good to see you again. It's been ages. Where have you been?" She opened the door wider. She was topless. She wore some sort of a panty brief, but her breasts were totally bare.

Luke almost gulped. He stopped just in time. "Hi, Wanda. It's good to see you again, too." He wondered if she caught the double entendre in that simple remark.

Luke had always felt Wanda was the prettier of the two, although they both were good-looking women. She wore her curly blonde hair short and flipped up. Her skin was a pale pink. Marcia was taller and dark-haired. She also wore her hair short, kind of pixyish in style. Marcia was good looking, but she had an edge that Luke couldn't define. She was harder, or flintier, or something. What a waste he thought, that they were lesbians.

"Come on in. I've got some iced tea or a beer or something, if you want." She opened the door all the way and stepped back, motioning to him.

Luke entered the apartment hesitantly. He was having difficulty keeping his eyes from her breasts. "Thank you. That would be good. A beer, maybe. It's a warm day."

"It sure is. One of those city heat waves." She closed the door, leaning forward to do it. Luke noticed that although she had leaned forward, her breasts did not swing pendulously. She was very tight and firm.

She went to the little kitchen, took two brown bottles from the refrigerator, popped the lids and walked back into the living room area. The apartment was just like Taylor's, only reversed. Luke noticed for the first time that Wanda's panties were transparent.

"Have a seat. Tell me everything that's been going on. Marcia won't be home until later. She's working."

She went to sit opposite him when something suddenly dawned on her. "Oh, I forgot." She looked down at her nakedness and smiled sheepishly. "I shouldn't expose myself like this when I'm around other people. I have to think about these things."

She went into the bedroom. She was back in a moment wearing a long "T" shirt that covered her body down to mid-thigh.

Luke had mixed emotions. She was certainly good looking and his manhood was responding, but he had also felt uncomfortable trying to hold a conversation with an almost naked woman.

She crossed the room and swung into the chair across from him, pulling her legs up beneath her. Her breasts still pushed against the cloth and a little flash of pink panty still showed but overall, she was covered up.

Wanda was a treasure trove of information. Apparently, Taylor had moved out last month. She had traveled with the man who ran the art school, but that stopped after a month or two. He had come to her apartment a few times, but they had fought. He beat her. Marcia had called the police once. They both drank a lot. According to Wanda, Taylor looked terrible. Her face was puffy and pasty. Taylor had gone home to live with her family, so he was not going to be able to see her. He thought about that. He was a little disappointed, but not overly so. It finally sank in. Taylor was a very selfish and self-centered person.

Luke told Wanda about the Marine Corps and about John. Wanda was interested in every thing Luke had to say. She had never met a Marine before. The conversation continued for a while. About an hour later, Luke felt he had to leave.

He couldn't be sure, but it seemed Wanda was making some subtle overtures to him. When they stood up, she pressed close to him. He was proud of himself for fighting his urges off, especially since it appeared Wanda might have been willing. Somewhere in the back of his mind was a morality that kept him from intruding on a relationship, even one like Wanda and Marcia's.

As he left, his step was light. He felt good about himself. He stuck his hand into his pocket and felt a slip of paper. He took it out. It was Margot's LA address. It occurred to him that Camp Pendleton was only a few miles from L.A. He might have a chance to visit her before he left for Korea. Then he stopped. Another thought entered his mind. In the Broadway musical comedy, *Finian's Rainbow*, the leprechaun Og sings a song near the end of the show:

"When I'm not near the girl I love, I love the girl I'm near. For Sharon, I'm carin' but Susan I'm choosin' . . . ."

Perhaps he was like Og. When I'm not near the girl I love . . . . He

smiled. Then he went to pick up his sea bag and headed for the Brooklyn
Navy Yard.

Mark and Maddie were back at Virginia Beach. They held hands
as they walked barefoot along the water's edge. Mark's pants were
rolled to the knee, but they still had gotten wet when the running
surf surged higher than expected. Maddie' Bermuda shorts presented no such problem. The sun had set, but the lingering twilight provided some visibility.

In a few hours, Mark had to catch a plane from Norfolk to
Washington, D.C. From there he would fly to San Diego. He would
pick up a group of replacements and fly to Japan for further transport to
Korea.

Mark had met Maddie's family the day before. They seemed like
good people to Mark, and he felt right at home. Maddie's younger
brothers and sisters reminded him of his own family. Her father told stories about World War II. Her mother beamed at Mark. She seemed to
approve of him. He would have loved to spend more time with them but
as it was, he regretted the little time he did, because it was time he could
not be alone with Maddie. Time was so precious to them. They did not
sleep at all the night before because they did not want to lose even those
few moments. They had spent the night sitting on the porch holding
each other.

"What time is your flight?" asked Maddie.

"Twelve forty-five. Same as it was when you asked a half hour ago,"
replied Mark, trying to be gentle with his kidding.

She looked up at him with a smile. "I guess I don't want it to come,
and if I keep asking, maybe it will go away."

He dropped his hand and pulled her close. "I know. I don't want it
to come either." He looked at his watch again. The hands glowed in the
dark. "We still have two hours before we have to leave. You said it won't
take more than an hour, right?"

"Yes. But you said you have to be there an hour ahead."

"We'll squeeze a little of that time out. We've still got at least two,
maybe two and a half hours."

She pressed herself tighter against him. They kissed a few times, bittersweet kisses. They held each other for long periods of time. They just
wanted to be together.

At midnight they pulled into the airport. Mark checked in and they
walked to the gate. The plane was on time and boarding started twelve
twenty. Mark was the last. They stood at the gate holding each other
until a sympathetic stewardess tapped him on the shoulder and told him

he had no more time. Mark ran down the stairs and across the tarmac just before they pulled the stairs away from the big silver bird. He was crying all the way.

Maddie stood at the big window that looked out onto the boarding area and sobbed.

14

Reunion

Miryang was a Garden of Eden. It sat in a natural bowl in the mountains. The grass was soft and spongy, a cool stream ran through the shaded glade, and it was *behind* the lines. The brigade, smarting from being stopped at Sachon before they could finish the job, was almost completely mollified by the lush surroundings. When they found out that there would be hot chow, mail call, and beer, the mollification was complete.

Weary infantrymen arrived by the truckload from noon until three in the afternoon. The first thing they did was strip their filthy utilities off and dive in the inviting river. Once they cooled down, they started to wash their gear and clothes. Since their packs were on trucks somewhere in the rear and no one had soap, sand became the major cleaning agent.

A few spare uniforms were trotted out, but not enough to go around. They also came in only a couple of sizes, creating odd mis-matches. The uniforms and the extra gear were distributed until they were gone.

As more and more of the Brigade filtered into the rest area, buddies started to find buddies and many happy reunions were held. Sad discoveries were also made, as men heard about lost friends.

Late in the afternoon, mess call was sounded and, for the first time in almost three weeks, the troops had hot chow. After chow, the beer was passed out, two cans apiece. Just as the group was settling down to drink their beer, the mail truck pulled up and bedlam ensued. A half hour later, the mail truck was gone and the mossy glade was again peaceful.

Matt and Jacques were sitting under a shady tree with their backs against the broad trunk. They had not received any mail. Matt had not expected any, but it was at times like this that he became a little melancholy. Jacques was piqued about *his* situation. Four of his girl friends had his address, but none had written to him.

"You would think at least one or two of them would write," he whined.

"You written to them?" asked Matt, rousing himself a little from his depression.

"No," Jacques said. "They are the ones at home. I am the one at war. They need to write to me."

Matt laughed. "That's a great attitude you have."

"I also have the women."

Matt looked at him with amusement. There was something to be said for that, although there was no need for a response. He stared off into the distance. They sat quietly, sipping their beer, letting the quiet and late day ennui envelop them.

"That food really tasted good, mon ami. Fried chicken was one of the foods my mother used to make."

"It sure did. I had six or seven pieces myself."

"So did I. And I had potatoes and the greens and the ice cream sandwiches." He patted his belly.

Matt laughed.

They were quiet for a while.

"We are going to attack another place tomorrow, mon ami?"

"That's what the lieutenant said," replied Matt. "Something about a mass of hills, that's been taken over by the gooks. I think those are the hills we can see off to the west."

Jacques looked to where Matt was pointing. "Bon. I do not like all this sitting around."

Matt, who had closed his eyes, opened one to look at the big Frenchman quizzically. Jacques had a slight smile on his lips. He had been kidding.

A little more quiet time passed. The day was warm, the food was good and Matt was getting sleepy. A thought occurred to him. "Where's Ivan?"

"I don't know," replied Jacques.

"He didn't get mail, did he?" asked Matt.

"He went over to the truck. The last I saw him, he was standing there waiting."

Jacques stood up. "Who would he get mail from?"

"I don't know. Think we ought to look for him?"

"He can take care of himself."

Matt stood up, also. "He sure can." Then he laughed. "I don't think I'll ever forget him flying through the air and landing on those gooks."

"And just ripping people apart like he did. He's an amazing fighting man."

While they talked about Ivan, he came into view, walking across the grassy area from near the road. He was carrying a large flat box, which was wrapped in brown paper and string. He had what resembled a smile on his face. As he neared, they noticed the wrapping paper had numerous postage stamps and markings on it. Most of them were in foreign languages.

"What's that?" asked Matt.

"Something I ordered from back home. I hoped to have it before we arrived in Korea, but it took a long time." His face was serious and noncommittal. He brought the package over to the tree and sat down. He proceeded to cut at the strings with his kaybar (combat knife). Matt and Jacques sat down next to him and waited in patient anticipation.

The box was three and half feet square, and a foot thick. When Ivan had removed the paper, he tore open the tape that held it shut and then folded back the flaps. Inside was a patterned cloth wrapped around something long. Ivan opened the cloth and picked the object up by the handle.

It was a two-sided axe. The blades of the axe were broad, a foot or so as measured from the handle and about eighteen inches from top to bottom. Matt reached out. The edges were sharp. The handle was a dark wood, wrapped in hide. It was a battle-axe, not too different than those Matt had seen at museums. The same type of axe Celtic warriors and Germanic tribes had used in Roman times.

Ivan stood up. He moved away from Matt and Jacques and started to swing his axe around his head. He had done this before. After a few thrusts back and forth he stopped and handed the axe to Matt.

"Here, you try it." He had a gleam in his eye. "This is a warrior's weapon."

Matt looked at Ivan's lidless stare and then took the axe in his hands. He swung the axe around, trying to do it the way Ivan had done it. It felt awkward. "I think it takes some getting used to."

Ivan grunted. He took the axe back and handed it to Jacques. "I will show you. It takes a little practice."

Jacques swung it around a few times. He seemed to handle it better than Matt did, but he was dubious as well. "Do you intend to take this into combat with you?" he asked, putting the axe back in Ivan's hands

"Yes, I do," said Ivan, as he caressed the blades. "The guns and the bombs and the grenades are good, but sometimes you need something else. I could have done better when we fought on that hill with the army soldiers if I had this."

They didn't doubt him for a minute.

Dateline Korea. August 17, 1950:

This is Wendell Turner, Associated News, reporting to you from the battlefields of Korea. I am going to try to put this into words that can be broadcast as well as be put into print. Please bear with me if they don't come out exactly right. What I am about to describe was a terribly emotional experience for me. I hope to convey that emotion to you, also.

As background, over the last few weeks the North Korean Peoples Army has been attacking a section of the highlands not too far from Pusan, where the Naktong River flows around the base of these hills. They crossed the river, using rafts, handmade floats, and pure ingenuity, and are now lodged firmly on the crests of most of the hills in the region. The U.S. Army's 24th Infantry Division attacked the positions on a number of occasions but had been unsuccessful in driving them out. As a matter of fact, while the NKPA units were being attacked, they were themselves attacking and taking some smaller objectives, thus increasing their hold on the area. If the Reds manage to consolidate these gains, they will seriously threaten the United Nations' last refuge in Korea.

Last night at a conference briefing, Army General Walton Walker, in command of the forces in Korea, told the gathered press of a new attempt that would be made in the morning to dislodge the enemy. As part of the plan, he had ordered the Marine Brigade back from the successful assaults they had been making in the Sachon area, to spearhead the southern portion of the attack on the Naktong Hills.

Back in early August, when the Marines had first arrived, they were thrown into the line to stop the "bleeding" that was taking place in the aforementioned southern sector of the Pusan Perimeter. Not only had they stopped the enemy but they also had pushed him back some thirty or forty miles. Now the "Fire Brigade" was being called on again to put out the fires, this time in the Naktong area.

They also gave us some charts so we could figure out the military structure, which can be confusing at times. I won't bore you to death, but some of this information may help.

An Army can be any size. It usually has a number of corps in it. A corps can also be varied in size. Its sub units are called divisions. A division is usually made up of three or four regiments with about 20, 000 troops. A regiment has about 5000 men and is divided into battalions of about 1200 to 1800 men. Three or four companies make up a battalion. Each company has three rifle platoons, a mortar platoon, and a machine gun platoon. These platoons are further broken down into squads, for riflemen and sections for the mortars and machine guns. I see here that the smallest unit is a fire team of four men. Each squad had three of these.

The next day, before daylight we were taken out to a hill, which overlooked the Marines' area of operations. As the sun rose and the artillery shelling began, we were witnesses to a spectacle that we believe few of us will ever forget.

At about 7:00 a.m., while the morning fog was lifting, artillery rounds started to impact on the hills in front of us. We could hear the rattle they made as they flew over our heads. In a little while, the shelling stopped and Marine Corsairs, those are gull-winged, propeller-driven, fighter planes, appeared over head and started to make bombing and strafing runs on the hills. The Marine spokesman with us told us the propeller-driven Corsairs were much more effective for this sort of activity than the newer, faster jets.

It appeared to us that some of the hills were being pounded unmercifully and little could live through those barrages. The spokesman somewhat reluctantly told us that it really was not anywhere near a heavy enough bombardment to ensure success for the assaulting Marines. Due to delays in disengaging from the attacks on Sachon, all the artillery units had not yet arrived and the preparation fell short of what they really would like to have had.

By 8:00 a.m., the sun was higher and the fog was gone, the first groups of Marines started to cross the open area approaching the base of the hills. These were D and E Companies from the Second Battalion. I don't know what I expected to see, but watching two columns of troops walk calmly forward, one on a dirt road the other through a rice paddy, was not something I anticipated. Their progress was orderly. They seemed to know what they were doing. To walk calmly to what could be a violent death took a special brand of courage. My heart went out to these men.

They proceeded this way until they reached the base of the hills. Then the left group, which had been slogging through the odiferous paddy, spread out into two thin lines, abreast of the hill. One was longer than the other. The longer line of men moved up the hill side-by-side, climbing hand over hand in spots. The smaller line waited and then moved upward about 200 yards behind the other line. The other Company, the unit on the right proceeded into a draw and the forward elements were hidden from view for a few moments. In the distance we could hear artillery and the muted sounds of combat as elements of the other parts of the Division engaged the enemy.

The material we had been given did not name the ridge the Marines were attacking, so the reporters started calling it No-Name Ridge. Later *we found out that the official name was Obong-ni Ridge. The Marines called it Bloody Ridge.*

While we watched the slow climb and assault we saw a Marine fall and tumble backwards, then another. My first thought was that they had stumbled, then I realized. I had just seen two men hit by enemy fire. The event was sobering. The line continued to move higher. A few came to the aid of their comrades. A few seconds later more men fell. The line slowed and became a little ragged as men sought cover.

We saw one Marine moving about trying to rally men to him. They responded. He led them to a rocky area where they could fire on the enemy. Some fell in the attempt, including the leader, but the Marines reached the area and began to return fire.

Another group, which had been safe behind a rocky outcrop, picked themselves up and ran to a higher, but less secure, spot. Some of them were cut down, too. Then we saw a third unit make a move to climb higher. It occurred to us that we were seeing a planned assault. The Marines call it fire and maneuver; one unit fires while another moves up closer and closer to the enemy. The bravery and professionalism in the face of direct enemy fire were awe-inspiring.

We also saw, Navy Corpsmen, move from fallen Marine to fallen Marine, offering aid. We saw corpsmen fall also. We saw Marines risk their lives to rescue fallen comrades.

The unit that had gone into the draw on the right of the big hill was slow to emerge. While we had been watching the unit climbing the front of No-Name Ridge, we heard a great deal of shooting emerging from that draw. But we could not see any of the activity causing it. Now we saw Marines, who apparently had been held in reserve, running to the draw. Some were climbing a small hill to the right of the opening. The crescendo of gunfire was increasing. Our spokesman was agitated. He had been monitoring the radio traffic and it appeared that the unit in the draw was being devastated by automatic weapons' fire from their right. He told us there was supposed to be some units from the Army 9th Infantry protecting that spot, but they were nowhere to be found.

The Battalion Commander requested artillery fire on the dug in enemy in an effort to free up the stranglehold they had on one of his companies. A few rounds arrived and then, inexplicably, stopped. The few rounds helped, however, and part of the unit broke free and began to climb the hill from the right side. We later found out that the artillery people were told to stop firing because headquarters believed there was an Army unit in that area, the one that was supposed to protect the Marines' right flank.

On No-Name Ridge, the next thing we noticed were small explosions here and there along the Marine lines on the front slope. Again, men were falling. Grenades. The unit had almost reached the top when the enemy launched their grenades. The Marines stopped.

Now the enemy rose up to attack down the slope. All along the ridge they stood out against the sky, looking like scenes we all have seen in a western movie, when a large group of Indians suddenly appears on a ridgeline.

They threw more grenades and started down. If they thought they would catch the Marines ready to succumb, they were mistaken. The Marines poured fire into them, thinning their ranks considerably. When the two groups met in a crash of bodies, the North Koreans just stopped. The Marines didn't budge. There was scuffling all over the hillside, before the Red soldiers broke and ran back up the hill. Many more fell in their attempt to flee. The Marines did not pursue. Later, we found out they had received the word to fall back. The Communist troops on the hill had been reinforced and the Marine unit was down to one-third of its original size. The First Battalion would pass through them and continue the attack later in the day.

When I started this report, I said that this had been an emotional experience for me. I actually cried a few times while I observed the action. The violence of the combat was shocking. The death of so many men was depressing. The horror of the situation was sobering. But the overall emotion was pride and wonder. Pride in these young Americans and wonder that they had the courage to face these challenges and overcome them. I'm glad to be an American.

The problems the Marines had at Obong-ni were, for the most part, caused by haste. The brigade was pulled back from Sachon and sent forward into other action before its supporting arms were ready, thus causing inadequate artillery fire and inadequate preparation for the attack. The lack of time to gather intelligence about its objective, had the Marines guessing about the enemy's strength and positioning and, resulted in a poorly planned assault. They didn't have the proper number of troops and they were without needed flank security. Of course the major problem from day one in Korea was that each battalion only had two companies to work with. A third company, in that initial assault by the Second Battalion would have carried the day handily.

Be that as it may, the Marines carried the day anyway. They bitched and complained about being chronically short of everything they needed, about not having the best support, about poor command decisions, but they still managed to get the job done. They accomplished these feats by a "can do" attitude, skill, and stubbornness.

One of the regimental officers described the situation, as being like a football game where the defensive team has to continuously bail the team out of bad spots handed to them by the offensive team. Their efforts are inspirational, but it makes him wonder how many times they can be put in this position and still perform.

By noon of the second day, the Marines were looking out over the valley and the plain in front of the Naktong River. The UN forces had broken through most of the defenses. Thousands of enemy soldiers were fleeing down the slopes and into the river. The Marines called in artillery, mortars and the Corsairs. It was a turkey shoot. It was particularly devastating for those NKPA troops who tried to swim the river. The battle for Obong-ni Ridge and the Naktong had become a rout.

Although the enemy had been driven out in most areas, there was still a pesky enemy contingent on one hill. Artillery, air strikes and tank fire were to no avail. They would have to be driven out with the bayonet. How and George Companies were sent to do the job.

The two units attacked by climbing up separate spurs. The intention was to meet on the top. There appeared to be nothing more than a reinforced platoon on the hill.

When How Company first crested the ridge, they were met by a withering blast of automatic weapons fire and immediately pinned down. Minutes later, George Company suffered the same fate. Both companies were spread out on narrow fingers of land, with sharp drop-offs on either side. There was little room to maneuver.

How Company tried a frontal assault with two platoons, which resulted in a gain of a few yards and a few casualties. They called for artillery but the rounds could not be placed accurately enough to hit the enemy platoon. Some fell dangerously close to the Marines. The artillery was called off. Air attacks were out of the question. The company's own mortars could not find a level place to set up. The ground was too open to allow them to set up their machine guns. They were literally between a rock and a hard place.

"Lieutenant, I have an idea. I think I see a way we can get them."

Matt had crawled up to the where Lieutenant Collins was lying, behind a small lump on the ground. Two or three rounds had pinged off rocks near Matt as he crawled over the exposed area.

"What you got?" asked Collins

"Off to the left of the gooks, there's a little flat land. One platoon could attack over that spot. The gooks aren't facing that way. It's at a right angle to them."

Collins risked a look. He couldn't see what Matt was talking about.

His face was abruptly sprayed by gravel as a round snapped by close to his head and hit an outcrop. The near miss caused his heart to leap. He dropped back down and exhaled with relief.

"You say it's flat enough for a platoon?" Blood trickled down his cheek from the shards kicked up by the bullet. He wiped it with a dirty hand. He was learning to trust Farrell's judgement. Even if he couldn't see it, if Matt had seen it, it probably was true.

"Yes, sir. Also if we back down a little from here, we'll be out of the gooks sight and behind a little rise. We can then crawl over the side of this spur and work our way across the draw until we can come up on that flat spot."

The idea sounded like it had promise. Besides, it would be better than just sitting here. He motioned to Matt and they backed off the spot where they had been lying. They crawled back a short distance, then came up to a crouch and ran back over the rise. A few rounds whizzed by, but they were high.

Collins looked at the spot Matt had been talking about. It was just as Matt had said. He called Gruene on his hand-held radio and received the okay from him. Gruene also promised to provide supporting fire when the platoon made their attack.

Dusk was approaching as the platoon slithered backward, and assembled for the movement into the draw and up to the side of the enemy position. The word platoon to describe Collins's group was an exaggeration. The unit, which had once had over fifty people, was now down to twenty-two. Instead of three, thirteen man squads, they had two eight-man squads, a fire team and a platoon leader and platoon sergeant.

It took about a half hour to get into position, but at last they were spread out in a skirmish line to the side of the NKPA unit on the hill. Collins prepared to lead the charge himself, using the two eight-man squads. He would leave Wingo with the fire team to act as a reserve.

He radioed Gruene that he was ready. Thirty seconds later, there was a marked increase in fire coming from the rest of the company. The support Gruene had promised was inundating the target.

Collins nodded to Matt and to other squad leader, and then he blew his whistle. The whole group rose to their feet and ran at the enemy screaming as they went. The fire from the rest of the company lifted just before they reached the trench line. The maneuver had worked. The surprise was complete. The Reds just stared at them stupidly.

In the dim half-light of dusk the attacking Marines must have appeared as ghostly harbingers of doom, emerging from the bowels of hell. Almost all seventeen of the Marines were in the trenches before the

Reds could get themselves together. Then, to give them their due, they fought like trapped animals. It was a no-quarter battle.

Matt and Collins were the first to arrive. Collins sprayed down the dugout with bursts from his carbine, taking down a number of the enemy before most of Marines were in the trench and it would be too risky to continuing firing.

One of the enemy soldiers managed to get off a shot at Collins though, and hit him in the shoulder. Collins fell at Matt's feet. Matt jumped over the fallen officer and ran his bayonet through the Red, driving him back as he did so. He pulled his bayonet free just as another Red came at him. Teeth and pieces of bone flew when Matt smashed him on the side of his face with a horizontal butt stroke. The mangled North Korean fell to his knees and then forward onto Collins's legs.

Matt looked back at his platoon leader. He was trying to get up. Matt yelled at him. "Stay down. We can handle this. Just protect yourself. We'll do the rest."

Matt turned toward the action. He noticed that the lieutenant was still trying to get up. He couldn't stay with him any longer. He was safe for the moment. Matt moved down the trench line toward the tangle of thrashing bodies. He arrived just in time to bayonet a Red who was drawing a bead on Lescoulie with his submachine gun. Lescoulie had his back turned, pulling Reds off one of his men.

When the platoon had first launched their attack, Ivan had done a strange thing. The others had plunged into the enemy trench at a point closest to them. Ivan ran past the trench, then ran along the rear, and plunged into it at the other end. As soon as he was set, his motive became clear. He was carrying his two-sided axe. He wanted room to swing it.

And swing it he did. Red soldiers just disintegrated in front of him. He was the grim reaper, harvesting bodies as he moved down the line. When he caught up with the nearest Marine, Lescoulie, he had left six dead North Koreans behind him, each one dismembered in some way.

The enemy had tried to resist but they were overwhelmed. They had inflicted damage on a few Marines however and one of the men in Jacques's fire team had been killed. In addition to his bullet wound, Lieutenant Collins had his leg cut open by a knife or bayonet. When the battle finished Matt had found him, lying across a dead enemy soldier. If he had only stayed where I had left him — Matt thought. Collins was bleeding heavily from both wounds. The Red was dead.

Matt took charge of the platoon and had them direct their fire on the rest of the enemy group, in order to take the pressure off the rest of the company. They now had the enemy in crossfire.

With this position neutralized, the rest of the balance of George company came forward and took up positions so they could fire on the other remaining members of the enemy platoon, who were on a little rise to the left. This group was tenacious, however, and still able to keep How Company pinned down. Darkness fell before they could be rooted out. During the night, without being observed, the North Koreans slipped out and disappeared. The battle for Hill 311 was over.

McAndrew and his rocket team were running down the road between No-Name Ridge and the village of Tugok. Their helmets bobbed on their heads as they pushed themselves hard. The considerable amount of gear they were carrying clanked and rattled. In addition to their rifles, canteens, and cartridge belts, McAndrew and Marsucci had the rocket launchers and two 3.5-inch antitank rockets. Hankins and Anderson each carried four rockets.

Where the road turned to the left and moved around the base of Hill 125, Lieutenant Gibbons, their platoon leader, stood waving to them. They ran over to him and just before they reached him, he turned and ran a little way up the hill.

"McAndrew, get the 'Sisters' set up here to fire at that turn in the road. We got tanks and infantry coming down from the north."

The four men scrambled to get themselves into position. The urgency in the lieutenant's voice matched the urgency that the platoon sergeant had displayed when he sent them forward. McAndrew turned and looked across the road. Back about fifty or sixty yards, a 75 millimeter, recoilless rifle crew was setting up. They had an infantry squad with them. Gibbons turned back to McAndrew.

"What I know now is that there are four T-34 Russian-made tanks and about a platoon of infantry approaching. The guys in B Company spotted them from up on the ridge. So far, we called for an air strike and we've got some of our own tanks coming up. We don't know how long it will take for the birds or the tanks to get here. We and the 75 over there are the first line of defense. If those tanks get past us, they will be into our regimental and battalion CP area."

It was the text book way of outlining a mission. The gravity of the situation was not lost on them.

"Gotcha, lieutenant. We'll get 'em."

He turned to Marsucci. "Angie, you set up here. You got room for a shot and for your back blast. Looks like you can move over there for a second shot. Check it out to be sure." He pointed to a spot about thirty feet away.

"I'll set up here with my tube. I'll go higher for my second shot."
He pointed at an area about twenty feet above Marsucci's spot and
another, higher up the hill. He looked at the lieutenant for approval.
Gibbons nodded his head.

The rocketeers were just settling in when they heard the first of the
distinctive and ominous sounds made by tanks on the move, the clanking and rattling of treaded vehicles. The sound was chilling, promising
the introduction of huge, heavily armored behemoths into battle against
vulnerable human beings.

At first, they weren't sure whether the noises were coming from the
front or the rear. If from the rear, it meant their own tanks were arriving. If from the front, then — well — the enemy was near. After another moment it became clear. The tanks were in front of them.

The Russian T-34 had a reputation of invincibility. During World
War II, the Germans, masters of tank tactics, were not able to defeat
them. Many in the U.S. Army felt that American tanks were no match
for the T-34s and that the antitank weapons available were also inadequate. The Marines felt otherwise. They believed that the American M-
26 tank was more than a match for the T-34 and the 3.5-inch rocket and
the 75 millimeter, recoilless rifle in the hands of good rocket launcher
teams would be able to stop them. We were about to find out.

The rocket crews were not able to see the tanks. The clanking and
rattling grew louder. Then there was new sound, a growling sound.

"What's that noise?" asked Marsucci, straining to hear better.

"Don't know," said Hankins. "Sounds like a motor."

"It's a plane. No, two of them," yelled Anderson pointing, sky-
ward.

They all looked up. Just emerging from behind the hill were two of
the gull-winged Corsairs. The planes rose a little to clear a peak and then
dove at the tanks. The rocketeers were not able to see the results but up
on Observation Hill, a contingent of high-ranking Army and Marine
officers, were granted a front row seat.

The planes made three passes. They dropped two five-hundred-
pound bombs on the first pass and then strafed and fired cannons on the
other two. They knocked out one tank and scattered the infantry who
accompanied them. The other three tanks continued toward the turn in
the road. The planes pulled up waggled their wings at the ground
pounders for good luck and left to rearm.

McAndrew and his people waited. Gibbons sat on the ground near
McAndrew's team and waited also. He held his carbine in his lap. If any
infantry were still with the tanks, he would do his part.

As the roar of the airplane engines diminished, the clinking and rattling of the tanks increased. McAndrew's eyes strained. It was early evening and the light was going down, too fast for McAndrew. Then, he saw something. The bulb of the flash repressor on the front of the 85 millimeter gun on the first enemy tank inched around from behind the hill.

McAndrew edged forward, trying to make his body a more stable platform from which to fire. Anderson had already loaded the rocket for him and tapped him on the head. McAndrew looked through the site and estimated the distance.

"Come on, baby. Come on. Just a little more," he whispered to himself, coaxing the iron monster into his web. The tube of the tank's cannon grew longer and finally he was able to see the turret.

"Just a little more, baby. Just a little more."

He lowered his aim. He was not going to fire at the turret, too hard to penetrate. Leave that for the 75's. He would knock out the tread.

"Another few feet and you are history, comrade." He continued to talk to himself as he squinted into the eyepiece.

At last, the whole side of the tank came into view. He squeezed the trigger. There was a half-second delay as the magneto sparked the rocket engine, followed by a "Whoosh" as the projectile flew toward its destination leaving a fiery trail. Seconds later, the round impacted on the right-hand tread of the tank and blew it off, throwing metal pieces in a thousand directions. The hull appeared to have been penetrated as well.

The T-34 pivoted wildly as its right-hand tread became useless and the left-hand tread dug in causing the spinning motion. The crew of the tank started to fire all their weapons in panic, but they fired haphazardly. Out of control, they exposed their left side to the rocket crews. Marsucci launched his round into the left side tread. There was a white-hot explosion and metal chunks flew again. The tank came to a complete stop. At that point, a 75 millimeter rocket smacked into the turret and the tank burst into flame

While the 75 millimeter crew was reloading and the Sisters were scrambling to their secondary positions, the first of the Marine's M-26 tanks came on the scene. They launched two 90 millimeter cannon rounds into the crippled T-34 and it exploded.

The second Red tank picked up speed and started to move around the burning T-34, intent on engaging the Marine tank. Just as it cleared the first tank, it was hit in the right-hand tread by both of McAndrew's rocket launchers. The tank came to a halt, unable to move. As its gun swung around, the 75's put the finishing touch on it with a direct hit on the turret. The Red tank's 85 millimeter gun dipped and stuck in the ground looking like a wounded, long-beaked bird. The enemy tank crew scrambled to get out. A waiting rifle squad gunned them down.

The second of the Marine tanks swung into position next to the first tank and fired rounds into the crippled T-34 until it exploded.

The third T-34 pulled behind the two burning tanks and swung its gun around looking for targets. It too went to its final resting place in a fiery blaze of glory. The 3.5-inch rocket teams, the 75's and the two tanks all fired all at once. There was one giant explosion. The last of the Red tanks was reduced to melting and smoldering rubble. The base of the iron monster remained, but there was a huge hole where the turret had been. There were no survivors.

The cheering on Observatory Hill could be heard throughout the valley. Normally reserved senior officers lost control and slapped each other on the back and yelled.

"Son of a bitch," said one Army colonel. "I saw it, but I still don't believe it."

The myth of the T-34 was defeated.

As night fell and the fires in the burning tanks ebbed, the rocket teams walked back to their company area singing. The number was "Accentuate the Positive," a tune the real Andrews Sisters had sung with Bing Crosby. The troops were in perfect harmony. Their namesakes would have been proud.

The next day, August 19th, was mop-up day. The brigade spent the day patrolling and setting up defensive positions. The day after, they received the word that they were turning their positions over to some Army units and the Marines were going into the newly designated Eighth Army's reserve, near Masan.

"I can't believe it. We are actually going to get new uniforms and equipment," said Matt as he looked out across the Bean Patch. The area had been a soybean farm. Trucks had pulled up earlier and boxes of clothing and gear were being unloaded.

"I hope they have boots," said Jacques. He held up his shoes. They had holes in the bottom from wear and on the top from bullets and frag-ments. One of the heels was gone.

Ivan said, "I think we all need something." He was putting the fin-gers of one hand through multiple holes in his uniform.

Matt looked at them and then the rest of the squad. Things had been happening so fast that they hadn't had much time to think about how they looked. Now he realized they looked like a band of raga-muffins. They all had damaged utilities. Matt was missing a sleeve. Ivan's were covered with blood. Fortunately, it was not his. Jacques' clothes were torn at the elbows and the knees. And they all smelled.

The rest of the brigade was in a similar state of bedragglement. In addition to uniform problems, their combat gear was in miserable condition. A great deal of it had been thrown away or it had been lost or destroyed.

After the uniforms and equipment were issued, they got to take showers. Hot chow was served for the second time since they'd been in Korea. It was welcomed like a lost treasure.

Beer was passed out, compliments of breweries back in the States. Some do-gooders back home had objected to the idea of giving beer to troops who might be only seventeen or eighteen, but the prevailing opinion was if they are old enough to fight they are old enough to drink. Many Marines wondered at the mind set that could send men off to die, but could not accept them drinking a beer. There was no logic to it.

Within the platoon area, the squad set up their own space. They had used bamboo that grew nearby and a combination of ponchos and pieces of canvas to provide a little protection from the sun and the rain. Although an enormous amount of supplies had arrived and been distributed, tents were not in the mix.

Now that they were the Eighth Army's reserve, the whole brigade, except for the artillery units, had moved to the "Bean Patch." It was near Masan, about thirty to forty miles from the Naktong area. Their artillery units were still attached to the Army's forward units and they were being used around Naktong.

"We are to get some new people, mon ami?"

"Yeah. Replacements are on the way. Should be here in an hour or two."

Jacques nodded his head.

"They also put out a call for volunteers from the service units to go into infantry units. Wingo says the rifle platoons are almost down to half strength."

"That is serious. We need help," said Ivan.

"Are they getting any response from the service units?" asked Jacques.

"I don't know. I think so. A lot of guys who join the Marines want to be ground pounders like us, but they have to fill other slots. This is their chance. I think we'll get some."

"What about the lieutenant?" asked Ivan. "Do we have any more information on him?"

"I haven't heard anything. When we came down from Hill 311, he was stable, but I haven't heard any more. He's going to be gone for awhile. He should be okay but he won't be back here. Sergeant Wingo will know more later. He's at a battalion meeting."

"Do you think he'll know what we will be doing?" asked Ivan.

"I would guess so. Right now we are the Eighth Army reserve, but you know that. Our job is to rest, fill in our units with the replacements, train the replacements, and restock our supplies. That's all I know. Wingo might have more."

The day was warm. They had eaten well. They had drunk a few beers. They were sleepy. Tomorrow would be busy. They had to train people, finish the resupply, and coordinate other activities. Now, it was the time for a nap. Matt and Jacques spread out and closed their eyes. A few minutes passed.

Ivan was wide-awake. "The Army unit that replaced us . . . they will not last."

Matt opened one eye. He had started to doze. "What makes you say that? They've got some veterans."

"I saw it in their eyes. They are too green. Their officers make it too easy on them."

Matt was a little more alert. "Why do you say that? Did you see something?"

Ivan grunted. He looked at Matt, no humor in his eyes. "I see many things. When we were turning over our positions to them, I noticed that there were not too many of them in the group. I asked if they were the whole platoon. They told me no. I asked where the others were. They told me they would be along. The officer told them if they had difficulty getting up the hill, it was okay to wait and come up later."

Matt looked at Jacques. Jacques had one eye open, then he sat up. He looked at Ivan. "Was there anything else?"

"Sleeping bags."

"Sleeping bags?"

"Sleeping bags."

"Why are those important?"

"Some of the men did not have sleeping bags. The ones who did not have them had deliberately left them behind to lighten the load. The officers made the ones who had sleeping bags share them."

"Great leadership," spat Matt sardonically. "How do you share a sleeping bag? Anything else?"

"Many things. The officers wanted work parties to go back and bring up more ammunition and they asked for volunteers. They got none. A sergeant ordered some to go. Some refused. They said they were spent from the climb. He let them off and went to find others."

"No wonder they're so screwed up. Someone needs to kick some ass."

They were quiet for a while. Most of the camp was quiet too. Then Matt had a thought. " Prisoners. I've been wondering about that."

"Prisoners?" asked Jacques.

"Yeah, prisoners. During all the fighting and retreating the Army was doing until we got here, they had an enormous number of people taken prisoner. They just lost a bunch more the other day while we were taking Obong-ni. They got them back when we finally overran all the enemy positions but these, guys, had in fact surrendered."

Ivan and Jacques were trying to digest that. They didn't know about any Marines taken prisoner. "I guess there are situations, where you have to surrender but they've got to be few and far between."

Jacques nodded. Ivan said, "I will never surrender."

"I wouldn't, either," said Matt "but I can see where some people might."

"The report the general read this morning. He talked about the statistics, how many we lost, how many killed, how many wounded, how many unaccounted for. Do you remember the numbers?" asked Jacques.

Matt thought a minute. "No, not exactly. I do remember he said something like 100 killed and 300 or 400 wounded, but that there was less than ten unaccounted for. That means that, *at the most*, they took ten Marines prisoner. But, that's not too realistic. More than likely, the ten unaccounted for are probably still out there somewhere, dead."

Ivan nodded. "We bring our bodies back. Somehow we missed those."

Matt looked at Ivan. He smiled inwardly. He was different. He came from a different culture, but he thought like a Marine.

The afternoon wore on. They dozed, ate a little of the food they had saved from the chow line and talked some more. Others from the platoon joined them. They had a common bond now. They had lived together, fought together, and survived together. They knew they could depend on each other. They also were developing a dislike together for the Army troops they had to work with. Other members of the platoon had stories similar to Ivan's. There were stories of units running without firing a shot, when attacked. There was even a rumor that, the Marines had been pulled from the line and put behind the Army troops to keep them from running.

Stories were now filtering back that, although the Marines had totally annihilated the enemy divisions they faced during their part of the Naktong battles, the Army units who had replaced them were struggling with their defensive assignments and were barely holding on.

There were complaints by the Marine brass blaming the Army troops for pulling back when they were supposed to guarding their flank, resulting in more casualties than there should have been. The Army kept insisting the problems were caused by miscommunications. The Marines felt that there were too many "missed communications."

"You know," said one Sergeant who had also fought in the Big War. "We're good. We're very good at this combat business. I don't think there's anybody better. But, if those Doggie units are run right, they won't be that far behind us. During the war, there was some good Army units. We respected them. These people we got here are shit. We kicked the Gooks asses going to Sachon. We did it in just a few days. We knocked the gooks off the hills up at the Naktong in just a few days. Those Army units should have been able to do that, too. They might have taken longer than us. They would have had to fight harder, but they should have been able to do it. I don't know what their problem is."

They sat around for a half-hour, grousing about the poor grade of soldier they had to work with when Sergeant Wingo showed up. He had word on the replacements.

"All right, squeeze in here and listen up," he said in his soft drawl. He gathered the Platoon around him.

"We got replacements. We're going to be a real Platoon again, not one hundred per cent, but almost. We got enough to make three, eleven or twelve man squads. We got a new sergeant. He's a buck sergeant and we got a new platoon leader."

The men looked from one to another trying to grasp what this would mean. Wingo went on.

"The sergeant, his name is Wallace, he'll bring the men over when they get finished drawing their gear. He's been around. Half the guys we're getting are new, just out of ITR (Infantry Training Regiment). We got to help them. The other half are volunteers from supply and communications and clerks and stuff." He scratched his head. "I guess most of them will need help, too."

The brunt of the troops felt that any help was good. Others wondered how new guys would react in combat. Would they be an asset or a liability?

"I've already assigned the new guys to squads. I got lists here. I talked to the new lieutenant and he told me to do it any way I wanted. He'll come over shortly, too. He said he had to meet with Lieutenant Gruene. That's about it. Oh, yeah. The new sergeant, he'll take over the Third squad. Farrell, you and Posvar keep the squads you got. Here's the lists."

Matt was pleased that he still had his squad. He looked at his list. The names meant nothing to him. There were four names on it. He had seven, at present. That was eleven, one short of authorized, but very good.

The platoon went back to bitching about the Army, when the new sergeant came over with the replacements. There was a little confusion as the squad leaders sorted them out. Finally Matt had his complement. He looked at them, three new men and one ex-clerk. He sighed. They looked so young.

He made Womack a fire team leader and gave him two of the men, the clerk and one of the new men. He also moved one of the other veterans into his team, giving him four. He assigned one of the new men to Ivan and one to Jacques. Ivan now had four. Jacques had three. He was pleased how it worked out. When they actually got into the training, he decided he would spend the majority of his time with Womack's team.

Mess call sounded and the troops filed through the lines, scarfing up plates of "mystery" meat, mashed potatoes, green beans, and apple cobbler. For some reason the mystery meat tasted good tonight.

The platoon finished and slowly found their way back to their platoon area. It was almost dark when Sergeant Wingo brought the new lieutenant over. The Platoon assembled in a semi circle. Matt and Jacques and Ivan stood in the rear. Sergeant Wingo was going to put them into formation but the Lieutenant waved that off.

Wingo wasted no time on preliminaries.

"First Platoon, this is your new Platoon Leader. Lieutenant Flaherty."

Matt nearly fainted. It was Mark.

15

The Alarm Rings Again

"And just who are these 'Yellowlegs' you fear so much?" General Pang said with exasperation. "Are they giants? Are they gods? Are they supermen?"

Colonel Park was sitting in an aid station. A medical man was bandaging his right arm. He was wearing only his underwear and felt self-conscious in front of the general. His uniform hung on some branches behind him. It had partially dried in the warm air, but it had been soaking wet when he removed it an hour before, the result of his hasty swim across the Naktong River. "We don't know who they are. They are not supermen but they fight like tigers. They don't give up. They don't run. They are not like the others."

"Where did they come from? Why have we not seen them before?"

"I cannot answer that, sir. One day they were not there, then the next day they were attacking us." He flexed his arm a little to test the bandage. "They attack hard. They are skilled in how to attack a position. They move well. When we thought we had them pinned down, they found a way out. We attacked them and they were a stone wall. They produce enormous firepower." The colonel's face was strained. The memories were not pleasant.

"They drove us off a few positions and when we counterattacked, they held. One time we did manage to push them off a crest and then they counterattacked and drove *us* off. We suffered enormous casualties. We lost whole platoons. We lost whole companies." His voice trailed off. "Our soldiers call them, 'Yellowlegs.' They fear them."

"That was obvious when your whole regiment fled from them," the general said with disgust. He pitied Colonel Park, but he also understood his position. Right now Park only had about one third of his regiment left.

"When did you first see them?"

Colonel Park thought a moment. "When they attacked the ridge we were holding near Tugok. That was on August 17th."

Now it was time for General Pang to think a little. He said, mostly to himself, "August 17 … three days ago. We had just settled in. let me think. We were moving more people in for our big push. We had just driven a number of the lap dogs out of positions to the north. But we had those problems near Sachon a few days before . . . ." He paced as he thought. Then something occurred to him. He spun quickly around and faced Park.

"Describe the attack."

"Sir?"

"Describe the attack. How did they advance? What about supporting arms? Did they use tanks? Planes?"

"Yes, sir. They used artillery and planes. We were well dug in. The impact wasn't that great. It was mostly the infantry that drove our people off the hills."

"What about the planes? What kind of planes? Were they jets?"

Park frowned as he tried to remember. It was hard. He had kept his head down through most of the air attacks. "No, general. I don't think it was jets. The planes were slower. They used propellers. They had bent wings . . . ."

"Bent wings!" General Pang shouted. "Bent wings. The American Corsairs, the same planes that destroyed the 83rd Motorcycle Regiment. Did you see any markings on the sides?"

"I really don't remember, general. I can't read their language anyway. Markings would mean nothing to me."

"The writing said 'Marines,' colonel," General Pang said with grim satisfaction. "Those are U.S. Marines in those planes. You fought against Marines on that ridge," declared General Pang. "I suspected, after the problems we had on the road to Sachon that we were seeing carrier planes, both from the Imperialist's Navy and the Marines but I was unsure if they had landed any troops. Now I know."

"But general, should that make a difference? They are still soldiers."

"Colonel." He took on the mantle of a teacher trying to educate a slow child. "The Marines, 'Yellowlegs' as you call them, are not 'just soldiers'. They are elite soldiers. They are specialists in amphibious warfare and in assaulting the enemy. They also are thugs and murderers and other criminal types."

He walked away from the colonel and called for a messenger. "This is challenging day for us, colonel. But we will prevail. I am going to commit my reserves to fill your regiment again. I will bring in some more troops from the north. We are going to attack again. We crossed the Naktong before and took the high ground. We will do it again."

The general was excited. Plans whirled in his mind. The Marines were here. He would accept the challenge. "We will also make a more determined attack in the northern part of the perimeter, but we will concentrate here, at Naktong. We have to move fast to shove all these interlopers out of Korea. In addition to the Marines, I have received word that units are arriving from some of the other imperialist countries, too. Time is important."

He turned and looked for the messenger. He wanted to get his staff together and make plans.

Matt's first impulse was to slide behind Jacques and hide. Then he realized the futility of that. Mark was his platoon leader. He couldn't hide from him. He had no choice. He stood his ground and looked at his brother, like any other curious Marine when introduced to a new leader.

Mark looked good. He looked like a real Marine in his field gear. His gold bars stood out, even in the dim light. The only problem was he looked green, just like most of the other replacements.

At one point, Mark glanced at Matt. But Mark didn't acknowledge that he recognized him. That was not surprising. Mark wouldn't be expecting to see him here in Korea. His changed looks probably also accounted for Mark's lack of awareness. Or, he thought. Perhaps Mark was just playing it close to the vest. He decided he'd find out soon enough.

"Please, sit down. I want to say a few words to you."

The group settled themselves on the ground.

"I just want you to know that, although I'm your new platoon leader I feel I've got a lot to learn from you. You've already been here. You've fought some battles. You've proved yourselves. I haven't proved anything yet. I need to earn your confidence."

He stopped and looked at them for a moment. It was almost dark. The platoon was silent. "I am Naval Academy graduate however and that is supposed to be a good background for what we need to do. I hope it is."

He walked a little closer to them.

"I hear Lieutenant Collins was a good platoon leader. I'm sure you all miss him. I hope I can do as well as he did. I'm also sure I will do some things different than him. Bear with me as I learn my way around."

He looked them over. "I don't know anything about any of you yet. I get to look at your records tomorrow. I'll know more then. I know you've seen a lot of combat in a short period of time and that you need some rest. I'll help with that as much as I can. I was told we need to do some training however. We need to incorporate the new people into the platoon . . . like me." He laughed nervously. Most of the platoon members smiled. "And I guess we need to sharpen up some of our skills. We need to be able to do our job when the call comes again. Sergeant Wingo will start you on that tomorrow. I'll step in with you as soon as I get a little better oriented. In the meantime, listen to Sergeant Wingo and the squad leaders."

He looked at a memo pad he had in his hand. Then he looked up. "One more thing, I'm sure you've heard all sorts of rumors about us making a landing somewhere. Well the rumors seem to be true. The First Marine Division is being assembled piece by piece. It will be composed of the First Marine Regiment, the Seventh Marine Regiment, and us, the Fifth Marines. As a division, we will probably make a landing somewhere but naturally the destination and the date are still a secret." He looked at them. Their interest had been piqued. "I guess that's all I wanted to say now. Are there any questions?"

They had many questions about the landing but Mark wasn't able to give them any more than he had already told them so the questions died down. The lieutenant then dismissed the troops. The group started to break up. Matt noticed a quick glance from Mark as he left the area with his squad. He had noticed him! He was just playing it cool.

The next day, the training commenced. Matt was tied up with his squad most of the morning as they went through the basic squad tactics over and over again. One part of his mind was on Mark and how this was going to play out, but even with that distraction, he was able to get the training done. Mark wasn't with them the early part of the day, but in the afternoon he showed up with the service record books and set himself up under canvas tarpaulins and started to read.

When he finished reading, he told Sergeant Wingo to start sending the men over to him one at a time. Matt was the fifteenth to be interviewed.

"By what wild reach of luck did you find out I was in the Marine Corps and then end up in the same platoon with me?" Matt asked incredulously. "I almost passed out when I saw you last night."

Mark laughed. He had been sitting on a campstool. He stood up and looked around. No one was paying any attention to them. He moved over and hugged his big brother. "Good to see you again, Matt. At least I can be civil even if you can't."

Matt returned the squeeze and then pulled back. "Mark. It's really good to see you, but how in the hell . . . ?"

"In good time, Matt," he interrupted. " It's a long story. Grab a seat. Let's make believe we're just going over records."

Matt sat down. Mark looked at him. His brother sure did look different, shaved head, tattoos, and scars. He was also more muscular. He looked like he could use a few good meals, though. The toll of combat he figured. "How long has it been? Three years?"

"Closer to four."

"Has it? God time flies."

They looked at each other, absorbing.

"Well?"

"Well, what?" Mark asked, smiling.

"Goddamn it, Mark, the story. Tell me the story."

Mark teased again. "Oh, that story."

Matt turned his head on a threatening angle, fire in his eyes.

"All right, all right. Let's see. Where do I start?"

"Try the beginning, shithead . . . uh, Lieutenant Shithead."

"That's a court-martial offense corporal," Mark stated in mock indignation. Matt was getting angrier.

Mark relented. "Okay let's get to it." He leaned forward. "First it was the picture."

"What picture?"

"The boxing team."

Matt looked puzzled for a moment, then he remembered. "You saw *that* picture? I knew I shouldn't have done that, but everyone else wanted it." Memories flooded back "That was a good time. We were undefeated, you know." Then he was back to the moment. "How the hell did that happen? How did you see the picture?"

Mark told him the story. Matt marveled at the coincidence. When he finished the photo story, he also told him about the family, specifically how Mom and Maggie were doing. He told him about Rory and Helene, Gannon and McQuinn. He also told him about Maddie. He left out Luke and John's story for now.

"So, you have a girlfriend." Matt looked at his brother fondly. "Good for you. Somehow, I figured you'd be the last of us to get tied up though."

"I'm not tied up. It's just . . . that I like her," he finished lamely.

Matt laughed. "Your eyes and your voice betray you, Chunk. She has her hooks into you. You are a goner."

Mark sputtered a second, then laughed. "Is it really that obvious? I hadn't admitted to myself yet?" Mark had heard his old nickname, Chunk, and that also brought back memories.

"Uh huh. It's *that* obvious. Nothing wrong with that. She sounds like a good woman."

They sat quietly for a minute. The day was warm and muggy. They could see hundreds of Marines moving around practicing various formations. The road behind them was alive with vehicles moving from the Bean Patch to the docks at Pusan and back again. Supplies were going both ways.

Finally, Matt broke the silence. "What's up with Luke and John? What are they doing?"

Mark looked at Matt a second. "Hold onto your hat, Matt."

Matt waited. Mark's remark produced a sense of anticipation in him.

"They both joined the Marine Corps."

Matt didn't say anything. He just sat and stared.

Mark continued, "Apparently, John talked Luke into it. Luke was living with some broad in New York City and they broke up and John convinced him it would be a good move."

"Who convinced *John* it would be a good move?"

"He did that himself. You don't really know John anymore. He's been kind of wild, but he's grown up a lot. He looks just like you, except for the hair. He got in trouble a few times. Gannon and McQuinn were great. They gave him some "guidance" and he straightened out. McQuinn's been real good to John and to the family. He told John if he saw you, you should contact him. He may be able to help out."

Mark looked at Matt for his reaction. There was no immediate response.

Finally, after a minute of thinking, Matt said. "I'm glad to hear McQuinn's been good to John. I had him figured as a straight shooter. As to the other thing, I'll think about it. There's nothing I can do now anyway."

"I guess not." Mark stated, looking around at a totally different world than Kingmont.

"Well, now that those two shitheads are Marines, do you know where they are?"

Mark coughed. Matt noted the cough. He looked Mark straight in the eyes. "They're not coming here?" He already knew the answer.

Mark nodded. "They're also in the Fifth Marines. Don't know what units yet. I just came as part of a replacement draft. They'll be coming to fill out the Regiment for the next phase. Apparently the timing was just right. The First and the Seventh already had their troops set. The Fifth had to be brought up to strength."

Matt's face was blank. He didn't know what he felt. He'd be glad to see them but under these circumstances?

They were quiet a moment or two. Then Mark cleared his throat.

"Things have changed a lot in Kingmont since you left, Matt. The lawyer I got to help with the estate stuff after the ... uh ... Van Scooten died . . . uh, he opened a few eyes around the town. I don't think you would have any trouble with the law anymore. I think McQuinn thinks it was a justifiable homicide too."

"What do you think, and Luke and John?"

"We all feel he had it coming."

Matt grunted but said nothing.

It was time for their interview to end. They agreed to keep their relationship quiet. They would play the role of platoon leader and squad leader. Junior officers often developed friendly relations with NCO's, so there would be nothing unusual if they socialized on occasion. Matt wasn't sure what to say to Jacques and Ivan. He'd think of something. Then he decided to just be honest.

Over the next few days, the training continued. A battalion of green Korean Marines joined them. Some of the U.S. Marine NCO's were delegated to provide training for them. Sergeant Wingo was one of the NCO's tapped for this duty. The Korean Marines were in excellent physical condition and they were hungry to learn. They also turned out to be fast learners. They were anxious to strike back at the invaders of their country.

The brigade continued to prepare for its new mission, which was to join the rest of the First Marine Division and make a landing.

Then, the fire alarm rang — again.

True to his word, General Pang had been able to mass 133,000 troops in the area for his big push to drive the UN forces out of Korea. The UN forces numbered less than half that amount. Pang had filled in the depleted units with new recruits and he imported a few divisions that previously had been left to guard Seoul and other captured territory.

On September 1st, they launched an assault all along the northern and western part of the Pusan Perimeter with particular emphasis in the Naktong area. The U.S. Army's 2nd and 25th Infantry Divisions were almost completely overrun. When the day had started, the NKPA was on the west side of the Naktong River. By nightfall they had advanced more than 4000 yards to the east, retaking Obong-ni ridge (Bloody Ridge) and other hills in the area. In addition, they now occupied the hill where Wendell Turner had recorded his story of heroism and the hill where the Army Generals had cheered the rocket and tank battle. The new front line actually pushed past the point where the four dead Red tanks still rested.

The next day The Fire Brigade was moved once more into position to attack the same ground they had fought over two weeks earlier. After that, they launched their attack against the same Division they had kicked off the hills the first time, the NKPA 4th Infantry Division. Ironically, the Army's 9th Infantry was once again on the Marine's right flank and the Marines found themselves in a position to blunt an attack the Reds were making on the 9th.

For the next two days, the Marines made the Reds pay the price for their aggression. They moved from objective to objective with dazzling precision. Early on, due to low hanging clouds and rain, they were not able to use their air support, but the artillery, mortars and tanks took their toll. When the weather cleared a little, the "Bent Wing Devils" torched and slaughtered the Communist troops.

The battles were not without casualties for the Marines. Infantrymen still had to seize and occupy objectives. Troops died or were hurt, but overall the combined efforts of all the combatants carried the day for the UN forces.

"What's that over there? I see something white."

Womack was leading the point fire team as the company moved forward from their last objective to the next one. They had just kicked an enemy platoon off a small hill.

"Where? I can't see anything in this goddamned rain."

"Over there, by that clump of brush." Womack pointed. "Better get Matt up here."

Lugo still couldn't see what Womack had seen but he ran back to a turn in the valley wall where he could wave at Matt. Matt came forward at a trot. Lugo told him Mac had seen something. Matt moved forward.

"What you got, Weenie?" He had forgotten his pledge to not use the name.

Womack was kneeling. The rain was puddling around his knee.

"There's something white up there, behind those shrubs. It stands out."

Matt looked through the downpour. He saw it, too, about thirty or forty yards away at the base of a small hill.

He turned to Lugo, "Bring up the rest of the squad."

Lugo ran back. Matt turned to his fire team leader. "Maybe it's nothing, but we can't take chances. This is 'Indian' territory."

The squad ran up. Matt spread them out into a skirmish line and they moved forward slowly. The rest of the platoon was still some distance back.

As they neared the white object, they saw more white objects. Then they saw green lumps. They crested a small rise and spread before them were forty to fifty dead American soldiers. They paused, stunned.

Matt moved among the bodies. The others slowly joined him. Most of the dead had bandages on various parts of their bodies. Some of them had white bands with a red cross on their arms. One of the dead was an officer. He had a major's oak leaf insignia and a caduceus on his collar. A doctor!

Ivan had joined Matt. "This must have been an aide station. The ones with the bandages were wounded men." He pointed from body to body. "The ones with the red cross were corpsmen. Why would they do this?"

Matt was just as bewildered. "I don't know Ivan. This one is a doctor." He pointed to the dead major. "And you're right some of the others are medics. The Army calls them medics."

He looked around more. Every one of the dead soldiers had either been wounded or had been a medical person. They looked closer at the corpses. Many of the wounded showed bayonet wounds which weren't covered by bandages. The enemy had killed them while they lay wounded in an aid station. Anger started to spread through the squad.

The rest of the platoon came up. They were equally repulsed by the spectacle. Mark and Sergeant Wingo decided that they couldn't slow down to properly account for these bodies, but they sent word back by runner to the rest of the company. The battalion would take care of it.

The platoon moved off. About a hundred yards from the massacre sight they found evidence of a battle. There were dead soldiers and dead North Koreans on one small hill. There were more dead Soldiers than NKPA's. There was evidence of a hasty retreat including discarded American weapons and gear. Apparently, anything that would slow a soldier down had been tossed away.

The platoon sent back word and continued its march. After a few minutes, Ivan, who had taken up a position behind Matt in the column, asked a question. "Did you see any bodies of soldiers who were not bandaged or were not medical people? Back at the place where all the dead wounded were."

Matt hadn't thought about that. He didn't see the point. "I can't say I did. Why?"

"They had no defenders."

Matt gave that some thought. Then what Ivan was saying dawned on him. "You're right. That was the aid station for the unit on the hill. When they ran, they just left their wounded behind." He was furious. "What kind of American does that? What kind of a war are we fighting here?"

"Perhaps the American defenders were taken prisoner?"

"Bullshit. Since Naktong, the gooks aren't taking prisoners. Those shitheads ran and left their own men."

George Company fought for the three days that it took to shove the Communists back to the other side of the river. The new people in the unit received their baptism of fire and stood up well, especially Mark. He led an attack on a mortar platoon and, with his platoon, took the position after some fierce hand-to-hand fighting. Matt was very proud of him.

Along the way the Marines overran the NKPA 4th Division headquarters and reaped a harvest of intelligence material. There were enough, orders, maps, plans, and other high level papers to give the intelligence people work to do for months. They also unearthed millions of dollars in worthless North Korean money. The troops had a field day with their "windfall."

As the Brigade was about to put the finishing touches on the enemy rout, they received the word to halt and then to pull back. The "word" had changed again, but this was good "word." They were being replaced. The long anticipated merging of the elements of the First Marine Division was about to take place.

Dateline: Korea. September 10, 1950

This is Wendell Turner reporting to you from Korea. I'm sitting on the docks at Pusan, watching the Fifth Marines load onto ships for deployment elsewhere. The majority of these troops have just completed more than a month of incessant fighting as the United Nations Eighth Army struggled to restrain the Communist aggression in Korea. The Marines, affectionately known as "The Fire Brigade," became the darlings of the Army high command as they were thrown into many hot spots along the line and successfully put the fires out.

Their efforts started in early August, when the Eighth Army, after retreating for a month and a half, attacked for the first time in the war. The Marines, who had just arrived in Korea, spearheaded the assault, in the red-hot southern area. This area had been a big problem for the United Nations troops. The Marines took the fight to the enemy, and had driven the enemy back some thirty or forty miles when the second "fire alarm" was sounded. The enemy was breaking through in the Naktong

Mountains area.

The under-strength and tired Marines rushed to the area and attacked No-Name Ridge as reported to you a few weeks ago. They put that fire out also, routing the enemy as they did so.

After a few days of much needed rest and re-supply, the call went out again. Back to the Naktong. Back to the ground they took before. The enemy had launched a massive attack and the UN units in the area were not able to contain them. The enemy's success was fleeting. It became their misfortune to run into the same Marines again. The Marines contained them, and in the process put the NKPA to rout once more.

One old sergeant told me "The first time we ran into them we knocked them down with a hard left jab. The second time we used a solid right for the knockout."

One high-ranking Army officer told me that the three operations The Fire Brigade participated in were "three of the most important engagements of the Pusan Perimeter. If there had been a single failure it would have had a devastating effect upon the entire UN front."

The Marines need to add another line to their hymn. The Pusan Perimeter is certainly the equal of "the shores of Tripoli."

16

Inchon

John could barely see those around him in the dim light of early morning, as he swung his leg over the rail of the ship and grabbed the risers on the landing net. It was just as well. A dizzying forty feet below, the hemp roping curled into a landing craft that rocked and slid around on the roiling waters. A few sailors, were pulling on the net, trying to keep the boat as close as possible to the troop carrying transport. They were having limited success. The coxswain for the landing craft was alternately forwarding and reversing the engine, also attempting to keep the flat-bottomed craft in its position so the boarding troops could drop into the boat safely.

All around John, other battle-clad Marines were climbing over the rail or were strung out on the net as they also descended into the slipping and sliding boat. Tension was high.

As John maneuvered down the ropes, his training kicked in. Do not hold on to the cross ropes of the net. Hold onto the risers. The next Marine above you needs to step on those cross ropes. He can't see your hands. Leave all your gear unbuckled. If you fall into the water, you want to be able to drop it quickly so it won't pull you down.

John looked around for Luke and couldn't find him. They all wore Mae West life jackets, helmets, field packs with entrenching tools, cartridge belts with suspenders, canteens, and first aid packs. They all wore yellow leg puttees, and carried weapons, hand grenades, and bandoleers of ammunition. It would be hard to find him. They all looked the same!

Luke was in the first squad and John was in the second. This landing boat was to take the most of both squads to the beach. He was sure Luke would be aboard somewhere.

When John had almost completed his descent, he jumped the last few feet. The waves chose that moment to rise under the craft and lift it so that he landed with a particularly hard jolt. He was jarred for a second, but then he pitched in to grab the net and help the next guy. A petty officer barked at him.

"That's why they tell you not to jump, asshole."

John glared at the sailor but held his tongue.

Others around him were also grabbing the net to pull it away from the APA, making it easier and safer for the Marines descending behind. Although it was not a stormy sea, the swells were "slippery" enough to make the loading especially perilous. The landing barge was never in one place for more than a second, moving it three or four feet higher or lower each moment. Sometimes, the boat swung at an angle to the mother ship. All in all it was amazing that no one was lost during the process of debarkation.

With its engines churning the pewter sea, the now loaded boat swung away from the troop ship, and headed for a rendezvous point in the open water. The scene was being repeated in the half-light of early morning all across the churning bay. From a distance, the look of the troops surging over on to and then down the landing nets was not unlike the look of a seeping gray-green waterfall slowly tumbling and cascading into the landing boats.

When the barges reached their assigned area they were met by a guide boat, which then formed her charges into a circle. They now had to wait for the rest of the boats in their section to load and for the sections that had embarked earlier to make their run to the beach. Although there were many boats afloat and the murky waters bubbled with activity, the only troops being loaded at this point were the members of the Third Battalion of the Fifth Marines. They would be the first to land.

As John's boat growled away from the *USS Barney Williams*, affectionately dubbed the *Barnacle Bill*, and headed for the rendezvous point. John looked around again for Luke and finally he saw him. He was in the back of the boat with his squad. John's squad had ended up near the front. He waved. Luke waved back, although the wave was a little tentative. He wondered if Luke was feeling seasick. He was having a little trouble himself.

The water was calmer out in the open, but the flat-bottomed boat still slid and bounced around with nauseating persistency. Fortunately, the spray coming over the side as the craft dropped into troughs and crested waves helped to wash away the remnants of the half-digested meals.

Lieutenant Boomer stood next to John. He also appeared a little queasy as he looked out over the ramp at the boats on front of them. They were starting to form the circle. The young officer turned and gave John a little smile.

"Great day for a boat ride, eh, Flaraty. When we get there, we get to pick the best spots to eat lunch and pick up girls, too." He looked back over the ramp again. "Waves are a little low for any real surfing though. But then, you can't have everything."

John saw the attempt at humor. He forced a smile through his queasiness. "We could have gone on another day, sir. That wouldn't have bothered me." He thought. Boomer is a good guy. The rangy blond from California impressed him. He was a surfer, among other things.

Boomer gave a small laugh and then looked around at the rest of his troops. Two of his squads were in this boat. His third squad plus his other people were in the boat behind them. The remaining Item Company platoons were also in boats in this section. The other companies in the battalion, George and How, had already formed up half-mile in front of them and were getting ready to make their runs to the beach.

When John and his platoon had first assembled on the decks of *Barnacle Bill,* thundering volleys of naval gunfire had boomed out all around them. The Navy was softening the landing area. He hadn't noticed the gunfire for a while, but now it was starting to intrude into his consciousness again. It was a constant rumble of noise as ship after ship unloosed volleys toward the port. He could see the orange flashes when they fired and then, through the smoke, he could see yellow and white flashes when rounds impacted on land. The beach must be like a vision of hell, John thought.

Dawn was beginning to show in the east when their section received the semaphore signal to form up at the line of departure. They came out of the circle they had formed, into a queue, much like a row of duck-lings following their mother. They then headed for the guide boats, which delineated the final checkpoint before attacking the beach. When they reached that point, they would still be six miles away. Other circles were also breaking and heading for the same point of departure. The earlier boats were already at the line.

For John and Luke it was all very exciting and scary. But this was what it was all about. They felt like Marines. This reminded them of all the scenes they had seen in the movies and the newsreels. This is what they had signed up for — the naval gunfire, the landing boats, the smoke, the planes roaring overhead, the sea spraying over the gunwales. It was perfect.

The date was September 15, 1950. They were headed for Green Beach on the small island of Wolmi-do, in the harbor at the port of Inchon. Their mission was to take Wolmi-do from the North Koreans and hold it, thus securing the left flank of the division's landing zone. The rest of the Fifth Regiment, and The First Marine Regiment would land later in the day.

Five days earlier the *Barnacle Bill* had tied up at the port of Pusan, along with a number of other ships which carried elements of the First Marine Division to Korea. With the exception of stormy seas when they neared Japan, the trip across the Pacific had been uneventful. Continual training helped to ease the boredom that three weeks at sea could impose on robust young men. Although the *Barnacle Bill* was big enough to hold a whole battalion of troops, it was still a small vessel in many ways. Two or three turns around the decks and you had done it all.

Weapons were disassembled and reassembled again and again. They were cleaned and polished to mirror perfection. Knives and bayonets were sharpened until they were keen as surgical instruments. Packs were packed and repacked. Enemy manuals were studied. Tactics were reviewed and rereviewed. Calisthenics were held two and three times a day.

Card games and dice games erupted throughout the ship. Monthly paychecks changed hands regularly. The food was great. The crew was great. The Marines developed a real affection for the "swabbies" of the *Barnacle Bill.* But all good things must come to an end. Finally, on September 10, they reached Pusan.

John had two sixes and a ten showing. His down card was a ten. Dipsey had two jacks and a five showing. The other two guys had nothing higher than a nine. The fifth card was waiting to be dealt.

The air in the hold was stuffy. Each of the Marines was shirtless. Perspiration dotted their brows. There was twenty-seven dollars in the pot. It was his bet. The two jacks had checked. He fingered the cards thoughtfully. The last of his money was in front of him, three dollars. He checked too. Save the money for the final card.

He drew a five. He had to go with the two pairs. Dipsey drew a deuce to go with his jacks and his five. John thought some more. Dipsey could have another jack underneath or a five or a two. Any of those cards would beat him. The other player's cards showed a couple of deuces and a five however and he also had a five, so the chances that Dipsey had drawn a five or a two were low. But he still had the jacks—.

He decided.

"I got three bucks." He pushed the bills forward. "It's all in. That's my bet. You take it?"

Dipsey looked at John with a slight smile.

John worried that Dipsey would out bet his three dollars, causing him to have to borrow or to fold.

"Yeah, I'll take it." He matched the pot. "Call."

John rolled his ten over and showed the two pairs. Dipsey looked at John with a crooked smile. He rolled his down card. It was a two. He also had two pairs but his jacks were high.

John sighed and stood up.

"I'm out until next payday, whenever that might be. Good thing there's no decent place to take liberty." It galled him to do it, but he shook Dipsey's hand. "Thanks for not pushing me."

Dipsey scooped up the money. The other two players were quitting, too. "No problem. I'll buy you a beer if we get somewhere we can get beer."

"Thanks, Dips. You're a real gentleman."

"It's the least I can do," Dipsey said with a smirk.

John took his cap from his back pocket, put it on and started back to the troop compartment and his bunk, the second bunk from the bottom in a five-tier stack. Maybe he could catch a few winks before chow. As he walked down the passageway, he saw Luke approaching him, accompanied by another Marine.

"John, I've been looking for you. This guy is a messenger from topside," he pointed to his companion. "He says there is some lieutenant on deck looking for us."

"He asked me if I knew you guys. I said I know you a little bit, so he told me to find you and bring you up."

"Do you know what he wants or who he is?" John looked from the messenger to Luke. They both shook their heads.

"Well I guess we'll find out." Luke turned to their guide and said, "Lead on, MacDuff."

The messenger looked at Luke with a strange look. Luke looked at John. "I guess he doesn't read much."

John shrugged. He wouldn't have known about the expression from *MacBeth* either, except that Luke had told him about it.

John retrieved his T-shirt and blouse and then they climbed through a few passageways and up a few decks and finally emerged on the main deck. They day was gray but warm. Their guide led them to the gangway. A stocky lieutenant was standing there talking to the Officer of the Deck. They came to attention behind him and saluted. The officer turned around. It was Mark.

Two minutes of hugs and backslaps followed. Finally Mark got them under control, looking at the Officer of the Deck sheepishly.

"Good to see you guys again."

"Good to see you too big guy ... uh ... lieutenant," said John.

Luke beamed in agreement. "Me too, Mark."

"I understand you guys can't get off the ship yet. Something about too much confusion and shit until they get an area set up for you. But, I have a surprise for you. I'll bring it here. Meet me back here in an hour."

Luke and John both started to speak at once, but Mark shut them up.

"In an hour, okay? Here at this gangway, okay? I'm not going to say any more. Just be here." He stood straight. "That's an order," he commanded, his eyes twinkling in merriment.

Mark went down the walkway to the dock.

The next hour was seemed eternal. Chow call sounded and they ate a little but they were too keyed up to eat much. They really wanted to visit with Mark regardless of what the surprise might be.

Finally, the time came. They were at the gangway when Mark came up the ramp. He had papers in his hand. He showed them to the Officer of the Deck. The OOD, a thin young ensign, read them, turned to John and Luke, and looked at them quizzically and told them they had they had been assigned to a detail on shore and they had to go with Mark who was in charge of the detail.

Happily, they got in line behind Mark and walked off the ship.

"I wasn't able to bring Mohammed to the mountain so I'm bringing the mountain to Mohammed," he stated cryptically.

John looked at Luke and shrugged. Luke shrugged back. He had heard the expression, from the Koran if he recalled correctly, but he didn't understand Mark's use if it.

They pulled away from the docks in a jeep, Mark driving and still mum about the surprise. In fact he wouldn't say anything except to give them short and to-the-point orders. He took them to an area a mile from the docks. John noticed a sign that said something about the Fifth Marines. He pointed it out to Luke. They decided this was the staging area for the Fifth and that their units would be assigned here shortly. They noticed that there were tents here and there, but most of the troops seemed to be living out in the open.

Mark remained merrily silent.

They pulled up to a makeshift canopied area, and Mark turned the jeep over to a corporal with a wave and a thank you. They walked to another canopied area. About a dozen Marines were sitting at some makeshift tables, talking and drinking beer. One Marine stood up and came over. He was a corporal. He held two cans of Schlitz out to them. They both did a double take. They hadn't expected to see him. He looked different, but there was no doubt. It was Matt.

"Well, I can't say I'm glad to see you two shitbirds, but I'll say it anyway. I'm glad to see you two shitbirds."

The words were confusing, but they got the message. There were hugs all around, and a few tears, the warmth and joy of the moment evident on all their faces. Mark stood on the side and beamed. John and Luke were bubbling with questions. The excitement was excruciatingly exquisite. They stumbled all over themselves to speak first. Finally, the situation settled down and they began to fill each other in on their respective histories. Matt introduced them to Jacques and Ivan. John and Luke were both enthralled with the two veterans and fascinated by the stories they told and the action they had seen over the last two months. They drank a few more beers. They felt the warmth of a close-knit family.

John and Luke tried to get Matt to talk about that night with Van Scooten. Matt grunted. Then he spoke carefully, "when we're done here . . . in Korea, maybe I'll go home and we can sort it all out. Right now it seems Mom and Maggie are doing good, thanks to you guys. They don't need me now. We still got a job to do here . . . ."

And that's the way it was left

The day wore on, a happy day, but dusk began to creep up on them. They would have to get back to the ship shortly. The ploy Mark had used wouldn't work too much longer. Earlier, he had found out his brothers were in Item Company, where he knew one of the platoon leaders. It wasn't difficult to arrange for a "special detail." Before leaving, he showed them the area they would be staying in the next night. It was adjacent to the George Company area. It was purely the luck of the draw that they were all in the same battalion, the Third. Their reunion continued over the next few days, then they boarded their ships and the whole division headed for Inchon, for their date with destiny

The scow-like rocket launching ships moved into the area in front of the first of the assault waves of landing craft and inundated Wolmi-do with one last giant barrage of fiery explosives. Ten minutes of "Armageddon" rained down on the little island. The timing was perfect. The rocket ships finished their task and pulled out of the landing zone just as the first wave of boats closed to within one hundred yards of Green beach.

Mark and Matt were in the first boat on the right of the first assault wave coming into the beach. Mark had just given the order to lock and load. The shelling had resulted in a great deal of destruction and fire. Burning buildings, shrubbery and trees dotted the landscape. Thick, black smoke drifted from the land into the faces of the invaders.

The first boats entered the smoke while they were still fifty yards from the shore. The powerful engines pressing them on, through the sooty vapor.

The smoke also did not inhibit the Corsairs as they screamed over the hidden, troop-laden craft and sprayed the beach with 50-caliber machine gun fire, so near to the landing boats that hot shell casings fell among the crouched Marines.

When the landing craft emerged from the smoke, they were only twenty-five yards from impact on the sand. The Corsairs finished their run and pulled up into higher reaches. Mark and Matt could see a small sea wall in front of them that could be an obstacle. Fortunately it was broken and tumbled down in a number of places.

Just as the boat was about to touch bottom, the coxswain gunned the engine to give it one last burst of power. The idea was to drive it a little way onto the tiny beach so it would be a steady platform and wouldn't swing in the surf. Once the troops unloaded, it would be light enough to float back out. Their boat made a perfect landing.

Mark grabbed the release handle and pulled. The big ramp on the front of the boat swung down and splashed into the low surf. Led by Matt and Mark, the platoon rushed off and quickly swung out into a line. They barely got their feet wet. They ran forward to the sea wall and stopped, crouching behind the shattered concrete.

Matt looked to the left. Other boats were crashing onto the sand. Ramps were coming down. Other Marines were spreading out onto the beach. One of the boats wasn't so lucky. They must have struck a sub-merged object. The front of the boat was lifted out of the water. The ramp was down, but the floor of the boat was high off the water. Marines were jumping over the sides or off the suspended ramp into water over their heads. He hoped they remembered about unbuckling. They all made it, but some of them lost equipment including weapons.

Weak automatic weapon fire was coming from some spot on the left. They didn't see any enemy to go after. Sergeant Wingo ran over to Mark to report the position of the rest of the platoon.

Mark chanced a look over the sea wall and saw a messy field dotted with barren and burned out shrubbery. He spotted a small ridge about fifty yards away and he ordered his men forward. They had to get off the beach. The next wave would be hitting shortly. Mark thought he could hear the landing craft engines in the smoke.

En masse, they ran across the open area and settled in behind the ridge with no difficulty. Either there were no defenders on this beach, or they had been shelled into submission.

A minute late, the rest of the company crunched ashore behind the lead platoons. Within fifteen minutes, Lieutenant Gruene had gathered his whole company and they turned to their right to advance up one side of Radio Hill, their first objective. Mark's Platoon led the way. The hill was about three hundred feet high and provided a good view of the harbor area.

The platoon encountered little resistance. The few dispirited enemy soldiers they did meet, surrendered to them quickly. By 0655 they had secured the top of the hill and raised a small flag.

How Company had come in on George's left and advanced across the small island. Their mission was to cut off the causeway which ran over to the mainland and to clear the bombed out industrial area. When finished, their next objective was to help George Company with Radio Hill. They would run into a little resistance fighting their way through the shattered buildings, but they took very few casualties. The mission to assist George Company on Radio Hill became moot

The third wave brought in the Battalion Commander, the headquarters staff and ten tanks. There were six M-26s, one flamethrower tank, two bulldozer tanks and one tank retriever.

The fourth wave delivered Item Company, which immediately turned to the left and struck out for North Point, Because they had no combat experience, Item Company was intended to be the battalion reserve. The battalion staff had been assured by a cursory sweep made by one of How Company's Platoons, that the area was enemy free. The staff decided to let Item get its feet wet in a supposedly trouble free situation.

Of course, Murphy's Law intervened.

Three hand grenades landed on the rubble-strewn road and rolled to a stop. Six Marines ran and dove in all directions, Luke and Pettigrew running into each other in their efforts to get away. They all managed to achieve some cover before the blasts. The rest of the point squad broke for cover when the small bombs went off. No one was hurt. Small arms fire followed the grenades and immediately pinned the squad and the platoon down.

"Where the hell are they?" barked Corporal Lisky. "Anybody see them?"

"To the right, a little hill, some openings. Maybe twenty-five or thirty yards," said Luke.

Then the shooting stopped. All was quiet. The squad members started looking around at each other. What do we do now?

Lieutenant Boomer ran forward. He dove down into the roadside ditch where Luke and Pettigrew crouched. A round snapped over his head.

"I see them," yelled someone behind them and a Marine BAR started to fire on the small mound. As the automatic rifle fired, three enemy soldiers stood up at the other end of the mound and hurled grenades. The grenades fell short. The BAR man hit one of enemy soldiers before he could drop back down.

"Lisky, get your men firing on that mound. Maybe we can keep their heads down," yelled Boomer. The squad had heard Boomer. They needed no command from Lisky. They all started shooting.

The Item Company Marines and the North Koreans exchanged fire sporadically. After a little time it was apparent that the enemy was not about to surrender. Boomer figured they would have to attack the mound or bomb it out. Captain Eisle, the company commander, had another idea. He sent for an interpreter. A South Korean Marine came forward and tried to talk the NKPA troops into surrender. The response was a flurry of grenades. Eisle shook his head. "That's the way they wanted to play the game, so be it." The Captain called back to the battalion and had the bulldozer tank come forward and bury them.

Three hundred yards down the road, some I Company troops heard voices coming from another mound. It turned out to be a many-holed warren. This time they brought an M-26 tank forward and it fired two rounds into one of the holes. A whole platoon of North Koreans scrambled out of the warren and surrendered. Bursts of flame followed them out. Apparently the tank rounds had hit a small arsenal hidden inside the mound.

Item Company had no more problems. They swept their area and called it secure. How Company had cleared the causeway to the mainland and the industrial area. George had taken Radio Hill so with the exception of the lighthouse at Solwolmi-do, and a few bypassed areas, the island was secured. By 1030 the bypassed areas, including another bunker that was buried by the tanks, were also cleared. George Company still had the lighthouse mission. Matt took his squad and two tanks out on the causeway that led to the lighthouse. And by 1130, that too was taken.

Wolmi-do was now totally in U.S. Hands. Artillery spotters, engineers and other support personnel rolled onto the island to set the stage for the next part of the invasion. The cost of the attack, on the part of the Marines, was seventeen wounded, none seriously. The enemy statistics showed 136 prisoners and 108 dead. There had been over 400 enemy troops on the island originally. The remaining troops were buried in the rubble.

"You know, when you first mentioned the tides here, I wasn't sure what you meant, or why that would be a problem. But I sure can see it now," ventured Matt.

The platoon was sitting in the trench line the NKPA had dug near the top of Radio Hill, looking out over the Inchon harbor. The harbor, which stretched for miles, was a sea of mud.

"Yeah, they told us the tides move twenty or thirty feet. That only gives us a couple of hours of maneuverable water on each side of high tide," said Mark.

Matt did some quick figures, then looked at his brother.

"Usually, it's about twelve hours from high tide to high tide. Right?"

"Give or take a little."

"If you can only use two hours on each side of high tide, you've only got eight hours a day you can use this port."

"Four of those hours will probably be in the dark, too."

"A planning nightmare."

"The fact that they wanted to take this island first, to protect the harbor, complicated the planning even more."

"Right. We had to come in on one high tide, and then they have to wait for the next one for the rest of the invasion."

"What time is it?" asked Jacques. He had been dozing behind Matt and Mark. Ivan was fast asleep beside him.

"Thirteen hundred," replied Mark, glancing at his watch.

"When does the rest of the attack start?"

"I'm not sure. I think about fifteen hundred. You'll know by the naval gunfire. . They'll start about an hour before the landing."

Jacques nodded.

They sat quietly for a while. Naval gunfire spotters and air and artillery forward observers were mapping positions of suspected enemy activity on the mainland. It was quiet enough to hear their pencils scratching on the maps and transparencies. The next bombardment would be aimed at the specific targets that they marked

Matt was starting to doze when he suddenly became aware of the silence. He opened his eyes and looked around. Everything was still. The air was still. The troops all around him were sleeping or resting quietly. There was no movement on the mainland. No planes flew overhead. The tide was too far out for even small boats to be moving nearby.

He looked out to sea. He could see the crenellated outlines of many ships in the distance but nothing was distinct.

Earlier there had been so much noise, from gunfire, explosions, aircraft, tank motors, boat engines, and people shouting. Now, nothing. The transition was drastic. It was eerie.

"Do you know how the rest of the division is coming in?" Matt asked, turning to Mark who was also getting drowsy.

Mark looked at Matt for a few seconds, as he willed himself more alert, and then he responded.

"Uh, let's see. The other battalions in the Fifth Marines will land over there on Red Beach. That's on the other side of North Point." He was pointing to the north. "Item Company and part of How Company should be able to watch them come in."

"Front row seats for Luke and John."

Mark smiled at the remark. "Sometime after the other battalions land we will cross the causeway and join them."

"What about the First Marines?"

"Uh, Blue Beach. They'll be way over there." He swung around and pointed to the south. "On the other side of the port. See that point that sticks out? They'll be on the other side of that."

Matt nodded. He could see the point.

"We should get good view. Not as good as the other guys, but still pretty good."

Ivan and Jacques woke up while Mark was talking. "It is nice to have an officer to get information from. Too many times, we peons are kept in the dark. It is nice to know," said Jacques.

Mark blushed. He had a philosophy about this. "I agree, Jacques. I think we should keep everyone up to speed all the time. I think it makes for a better Marine. Most of the times I think the commanders just forget or they don't even think about it. I'll try to be different. I'll keep you guys abreast of everything I know."

Ivan nodded. "Good."

Mark's H-Hour estimate of fifteen hundred proved a little optimistic. The actual landing hour was pushed forward to 1730. The tides were just not to be hurried. This would only give the landing forces about two and a half or three hours of daylight, so the byword became haste.

"That's pretty scary," said Luke. "I wouldn't want to have to climb ladders while someone is shooting at me."

John had borrowed some binoculars from Lieutenant Boomer and was observing the landing to their left close up. The sea wall there was high, necessitating the use of scaling ladders. There seemed to be confusion as anxious green clad troops stacked up waiting their turn.

Suddenly John and Luke were jolted by a roaring voice from behind them.

"Goddamn it you shitheads, start putting some fire on that machine gun over on the left. Help those guys out." It was Technical Sergeant Meek the grizzled, lumpy-faced, company gunny.

The disciplined Marines scrambled immediately. Within seconds, twelve men were firing over the heads of the landing force into the enemy gun position. It was at least 500 yards away but rounds were hitting near the opening. The enemy machine gun fire slowed.

John was lying down, trying to achieve a steady shooting position. He wanted accuracy. He set his sight elevation at 600 yards. He put a little left windage on it because of the breeze. He looked through the peep sight, and set the front sight blade at six o'clock on the opening in the concrete bunker. Yellow flashes sparked intermittently from the opening. When he saw the next flash, he squeezed the trigger.

The flashes stopped for a few seconds then started again. The recoil had rolled John a little, but he had attained the steady position he wanted so his body rolled right back to a good firing position. Within a second, he had the bunker aperture lined up at six o'clock again and fired. One more time and the bunker was silent. The movement on the beach sped up. One Marine, when he reached the top of the sea wall turned around and looked back at John. He waved at him.

Gunny Meeks came over to John.

"It looks to me like you were the one that silenced that gun, Flaraty. That was good shooting." His fleshy lips were wrapped around a lump of tobacco and when he spoke he sprayed brown saliva. "Got to be at least five, six hundred yards. Good work." He moved around the men, alternately praising them for the help they gave and chewing them out for failing to react quicker.

"Here comes the cavalry," panted Angie Marsucci as he and the rest of the Andrews Sisters jogged down the road toward Ascom City. Their launcher tubes and other equipment rattled and clanked against their bodies as they ran.

"Yeah, but they had horses. We got to do it on foot" panted back an equally winded McAndrew, stumbling along next to his buddy.

Two days after the landing at Inchon, the whole First Marine Division had gotten into high gear and was now twenty miles inland. The Sisters, however, had been called forward to meet a threat.

As on the other occasion, back inside the Pusan Perimeter, Lieutenant Gibbons was waiting for them. He stood at the base of a small hill on the left side of the road. Also as he had done before, he set up the positions for them. The two launchers were placed halfway up the side of the hill. At the bottom of the hill was a recoilless rifle team. They were all pointed to the northeast toward a place where the road turned to the east and went behind a small rise in the land.

Near that turn, on a hill that overlooked the bend in the road was the infantry platoon that had called in the report, which sent the tank killer teams scrambling. The report had been chilling. There were six T-34s coming down that road, supported by about 250 enemy infantry.

Behind the Andrews Sisters, however, they could hear the unmistakable but welcome sounds of the five M-26 tanks coming up the road to join the battle.

The infantry platoon that had first noticed the advancing behemoths stayed hidden and let the enemy tanks pass their position. The enemy troops were either riding on the vehicles or trailing behind. When they reached the place on the road where the rocket and recoilless rifle troops could see them, they were trapped.

The platoon opened up on the enemy infantry with all of their weapons, rifles, BARs, Machine guns and carbines. The NKPA infantry died in bunches. The murderous fire swept the tanks clean and cut down the walking enemy like wheat scythed in a field.

A rocket team from the platoon on the hill sneaked down behind the tanks and let loose with a 2.35-inch rocket round. The lead tank was immediately stopped, as a tread spun off, shattering into a thousand pieces. The more powerful 3.5s were replacing the 2.35-inch rockets, the old bazookas, but some units still carried the older weapon.

The rocket team then pumped two more rockets into the tank and it burst into flames. The Andrews Sisters and the recoilless rifles opened up on the remaining tanks. Causing them all to stop. One of the T-34's tried to swing into a nearby rice paddy to obtain some maneuvering room. Just as he did so, the Marine tanks showed up and cut loose with their 90 millimeter guns. The rocket and rifle teams continued their fire.

So many rounds impacted on the enemy tanks in the next few seconds, that the smoke and flames they produced restricted visibility for a full five minutes. When the smoke cleared a horrifying scene of destruction was revealed. There were more than 250 dead soldiers lying around the road and the tanks were smoldering ruins. Almost every single member of the enemy force was dead. Not one single Marine was even nicked.

The platoon came down off the hill to survey the damage. The rocket teams moved forward, equally curious.

"God, All Mighty, whata scene," said Anderson.

"If I hadn't seen it, I wouldn't have believed it," said Hankins.

McAndrew and Marsucci just stared.

Some of the tank crews came forward to admire their handiwork. They looked from tank to tank. They had to stand back a little because of the heat and the danger of rounds cooking off.

"Those 90 millimeter rounds sure do a lot of damage," said one of the tankers.

"So do the rockets," said McAndrews.

The tanker looked at McAndrews.

"Your tinker toys didn't do this. We did."

Marsucci bristled.

"Hey shithead, we stopped 'em first. You just cleaned up."

"Who the hell you calling a shithead?" The tanker now joined by other tankers started, to move forward.

Lieutenant Gibbons stepped in.

"Halt! Everyone stop!"

He looked at the tankers. They were still moving forward.

"I said, halt!" he yelled in a louder voice. He turned to look at the Sisters. They had stopped but they were together. They were ready to fight.

The first tanker looked at the lieutenant and stopped.

"Lieutenant, these shitheads . . . ."

"Silence, Marine."

The tanker shut up. Gibbons looked at the man with the funny tankers helmet.

"I heard the whole thing. What a stupid, fucking thing to fight about. We just knocked off six tanks and more than two hundred troops and all you want to do is fight each other. You all get credit." He waved his arms inclusively. "You all fired at the same time. What about the guy with the 2.35 rocket?" He pointed back toward the hill. "He knocked out a tank all by himself." He looked at them with real anger. He couldn't believe anyone would want to fight over this. Maybe it was the pressure, the tension.

"Get back to your vehicles. Any more of this shit and you get run up."

The tankers started to back away, reluctantly. Finally, they turned and moved back to their iron monsters. The original complainer was still grumbling.

The Sisters also calmed down. They turned to look at their handiwork. Others joined them.

The Marine tanks had just turned and were lurching their way back to their original position in the attack columns, when a convoy of jeeps came around them and roared up to the spot where the troops had been admiring their work. They came to a halt, in a cloud of dust and disgorged fifteen or twenty people. A few started to take pictures of the burning tanks and the corpses. Others just moved forward to get a better view. The press had arrived. The lead jeep stopped over a little culvert that ran under the road. In the jeep were General MacArthur and more brass than the Andrews Sisters had ever seen in one place.

The general wanted to see as much of the frontline fighting as he could, so he had bullied his way past his subordinates objections to reach this point. He stood looking at the burning tanks and he marveled. He noted the rocket team standing on the side of the road and walked over to them.

"Did you do this son?" he asked McAndrew.

"Yes, sir. Me and my teams here," he pointed at the other three Marines.

"Wonderful. Did you have any help?"

"Uh, yes, sir. The tanks helped."

"And the recoilless rifles over there, too, sir," said Marsucci, not to be left out.

"That's what it takes doesn't it son? Teams of people. It takes teams to kill tanks."

"Yes, sir. It sure does, sir," said Hankins.

MacArthur looked around again. Black smoke curled up from a half dozen places around the road. He wanted to get closer to the tanks, but they were still too hot. Even though the fight had been over some time ago, the acrid smell of explosives was still in the air.

He looked at the Marines again. They looked at him in his old battered cap, sunglasses, corncob pipe and leather jacket, and smiled.

"Keep up the good work, men. We'll get these people out of this country real soon with men like you. Then we can all go home."

Almost involuntarily, they all saluted.

The general got back into his jeep, as did all the brass and the reporters. The jeeps turned around and went back down the road to the rear.

A few minutes later, McAndrew heard something from the culvert under the spot where General MacArthur's jeep had stopped. He moved over to the opening and heard another noise. He motioned the rest of the Sisters over. McAndrew and Anderson covered one end of the tube under the road, Marsucci and Hankins the other.

McAndrew called out. No response. He placed his M-1 into the opening and fired a round. Then he fired again. He heard the sound of shuffling and them a head emerged and then another and another. All in all, there were seven NKPA soldiers in the culvert. They had been within a few feet of the Commander-in-Chief of all UN forces in Korea and a number of other high military officials and they did not realize it. One well-placed grenade could have changed the whole color of the war. They were fortunate themselves however. They were the only Red survivors of this engagement.

On the way back to their unit, the Sisters had a disagreement over their victory song. They finally settled on a number of reward and celebration, *Drinking Rum and Coca-Cola.*

17
The Juggernaut

The First Marine Division continued on its way, moving easterly from the west coast where they had made their landing, and heading for the South Korean capital, Seoul. The word, Seoul, means capital in Korean. They rolled over opposition easily until they reached the outskirts of the city, where North Korean resistance stiffened. Some of the North Korean units that had been in the southern part of the country investing the Eighth Army at Pusan had been brought north to reinforce their units defending Seoul, after the Marine landing at Inchon. Ironically, removing those NKPA units from the Pusan area was just what the Eighth Army needed to allow them to launch their breakout.

Luke cautiously peered around the corner of a building looked up the length of the littered street. Battered two and three story buildings leaned over the roadway. Concrete and steel chunks were scattered on the pavement and against some of the bombed out structures. A pile of such materiel blocked the intersection at the end of the street. He guessed that the pile was a defensive position and hid some of the NKPD troops using it as a barricade.

He looked across the street. He saw a large doorway with two wooden doors in a wall to his right front. The second floor of the building had collapsed. The doorway, however, would provide some cover. He decided when he made his dash across the street that was where he would head. "Doc" Pettigrew was behind him. Corporal Lisky was behind Pettigrew.

He pointed the doorway out to Pettigrew. Pettigrew nodded. Luke then waved to get Sanchez' attention. Sanchez, who was a few yards back, was the BAR man. He also nodded.

Luke took a breath and ran across the street, dodging the bigger lumps of stone. Pettigrew was right on his tail. They made it without incident, slamming into the wooden doors at almost the same time. They looked back. Sanchez had swung out into the street to protect them, finding his own pile of rocks. The BAR's biped was propped on top of the rubble. The rest of the squad was still behind the building. Luke and Pettigrew looked forward at the rock pile in the intersection and saw movement. There *were* enemy troops there. They hadn't seen the two Marines cross the street in time to react. The Reds now scrambled, trying to set up a defense.

Luke noted they had a rocket tube, exactly what he had feared. An Army tank was moving up behind the Marines to help them with their assault, but they had to protect that tank from this rocket launcher. Luke called across the street.

"Tell Lisky they got a rocket launcher. We'll need help." Sanchez nodded and yelled something back.

Luke's adrenaline was flowing. He was sacred but he also very much felt alive. All his senses were sharpened. He could see better, hear better and react faster. His company had been fighting for three few days without letup, but for some reason he was not tired. He looked again at the rubble barricade. He could see five or six enemy soldiers now. Then he heard the tank.

The tank, an M-24, was rattling down the side street where the rest of Luke's squad remained. It was about to swing out onto the main thoroughfare, facing the barricade. The M-24 was the generation of tank before the M-26. Its main gun was 75-millimeter gun as opposed to the 90-millimeter gun on the M-26. It was still a good tank. There hadn't been enough Marine tanks for the invasion of Seoul so the Marines borrowed some Army tanks and crews.

The iron horse paused for a moment and then pivoted on its tracks and moved in a jerking fashion onto the street. Tanks turn by stopping and starting the treads on each side so that the vehicle slides from place to place a little at a time. It sometimes looked to the observer, like a stop action movie.

Luke looked at the barricade again. He could now count about fifteen or twenty soldiers and another rocket tube. The Reds had also seen the tank. Luke looked at Pettigrew. They had to do something.

Luke's position in the doorway hid him from the enemy. Luke and Pettigrew decided they could get off a couple of shots at the enemy rocketeers and then drop back. That would buy some time for the tank to swivel and fire on the position.

Luke rose up, Pettigrew next to him. They fired as fast as they could, emptying their eight-round clips. Some of the soldiers behind the barricade went down. The enemy *had* been surprised. Luke couldn't be sure if they got the rocketeers or not however. He dropped back to reload. Pettigrew was already fumbling a new clip into his breech. They heard the BAR being fired by Sanchez and then they heard the larger, deeper-throated 50 caliber machine gun from the tank. Luke looked out. He saw the rounds smacking into the stone blocks of the barricade and ric-ocheting down the street.

One of the enemy rocket tubes appeared slowly over the top of the barricade. Luke watched. As soon as Luke saw the gunner, he poured his whole clip into the area. The tube dropped, clattering to the front of the pile of rubble.

The tank moved closer, rattling and clanking and crunching over fragments. Then it fired its first round, rocking back on its treads, and blowing a giant hole blew in the middle of the rock pile. Bodies flew. Enemy troops started to run. Luke and Pettigrew fired into the fleeing group. The rest of Luke's squad had emerged from behind the building and joined in the slaughter. The tank fired a second round at the barri-cade. It disintegrated into flying bits.

A head appeared in a second story window across from Luke and Pettigrew. It was another Red soldier and he held another rocket launch-er. Pettigrew fired one round, the soldier was falling from the window down to the pavement. Luke and "Doc" Pettigrew had "killed" three rocket launcher teams in just a few minutes of action.

The tank commander, an Army sergeant, popped the top of his tank and stood up to look around. He smiled beneath his funny look-ing helmet when he saw the dead rocket man. He looked at Luke and Doc and waved his thanks. Corporal Lisky climbed up on the tank and told the Sergeant that Luke and Pettigrew had gotten two others too. He yelled down that beers were on him when they were able to secure for the night.

They resumed their march and moved slowly down the street, the squad looking in all directions, the tank lumbering along in their midst.

Proceeding slowly, they had progressed a few blocks when they came under fire again from an automatic weapon on the roof of a small building. The first few rounds hit two members of the squad. Lisky got on the tank phone and told the tank where to fire. The tank knocked the gun out with one round. They took the time to pick up their wounded and return them back to the rear.

The squad walked and the tank clattered down the street. During the first fight at the barricade they had sent for help. Two 3.5 rocket section s finally showed up and then they also fell in behind the tank.

Two streets over, John's squad was fighting its way along another battle-cluttered street. Downed light poles canted at crazy angles. They did not have a tank, so they were making do with rifles, BARs, 3.5's and machine guns.

"Flaraty, over on the right. See it?"

Lugo was pointing to a window on the second floor.

John looked at the window intently. Then he saw it. It was the muzzle of a machine gun.

"I got it, Frank." John turned around. "Let's see if the rocket guys can get it. I'm getting tired of running up and down stairs."

Lugo called back. Two rocket teams came forward. They both zeroed in on the window and blew the whole corner of the building off. There was no trace left of a gun or an enemy.

John smiled in grim satisfaction. "That's the way to fight a war."

They continued down the street. No shots were fired at them, so they made good progress. The squad was deployed in a wedge formation and no one made a move without being covered. As good as their tactics were, however sometimes some things can't be anticipated. They had already passed one three-story building when they received fire from that building. Two men went down, hit from the rear.

John acted on instinct. He dashed to the side of the building, so he was out of the line of fire. His fire team followed him and they were pressed against a wall right next to a window. John pulled a grenade off his suspender and motioned to Lugo. Lugo nodded and motioned to the BAR man, Lawton. Lawton nodded.

As soon as Lugo saw the BAR man nod, he jumped forward to the window and smashed it in with the butt of his rifle. John had already removed the grenade pin, so he released the spoon reached around the window frame, and threw the grenade through the broken window. The grenade blew. Glass and debris flashed past them. Lawton moved forward and fired a burst into the room. All four jumped through the yawning opening. The room was empty, but it had two doors leading elsewhere.

They fired a burst into each door and then swung them open cautiously. One led to another room. It was empty. There was no door in that room. The other led into a hallway, with stairs going up to a second floor. There were no signs of habitation. John poked himself cautiously around the corner into the hall. No one was in sight. He led the group out slowly, looking in all directions. They approached a door situated at the end of the hall carefully. Lugo was the last in line. He kept an eye on the stairs. The door at the end of the hall went to the outside. They were going to have to climb the stairs.

"Shit," said John. "This is the fourth stairway today."

Lugo laughed nervously. "I'll go first this time. You back me up."

John nodded. He had gone first on the other three.

Lugo nodded to Lawton. Lawton released two short bursts from the BAR into the ceiling. Plaster showered down like white smoke with pieces. As soon as Lawton lowered his weapon, they charged up the stairs, Lugo in the lead with John right behind. The BAR man and his helper brought up from the rear.

At the top of the stairs they faced a door, in front of them and a landing that ran around the stairway opening to the next set of stairs. They quickly spread out on both sides of the door and Lugo nodded to Lawton. Lawton fired a long burst into the door. They heard a cry. Then an automatic weapon fired back at them from within the room. All four Marines dove for the floor. The bullets passed over their heads, but the door now had a large, jagged opening in the middle.

John used the opening to throw a grenade through. The explosion was followed by silence. He crept over to the door. It was shattered and hanging by one hinge. Inside were two Red soldiers. One was dead. The other was barely alive or so it seemed.

John and Lawton climbed the stairs to the third floor just to make sure there were no other Reds above them. The top floor was empty. As they descended again, they heard two shots from the room with the "dead" soldiers in it and they rushed to the door. Lugo was down with a chest wound. Kelly, the other team member, was just pulling his bayonet out of the Red who had been wounded before.

"The bastard was faking it," screamed Kelly. "He only had a small wound"

He was dead now. John went over to Lugo. He was gasping for air. Pink bubbles of blood were seeping out of the wound in his chest. John pulled his shirt open and pressed his hand on the wound. He had to stop the loss of air from the lung.

"Kelly, call down to the street to send the Corpsman. Lugo's hit bad."

Kelly went to the window. Within minutes two corpsmen were in the room working on Lugo. The rest of the team had to leave. The squad had to keep moving.

Thanks to John's quick thinking, Lugo would survive but he was headed back to a hospital in Japan. Lieutenant Boomer told John to take over the fire team.

A few streets away, Matt's squad moved in a wedge formation down a broad avenue. Two rows of trolley tracks ran down the middle of the street. Jacques' fire team was on point. Ivan's was on the left, Womack's on the right. Matt did not have the luxury of a tank or a rocket team. They would have to do things the old-fashioned way — bullets, grenades and satchel charges. The rest of the platoon was about fifty yards behind them. That group had flamethrowers.

The buildings in this part of the city were three and four story structures, which provided many places for hidden riflemen. So far, Matt's squad had encountered little resistance, however. Their job was to try to keep moving, to take on any resistance they met, but not to clear the buildings room by room. That would be left for those who followed. MacArthur wanted to secure Seoul by September 25, the three-month anniversary of the North Korean sneak attack.

They proceeded cautiously, wary eyes scanning rooftops and blasted windows. Power lines were down. Light poles hung at rakish angles, supported by tangled cables and burned out vehicles. The street was littered with broken concrete and stone. A steady stream of dazed Koreans moved along the left side of the street, making their way out of the beleaguered city, with their belongings on their heads or piled high in small hand carts. Ivan eyed the line of refugees suspiciously. It would be easy to hide a gunman in that group.

Jacques's team approached a large intersection. Trolley tracks ran down the middle of the cross street. Jacques wondered what the Koreans did if trolleys running east and west crossed the track intersection at the same time as trolleys running north and south. He smiled at the thought.

The cross street was a tree-lined boulevard and had probably been quite pretty before the bombing and shelling. Now the trees were blasted stumps. The battered buildings held shattered storefronts. Embattled refugees trudged along this street, also.

Jacques looked to the left. A few streets over he could see what appeared to be troops moving in the same easterly direction. To his right he could not see more than one street due to a curve in the road. He turned back to Matt, some twenty-five yards behind him. He waved him up.

"How do you want to handle this intersection, mon ami? It is a very wide area."

Matt looked up and down the street. "You are correct, my astute legionnaire. Let me see what Mark wants to do."

Minutes later, they were all looking around the corner of a building, trying to decide the best approach. They decided to use a squad rush movement, where one squad at a time moved through the intersection as fast as possible while the other squads set up to support them with fire if needed, similar to fire and maneuver tactics.

Before they could put their plan into operation, however, they heard the unmistakable rattling, clanking, gear meshing sounds. It was a tank.

And it was coming around the right turn in the street about 100 yards away. The group was galvanized into action.

"Get Wingo up here with some satchel charges" Mark yelled to his runner. "Send Cormack and his flamethrowers up too." The runner dashed back to the rest of the platoon.

"Matt, think you and your guys can work your way along the street on the right without being seen and come up alongside the tank?"

"Yeah, I think so. They can't see too well to the side. If we wait until they're almost even with us, it should work. You want us to place the charges?"

"Right. We'll draw their fire. You come in from the side and put the satchels in the treads. When the treads get blown, we move the flamethrowers in. That should suffocate them. See any better way?"

Matt thought a moment. He could hear the tank getting closer. "No. Sounds good to me. Maybe we can work around behind the tank and place charges on the other side, too." His mind was alert, thinking fast. "Actually you've got the dangerous job. You have to draw his attention."

"Yes, I know." His smile was a nervous smile. We'll have to shoot and move so he can't zero in on us. We can't do much with our rifles, but if we can just occupy him . . . ."

"Until *we* get done," Matt finished the thought with a smile. "You'll have to get them to stop. The satchel fuse needs a few seconds."

"I know. We'll do what we can."

Mark quickly set up the other squads for a "shoot and move" tactic. One squad would fire at the tank from the left and then run to the right, behind the other squad. Then that second squad would fire and move to the left, noting how the tank turret swung each time. If they were fast enough, and guessed right, they should be okay for a few minutes.

One of the runners ran up with the satchel charges. Matt passed them out to Jacques, Ivan and Womack. He kept one for himself. Slinging their rifles on their backs, they moved up to the corner on the right side and pressed against the building. The flamethrower operators moved up behind them and pushed into a doorway.

Matt peered around the corner. The tank was almost abreast of them. Sweat burned his eyes. He signaled his men to kneel. Just as the tank entered the intersection, the Second Squad fired up on them. The tank was slow to react. As soon as the riflemen started firing, Matt ran around the corner in a crouch, the rest of the squad trailing behind. He dropped Jacques and Womack off and proceeded past the rear of the tank running around to the other side. Ivan followed.

They could hear the gears and the servomechanism whirring as the turret moved to face the rest of the platoon. The heat coming from the exhaust was intense. The tank's machine guns were firing, but the cannon hadn't fired yet. Matt and Ivan pulled the fuses on their satchels and dropped them inside the treads into the gears.

Just as they stepped back, they heard an explosion and then another. Jacques and Womack's charges had gone off. The tank lurched and then listed to its left. Matt and Ivan ran down the street to get away from their charges. Their satchels went off simultaneously. The tank shuddered and then pivoted to its right as the driver tried to move out of the area. It was too late. The treads were off on both sides. It was now a "tiger at bay," on its last legs but still dangerous.

As if to demonstrate its ferocity, the metal monster unleashed a cannon round at the infantry squads on the street. Concrete and wood chunks flew off the corner building and showered down onto the huddled troops. This was quickly followed by another round that roared through the hole made by the first round and exploded inside the building

While the tank was reloading and rotating the turret, one of the flamethrower operators moved up and "snapped" his match. The spurting gasoline ignited and the engulfed the tank from its left side. He poured it onto the tank until the paint on the turret began to bubble and burn.

The turret was still turning and the machine gun was still firing. The flamethrower man continued to shower the behemoth with fire, while moving slowly to his right to avoid the moving cupola. The second flamethrower man was kneeling at the corner. When the turret swung past him he jumped out onto the street and moved past the front of the tank to his left in order to get to the tank's other side. As soon as he was set, he started to pour burning liquid onto that side also.

When the first flamethrower ran out of fuel, his weapon shut off. He ran down the street as quick as he could to avoid retaliation. The second operator continued to pour it on and then the turret stopped moving. He shut off his "gun," a little flame lingering at the nozzle like a pilot light, and watched. After a moment, the hatch opened and a gasping North Korean tried to climb out. He was ripped to pieces by small arms fire. When he slumped over, Ivan ran up and climbed onto the tank. He stuffed the unfortunate soldier back down into the opening and then dropped a grenade behind him and jumped off the tank. Ivan had burned his hands on the hot metal but he seemed unaware of the pain. Seconds later there were a number of violent discharges inside the metal coffin as the grenade triggered the tank's ammunition supply. The tank was dead. The battle at the intersection was over.

18
Mail Call
Dateline: Korea. September 21, 1950

Wendell Turner reporting to you again from the battlefields of Korea. The Marines, after their dramatic landing at Inchon on September 15, have moved briskly across the Korean peninsula, and are presently investing Seoul, the capital of this war torn country. My present location, however, is in the south, near Pusan with the Eighth Army.

For the eclectic group of soldiers that make up the Eighth Army, breaking out from the Pusan Perimeter was not, in the traditional sense, a breakout — at least at first. There was no sudden penetration of enemy lines, attacking forces pushing through the main line of resistance and spreading out in the rear to exploit their gains. There was no rolling back of enemy lines or collapsing of resistance, no lightening spearhead racing to some objective. It was more a stiffening of the Eighth Army lines at first, followed by tentative probes that resulted in a few small successes.

One of the reasons for the slow breakout was that in the Naktong River area, at the time of the UN thrust, the NKPA apparently had been reinforcing their depleted defense with troops from northern areas. The ROK, or Republic of Korea forces, part of the UN contingent, had noticed this shifting earlier. The first UN efforts bumped into these reinforced elements of the North Korean forces in their efforts to cross the Naktong River.

The Eighth Army had also been reinforced with troops from Turkey, England, Greece and a few other countries. However, even though UN troop levels were growing the UN forces were not yet large enough to substantially offset the additional troops being brought in by the Communists.

As the new UN troops arrived, at first they replaced the Marines, who had been pulled out to join their division in the landing at Inchon. As more units were fed into the fray, they were able to build the pressure on the NKPA, but the North Korean's own influx of new troops made it possible for them to resist the pressure and hold the line. It became a frustrating and irritating situation on both sides. Each had moved new people into the area in order to launch offensives, yet both sides had to use their additional forces just to maintain the status quo.

One battle in particular demonstrated the frustrations of the situation. On Hill 174, near Taegu, units of the U.S. Fifth Cavalry Division had to take and retake the hill eleven times before they were able to hold it.

Finally, on the September 18th, a unit of the Army's 24th Infantry Division crossed the Naktong River against stiff resistance, and established a beachhead. The rest of the Division quickly followed and they were finally able to exploit their gains. The Eighth Army's balky engine began to come to life. Within a few days, they were driving forward at full speed. If predictions are correct, within a few more days, maybe a week, they will join up with the Marines and the U.S. Seventh Division in or near Seoul and the rout will be complete.

"Frank! Come in. How are you doing?" The tall, dark-haired man pushed away from his field desk and stood quickly. He reached out to accept the extended hand. "How long has it been, two, three years?"

"All of that, Mike. It's good to see you again."

"The last time was the conference in New York, right?"

"Right. We played golf the last day."

The dark man laughed. "You played golf. I drowned golf balls."

Frank smiled. "You *did* have a bad day."

"Bad? I started with a dozen balls, I found three balls lost by others and I still had to borrow two from you to finish the round. I call that a disaster."

They laughed again.

"Goes to prove you were spending time doing something else besides playing golf. Like God's work."

"You always did have a flair for Irish blarney, Frank." Mike's dark eyes twinkled. "Thanks for the compliment."

Mike turned and grabbed a camp chair and planted it next to his desk. He sat in his own chair and motioned to Frank. Frank took the proffered chair and sat down.

Frank was in his early forties. He had a square face, not unlike Spencer Tracey, and gray hair. He was a husky man. His baggy herringbone utility uniform did not fit well. It was easy to tell he was not used to wearing such clothes. He wore the double silver bars of a Naval Lieutenant on one collar point and Chaplain's Cross on the other. He held his cap in his hand. His full name was Lieutenant Francis X. Canavan, Naval Chaplains Corps. He came from the Boston Diocese.

Mike, whose full name was Miguel Pereira, was also a priest. He was a Captain in the Army, which is the equivalent rank of a naval lieutenant. He was taller and thinner than Frank, also a little younger. His hair was still very dark. He, too, wore a field uniform, called fatigues in the Army, but for some reason his uniform fit him better. He came from Rhode Island.

"It's really good to see you again, Frank but I wish it wasn't under these circumstances." His face took on a serious mien. He looked at his friend with compassion. "You know why I sent for you?"

"Your note said you thought you found had found Kevin's body." The information had come as a bit of a shock. He knew Kevin was in Korea working with the missions but he had no idea where he was. "Are you sure it's him?"

"We'll go out to the site in a minute. You can identify him." He turned in his chair and reached into one of the slots in his desk and pulled out a black book. He passed the book to his friend. "One of the local people brought this to our soldiers when we first entered the town. It took a little while to find out what she was saying but we finally found an interpreter."

Canavan stared at the book while he listened to Father Pereira. He had one exactly like it.

"Your brother apparently had lived and worked in this area for some time. The people liked him. He healed the sick, worked their farms with them, played with the children . . . ." His voice faded. He looked at his friend, his eyes filled with compassion. "He had loaned the book to the woman's son. Apparently Kevin had been teaching him how to read and speak English. When the Communists came, they killed all the men, including her son. They also killed Kevin. She hid the book. She didn't understand what it was, but she knew it was special somehow."

Frank still didn't say anything. His hands trembled. He continued to stare at the unopened tome.

"Our GIs, the ones who made the first contact with her," Pereira continued, "brought the book to me. After I spoke to the woman, she showed me the grave site. It's a mass grave. You'll see it. We've been finding mass grave sites quite frequently as we've pushed the North Koreans further north. Some have contained the bodies of GIs but most have been locals. They treated the prisoners and the local people badly. A sad chapter written by a cruel people." He was choked by the remembrance. "We would have bypassed this site except for this woman."

Father Canavan turned the book over in his hands. It was a mottled black, leather-covered Bible. Pieces of the leather had worn or broken off, leaving jagged tan and brown abrasions in various places. The book had seen tough times.

He opened it. On the left inside cover was a sticker that said "Ex Libris" in ornate print. Beneath that was a name written in neat script, "Kevin P. Canavan." On the right page, also in the same neat but faded script, was a note.

"To Kevin, on your ordination. May the Lord be always with you as you journey down the road to Salvation. Mother."

His eyes filled, tears ran down his cheek. His Bible had the same message.

Frank Canavan had been born in Ireland. His father and two of his brothers had come to America in the late twenties. The rest of his family, including his mother, two sisters, and his brother Kevin, had stayed in Ireland. The plan had been for them to come to America after Frank's father was settled. The Great Depression intervened, however, and the elder Canavan never did get settled. He died in poverty. Frank and his brothers went back to Ireland. America remained with him, however, and after a year or two in Ireland, Frank returned to the United States and entered the seminary. After his ordination, he worked as a parish priest until he decided he wanted to become a chaplain. During World War II, he served in the Pacific. His present assignment was with the First Marine Division.

His brother Kevin, the youngest in the family, became a missionary priest during the Second World War, and when that conflict ended he had come to Korea. He had lived with the Korean people for almost five years.

Father Pereira stood and went to Father Canavan. He put a hand on his shoulder. Canavan put his head down and sobbed quietly. After a few moments he stood up. With grief-strained eyes he looked at his friend. "Okay Mike, I'm ready."

The journey to the grave site in Pereira's jeep took fifteen minutes. Father Mike led him into a field. Frank could see the freshly turned earth. It was a big site. With each step, the odor of death assailed them. The chaplains reached into their pocket and took out the surgical masks they always carried. Chaplains spent a great deal of time with dead bodies. The masks weren't very effective in odor control, but they were better than nothing.

The townspeople had separated Kevin's body from the others. For all intents and purposes, the other bodies were still buried although a few body parts and scraps of clothing were exposed here and there. Frank stepped down into the excavation. The odor nearly overwhelmed him but he endured.

Kevin's partly decomposed body was still recognizable. Frank put his hand into his pocket, took out his vial of Chrism (Holy Oil) and anointed the body parts he could reach. He had to turn the body over to anoint the hands because they were still tied behind his back. It was then that Frank saw the gaping hole in the back of his brother's head. His emotions stirred.

Something caught his eye as he went through the sacramental ritual, a glint of metal. Trembling, he touched the metal piece. It was a medal, a miraculous medal. It was pinned to the inside of Kevin's shirt. Those who had handled the body had missed it.

Frank took the medal, blessed it and put it in Kevin's hand. He stood up and made the sign of the cross over the grave. Then he climbed back out of the hole. He said a few more prayers, turned to Pereira and nodded. They walked back to the jeep in silence. The Koreans passed them as they went back to cover the grave. Father Canavan nodded to them and thanked them.

By the time he reached the jeep his emotions had changed. His sorrow was still strong, but he had been able to push it back. The tied hands, the hole in the back of the head, were too much. New feelings took over. They weren't priestly feelings.

September 17, 1950

Dear John,

How are things in Korea? Rather sticky, I imagine. I just read where the Marines made a big landing at Inchon. I guess you were in on that. I pray you guys are okay.

I'll bet you're surprised to get a letter from me. I also wrote to Luke. I don't know whether you get to see each other much, but if you do and he sees this before he gets my letter, tell him he's got one coming too.

The reason I'm writing to you is because of Barbara. I don't know if I'm doing the right thing or not, but I really feel I have to do something. I think she's got it bad. Ever since that night we all spent together, she has been a different person. She mopes around a lot. She still goes for tryouts and interviews, but I don't think her heart is in it. You know how she came from Minnesota to Hollywood to be a movie star and I came from New York to do the same thing. We used to talk about that all the time, you know, what pictures are casting, who's trying out and all that. Now all she talks about is you.

This is really letting the cat out of the bag, but last night she told me that she really cared for you and that you made love that night, (yes she actually told me this). After that she was worried that now you knew she hadn't been a virgin that you wouldn't want her for a girlfriend! Also she doesn't know why she did it on the first date but that she was afraid you would hold this against her, too. By the way that night, Luke and I also . . . well, you know. That was our first date also.

I told her it didn't matter to guys, (I hope it doesn't matter to you), as long as you stayed faithful when you were married. She told me that you had talked about your backgrounds and that you were an Irish Catholic and shouldn't do those things. I told her Swedish Lutherans like her aren't supposed to do these things either, but sometimes it happens.

She says Irish Catholics are different. They only marry virgins. I told her, I don't buy that. I don't think it matters. Love is what matters.

After this conversation, with her and with the way she's been moping around, I thought I better let you know. She says she wants to write to you but she's scared. She's afraid you won't write back.

It would help a great deal if you wrote to her. I don't know how you feel about her, but even if you have no real feelings (which I doubt), even a simple friendly letter would go a long way. Don't mention my letter however (This letter).

By the way, the reason she's not a virgin is because she tried out for a part in a movie last year and the only way she could get the part was to . . . well, you know. She got the part, a bit part, but her scene was cut. What a lousy deal. She told me the producer was really mad when he found out she was a virgin. How do you explain some men?

I really like you John and I like your brother a lot more than I care to admit. Someday I would like to get more serious with him if he wants to. I think he's still carrying a torch for that bitch in New York, though. I only knew him for a few weeks back then when he used to come to the school where we both modeled, but I guess he had an impact on me. My heart did a real leap when you guys showed up at our apartment. I just wish you'd had more than two days.

I just read back through this letter and I probably have overstepped my bounds. I really like Barbara though and I want to do what's right for her. If you have any feelings for her, please write to her.

Your "movie star" pal.

Margot

John looked up from the letter. He was sitting in a warehouse outside downtown Seoul surrounded by other Marines also reading mail and talking among themselves. He was leaning back on his seabag. It had been delivered from Japan along with the mail. His company had finished mopping up in Seoul two days ago, and was waiting for the next move. His thoughts ran in all directions. He didn't know what he felt for Barbara. He had intended to write to her. He just didn't seem to have the time. He thought about that for a minute. He had plenty of time on board the *Barnacle Bill.* But then he didn't know what his feelings were, or what to say. Now that he was here, he hadn't had time to think about anything but "soldiering."

He read back through the letter again. "She really cares for you." That's what Margot, said. Wow! No one had ever said that about him. That made him feel good. "She's worried about you finding out she hadn't been a virgin . . . ." Wow! She talks to her girlfriend about things like that. He asked himself, how *do* I feel about her not being a virgin? I don't really know. I guess I don't have a problem with that at this point. Like Margot says, if we were married I would want that to stop, but something in the past, that's not a problem.

How did he feel about Barbara? She was very pretty, beautiful really. She was tall and slim, blonde, blue eyed, with small dimples in her cheeks. She reminded him of Ingrid Bergman. When he came back to the U.S. would he look her up? Sure he would. He would be glad to see her again. Maybe they could — but wait!

John looked down at the letter and read it through once more. He looked up again. No, that *would* be wrong. He might hurt her if he tried to "make" her again. A month ago, they just seemed to fall into each other's arms. He hadn't sought to take her to bed. It just happened. Now that he thought about it, it was wrong. Or, at least it would be wrong to do it again.

But what did he feel for her? The sex thing was getting in the way. Sex was okay if there was love, right? The church taught that sex was only okay in marriage. They had a point. But an awful lot of people had sex without marriage. Would they all go to hell? Probably not, but a lot of them would.

He stared off into space, still thinking. The quiet murmur of the other troops as they sorted through duffel bags, wrote letters, and read mail barely penetrated his consciousness. He really liked Barbara. He enjoyed her company. Knowing she really "cared" for him had given him a thrill. He had known other girls back in New York, but he hadn't felt this "thrill" with any of them.

He thought more about their time together. The sex had seemed natural, but he guessed she felt guilty. She was not the type of girl who fell into bed easily. That pleased him. It fit his own values.

John reached for to his seabag and rummaged around in it until he found the letter writing folder he had bought onboard ship. He opened it, put the date on the page and then wrote,

Dear Barbara,

I'm sorry I haven't written sooner but I've been real busy, with sailing and training and fighting. I really enjoyed our day and night together and I look forward to coming home and seeing you again. It would really please me if you wrote to me, too. I need to keep my morale up and letters from home sure help.

Right now we're sitting in a warehouse waiting for orders. We've just been through a lot of fighting in Inchon and Seoul. We're resting. I don't know what comes next. Some people are saying we should be home soon. I don't believe that. If we do I'll drop by. I'd like to see you again. I hope you don't mind.

We've got some good guys in our Platoon . . . .

The rest of John's letter was just a friendly recitation of his activities since they had parted. He left out a lot of the fighting parts. He also asked about her family. He was uncomfortable with anything more intimate. Perhaps this would come later.

When he signed the letter, though, he used a phrase he remembered from a melancholy song popular during the war years,

" 'til we meet again,"

John

September 28, 1950

Dear Mark:

I received your letter today and I was sooooo glad to get it. I don't know what I expected. I know you had to fly to San Diego then get on a plane for Japan with stops on some islands and then you were to get to Korea after Japan. All this would take time and you wouldn't have a chance to write, but still, it seems like it took ages. I knew you were somebody special to me, but I guess I didn't realize how special. My anxieties surprise me and give me away.

I see that you wrote it on September 11. You said that was your first day in Korea. I feel good that you wrote to me as soon as you could.

How nice to run into your brothers. It's like a family reunion. You're all in the same battalion. That's great. You can see each other a lot that way.

I was wondering. Some of the stories in the newspaper say that the enemy has more than 100,000 troops. You told me a Marine Division has 20,000 troops. Are 20,000 Marines enough? Sure you're Marines right? Five to one in right up your alley right? Just kidding again. I'm sure that isn't all. There must be some other help, too. Oh yes, I forgot. You've also got some Army and Navy people to help don't you? And you have fighter planes to help, too.

You said you were getting set to go aboard ship and make a landing someplace. You didn't know where yet. I saw in the paper that a few days after your letter, the Marines landed at some place called Inchon and that the Fifth Marines took an island in the harbor first. Were you in on that? I figured the landing you mentioned was that one.

The paper is now talking about the capture of Seoul. The whole division was in on that. I guess you were involved. The pictures of the city look horrible, just rubble and bombed out buildings. I pray that you are okay. There was a picture a few days ago of General MacArthur looking at some Russian tanks that the Fifth Marines had destroyed. I first thought the Russians were involved. Then I read it again. They've been supplying the North Koreans with tanks. They really are a despicable people.

I just read back over what I had written. Lots of detail. I see that I really search for news about you. I guess I got it, the bug that is, worse than I realized. I went back to the beach the other day, by myself, just to see if I could see you and feel your presence again. It worked a little. I sat on the sand where we had our first kiss. I remember that very well. I tried to find the spot where we sat after our swim the first day. I think I found it.

All the cottages are closed. I climbed up on the porch where we stayed. The cottage is all locked up. The swing was put away. I still felt you there with me somehow.

I'm starting to feel melancholy. I miss you a great deal, even though I've only known you a short time. I think I got it bad. I've never felt like this before. You seemed to be saying the same things in your letter. You've got it too. I will pray that nothing happens to you. I don't know how I would handle it if it did.

Let me mention one thing in passing. One of the men at school asked me out a week ago. I went with him. We went to a dance at a club he belongs to. He was a perfect gentleman. When he took me home, he wanted to kiss me. I let him do it but it meant nothing. That's all there was, one almost brotherly kiss. Today after reading your letter, I told him that I was waiting for someone and it wouldn't be right to see him again. He seemed a little hurt, but he accepted it.

I wanted you to know about this so we trust each other. I will wait for you, Mark, as long as it takes, if that's okay with you. Please be up front with me. Let me know if you approve.

I guess I'm written out at this point. I hope you have some time soon to write again. You mean an awful lot to me.

Love,
Maddy

"I wondered why they called it a wetting down party," said John, laughing, as beer foam trickled from his head and dripped off his nose. "Now I know."

Matt had been similarly "wet down" a moment before and was wiping his face with a rag Mark had provided. "It sure is hell to get promoted in the Marine Corps," said Matt. "Not only do you have to pay for the drinks, but you get a bath besides." He looked at his younger brother, which was like looking at himself. "Congratulations squirt. Keep up the good work"

John looked back. "Same to you, Matt." He stood up. "A toast to Sergeant Farrell."

They all stood. "To Sergeant Farrell." They banged cans together and chug-a-lugged the foamy Japanese brew. After sitting for a moment Luke stood up. "A toast to Corporal Flaraty."

They all stood up again, looked at John, banged cans and downed the freshly opened beers. They sat down looking a little bleary-eyed at each other while they considered their next toast.

Jacques stood up, "A toast to Corporal Spears." They all stood up again and saluted the almost-smiling black man." Beer ran off his shaved head and onto his shirt.

It wasn't often Marines were able to salute three promotions at once, but the fighting created a need for new leaders, and those who had performed well in the field were the natural choices.

Saluting the trio were Mark and Luke, the Andrews Sisters, who had become quite attached to the brothers, Womack, and Sergeant Wingo. The "bar" they were in had probably been a dive *before* the battle for Seoul. Now it was a rat hole. It still had a roof but most of the walls were broken through. Miracle of miracles, the owner, a grizzled old Korean, had managed to protect his cache of Japanese beer and a large number of Marines were happily jammed into the place, drinking the foamy delight for twenty-five cents a can.

The war, as they had known it, was over. The NKPA were gone from South Korea. This success was due, in no small measure to the First Marine Division. They had a right to celebrate.

With the salutes done, the group became quiet. They were letting the effects of the beer and the natural letdown slip over them. They were tired. They were happy. They felt they had done a good job. They wanted to rest and absorb the feelings. Others revelers in the bar shouted and laughed, but in their group a full ten minutes went by with no conversation. Luke finally broke the silence.

"What do you think happens next?" he asked to no one in particular. He was looking at Matt and Mark who sat side by side.

Mark was first to reply. "No one is saying much. The officers at battalion think we'll be held here for a while until a decision is made. Some people want to attack North Korea and teach them a lesson. Some think we did what we came for. The NKPA are out." He shrugged his shoulders. "I don't know what to think."

Matt spoke up, "I bet we'll go into North Korea. We got a big armed force here. MacArthur will want to take over the whole country now, while we got the people. He thinks like Patton. At the end of the last war, Patton wanted to keep going and get rid of the Russians. He thought it was a mistake to stop. MacArthur would say, don't make the same mistake again. He would probably make the point that the job is only half done."

Mark spoke up again. "During my last few days at Quantico, we had a speaker come down from the State Department to address our class. He gave us a little historical perspective, which I didn't have." He looked around. Most of the group nodded. They were interested. "As a matter of fact I don't think most people understand Korea at all. Hell I had barely heard of the place until the North Koreans attacked."

Most of the tired group nodded again.

"What he said was, that after the Japanese surrendered at the end of World War II, the U.S. and the Russians were given the assignment of repatriating the country. They had been under Japanese rule for so long that the infrastructure had to be rebuilt, the Japanese moved out, and the industry rebuilt. The area was to be held in trust. This same sort of thing happened in Berlin and Germany, in Italy, and other places. Here in Korea, the dividing line of responsibility was the 38th parallel. This was not intended to be some sort of border, just a line to apportion responsibilities. The Russians would rebuild the North. We would rebuild the South."

The group, though tired, was interested. Mark was warming to his audience.

"In the south, free elections were held under the auspices of the U.N. in 1948. Syngman Rhee was elected. The Russians refused to hold elections and appointed their own leader and created the North Korean Peoples Republic, in defiance of the UN General Assembly."

"So what your saying is that the 38th parallel was not really a border. It was just made that way by the Russians, right?" asked Matt.

"Exactly. Someone asked why the UN let the Russians get away with it, our speaker couldn't answer. I suspect he was protecting bad decisions made by someone in the government."

"Really?" asked John sarcastically. "Do government people make bad decisions once in a while?"

There were a few snickers.

"In any event, we did let them get away with it, and you see the result. The North Koreans want to unify the country. The way they do it is to invade."

"That makes it more likely that we will move into North Korea. I think MacArthur wants to do that, and I bet Syngman Rhee does, too," said Matt continuing his earlier idea.

The group remained quiet for a few minutes. The din in the rest of the bar remained at a high level.

Corporal McAndrew asked a question. "What do you guys think of the Army troops we been working with?"

Matt looked at the Corporal. "The 64-dollar question Buddy. What do we think of them? Jacques and Ivan and I have had this discussion many times. What do you think?"

"We've talked about it, too," said McAndrew. The other members of the Andrews Sisters chimed in with affirmative answers. "We can't make it out. They're just regular American guys like us, but they don't act the same. Is it the training?"

Massucci added, "We're Marines. We volunteered for the best so we should be the best. We get the best training and all that, but I don't think they should be so far behind us. There's got to be something else. They actually throw their weapons away and run. They let themselves get taken prisoner. I haven't seen any Army unit stand and fight. When it gets tough, they 'bug out.'"

"During the last war, I saw some really good Army units," said Sergeant Wingo in his Texas drawl. "They were well trained, they had good leaders for the most part, and they fought hard. On Saipan, one Army regiment was moving too slow during a big push we were making. They were right in the middle of the line, so the two Marine regiments on either side of them had to hold back and take unnecessary casualties. A Marine general commanded the whole push. He removed the officer in charge of the

Army regiment and replaced him with another Army officer. The unit picked up and took right off and did a good job. There was nothing wrong with the troops. It was the leader. I don't know why they're different now either, but I suspect it's got to do with their officers, like that guy" He looked at Mark. "I don't include Marine officers in that, sir."

Mark looked at Wingo and smiled. "It's a good thing you made that clear sergeant." Then he laughed.

"There was a big stink about that," said Matt. "The military protocol is that a commander from one service does not remove a commander from another service. Some in the Army have never forgotten that."

"Maybe they're too caught up in that kind of stuff to be good officers," said Ivan, cutting to the heart of the problem. "Their leaders are too soft on the troops. We saw a lot of that at Naktong."

Matt and Jacques nodded in agreement.

"When they take over a defensive position, they actually set up "bug out" routes, in case they get overrun," said Jacques. "They actually plant the idea in the troops' heads that they can run. I fought all over North Africa and Southern Europe with the Legion. I never heard of a "bug out" route. There are no "bug out" routes mentioned in any of the Marine training manuals. I bet there are none in the Army manuals either. Where does the idea come from?"

Wingo offered a solution. "It's part of the 'Mommy' syndrome."

They looked at him with questioning eyes.

"Mothers have no idea what happens in combat. Oh, they know people can get killed, but they don't realize that the number of people who do get killed can be minimized by hard training, teamwork, standing together, fighting hard, and giving no quarter. They don' realize that more people get killed by folding before an enemy, as opposed to standing up to him. More people are killed or captured by being timid. They think that if you just don't antagonize the enemy too much you have a better chance of going free. If you run, you'll be better off."

He stopped suddenly. He looked around. "I'm not too good at making speeches and sometimes I don't say things the right way, but I know what I mean." He looked a little sheepish.

They nodded their heads. They knew what he meant.

Matt said, "I think our government operates that way too, a lot of the time."

They all nodded again. They had seen examples of that too.

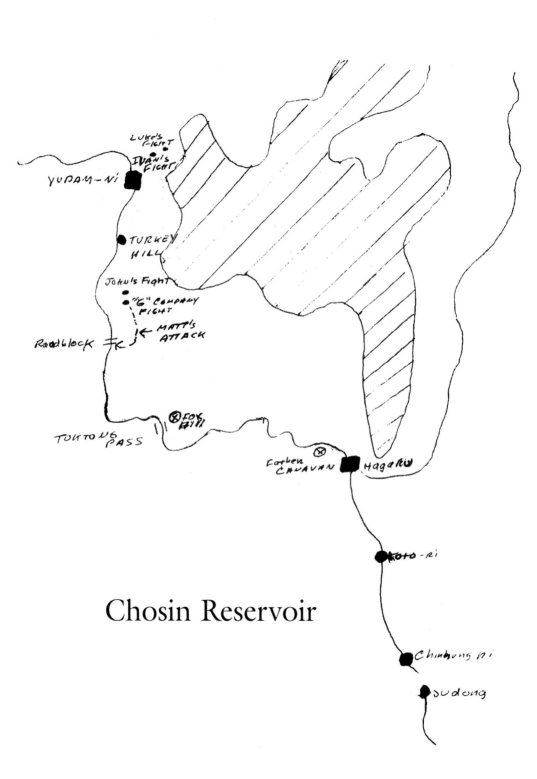

LUKE'S FIGHT
IVAN'S FIGHT
YUDAM-NI
TURKEY HILL
JOHN'S FIGHT
"G" COMPANY FIGHT
MATT'S ATTACK
Roadblock
TOKTONG PASS
FOX HILL
Cothen CARAVAN
Hagaru
Koto-ri

Chosin Reservoir

Chimhung ni
Sudong

19

The Road To Destiny

Thunderous applause rose from the throng, as the mustachioed master of ceremonies introduced the star. "Thank you. Thank you. Thank you," said the oddly dressed performer as he strolled flat-footed, across the makeshift stage, golf club in hand. When the applause stopped, he grabbed the microphone and faced his audience. "Thank you, again. Although I'm not really sure, I should be thanking anyone." He looked around the assembled throng, a smirk on his cocky face. "I know the USO moves fast but this is the first time I've hit the beach *before* the Marines." The large assembly of sailors and airmen burst into a roar of laughing approval. They enjoyed a joke at the expense of the proud ground-pounders. The ironic part was, the statement was true! The Marines, who were intended to come ashore here ten days ago, were still at sea. They were reluctantly participating in "Operation Yo-Yo" as the troops dubbed it.

The USO had flown Bob Hope and his troop of pretty girls, swing music, and corny comedy into Wonsan the day before, anticipating that the Marines would already be there. The city was safe enough. The First ROK Army had swept through a few days earlier and cleared the area of any North Koreans. The First Marine Division was scheduled to land before the Koreans arrived, but had been held up due to a heavy concentration of mines in the approaches to Wonsan harbor and in the harbor itself. The Navy had to clear the mines before risking the ships carrying the Marines.

Initially, the troops hadn't been told about the mines so that when the ships started steaming north and south at twelve-hour intervals, they imagined all sorts of possibilities, including sailing for home. When they found out about the mines, the "Operation Yo-Yo" title emerged.

The only troops in Wonsan for Bob Hope's show were advance elements of the naval landing forces and Marine pilots and aircrews that had flown in just prior to the entertainer's arrival. The ROKs had moved north of the city to provide security.

In history, it has been shown that it is as difficult to handle a victory as it was to obtain the victory in the first place. For the UN, the situation in Korea presented the very same challenge. In other words, what happens next?

During the latter part of September, as it became evident that The North Korean Army would be out of South Korean shortly, messages were exchanged between, General MacArthur, President Truman, the UN General Assembly and others. The choices would not be easy but the time to answer the question was at hand.

The UN forces had driven the interlopers out of South Korea. Both sides had paid dearly in personnel and materiel losses, but the war could be over. The rebuilding could start. Both countries, minus the deaths and the property damage, were back to the status quo. North and South Korea would remain — one communist, one free. Certain factions felt this was satisfactory.

On the other hand, the North had invaded the South, which was outright aggression. Shouldn't they be punished for this? Shouldn't they somehow have to pay reparations? Would they attack again? Were they really defeated? Other factions felt strongly about this aspect of the problem.

And, on still another hand, North Korea was a client state of the Soviet Union. What would happen if the UN moved into North Korea to punish them? There were those who didn't want to risk a confrontation with the Russian Bear. Communist China, which shared a border with North Korea, was also a factor.

The fourth viewpoint was that of Syngman Rhee, the septuagenarian president of South Korea. He wanted one Korea without the Communist/Non-Communist division. In other words, he wanted total victory. His point was well taken. Korea had been one country for centuries. When the Allies drove the Japanese out, Korea was supposed to be returned to its former status as an independent country. This seemed to be the moral approach. Morality and politics don't often go hand in hand, however.

After many meetings in the US, at the UN, and in other parts of the world, the final decision came down on the side of ending the war — but not just yet. On September 27, the Joint Chiefs of Staff issued their orders . . . .

Your military objective is the destruction of the North Korean Armed Forces. In attaining this objective you are authorized to conduct military operations, including amphibious and airborne

landings or ground operations north of the 38th parallel in
Korea, provided that at the time of such operations there has
been no entry into North Korea by major Soviet or Chinese
Communist Forces, no announcement of intended entry, nor a
threat to counter our forces militarily in North Korea.

General MacArthur had his orders. There were further paragraphs
restricting operations near the Chinese border and other paragraphs
specifying the use of South Korean forces only in certain areas.

In South Korea, plans were put into operation for the invasion
North. Before the troops were unleashed however, one last effort was
made to effect a peaceful settlement.

General MacArthur broadcast a surrender message to the North
Korean Army and their leaders on October first. The only response to
the message came, ominously, from Red China. Two days after the
broadcast, the Chinese let it be known, through the Indian Ambassador,
they had no diplomatic relations with the U.S. or the UN, that if UN
forces crossed into North Korea they would intervene. The Indian
ambassador, sensing a certain amount of ambivalence on the part of the
aging Mao, queried him about how China would react if only South
Korean forces entered North Korea. Mao agreed that if the only forces
to enter North Korea were Korean forces then they, Red China, would
not intervene.

The Chinese message was disregarded by the western powers.
Also, since no reply to MacArthur's surrender message had been
forthcoming from the North Koreans, the orders to the UN forces
were implemented, but changed slightly. MacArthur was now
empowered to "take all appropriate steps . . . for the establishment of
a . . . democratic Government and Sovereign State of Korea." The
only restriction MacArthur had was not to enter Manchuria or Russia.
The only concession he made to the Chinese was that the Armies of
the Republic of Korea would be in the forefront of the invasion. The
curtain was about to rise on a whole new war.

On October 25, the angry and frustrated Leathernecks finally landed at Wonsan. During the time the Marines had spent loading at Inchon
and participating in "Operation Yo-Yo" at sea, the Eighth Army had
moved north overland and had taken Pyongyang, the North Korean
capital. The Eighth Army and the Second ROK Corps were in posses-
sion of the western portion of the lower half of North Korea.

The plan now was for the newly designated X Corps, spearheaded by
the First Marine Division, to move to the northeast. In a thinly veiled
reference to MacArthur's imperial ways, some pundits named X Corps,

"The Tenth Legion."

The Marines were to head inland, using the road that wound along the eastern edge of the Taebak Mountains. The orders were to advance to the village of Hagaru-ri at the southern edge of the Changjin Reservoir and to establish a base for further operations. A village a few miles north of Hagaru, called Yudam-ni, would be added to the order later on. The distance from Hungnam to Yudam-ni was 78 miles. It was about to become the bloodiest, cruelest, most heroic 78 miles in the history of the Marine Corps.

Colonel Bowker strapped himself into the observation plane and looked at the pilot hopefully. The pilot, a red-headed lieutenant, named Green, naturally called Red Green, nodded to the colonel, gave him the thumbs up signal and then directed his attention to the takeoff.

The colonel was not enamored of flying and the workhorse OY, did not inspire additional confidence. He thought of it as an olive-drab Piper Cub which, in fact, it was. He was also reminded that it looked a great deal like some of the "hollow" model airplanes he made when he was a boy. They were nothing more than balsa wood frames with a paper skin. To him, the observation plane seemed equally as flimsy.

Within minutes they were at 5000 feet and heading northeast. The small airport at Wonsan disappeared behind them. The colonel loosened his lap belt and looked around. The take-off had been smooth. He forced himself to overcome his reservations. After a few more minutes, he took his maps out of their case.

Colonel Arlen T. Bowker, was the Division Operations Officer. His primary function was planning and strategy. Colonel Bowker had been one of the masterminds behind the Inchon invasion and the attack on Seoul. He was a highly competent Officer.

He had been studying maps of the Division's expected area of operations for weeks, but this was going to be his first look at the ground over which the unit would have to move. Military planners did not often actually see the terrain they had to manage. Bowker welcomed this opportunity.

He looked out the window. The sea was on his right as they were starting to approach a small city snuggled around a crescent-shaped bay on the coast. Must be Hungnam, he thought. It would be their major port for unloading supplies as soon as the rest of the mines were cleared.

He spread the Japanese map out on his lap. Someone had provided a translation for most of the Japanese words on the chart. The rest of the symbols and measurements were pretty standard. He'd just have to remember that they were in meters and kilometers, not feet. He glanced out the left side of the frail observation craft and obtained his first look at the road leading north from Hamhung that would be, their main route of advance. It would be known as the Main Supply Route. In later years Marines would just refer to it as "The MSR."

The red-headed lieutenant put the plane into a slight bank as he turned to the left. Within moments, they were level again. Another town appeared in their path, Hamhung. Could mix those names up easily thought Bowker. Hamhung, eight miles inland, was a little smaller than Hungnam.

The first village of any note after Hamhung was Oro-ri, which was another eight miles further along the road. Next came Majong-dong, which was about fourteen miles from Oro-ri. The road was level, two lanes wide and graveled. After Majong-dong the land would become rolling as it passed through some small hills and valleys. It also started to rise in elevation. Bowker noticed the plane was now at about 8000 feet. The land was brown and barren looking. It was farmland, but it appeared to Bowker, to be used for subsistence farming only. In the distance he could see autumn-stripped trees.

Sudong was next and then Chinhung-ni, where the two-lane road ended. From there on it was a one lane, dirt road. Sudong was seven miles north of Majon-dong and six miles south of Chinhung-ni.

Sudong was in a valley and surrounded by half-mile high hills. Bowker made a note on the map to be particularly careful here. It was a natural "pinch off" point. The Marines would have to get troops on those hills as they moved through here to avoid surprise attack. The road continued in the valley to Chinhung-ni, crisscrossing a small streambed a few times. The stream was dry, which would be typical for this time of year.

At Chinhung-ni, the countryside went through a dramatic transformation and so did the road. Koto-ri was the next village on the map. It was ten miles from Chinhung-ni, but the road rose 2500 feet in elevation in that ten miles. Also, eight of the ten miles traversed Funchilin Pass, a series of switchbacks, hairpin turns and the most dangerous sections anywhere along the road.

The road was carved into the side of the mountain about fifteen hundred to two thousand feet above the floor of the gorge and about the same distance from the top. When you traveled along the shelf-like road, you literally had a chasm on one side and a wall on the other. The road was also narrow. Bowker noted that the division's trucks might have a difficult time passing through certain sections. The tanks would be even more of a problem. They required more room, particularly on the turns. He decided that they would have to put bulldozers and bulldozer tanks near the front of the column when they entered the pass. The road would have to be widened as they went.

Halfway through the twisting canyon, the colonel made note of a building beside the road. It was a power plant that operated only when water was released from the reservoir. Right now it was inoperative.

Koto-ri was on a tumbled-down plateau. It was a railhead for a narrow gauge railroad along the Changjin River. The railroad was not in operation. The river, alongside the town was the river that ran from the Changjin (Chosin) Reservoir down through the Funchilin Pass. The area could be used as a base. There might even be enough room to construct an airstrip. Colonel Bowker added to his notes.

Next along the road was the division's destination, Hagaru, eleven miles from Koto-ri. The road to Hagaru followed the river and the railroad tracks across a high plateau. The land was relatively flat, but with a few small hills near the highway that created numerous ambush positions and "pinch points" along the way.

The OY crested a rise just before Hagaru and entered another high valley. The tip of the Chosin Reservoir could be seen directly to the front. A road junction and a number of buildings occupied the plain. Some looked abandoned. Others looked as if they were still occupied. One of the roads ran to the east side of the reservoir. The other ran more to the north, around the west side of the large body of water. Bowker made additional notes. This valley could serve better as a base than Koto-ri.

He directed the lieutenant to make a few circles around the area so he could get a better feel for it. Yes, this would do nicely. There were hills all around and they would have to get security on those hills but the area was big enough for a division. It was even big enough to construct an airstrip, a lifeline for supplies and personnel.

He was about to tell Green to return to Wonsan when he had a thought. He wanted to see what the road to the next village on the west side of the reservoir looked like. He glanced at the map. It was about fourteen miles from Hagaru. It was called Yudam-ni. Their orders thus far, would only take them to Hagaru, but Yudam-ni was the next logical step. He wanted a look.

A few miles after the road left Hagaru it began to twist and climb much like sections of the road at Funchilin Pass. It finally crested at 4000-foot high Toktong Pass and then descended through dark and daylight deprived valleys, flanked by almost vertical hills and mountains, until it reached Yudam-ni. Bowker felt a chill. There were a thousand places along this road to ambush and trap an infantry column. It would also need widening.

Yudam-ni itself was unremarkable. He did note that it was a valley closely surrounded by hills. Subconsciously he thought of it as a place that would take the whole Division to defend.

On the way back to Wonsan, he stared idly out the window, letting his thoughts run free in his mind. Something kept forcing itself into his consciousness. A word? Was it fear? No. Was it difficulty? No. Then he got it. The word was Caution. His eyes glowed with intensity. They should move slowly. He grabbed his note papers. He wrote, "Move deliberately, maintain contact between all units, go slowly. Keep units on all the hills, large units, company size. Send recon (reconnaissance) people out a few miles ahead and a few miles on each side. Consolidate forces before each move. We will be strung out, but we can keep each other covered if we are deliberate. Maintain constant air contact. Make sure some artillery is always in place to cover the route of advance. Don't move all the supporting arms until the advance elements are set up." He scribbled furiously. He felt he had a handle on how this attack should be done. He started to feel more comfortable.

When they neared Sudong, the pilot suddenly straightened and pointed out to the right side. On a hill above the road, was at least a company-sized unit of soldiers traversing an open area. Upon seeing the plane, they scattered. The OY swung low over the spot. A few of them fired weapons. Red pulled the observation craft up quickly. There was no armor on this bird. They moved rapidly out of the area. Before they pulled up, however, Bowker had a good look at them. They were not North Koreans. They wore mustard-colored uniforms, not the North Korean brown. They were Chinese.

Bowker's worries returned. The sighting troubled him. Information about Chinese intervention in Korea had been filtering into the First Division for the last few weeks, but now he had seen it for himself. This was going to be a new war.

As they completed the last leg of their flight, the colonel went over the maps again. Eventually the names of the places on the charts would become seared into this mind. It was only seventy-eight miles from Hungnam to Yudam-ni, but every name would become indelibly etched in Marine battle history. From this day forward, names like Majong-Dong, Sudong, Chinhung-ni, Funchilin Pass, Koto-ri, Hagaru, Toktong Pass and Yudam-ni would bring back images of heroism, valor, skill, and unbelievable suffering. This then would be the MSR, the main supply route. It would also be the highway to destiny for the Marines, seventy-eight miles of tortuous roads, overwhelming enemy forces and murderous weather. This would be the route by which they would enter the valley of death and then emerge victorious two weeks later, routing and smashing ten Chinese Communist divisions as they went. Destiny called.

Captain Gruene stood in front of George Company while the gunnery sergeant moved the troops into a semicircle around him. They were assembling in a bowl like depression in a field a mile or so north of Wonsan. The sky was heavy with low clouds. The temperature was in the high forties, but the frigid breeze coming off the mountains promised something much colder. Ominously, they had been issued some of their cold weather equipment that morning.

When the gunny was satisfied that he had arranged his company properly, he called them all to attention, turned on his heel, saluted his CO and stated "George Company is ready for instruction, sir."

"Thank you, gunny. Have them sit and get comfortable. The smoking lamp is lighted." The gunny issued the command, and two hundred plus Marines settled into place. Cigarettes, cigars and pipes emerged. Lighters flared. Smoke rose. Looks of anticipation showed on the troop's faces. The captain had just come from a regimental meeting. He was sure to have some "poop" on their fate.

He scanned the group. He liked what he saw. As far as experience was concerned, they were bit of a mixed bag. Overall he was satisfied, though. They had fought well through the early days at Pusan, Inchon, on the road to Seoul and in Seoul itself. His officer and NCO corps was good, very good. Sadly they were the result of survival of the fittest, but he knew he could depend on them. The less able had fallen in combat. Those that were left, were the best. That's what military people meant when they used words like "battle hardened" or "battle tested." These were the survivors. They had done the job and survived.

The privates and PFCs were, for the most part, also battle tested. Replacements had been added as they moved through the campaigns, but there had been enough action along the way that there were very few who did not have at least some combat awareness.

"I thought you would like to hear what the official 'skinny' is." He smiled at the group, using, along with "poop," one of the Corps' favorite expressions. "We've been feeding off half truths, rumors, and misinformation for so long, I'm sure most of you have given up trying to figure it out what's really going on."

There were smiles and nodding heads.

"First, the Eighth Army is in Pyongyang and is consolidating its gains. The Second ROK's are on their right flank. The First ROK is moving up a road from Hungnam on the coast. They will be to the right of the Second ROK, but there will be mountains in between. We will move up behind the First ROK's and pass through them somewhere along the way."

The troops found his resonant voice and soft Texas drawl pleasing to the ear.

"The Tenth Corps people . . . . Oh yes, in case we haven't told you, we, the First Marine Division, are part of the Tenth Corps, along with the First ROK's, the Army's Seventh Division and the Third Army Division which will join us later. The Tenth Corps people tell us that the war is almost over."

He looked around. They were fully alert.

"General Smith, our CG, doesn't think so. The Army people think all we have left to do is clean up the fleeing North Korean forces, a mop up operation, if you will. We've driven them out of South Korea. Now we'll destroy their Army and go home. General MacArthur has put a date on it, November 24 and we'll be heading home."

Today was October 27. Home by Christmas was the buzz that went through the group.

Captain Gruene noted the excitement. "Don't get your hopes up. Remember what I said about General Smith. He thinks were getting into a danger zone here, and he thoroughly pooh-pooh's the whole concept of an easy mop up."

He was intent as he looked around at his people. "Consider this. We're fighting in their country. People fight harder on their own land. We drove them out of the South and they lost a lot of their equipment, but they still have plenty more. Russia is supplying them. Also . . . ." He looked around for the effect his pause created. Their attention was rapt. "There is evidence that Red China is coming into the battle."

"How so?" asked one of the sergeants in the Second Platoon.

"First there have been many reports of sightings. Spotter planes have seen small groups moving through the mountains. In addition, the ROKs, over near Pyongyang, and the ROKs in our sector, have fought a few small battles with them along the road that goes up north. Also, they captured a bunch of them near a town called Sudong. They come from two or three different regiments."

"What is Tenth Corps' response to the ROK's reports and the prisoners?" asked one of the lieutenants.

"General Almond has indicated that his intelligence people think the ROKs might have been mistaken about whom they were fighting."

Looks of disbelief crossed many faces. "The Army doesn't trust a Korean to be able to identify a Chinaman? Bullshit" said one old-timer.

"What about the prisoners. You said they came from different regiments. Doesn't that indicate a large unit in the area?" asked someone else.

"A group of 'advisors' or 'volunteers,' nothing to worry about," replied Gruene.

"That's also bullshit," said the first sergeant.

"Of course it is. There is every indication that we will find ourselves fighting Chinese Communists as we move north. The Army is just sticking their heads in the sand."

"Why would they do that?" asked Mark. "Why wouldn't they take the normal precautions that are indicated by this intelligence? These people aren't stupid. The Army people I mean, they did a good job fighting the last war. Why the denial?"

"Major Martin, our battalion intelligence officer thinks that they don't want the Chinese to be here in North Korea because, if they are, then we might have to stop our attack and pull back and wait for word. Some of the early orders tell us that we can advance as long as there is no entry by major Soviet or Chinese forces. Although the orders have been changed, they still don't want this to be a major contact and have squeamish people in the government back out."

The group was silent. They were digesting that.

"Colonel Litzenburg from the Seventh Marines feels that we are almost definitely going to be fighting Chinese. He had one of his officers, a reserve captain who wrote his Ph.D. thesis on the Chinese Communists, give a lecture to his officers. Colonel Martin took notes."

He peeled back a few pages on his clipboard and started to read from his brief jottings. "Mao Tse Tung is the leader. He is a dedicated Communist. He has led the Chinese Communists for many years. They threw the Nationalists out two or three years ago and the Communists have been running the country ever since."

He shuffled through a few more pages.

"The Chinese are a very old culture. They have had many leaders, mostly totalitarian emperors and warlords. The Communist system of group ownership and everyone being equals appeals to them. Don't forget they lived under cruel warlords for centuries. They don't see how the Communists are using them. They believe in Chairman Mao, as they call him. Their army will be very dedicated.

"Mao has written a book about his philosophy and his tactics. His tactics are mostly guerrilla tactics. His troops live off the land, make do with limited weapons and support. Many of their weapons will be U.S.-made weapons which we gave to the Chinese Nationalists, but which the Communists captured when they drove Chang Kai Chek out."

He continued reading. "They march and fight by night. They

hide by day. They are masters of ambushes and booby traps. They do not seek mass encounters with the enemy. They prefer to break the enemy into small pieces and chew him up. They also want to bleed him to death."

Captain Gruene looked up. "It is new enemy for us. I don't doubt that we will beat him, but we have to know how he thinks and how he operates. Colonel Litzenburg thinks this could be the start of the next big war. If it is, we want to win these first battles."

He folded his papers and looked at the group and smiled. " You need to know about your enemy, but you don't need to fear him." He saw acceptance in their faces. "You are every bit as good as the Marines who were in the First and Second World Wars." He saw pride. "You proved that at Pusan, at Inchon and at Seoul." He liked what he saw. "You don't have to prove yourselves." He looked at each of them. He saw determination. "The Chinks have to prove *themselves*." The Company rose to their feet, as one. The captain raised his arm. They joined him with raised arms and roared their defiance.

Tears came to his eyes. He roared over their shouts. "Do you remember the old Marine Raider challenge?"

Someone yelled, "Gung Ho."

"Yes," his face glistened. "Gung Ho!" He roared.

They all yelled, "Gung Ho!"

On November 1, the Seventh Marine Regiment left the Wonsan area by truck to Hungnam and then north. The Fifth Marines followed shortly after. The First Marines would stay near the coast consolidating the area until the Army's Third Division arrived, then they would join the rest of the First Marine Division as they plied their way north. The Army's Seventh Division moved slowly off to the northeast sending small units ahead to locate the Yalu River.

The Seventh Marine Regiment first encountered the Chinese just south of Sudong on November 3, and over a three-day period fought a series of day and night battles against three Chinese divisions. To everyone's surprise, after the three days, the Chinese disappeared. The Seventh had destroyed one division and crippled another badly, while suffering only minor losses themselves. They had no idea why the Chinese cut off the battle.

In the Eighth Army's sector, north of Pyongyang, a similar event occurred. They were also attacked for three days, but unlike the Marines, the Army fared badly, losing a large number of troops and equipment to the Chinese. Then the Chinese disappeared. The mystery remained. Why did the Chinese launch a hard-hitting effort for three days and then back off?

Back in the east, the Seventh Marines moved forward, and, on November 10, the Marine Corps birthday, they entered Koto-ri and paused to catch their breath. Full winter clothing and other winter gear was issued. Five days later, the Marines entered Hagaru along with below zero temperatures.

20
Cold

Pow! The M-26 tank rocked back on its treads and then snapped back to its original firing position. Snow and dust flew and hid the iron horse momentarily. The 90 millimeter round left the muzzle of the tank's cannon and hurtled across the frozen plateau into an enemy rocket launcher position, squeezed into a snow-covered rock pile. The sound of the impact was an enormous ka-boom, which took about three seconds to come back to them. Matt, Jacques and Ivan saw the flash and the pieces whirling through the air before they heard the bang.

"Merde, those tanks are accurate. That's got to be a half mile away," said Jacques admiring the work of the tankers. There was another dull and distant boom as the echo of the blast returned from across the frozen Reservoir.

"A hard way for men to die," said Ivan simply.

"He would have launched that rocket at us if he had the chance," said Matt. "He wouldn't have given it a second thought. We'd be toast."

"You may be correct my friend, but I still long for the old ways. When men faced men. This is not the warrior's way."

Matt looked at Jacques. Jacques shrugged his shoulders. "So do I, but if you can't beat them, join them," said Matt. "We have to stay alive so that when the time comes we're still able to fight them *mano a mano*." He put his arm around Ivan's well-muscled shoulder. He still had his axe strapped to his pack. "You'll get your chance my ferocious friend. You'll get your chance."

Ivan stared straight ahead. He could wait.

The third squad was trudging through the snow in a skirmish line, headed for the smoking rocket site. They were wary. That rocket had held them up for about an hour. The tank finally did the trick. Matt and Jacques' squads, the First and Second, were maintaining their positions as a precaution. In a few minutes, the Third squad came back. There was nothing left at the rocket site.

"How far do you think we've moved in the last two days, since we left Hagaru?" asked Ivan staring out at the barren plain, broken only by frozen tufts of grass sticking through the snow.

"I don't know seventeen or eighteen miles. What do you think Jacques?"

"Yes, mon ami, I would say the same. The village we can see in the distance. I believe that is Sinhung-ni. That's about nineteen or twenty miles from Hagaru." Directly in front of them, through a frosty, foggy haze they could see the outlines of thatch-covered huts.

"There doesn't seem to be many enemy troops around here. Our platoon and some of the other platoons have been searching the area for two days and we have found very few Chinese. Why do you think we are here?" Ivan continued to question.

"Mark said we're consolidating. The whole regiment … we're getting all our people together. Then we're supposed to move north toward the Yalu. Right now we're . . . us . . . our platoon, just out in advance, checking the route out. We're the advance elements for the regiment." He looked at his friend in exasperation. "Don't you listen when Mark talks to us?" he chided.

Ivan looked at Matt with the hint of a smile. "I listen, but I still don't understand. We are Marines. We are supposed to be fighting. We should just challenge those Chinese. We do too much of what you call, 'pussyfooting' around."

Matt and Jacques looked at Ivan and laughed. Matt hugged their irrepressible friend. Ivan never changed.

A runner crunched through the snow toward them. Due to the distance he had come and the knee-high snow, he was breathing heavily. He had a message from Mark. Mark wanted them back inside the company perimeter. They were moving out. Matt and Jacques gathered their squads and started the trek through the fluffy snow to join the rest of the rest of the unit.

When they arrived back at the company position, they found that some of the troops had built fires. Like moths to a flame, they moved to one of them, pushing their way between the parka-clad men who surrounded it, doing anything they could to thaw out. The temperature had again, dropped to zero degrees the night before. It had been at or near zero for a few days now. The sudden impact of the extreme cold had been so devastating that a few men actually broke down and cried, or collapsed in supplication. These same men had faced the enemy without fear, but the cold had defeated to them.

The fire did little to help. After a moment, Matt walked away looking for Mark. Jacques and Ivan stayed. They looked around at their fellow Marines. They all looked alike, overstuffed teddy bears with guns. Each man wore a long, green parka with a fur-lined hood. They wore their camouflaged helmet under the hood and a tight fitting olive green wool cap under the helmet. The parkas were cinched at the waste by cartridge and ammo belts. They had packs and bed rolls on their backs.

Each Marine wore two or three layers of skivvies (underwear), two-piece longjohns, herringbone utilities, sweaters, snow pants and a field jacket under the parka. They had wool mittens with a trigger finger. Some also had gloves. A leather shell that cinched at the wrist to keep cold air out covered the mittens or gloves. Because of the bulkiness of the clothes, it was difficult to move without waddling.

"We look like green penguins," Jacques observed.

On their feet they wore shoepacs, rubber boots that replaced the regular combat boots. When a Marine was moving his feet stayed warm. In fact, even in extreme cold, his feet actually perspired. If he were stationary for any length of time however, the sweat would freeze, which caused frostbite. The Marines finally learned to keep their toes moving when stationary, and to change socks often. They carried the wet pair next to their body to help it dry out. Frostbitten toes caused casualties as frequently as bullets. It wasn't unusual, even in the middle of a firefight, to hear Marines reminding each other to keep moving their toes.

Sadly, the heavy clothing and the rubber boots made it impractical to wear their yellow leggings so the distinctive puttees were "shitcanned."

As if to punctuate how cold it really was, just as Jacques and Ivan were moving away from the fire to go to their platoon, one of the troops at the fire threw out the last of some coffee he had in his canteen cup. It had still been liquid when it was in his cup. It had turned to ice crystals by the time it hit the ground.

When Jacques and Ivan found Mark, he was with Matt and he was sitting on a stump chewing on a turkey leg. Thanksgiving had been two days ago. A Thanksgiving meal with all the trimmings had been provided back in Hagaru. Most of the Marines had managed to stash some food against their bodies for the next day but Mark had made it last two days. The meal was something the men had genuinely appreciated. It was the first hot meal most of them had had since leaving Hungnam, two weeks ago.

"Get your men together when we get done here." Mark garbled with a full mouth to his squad leaders. He threw the thoroughly gnawed bone away. "We're moving back aways to get ready to move to the other side of the Reservoir."

Quizzical looks crossed their faces.

"The whole regiment is going. Apparently, the Army is taking over this mission and the Fifth is going to spearhead an attack to the west from a place called Yudam-ni on the other side of the lake. We've got to go back through Hagaru to get there."

Matt looked at Jacques. Ivan would be happy.

"Right now, I'm not sure which units will move out first, but we all have to go back to the regiment CP area. From there, we move by trucks. Some will go at once. Some will wait for the trucks to come back, and some of us will hold the ground until the Army unit gets there." He looked around to see if they understood. "I don't know anything more at this point. It's about a two-hour walk back to the battalion and another hour to Regiment. We need to get started right away."

"Will we move out in a combat formation or a route column?" asked Matt.

"We'll be in a route column, but the Second Platoon will be behind us to be a rear guard. A squad from the Third Platoon will be on point." He smiled. "You never can be too careful. Even though we've seen very few enemy troops, we know they're out there."

Heads nodded. The squad leaders moved off to gather their men.

Later that day the First battalion of the 32nd Infantry arrived to relieve the Marines. Eyebrows rose among the Marines. They were sending a battalion to relieve a regiment? Tenth Corps assured them the rest of the 32nd regiment would be there in a day or two. The Marines were not to wait. The assault planned for the Fifth Marines was a top priority.

The Second Battalion was the first to move out from the regiment's position, some twelve miles from Hagaru. They made good time getting to Hagaru, but they slowed when they turned the corner to head north toward Yudam-ni. They had to fall in line behind a convoy of vehicles from the Seventh Regiment, which was completing its own movement to Yudam-ni. Most of the Seventh was already in the mountain village, except for one company and some supporting arms. These were the last units to go. The Seventh was to set up a blocking position and to help the Fifth launch their assault the next day.

When they finally reached Yudam-ni, the Second Battalion of the Fifth moved into a position in the village at nightfall, near to their jump off point, while the Seventh Marine units moved into the hills around the village to set up a defense. The rest of the 5th Regiment moved up the next day, November 27. The Third Battalion arrived in Yudam-ni at noon and the First Battalion arrived by nightfall. The Second Battalion did not wait for the other units to arrive before starting their attack. The other battalions would follow them. Their mission was to attack west and link up with the Eighth Army units that would attack north and then to the east from their positions. The idea was to form a pincer, which would trap the fleeing North Koreans.

On November 24, three days earlier, on the other side of the Taebak Mountains, eighty miles to the west, the Eighth Army had launched their offensive. The next day, 180,000 Chinese Communists, who had been hiding in the hills waiting for their opportunity, met them. The first unit to crumble was the Second ROK Corps that had been guarding the Eighth's right flank. Next, a whole Turkish brigade was overrun. Then came units of the 5th Cavalry and the 5th Infantry Division. By the end of the second day, November 26, they all had been routed and the whole UN Army was in retreat.

In addition to the fact that this was an enormous defeat for the UN forces, this pullback left the Marines with no reason to attack to the west. There would be no one to link up with. Thus there was no reason to be in Yudam-ni, nor to suffer the ordeal that was to follow. This whole situation could have been avoided if anyone had thought to inform the Tenth Corps of the collapse in the west. The Eighth Army was gone by November 26. The Marine assault started the *next* day and it should not have taken place at all.

Matt looked at John and Luke. His heart warmed. "I'm glad we're able to get together like this, even though it's just for a few minutes. I think we're all about to get into some deep shit soon and well . . . ." He trailed off.

"Me too, Matt," said Luke, grasping the impact of his brother's comments. John looked at Matt and smiled. "Who'd have thought we'd all end up in a tent in some shitty bombed out village in the Korean mountains, with the temperature below zero, surrounded by people who want to kill us?"

"You put it a little crudely," said Mark, "but the message comes across."

"How were you able to get off so you could come to the warming tent when we were here?" asked Matt.

"John stays in good with the gunny. He takes care of us," said Luke with a smile.

"I told him I had family in George Company. He accepted that," said John.

There were about twenty-five over bundled Marines standing in the small tent trying to coax a little more warmth from a small oil heater. A guttering kerosene lantern hung from the center post, providing the only light. Each group had a half-hour of "warm" time. Then it was back to the wind and the snow. They were able to unbutton some of their clothing, but not much. The temperature in the warming tent was still below freezing. Albeit, it was worse outside where the temperature was below zero, with a fifteen to twenty-mile an hour wind.

"In some ways, we're the lucky ones. The guys up in the hills don't get to a warming tent. They can't leave the line," said Mark.

"I guess it evens out. We get to attack tomorrow. They get to sit," said John.

"I'd rather attack," were the first words spoken by Ivan since they had entered the tent.

They looked at each other. Ivan had a way of defining himself in very few words.

"You will get your fill of fighting one of these days, my dark friend," said Jacques. "There is an old proverb 'be careful what you wish for, you might get it.'"

Ivan stared at Jacques, with his almost lidless eyes.

They stayed quiet for a while.

"You got plenty of fighting at Pusan and in Seoul didn't you?" queried John.

"I had some good fighting at Pusan. The fighting at Seoul was all long range, no man to man. It is not the same." He turned his head, his dark skin reflecting the feeble orange light of the lantern. "I can wait."

They were quiet again for a moment. There wasn't a great deal of talking in the tent overall. Absorbing warmth was the crying need.

Luke broke the silence. "I heard the Second Battalion didn't do too good in their attack today. They only got a little way and then they had to dig in."

Mark nodded. "Yeah, we all heard that. I guess it's true. They'll be ready to go again tomorrow and so will we. All the brass is together now setting up the plans." A thought occurred to him, "Where's your company set up, Luke?"

"Across that road in back of your company and about 500 yards to the north. We're facing north. Our CO told us the Seventh, which is up on the hilltops is spread out so thin that we got to be prepared if they get attacked and the Chinks break through. We're set up to cover part of the road and a draw."

"We've got the same kind of assignment, but we're facing south," said Matt.

John had been quiet for a while. He had grown serious, "Matt, I've been meaning to ask you something, but I haven't had the chance."

Matt looked at him "Shoot, squirt. I can't go anywhere." Then he stopped himself. "Is it personal?"

"No, nothing like that. It's just ... well, we're going into combat ... and I'm a corporal now and . . . I'm going to have to issue some orders . . . and . . . well how do you make people obey orders if they don't want to. I mean, I've seen some bad shit a few times . . . ."

Matt stopped him. "Look, Squirt, orders don't get the job done." He thought a little more, looking for a better way to say it, "Oh, you need orders at certain times. You've got to tell a man what he's supposed to do. He's got to know what's expected so he can do his job. Also, when things are confused, you can get things straightened out again by issuing orders. But if you're in combat and you got a hairy job to do, no amount of orders will get someone to do it. You may have to give that order, but the willingness has to come from the guy getting the order.

"He's got to believe in the order or believe in you. He has to accept the order as the best way, or maybe the only way. Men will attack machine gun nests, knowing there is a real good chance they'll get killed, but the reason they'll do it is because they believe it has to be done, or it's the honorable thing to do, or they are warriors or something. They believe. The order is just the way to get things going. If the training has been right, and the order is fair, and you have dealt with him right, you won't be turned down. That's what leadership means."

Mark added a point, "Your men will gain confidence in you and subsequently your orders, if you live by a code and they see that. Be the first to take risks. Share in the hard work, the shitty work. Take care of them. They'll take care of you. Sometimes officers forget this stuff and it costs them. Troops don't expect their leaders to do all the dirty work, hell, that's what they're there for, but they do expect them to do some of it and to help out and to protect them. They also expect you to be mature, to accept responsibility."

John was nodding. He smiled. He remembered a conversation back in Kingmont. He felt better. Lead by example. It was his own code.

"Tell them to attack. If they are fighting men, they will attack," Ivan put the finish on the discussion.

There was a rustle at the tent entrance. Someone shouted in a stage whisper. "Next shift." There were many moans and groans. The lantern was turned down. In a minute they were back in the real world, bundling up.

The sky was sharp. There were a million stars in sight. The clarity of the heavens seemed to put emphasis on the cold. The brothers all hugged. Ivan and Jacques clasped the two young Marines also. Then they went their separate ways.

When John and Luke got back to their company area, the gunny grabbed them. "I was just sending someone to get you. Get to your platoon. They got a job for you."

Lieutenant Boomer led his platoon up a draw that headed to the northeast. When they had gone about a half-mile, he stopped. There was no moon, but the clarity of the ice-cold air and the mantle of stars created enough light to maneuver. He hunched over and checked his lensatic compass. The luminous arrow showed 46 degrees. His line was a little off. He had to head more to the north. He snapped the compass closed, shoved it in his pocket, and motioned to the men nearest him that they would have to start climbing the hill on their left.

Fifteen minutes later, panting with the exertion, he stopped again. His platoon was strung out behind him. This looked like the spot. He called the Korean Marine sergeant up to him and indicated through signals that this was to be where he set up his machine gun section. They had gone over this earlier. The sergeant understood and rapidly deployed his two guns facing up the draw on his right side. They would be part of the defense around the Fifth Marine headquarters.

Boomer and the rest of the platoon moved up the spur to a spot with a commanding view of the peaks around them and the valleys between. Fortunately, it also had large boulders and natural depressions, which could provide a certain amount of cover if they were attacked. Their job was to be an outpost, to be the eyes and ears of the regiment.

The Seventh Marines were further up in the hills, but their area of responsibility was so big that they could only cover the front in broken lines. They tried to occupy most of the high ground but they left the draws for artillery and mortar batteries to cover with fire. The Fifth, which was preparing to assault to the west the next morning, would attempt to cover the natural channels into their regimental headquarters while they waited, hence the outpost.

The frozen platoon settled in. The frigid night settled on them.

21
The Agony on the Mountain

Cold as it was, John had a difficult time trying not to doze off. The fireworks on the big hill to their right had fascinated them all earlier, and that had kept him awake for the last few hours. He figured the Seventh Marines were getting hit hard. A succession of on again, off again, fire-fights and sporadic artillery missions had occurred since around midnight. Similar scenarios were playing out on the other hills around Yudam-ni.

But the last half-hour had been quiet, thus his drowsiness. John changed position. He was tucked halfway into his sleeping bag, keeping his legs warm. He must have worn a bare spot in the down letting in cold air in, so he moved his body. He and Goedeke, the new guy, were on watch. Lawton and Kelly were trying to sleep. He looked across the rocky crest at the First Squad area to see if he could see Luke, but other than a head bob here and there he couldn't make out anything. The "head bobs" were good however. It meant that at least some people were awake.

John shifted his gaze to scan the area in front of him. They were on the crest of a middle-sized hill. The land dropped away into a valley. To their left was a big hill. A saddle ran from their position toward that hill, but he didn't think it connected. This hill had been quiet. He didn't believe there were any Marines there. In front of him was a gorge and on his right front, across the gorge was the big hill with the Seventh Marines on it. It was quiet there now.

He started to think about what Matt had said. It made sense. He had good men. Although Goedeke was new, he seemed like a good man. They would understand what their mission was. If he had to give orders, they would follow because the orders made sense. He noticed they seemed to look to him sometimes. That would help. They needed his orders.

As he mused, a soft sound slowly intruded upon his consciousness. It was a gentle sound, like cloth brushing against a hard surface. He sat up straighter, trying to be quiet. The sound stopped. He strained both his eyes and his ears. There it was again, to his left front. Slowly he turned his head to the sound. From the corner of his eye, he saw Goedeke straighten. He had heard it, too. The private looked at John. John put a finger to his lips and signaled him to wait. They both moved their hands slowly to get their rifles into better positions.

He saw something. About twenty yards down the left front slope, someone was crawling. Although the stars provided light, there were also many shadows and John couldn't get a handle on the size or shape of the intruder. He decided to watch a little longer before acting. As if on cue, the fighting on the right-hand hill broke out again with a great deal of noise. John saw this as an opportunity to cover any noise he might make. He crawled over to Kelly and Lawton and woke them up. He motioned for them to wake the guys next to them and pass it along. Within a minute the whole platoon was awake. Lieutenant Boomer crab-walked along the crest and dropped down next to John. His eyes and eyebrows queried him. John pointed.

They could see several soldiers crawling along. They wore quilted suits. Most of the Marines in the front portion of the line saw them too. Boomer passed the word to hold fire until he could see what this activity was all about.

When the first two were about ten yards away, the Marines could see another ten or twelve climbing up behind. It was time to act. Boomer gave the order to fire. He also told his radioman to report the contact to Item Company headquarters down in the valley. He sent a runner to alert the KMC machine gun section back on the trail.

As soon as they were fired upon, the crawling Reds stood up and attacked. The ten or twelve were joined by thirty or forty more, and they launched their attack from close in. Out on the saddle, another thirty or forty attacked. They were within twenty yards of John's position.

The wave of attackers behind the infiltrators, went down quickly to the Marine's massed fire, but the rest of the enemy company, which had climbed right up to the Marines before the shooting began, swarmed over the position, unleashing a hail of submachine gunfire as they came. They then engaged the Marines in hand-to-hand combat. John had managed to get his bayonet clipped on just in time, As the first Red came over the rock at him, he held his rifle up and let the Red impale himself on the bayonet. The impact sent John to the ground, but he shoved the Red off and bounded back up. Goedeke was down, bleeding from a 45-caliber slug in his belly, thanks to a Tommy gun made in the United

States, in the hands of a quilted Red soldier.

Kelly and Lawton were struggling with three Reds, but the Marines seemed to be getting the better of them. John turned to his right. The whole hilltop was a boiling cauldron of fighting, cursing, desperate men. He was afraid to fire his weapon. He might hit a Marine. He decided to help Kelly and Lawton.

On the other side of the saddle, Luke and his team had cut down a few of the first attackers, but now they were being swarmed. One small Red came right at him firing what looked like a carbine. Luke ducked behind a rock, and when the Red came around of the rock, Luke smashed his face with the butt of his rifle. Teeth and pieces of bone flew. The man was wearing glasses. The metal frame and shards of broken glass embedded itself into his face and his weapon flew out of his hands and up in the air. It was a carbine, another American weapon.

Luke turned to seek out a new target. He hadn't bargained for what happened next. In front of him was the biggest man he had ever seen. He must be at least eight feet tall. The giant just stood there looking first at Luke and then at the soldier Luke had just killed. His expression turned from puzzled to fierce in a matter of seconds. He took one more look at the fallen Red at Luke's feet and then roared out his rage and attacked.

Luke brought his rifle up and fired. One round went off and the empty clip sprung free. He was out of ammunition. He didn't know if his round had hit the giant or not. The behemoth was on him. He kept his bayonet point in front of him, but the giant brushed it aside. Luke heard cloth tear. He knew he had cut something, but apparently the padded clothes had protected the attacker.

The giant smashed into Luke and knocked him down. Luke felt himself being picked up and spun around, held by the ankles. He was helpless. He flailed his arms in desperation. He saw a Marine try to slip in under him and stab at the big Chinese, but the big man was able to swing Luke low enough so that he hit the Marine like a bat hitting a ball. There was a loud crack. Luke's helmet flew off. The other Marine flew backwards and went down. Luke passed out.

Other Marines attacked the giant but he continued to swing the unconscious Luke around and fend them off. More Reds swarmed over the position and they shot at the Marines that went after their champion. It was a bad situation.

John had noticed the big man and the melee surrounding him, and decided to help. There were no Reds still standing in his sector. He and Kelly took off running. Kelly carried the BAR. As they ran, two Chinese turned to meet them. John stabbed out with his bayonet and caught one in the throat. Kelley smashed the other with the stock of his weapon. The two Marines stumbled on. Other Chinese turned to them. One fired a burp gun. Rounds whistled past John's head. One caught his helmet. He heard the clang and felt the jolt to his jaw as the bullet tried to jerk the helmet off his head. The impact stunned him for a second. Blood ran down his face from a small cut on his head and he fell to a knee.

Kelly had taken one of the rounds from the burp gun and was on the ground. He was trying to get up. One of the Reds clubbed him with his weapon and he stayed down. John forced himself back to his feet. Kelly had dropped the BAR. John picked it up.

He looked at the Reds around him. They were getting set to attack him. He swung the automatic rifle up to his waist and squeezed the trigger. No sense in worrying about "friendlies" now. He was surrounded and all he could see were Reds.

Before the magazine emptied, he had swung in a 360-degree circle firing the whole time. The Chinese in front of him disappeared, cut down by the continuous fire. They were all at his feet in a writhing mass of arms and legs. He looked down. He must have shot a dozen of them. He felt no pity. They were trying to get him. He got them first.

He noticed some were still alive. He had no rounds in the magazine to finish them off. His rifle, which was lying on the ground, was also empty. He pulled a grenade from his parka pocket, pulled the pin, looked around for the best escape route and then dropped the grenade into the middle of the downed enemy soldiers. He grabbed his rifle and ran, heading toward where he had last seen the big man. The blast from the grenade jarred him slightly on the back as he ran. Pieces of flesh stuck to his coat.

He had closed his eyes to the blast so he wouldn't lose his night vision. When he opened them, he saw that the big man was still swinging his prey. There were two or three Marines trying to work their way under the human weapon. John recognized Corporal Litsky, Luke's team leader. Then, to his horror, he recognized the person being swung. It was Luke.

He had to kill two or three more Reds before he could reach the Giant but he hardly noticed them in his rage. He ripped one apart with his bayonet and he crushed the face of another with the butt of his rifle. The third just fell, shot by someone else.

He never paused in his attack. When he arrived at the giant's position, he kept running. He drove at him, bayonet first trying to hamstring him. He managed to duck under the swinging Luke. He missed with the bayonet, but he crashed his body into the giant's legs. The force of his drive knocked the big man off balance and he fell, releasing Luke. The giant landed on John with all his bulk and try as he might to stay conscious the young Marine failed. The four hundred-pound weight crashing into him, forced him into unconsciousness.

Other Marines tried to rush in at this point but the big Chinaman was up almost as quickly as he had fallen. With one blow he killed two of his attackers and knocked another out. All at once there was silence. There was no one left to fight, the only movement coming from the surviving Communist soldiers.

The giant looked around. All the Marines were either killed or unconscious. His comrades called to him. He began to recover his control. He looked around in front of him and then behind to find his friend. He found him under a group of bodies, some Chinese, some Marine. He pulled him out and carried him away in his arms. It was the small Chinese soldier Luke had smashed in the face.

Mark looked at the squad leaders. It was dark, but he could make out who was who.

"The situation is this. Earlier tonight we sent the First Platoon of Item Company up onto a spur to the northeast." He pointed in the general direction. "They took along a section of machine guns from the KMCs. The machine guns were to be dropped off at a point where they could cover a draw that came down from the mountains into the Fifth Marine HQ. The platoon was to go on to the spur and to set up an outpost."

Behind the squad leaders, the troops in Mark's platoon were receiving extra ammunition and grenades.

"A little while ago, two of the KMCs came down from their spot. They had both been wounded. They said that there had been an attack up the draw and they had killed many enemy soldiers, but there were too many of them and they overran the position. We know the HQ people, behind the KMCs, fought off an attack that came down that draw so it sounds like the KMCs were correct.

"Just before the KMCs were hit, a runner came down to them from Boomer, that's the Item Company platoon leader and he said they were being attacked. At the same time, battalion got a radio message confirming that attack. Since then, battalion has heard nothing."

"That accounts for the noise we heard earlier," said Jacques. "We knew it was too close to be the Seventh up on the hills."

"That's what Gruene thinks, too," said Mark. "In any event, we got the job along with the Third Platoon to go up and get them out." He looked around at the group. "We also need to find out how big this penetration is."

"What's the plan?" asked Matt.

Mark looked at his brother peevishly. "I'm getting there, Matt. We need to go through this by the numbers."

"Sorry, Mark. Go ahead." He didn't want to upstage Mark, but he was worried. He knew that John and Luke were in that outpost Platoon."

"Our plan is to move up to the spur, take up defensive positions, and then one platoon will look around while the other maintains a base. We'll go first." He looked at Matt. "Your squad will lead off. Lescoulie will be next. Wallace, you'll be the rear guard. I'll be between the First and Second Squads. The Third Platoon will follow us."

He looked again at Matt. "Get a fire team out front. Wedge formation, we'll follow in a column. No talking after we leave the valley. Hand signals only."

He looked at Matt again. "Any questions?"

"No ... Oh when do we leave?"

"Five minutes. Meet back here. Sergeants Wingo and Crider have been giving out ammo. You just need to give your orders and then we're ready."

Matt smiled. Mark was doing things by the book, but then the Marine Corps' book was pretty well written.

Forty-five minutes later, they came upon the machine gun position. There were five dead KMCs, three dead Reds, and one smashed machine gun on the site. The other gun was missing, presumably taken by the Chinese. In front of the position and down into the valley were scores of dead Chinese. The evidence allayed any doubts the Marines had about the KMCs. The Korean Marines had done their job. The relief force pressed on.

The mountains had become quiet. The two platoons moved up the slope deliberately, trying to maintain silence. They had hoped for some combat activity in other areas to mask their approach, but that was not to be.

A half mile from the machine gun position, Ivan, leading the point fire team, crested a rise and stopped. Spread before him was the outpost, or what was left of it. He waived Matt forward.

In the dim light, it was difficult to pick out all the casualties. The rocks and clumps of snow added to the confusion. There were at least one hundred dead or dying people on or around the position. Most were Chinese, but there also was a large number of Marines.

Matt followed Ivan as they picked their way through the debris, eyes and ears cocked for remaining enemy troops. The squad had moved halfway across the area when Mark caught up with them.

"Found anything yet?" A strange question, considering the number of bodies lying around. But they both knew what he was asking.

"No ... nothing so far," answered Matt, eyes searching as he spoke. "I recognized one or two guys, but nothing on John or Luke yet."

"Okay." Mark breathed a little easier. "Matt, you keep your guys looking for survivors." He turned and called back to Sergeant Wingo. "Tex, you take Lescoulie and Wallace's squads and move through the knoll there to the other side. Set up a defensive position. We don't know what we're facing here. We got to be careful. An awful lot of fighting took place here."

"Aye, aye, sir," replied Wingo looking around. "Lescoulie?"

"Yo."

"Get Wallace and bring your squads up to me. We got to set up a defense." Moments later the two squads had passed through the position and were set up.

As Matt's people moved through, checking each body they found a few Marines injured but still alive. They also found a few live Chinese, who were put out of their misery before Mark found out and stopped the killing. Lost buddies create hatred. The Third Platoon had come forward by this time and the corpsmen from both platoons were working on the wounded. The Third Platoon set up defensive positions while the two lieutenants decided the next step.

As the two platoon leaders conferred, Matt found John. He was sitting on the ground propped against a rock. He had lost his helmet and blood had frozen in a jagged stream on his forehead. He stared straight ahead, vacantly, mumbling and rocking back and forth. He was cradling a battered and broken Marine in his arms. It was Luke.

Matt squatted next to him and put his hand on John's shoulder. "John. It's me, Matt."

John continued to stare straight ahead. Matt could see tears frozen to John's dirty face. His clothes were tattered and bloody. Matt wondered about the head wound. Suddenly, John was talking.

"The big motherfucker was just killing him. He was swinging him around like a bat and hitting people with him." He started to cry again and hold Luke closer to his body. Matt noticed that when John moved Luke, Luke flopped around like a rag doll. He looked like he had no bones.

"John, it's Matt," he said again. John continued to rock, holding tight to his broken brother.

"John."

He continued rocking, more tears freezing on his cheeks.

"John!" louder this time. "It's me, Matt."

John turned and looked at him with pain-wracked eyes. Awareness of who was speaking to him seeped in. "Matt, he didn't have a chance. The guy must have been eight feet tall. He just used Luke like a toy. Luke didn't even have a chance to fight like a man."

Tears came to Matt's eyes. He looked down at Luke. There was no doubt. Luke was gone.

Ivan looked at Luke too. His mind churned. What kind of a man fights like that? Thoughts of revenge, savage revenge, coursed through his being.

"John, we need to keep going. Let me turn Luke over to the corpsmen."

John looked at Matt. He didn't relax his hold on Luke. He hadn't heard what Matt had said.

"Matt, that big motherfucker didn't give him a chance." Fresh tears rolled down his face and froze. "He's my brother. I love him. That big . . . ." He started shaking. "That big goon just crushed him on other people . . . . He's . . . ." He trailed off. Then he broke down and began to sob. Matt sat next to him and took both of them in his arms. They rocked for a few moments.

When they told Mark, he turned away and cried. After a short time he regained control and went back to running his platoon. They had found seven live Marines, all wounded. It was agreed that the Third Platoon would continue on to Hill 1384, along with two squads from Mark's platoon. Mark would stay with his first squad and they would protect the rear as well as the wounded and the corpsmen.

In the meantime the fighting had picked up again on all the hills around them.

22
Zulu Time

Ivan was pensive. Although he almost always stood back and thought about situations before deciding on a course of action, this time he spent time observing as well as thinking. With his bull's-eye stare, he watched John holding Luke and sobbing. He noted Matt's wooden motions, his unspoken anguish. Earlier he had seen Mark busying himself with trivia, things that corporals should do, not officers. He reasoned that was Mark's way of not thinking about what had happened. He observed the big Frenchman's helplessness. How did he feel? Ivan ached for his friends. He hadn't known Luke for long, but he had come to love him. Fighting together, suffering together, men bonded.

He looked at them individually, then as a group. He didn't cry. In his world men didn't weep. But he knew these men were not lesser warriors because they wept. Each man handled the situation differently. There was no weakness in them. He knew these men well enough now to realize they were all strong and brave. He wanted to help, but he was at a loss. He didn't know how to help.

Other ideas entered his consciousness. He felt he owed Luke something. He felt he owed them all something. They accepted him for what he was. He was alone in a foreign army and a foreign land. He had no one else. They had become his family. He had not seen prejudice in Africa, but he had learned how it felt in America. He was the different one. He knew his life could have been much harder if not for them.

And Matt and Jacques? The three had suffered together. They had grown and developed together. Hadn't they protected each other's lives on more than one occasion? Hadn't they fought as a team? Didn't he owe his life to them? Weren't they his brothers? Didn't they need him? He churned with the need to help.

Eventually, his thoughts returned to the present and he turned from watching his friends and walked away, back to where his fire team was set up. He puttered around, checking his men's line of fire, making sure they were alert and prepared. He fussed for a while and then he stopped. Picking up his duties didn't help. He *needed* to do something for his "family." His dark face peering from his fur-lined hood, he continued to brood. His equally dark eyes were not focused. His mind however was working … working on something … anything.

Clouds had moved in again and light fluffy snow was falling. The crystalline night was gone. Although the whiteness of the snow reflected more light with which to see, the falling snow itself limited visibility. The cold was still palpable and deadly.

He looked around at his men. They were quiet, resting. They were tired. Sleep over the last few days had become a sometime thing. The snowfall increased and like the rocks and shrubs around them, it covered them with a gossamer mantle. Except for occasional movement, it was hard to tell a granite lump from human one. He continued to look around and think without seeing.

Then his face changed, not all at once but gradually. He had *noticed* something. It triggered thoughts. An idea emerged.

A half-hour later he and his fire team were moving stealthily amidst the rocks and tangled shrubbery at the foot of the rise. Above them the rest of the squad was tending to the wounded and waiting for the other platoon to return from Hill 1384. He had told one of the wounded Marines, to tell Matt that he had taken his men on a scouting mission to the west. Matt would be angry, but Ivan had decided. As he had stood there watching the snowfall, his course became clear to him. Before the new snow began to cover the old, he had noticed footprints near his team's position. They headed down the slope to the west. Ivan made sure he had his axe. One set of footprints was very large.

Mark sat quietly, looking at the defensive position they had set up. The rifle squads, half covered with snow, faced out, taking advantage of what cover they could for personal protection. The machine gun was aimed across the saddle. He could see the gunner and his assistant working on the gun, making sure it would operate properly in the metal choking cold. It was not yet daylight, but for most tasks, the ambient light reflecting off the snowy mantle provided a satisfactory level of illumination. Behind the perimeter, the corpsmen moved carefully among the wounded. They also stacked the dead.

Mark and Sergeant Wingo had placed the platoon in their positions earlier, although Wingo had done most of the work. Mark was finding it difficult to think about things like that.

As he stared vacantly into the falling snow, he felt a presence next to him. He turned and looked up. It was Jacques.

"May I join you?" the tall Frenchman asked.

Mark's thought process was slow. "Uh, what . . . oh yeah. Sure, sit down, Jacques." He looked for a place to move, to make room. Jacques touched Mark's shoulder. No need to move, mon lieutenant. I can sit here." He dropped onto the ground next to his platoon leader.

"I understand that you have had many burdens over the years, family burdens, being in charge of a platoon and now . . . this, the loss of a brother. My heart goes out to you my friend. I grieve for you."

Mark nodded his thanks. He didn't trust his voice.

"Matt has told me that you held the family together after, uh . . . what was his name, oh yes, Van Scooten. After he died."

Again Mark nodded.

"He was always very proud of you, " said Jacques quietly.

A light flickered in Mark's eyes.

They were quiet for a minute or two. In the distance they could hear the rattle of machine gun fire and artillery explosions. The actual fighting was far away. The light breeze now swirling the snow was carrying the distant sounds to them.

"Did Matt ever tell you what took place that night?" Jacques probed.

Mark's thoughts went back to that time. It seemed so long ago. "No . . . he never did. He just said he took care of my mother's problem. Did he tell you?" The flicker in his eyes remained.

"No, mon ami, uh, mon lieutenant, he never did. He said something like he said to you. 'He took care of the problem.'"

Again they were silent for a time.

"It sure changed our lives." Mark had additional thoughts. "Matt was gone. Mom was adrift. The Van Scootens threatened. I was unsure about what to do. Maybe John and Luke would not have come into the Corps . . . ."

Mark and Jacques sat side by side watching the snow. The far off sounds of combat had lessened. There were light flashes here and there as artillery missions were fired on distant hills. The platoon lay quietly in front of them, waiting for the dawn.

"Luke should never have been here," Mark said, as he continued to stare ahead. "The Sullivan Rule was supposed to protect families."

Lescoulie heard a catch in the lieutenant's voice. "It was a screw up. The military is famous for screw ups." The catch in Mark's voice became more of a sob.

"Wasn't it just a mistake in spelling?" Lescoulie probed gently. It was not really the military's fault. "His and John's name is spelled different than yours on all the papers, And Matt, he has a different name altogether."

Mark nodded. He really understood all that. He just had to blame someone.

"They really aren't alike, are they, Luke and John, I mean?" asked Jacques after another period of silence.

"Hardly," laughed Mark sadly. "Luke was a poet, an actor, a romantic soul. John? Well, John was one step away from being a juvenile delinquent."

Mark stopped. "That really isn't true. He was just immature when he was younger. John is tough. He thinks in black and white terms, good and evil, no in between. He responded to discipline though." He rambled a little.

Mark looked off into the distance again. "Luke could see nuances, shades of gray. He was passionate about music, art, and the theatre. He was still all man however. He was a little too trusting, but once crossed . . . ." His voice caught in his throat again.

The big Frenchman put his arm around him. Mark cried quietly.

A few hours later, Ivan stumbled back onto the hill where the platoon waited. He was holding up one of his men who seemed unable to walk. The snow had stopped. The sun had risen but it was behind the clouds, creating the omnipresent gray mantle of dim light. Ivan was covered with blood, thankfully very little his own. The Marine he supported was almost unconscious

Matt, Mark, and John ran over immediately. He looked at them, then turned and lowered the wounded Marine to the ground awkwardly. He straightened up and saluted them with his right hand, his eyes alight with fierce pride.

"Sir, I report that I lost two men killed and one wounded in a night battle, but we killed twenty-three of the enemy." He slid the axe off his shoulder and with his right hand he took something from his left hand. The left arm, which had been holding the burden, dangled at his side, appearing useless. He swung the object in front and rolled it toward the brothers. It came to rest at John's feet.

"Your family honor is avenged."

The object he placed at their feet was the head of the giant Chinese soldier.

23

Time Heals All Wounds --Slowly
Dateline: Korea.

Wendell Turner, back with the Marines in Korea, North Korea, that is. And I put the emphasis on the word north! Boy, is it cold! Estimates vary, but the best opinion is that the daytime highs are around ten or fifteen below zero and the nighttime lows reach twenty-five to thirty below zero.

As you know, I can't tell you exactly where we are but I can try to give you a picture of what is happening. Yesterday, I flew from one base to another in a two-passenger helicopter. Was that ever an adventure. Cold and high altitudes have a deleterious effect on helicopters. As my old grand-pappy used to tell me, "Machines don't like the cold any better than we do. They get cranky." That 'copter was cranky. I thought we were going to have to set down at least four times during the half-hour flight.

Over the last few days, the battles have been "helter skelter" affairs. That's not to say they weren't ferocious. Some of the bloodiest battles of the war have been fought here. Thousands of men on both sides have died after suffering horribly in the cold. The front has been fluid however. The Seventh Marine Regiment was on most of the hilltops around this small village, but due to the terrain, there were many gaps in their line. The Fifth Marine Regiment, which was planning to attack to the west, was in the valley while they waited to start their assault. They were also covering the draws that ran between the Seventh's positions on the hills.

The first day, the enemy in massive night attacks, using human wave "grinding" tactics overran a number of the units on the hills, and then ran into the units covering the draws. The units on the hills fought them almost to a man. Custer would have been proud. Two Seventh Marine companies covering the western hills were reduced from over two hundred troops each to a handful, twenty-six in one case and eighteen in the other. But they held! That's what so wonderful about these heroic young Americans. They don't quit. The next day a count was taken of enemy dead. They found two thousand at one hill and fifteen hundred at the other.

In areas where the Chinese overran the positions, the Marines fought and the Chinese paid a terrible price, but their numbers were too great. The Reds ran past the embattled outposts and continued down to the valley, leaving the hill defenders behind them. That's when they ran into the Fifth Marines who were defending the draws. That's when the battles became wild and free ranging. In most places, the fighting was hand to hand. The fights were small unit fights, ten or fifteen Marines at a time fighting with two or three times that number of enemy. Units became mixed. Marines who were part of one company finished the night with another. Seventh Regiment Marines ended up in Fifth Regiment units and vice versa. It was a night to remember.

By morning, the shooting let up. Stock could be taken. The wounded were brought down off the hills, as were the dead. Replacements climbed up the slopes to shore up the defenses. The Seventh Marines had lost so many men, that their units had to be replaced by Fifth Marine units. Attacking to the west had become a less probable mission for the Fifth. Survival of the whole force was the primary goal. A Marine commander, using prisoners and captured information, estimated that the two regiments had been attacked by at least five divisions of Chinese.

The next night brought more attacks from the Communists, although they were not as severe as the first night. The lines held with only minor penetrations. The second day dawned with the expected gray, slanting winter light and snow, large fluffy flakes that swirled in all directions in the ever-present wind, but little military action. Local storms over the last three days and twenty-mile-per-hour winds off the reservoir have been factors throughout all the battles.

One of the Seventh Marine Companies covering a vital pass in the mountains south of here, was surrounded. A rescue effort was made, but was called back. Marine pilots, who had been covering the area, reported that the relief battalion heading toward the surrounded company was moving into a huge concentration of Communist troops that were moving into a position between their base and the beleaguered Marines. Information from air observers about large enemy units on the move, added to the reports they were receiving from the line companies, explained the relative quiet of the last two days and nights. The enemy was reorganizing. The unsettling conclusion arrived at by the Marines, was that they themselves were totally surrounded — And surrounded by a very large number of enemy troops.

While the Marines were pondering this development, a change in orders came through, abandon the attack to the west and return to the base at Hagaru. An apocryphal order at best.

Today, when reporters questioned General Smith about a statement he had made when given the order to "retreat. He had said, "this is not a retreat, it is an attack in another direction." Some of the fourth estate felt that statement to be self-serving bravado, designed to sugarcoat the word "retreat." Smith, who is a courtly gentleman and not given to hyperbole, was taken back by that opinion. He took pains to explain. "Gentlemen, when one is surrounded by an enemy an attack in any direction is an attack, not a retreat."

Perhaps my judgement is a little biased toward these fine, fighting men, but I think the general's comment says it all.

Mark stared out at the snow-capped hills around him. Some were only faintly visible. Some were near enough to see plainly, even through the light fluffy snow that was presently falling. In the distance he could see a frozen arm of the Chosin Reservoir where it cut into the mountain valley and stopped at a small village. The village appeared empty.

He was standing near the crest of Hill 1282. George Company had moved onto the hill during the night. The open area in front of him was littered with bodies. Chinese bodies. A huge battle had taken place here. Two days ago, the dead Marines had been brought down to the valley behind the hill, but their deceased opponents remained, awaiting some future burial proceedings. To the right was Hill 1240. A monumental battle had been fought on that hill, also. Thousands of enemy had died. Only a little more than one squad survived from the two hundred plus who had originally held the hill. Mark imagined Chinese bodies strewn about that hill also, waiting to be put to rest.

For Mark, and the others, the last two days had been a walking nightmare. Luke's death had been devastating. Mark struggled. He wanted to cry. He wanted to quit. He wanted to grieve. He wanted to sit down and rest. He wanted it to be over. He wanted to give up.

But he didn't. He couldn't give up. He knew his responsibility. Mark had to summon every bit of his self-control to continue, and he did. He had to tell himself that he was an officer. Others depended on him. He could not succumb to personal grief. He could not give in. He had to go on, and he did.

Matt and John had also taken Luke's death hard.

Matt had lost not only a brother, but also the brother that he felt had the most to offer the world. He was the poet, the thinker, and the gentle spirit in the family. He was the one who was above the petty things in the world. He had a romantic ethos. Although he had become a good Marine, he was the least warrior-like in the family. He shouldn't have had to face the harsh reality of combat, especially the way it happened. And he shouldn't have had to pay the ultimate price. Matt performed his duties perfunctorily. His insides were in such turmoil he couldn't bring himself to think a minute ahead. He needed to grieve.

John had lost his best friend. Luke had been his buddy, his pal, and his confidant, as well as his brother. He had also died ignominiously. John knew that they all ran the risk of dying — they were in the killing business —but death, if it came, he always had envisioned differently. Dying while landing on the beach, or in hand-to-hand combat, or attacking an enemy, were the deaths of a fighting man, not death that came while being used as a club to beat others to death.

Ivan had upheld the honor of the family. He loved Ivan for that. He wished he had done it, but it didn't bring Luke back. He turned surly. He lashed out at everyone who talked to him. Jacques was the only one he listened to. He might have listened to Matt, but Matt had his own demons to exorcise.

Jacques was the steadying hand in the group. He had lost a friend who was also the brother of his best friend, but he could be philosophical. "Se la guerre." He had been there when Mark needed him. He would be there for all of them. He ached and he grieved, but he went forward.

"Lieutenant, I have repositioned the Second Squad for you. I moved them over a little. They will be better able to cover that sector on the right." The big Frenchman was filling in for the platoon sergeant. Sergeant Wingo had gone down to battalion along with the other platoon sergeants to see about getting replacements. They had taken a few of the more seriously wounded, with them.

Ivan was also hurt bad but refused to go. He did agree to wear a sling and have his ribs taped, after Matt had threatened him but he was not leaving his friends. The first day after the duel, Ivan had spit up blood often but it had stopped. He regarded that as a sign his internal injuries were not too serious.

Due to casualties, both combat and frostbite, George Company was down to less than a hundred people. Mark only had twenty-five in his platoon.

"What . . . oh, yes . . . thank you, Jacques? That helps a lot." He wrenched his mind back to the situation at hand. They had to be able to hold the hill in case of attack. Hill 1282 had already experienced one giant battle when their predecessor, Easy Company of the Seventh Marines, had fought off more than two thousand Chinese.

Another attack could be imminent. The last few days had seen only sporadic enemy activity but things could change any time. The Seventh Marines had the job of holding these hills before, now it was the Fifth Marine's responsibility.

Ivan was the talk of the company. The other Marines had always been a little in awe of the stolid black man, but now he was a god. A patrol had been sent down to bring back the bodies of the two members of his fire team that had been killed. They brought back more than bodies. They whispered about the devastation the four-man crew had wrought. They counted twenty-seven enemy bodies, four more than Ivan reported, and the headless body of the biggest man any of them had ever seen. The fact that the Zulu prince had a broken shoulder, that the bones "clicked" when he moved, and that he refused evacuation all added to the legend.

"What's Matt doing?"

"He's behind the rocks there." Lescoulie pointed to a spot to the rear of Matt's squad. "I think he's sharpening his bayonet. His face is very dark."

"Is his squad set up right?"

"Yes. He can do that without thinking, which I think is exactly how he did it."

Mark wasn't sure what Jacques meant by that, but if the squad was positioned right, that's all he could ask for.

"Is Ivan with him?'

"Yes, sir"

"I don't know what to do about him. He shouldn't have gone off on his own. He got two men killed and two others wounded, including himself, but . . . he killed twenty-seven of the enemy and avenged, for want of a better word, our family honor."

"I suppose, mon ami, uh, lieutenant, there is nothing you can do." Jacques answered knowingly. "He is more the hero than anything else. It sounds cold but twenty-seven for two is good statistics."

Mark looked at Jacques, indecision on his face. "I guess you're right. The rest of the platoon has no trouble with it. I guess that, sometimes, I'm too scrupulous. I need to be less picky." He still looked pained. "It is hard to make proper judgements when your family is involved." He looked at the big Frenchman for approval

Jacques nodded. "In my opinion, you are doing the right thing . . . sir." He smiled at Mark

Mark smiled back. After a minute he asked, "How's John doing?"

"I have him in my squad. He's like Matt. He does what he has to do, no more. He hurts. The others stay away from him. He is very angry right now."

"I understand. I feel the same way." He looked out at the hills again. Then a thought occurred to him. "That platoon they were in, both Luke and John, it's gone isn't it? The whole platoon?"

"Yes, sir. John is the only healthy survivor. There were a few who were wounded, but they can't fight any more. The platoon exists only on paper."

Mark looked out at the tumbled landscape again. "What a godforsaken place Korea is. Who wants this goddamned country anyway? Why should men die for it, good men, like Luke? Why should men get hurt for it, like Ivan?"

"Because they took an oath, they did their duty? Because of … honor?" replied Jacques quietly

Mark looked at him with understanding. "Yes, I guess so. They also want to be warriors. This is the price we pay for that." He looked at his troops, strewn about in their fighting "holes," some trying to cook frozen cans of food over Sterno cans, others lying half in and half out of their sleeping bags trying to grab a few minutes of sleep. They were dirty, cold, tired, hungry, sick, and who knows what else. They all had diarrhea and respiratory ailments. Runny noses were epidemic. The body odor would have been unbearable but for the cold. They all weighed a great deal less than when they first entered these mountains. They wore filthy, ripped clothing. Samples of what they *had* been able to eat were showing up as stains and smears down the front of their parkas. But, he admired them. He loved them. He would die for them.

Then he turned to the tall Frenchman and said somewhat philosophically, "I don't know Jacques. Is it all worth it? Or am I just saying that because I'm feeling blue?"

"I would say a little of both. It is worth it and you do feel blue. I have never talked to you about this, but I have talked to Matt and he felt America was right to be here. He felt Communism is our next big enemy and we had to fight them wherever they show up."

"I guess I remember him saying something like that years ago, when we were both at the academy . . . ." His voice trailed off. He looked around at the godforsaken terrain and asked, "But why Luke?"

"That I don't know, mon lieutenant." Jacques said quietly. He was about to add more when his reply was interrupted by a crack as a round whistled over their heads. They dropped to the ground. The other Marines scrambled for cover also, knocking over half-cooked meals.

There was another crack, then another. Mark looked around

furiously. Where were the shots coming from? Another round struck the ground near him. He rolled over to his left and scrambled on hands and knees to a spot behind a rock. Lescoulie was crawling toward his squad. A Marine in Matt's squad fired off a round.

"There's a couple of gooks in the middle of the bodies, right out front," yelled the Marine. "About two hundred yards."

A machine gunner picked up the spot and fired short bursts. He was immediately met by automatic weapons fire in return, from another spot behind the bodies. More Marines saw targets and fired back. More Chinese fired and then launched mortars. The Marines fired mortars in return. For the next fifteen minutes the firefight was hot and heavy, then it stopped. The Marines waited for an attack. It did not come.

Ten minutes went by and, with the exception of a few sporadic shots, nothing happened. Mark, who had stayed behind the rock, the whole time darted out and ran to his platoon headquarters. He attracted two enemy rounds almost immediately. One landed in front of him, the other at his heels. He made it over the crest of the hill, tumbled into his CP, and breathed a sigh of relief.

A moment or two later, somebody else on the line moved and was struck at once. One of the corporals to Mark's right was also hit by a lone rifle shot.

Mark wrestled with what he was seeing. The Chinese seemed to be playing a new game. Why would they shoot but not attack? What strategy dictated what they were doing, as a tactic? It looked like the Chinese were trying to make them hold their positions. That's it! They wanted them to hold. Perhaps the Gooks anticipated being reinforced. That was a chilling thought. Mark glanced at his radioman. The man shrugged his greeting. He had the handset clipped to his collar so he could hear if called but he was still able to use his hands for other things. At that moment, he was trying to warm some C-ration cocoa over a Sterno can

"No word from the CO?" asked Mark.

He knew the answer would be no. His radioman would have alerted him if Gruene had called. But he had to ask. The rumors that they would be moving had been flying all day, but no word had been forthcoming. He was anxious to know either way. He needed to be doing something so he wouldn't have time to think.

"No, sir. Nothing yet." The radioman continued to stir the lukewarm foamy mass in the C-ration can. Mark looked at the can. For some reason the cocoa looked good to him. He was about to ask if there was any more cocoa in his pack when a movement caught his eye. In the distance, to their rear, he saw Sergeant Wingo, wending his way up the slope. He had a small number of troops with him.

"Yo, lieutenant. We got some help," yelled Wingo.

Before Mark could warn him, shots rang out from the front. Wingo ducked. The Chinese had seen them too. The sergeant moved at a crouch toward the CP.

"Things are a little hotter here than when I left, I see. How long has that been going on?" He kept inching forward.

"Just a short time. They seem to be trying to keep our heads down. How'd you make out with replacements?" Mark asked, looking at the six men behind the sergeant.

"I got a little help." He waved at the men. "I had to send some over to the Second Platoon with Sergeant Gross." He slid behind the top of the crest and sat down, panting. His contingent joined him. Mark didn't know two of the men, but he knew the other four, the Andrews Sisters.

"What's a nice officer like you doing in a place like this?" asked Buddy McAndrew with a big grin.

Mark's spirits picked up at the sight of the wise cracking rocketeer. "I would ask you the same thing, but I'm too glad to see you," he grabbed Buddy and hugged him.

The other guys smiled and looked around. Marsucci saw the dead Chinese and said, "It doesn't look like you need much help to me."

Mark looked where Marsucci was staring. "That wasn't us. It was the last guys who were here. They held off two thousand Reds two days ago. We replaced them. Right now, we're pinned down."

Marsucci nodded, observing the front. Andy Hankins unwittingly asked the painful question. "How are your brothers doing and that guy Matt and the Zulu and . . . ?" He stopped. The look on Mark's face brought him up short. He realized what had happened. "Oh no … all of them?"

"No . . . not all." Tears filled Mark's eyes. "They got Luke and Ivan's hurt . . . ." He trailed off.

"Aw, lieutenant. I really feel bad. I shouldn't . . . ."

"It's all right, Andy. You couldn't know." Then Mark regained control. "How did you get to come up here?" He looked at them. "Aren't you needed in case of tanks?"

"I guess they don't figure on enemy tanks in the mountains like this and the line companies need people," said Buddy. "Besides we ain't got any ammo for our blow guns. All hell's breaking loose down there. The word is we're moving out. They're filling up the rifle companies as much as they can with us special types."

"The word *is* out. We are moving," said Sergeant Wingo. "The final plans aren't ready yet, but we'll be hearing soon." He looked at

McAndrew, a little annoyed that he had told Mark before he had a chance.

McAndrew didn't notice. "When we heard you guys were here, we volunteered. Figured we could meet up again."

"Well, you made my day, Buddy. That's great. You guys go to Matt's squad. He needs a fire team. Mark didn't want to think about the reason Matt was missing a fire team and he shoved the thought out of his mind. Mark spoke to his platoon Sergeant, "Sergeant Wingo!" The other two men were both cannon cockers. Their unit had run out of ammunition so it was being disbanded.

"Yes, sir"

"Put these cannon cockers in with Lescoulie. He needs the most help, after Matt. Tell him the Andrews Sisters have come to help us. He can tell John. That ought to pick up morale a little." He turned to the new men. "Glad to have you." They each nodded a little uncertainly.

"Aye, aye, sir" said Wingo.

While Mark had been talking to the Andrews Sisters, his platoon was learning to keep their heads down. The Chinese had begun tossing grenades toward their lines. The grenades were still too far away to be effective but apparently the enemy was inching closer.

There were no new orders. The day wore on. The sporadic fire continued. Mark sipped the cocoa. The first sip was warm, the second was tepid, and the third was cold. He threw the remainder away. It clunked when it hit the ground. His radioman was dozing. He started to doze himself. He awoke with a start to a strange sound. Something was crackling. His radioman touched him. He was holding out the handset.

"Lieutenant Gruene wants to talk to you."

The crackling had been the static on the radio. He hadn't recognized it. He needed sleep badly.

He took the hand set. "One, six here." He couldn't resist being formal.

"Mark. I got good news and bad news," a Texas drawl crackled through the static. "We're getting out of here. The whole regiment is coming down. We're going to go back to Hagaru. That's the good news."

Mark's heart leapt. Then he wondered about the bad news.

"The bad news is that we have to disengage as soon as possible."

Why would that be bad news? Then Mark remembered his tactics. One of the most difficult maneuvers on a battlefield was to disengage from an enemy while he was shooting at you and then to head in a different direction.

"I'm trying to line up some help. Just get ready. We've got to move soon."

"Roger that. Out" said Mark.

The "word" was passed quickly. Mark spoke to Matt. Matt's spirits seemed to lift a little when he saw the Andrews Sisters and he heard about the pull back. John also showed a little life. Lescoulie looked at Mark and smiled for the first time in days. Mark wondered about the smile. While they were getting ready, Jacques managed to move quietly over to Mark and pull him aside.

"Mon ami, I hope you don't mind, but I spoke to both Matt and John in the last few hours. I told them you needed their help. I told them they couldn't keep sulking around. They had to put Luke behind them. I appealed to their manhood. I am not sure they liked to hear it, but I think they are responding."

Mark looked across at Matt's squad. He was barking orders. His people were moving around, obeying. The situation looked better. He turned and looked for John but he could not see him.

"Thanks, Jacques. I'd never step in the way of anything you wanted to do. If a little tough talk gets them out of the funk they're in, great. The important thing is that we have to move on." He thought for a minute then asked, "What were their initial reactions?"

"Matt stared at me for a full minute and then slumped. He grabbed me, and hugged me, and told me he had been acting like a spoiled brat. His last words were 'never again.'"

Mark smiled. That was the old Matt. "And John?"

"John told me to mind my own business and walked away. Actually he crawled away. The enemy is still shooting at us. After a few minutes, he came back and apologized. He said something about being mature. He said he would do his job just as hard as he did before. He told me he was glad to be in this platoon."

Mark smiled again. Perhaps Jacques had found the key.

The maneuver to disengage was a gem. Four planes had been assigned as air cover for their withdrawal. In addition to solving family problems, Jacques had suggested an idea to Gruene as to how to use the Corsairs. The idea was accepted and passed along to the forward air controller and the artillery forward observer. Two Corsairs would fly low over the hill making a dummy run, because the two groups, both Marine and enemy, were too close together to make a real aerial attack, without the risk of hitting the Marines too. The Chinese should take cover when they saw the planes coming. As soon as the planes approached, George Company would pick up and run to the rear.

Another two-plane flight would follow behind the first. If the company was still too close to the enemy, they would make a dummy run also. The third time, the planes would come in firing. When they pulled up, artillery would be unleashed on the position. The whole idea was to keep the enemy heads down while the Marines were at their most vulnerable point.

The idea worked to perfection. On the first pass the Reds kept their heads down and the company pulled back. On the second pass, George was far enough off the hill that the Corsairs, not needing a second dummy pass, blistered the enemy lines with machine gun fire and napalm. By the third pass, George was hundreds of yards down the hill. The planes blasted the hill again. After they pulled up, the artillery pounded the area for fifteen minutes, igniting ammunition and booby traps the company had left.

When George Company arrived in the valley, they were surprised to find that their battalion was the last unit to come down from the hills. The other elements of the two regiments were already making their ponderous way down the MSR. Other parts of the Third Battalion streamed into the flat area from several locations. Due to the maneuver they had used, George Company had managed to come down without being followed by the enemy, but other Companies had not been so fortunate.

In some areas, the troops had been told to move rearward by using specific valleys and gorges. The Artillery people had set up 105 millimeter howitzers to fire direct fire into the gorge after the Marines passed by them. The 105's could fire directly at an enemy as well as they could fire high arc fire. It was the same as any gun, and using canister or "grape shot" rounds, they were capable of blowing large holes in hordes of advancing troops. Both sides in the American Civil War had used similar tactics. Some of the Red units learned about the devastating effects of grape shot the hard way.

"Where's John?" asked Mark, as he watched his platoon head toward the southbound road. The engineers were waiting for them to cross the dry riverbed before blowing the bridge.

"He volunteered for a detail," answered Sergeant Wingo. "The Gunny needed some troops to help load the last of the trucks."

"He volunteered? John?"

"Surprised me, too," said the Texan. He looked at Mark and made a helpless gesture.

Mark turned and looked back to the place where the trucks were almost finished loading. The landscape was littered with debris. The valley looked more like a garbage dump than the remains of a headquarters. Piles of boxes, broken vehicles and unused equipment were burning. Booby traps were being set. Bulldozers were filling in a big, but shallow grave. Contrary to tradition, the Marines would have to leave their dead here. There just weren't enough trucks to carry the dead and the wounded. A difficult decision had been made.

As the last of the 3rd Battalion units finished their jobs and passed across the bridge, they could see the tail end of the rest of the regiment ahead of them, a quarter of a mile down the road. They also could see thousands of black dots on the hills surrounding the valley, waiting for them to leave. The bloodbath at Yudam-ni was over. Now the bloody gauntlet to Hagaru began.

24

The Bubble

Captain Richard "Moses" Drotsch and Lieutenant John "Redman" Eagle were on station, flying their Corsairs over the barren hills of North Korea waiting for the word on where they would be needed next. Eagle was Drotch's wingman.

"That was a heck of a job we did on that last hill, Redman." Drotch's New York accented voice crackled over the tinny sounding radio. "There's no hill left."

"The artillery helped, too, Moses," crackled back Eagle in clipped precise phrases. "I was glad to see the grunts get out of there though. I don't think they could see what was massing in front of them. What do you think? The gooks had maybe a thousand men moving up?"

"Yeah. Probably a thousand, eight hundred for sure."

"It looked like there was only about a hundred Marines on the hill. It would have been a blood bath."

Drotsch did not reply. His plane was floating and he was observing.

"That was a neat idea about the dummy run to keep their heads down. I wonder whose idea that was."

"Dunno."

"That other hill, the one Skip and Thomas worked over, there were hundreds of gooks advancing on that hill, too."

"Yeah." Drotsch looked back toward the hill they were talking about. "There was only about a hundred Marines there, too. I think it was the right time to move. I don't think those guys down there can handle ten-to-one odds firefights anymore. The division has got get consolidated."

The two Corsairs banked over the northern part of the hills around the Yudam-ni valley, and as if to reinforce their misgivings, they noticed that in addition to the enemy troops already on the floor of the basin, thousands more Chinese troops were streaming into the valley. The

Chinese seemed to be everywhere.

"What are those blasts you can see in the valley? Are we still firing artillery back at the Reds?" asked Redman.

"Don't know for sure. I think they moved most of the artillery onto the road. They'd keep some available, but I don't think it's them. I suspect its booby traps. The air traffic we heard earlier, they talked about burning everything they couldn't take, so that explains the fires, but my guess is that some of the troops wanted to get in a few last shots at the gooks."

They did another slow bank in order to keep the valley in view.

"I heard about one trap they use. They take an empty C-ration can, pull the pin on a grenade and slide the grenade into the can. The side of the can keeps the spoon from flying off and blowing the grenade. They leave a box of rations in plain sight with this can in it. When the unsuspecting Red picks up the box, the grenade falls out, the spoon pops off and poof, one less gook."

Redman shuddered, his bronzed face forming a frown. "It's a vicious war down there isn't it?"

"Yeah," said Moses. He was silent for a while, then he said, "We get a little insulated up here. We attack men with cannons and napalm and all that, but we don't see the blood and the arms and legs flying off and all that shit."

"We don't have to sleep on the ground in sub-zero temperatures, eat frozen food and shit in our pants . . . ." Redman trailed off. "My heart goes out to them."

"Don't forget, some of our guys are down there too, calling in missions. Someday, it will be our turn."

"I can't wait." Eagle said with cynicism.

A sharp order crackled over their frequency. "Get off the radio and await further orders." Drotsch smiled. He looked across to Eagle on his left. Redman waved back. The two gull-winged predators continued their slow floating vigil.

Colonel Carl Woessner, the operations Officer for the Seventh Marine Regiment, and Colonel Mike Hargraves, his counterpart from the Fifth Marines, had just completed their newest planning session and were in agreement. They were on their way through the stalled convoy to the regimental commander's jeep to present their findings. In short, the plans they had made two days ago for the breakout were still sound. No need for any changes other than a little tweaking here and there. The plan was simple in conception, difficult in execution. In order to maintain contact and mutual protection, the whole convoy would move down the road as one, like a giant bubble, the contingent moving only as fast as its slowest part. A unit in the front would clear the way, a unit on the right and on the left would scour the hills, and a rearguard unit would face backwards as they moved.

The main body of the two regiments would be in the middle along with the wounded and the equipment. Artillery units would leapfrog down the road, keeping guns in position to support infantry units at all times. Marine, Navy and Air Force planes would be on station to help, as long as the weather permitted. They knew the bubble would contract and expand as they moved, but they also knew it would not break

Reviewing the plans one more time was necessitated by the intelligence picture developing. Captured prisoners had recently confirmed that there were at least five different Chinese divisions in the area. Also, aircraft had spotted large numbers of troops moving through the hills. Their estimates put the numbers in the tens of thousands. The airmen also observed that the Red units were moving quickly, apparently in an attempt to get into position alongside and in front of the Marines.

The two officers had agreed that although the intelligence reports were grim, the plan was still good. The newest report placed one Chinese Communist Division on their left flank, two on the right flank, one behind them and one in front. They were outnumbered at least five to one. The bubble remained still the best way to move the troops.

They found Colonel Litzenburg, the Seventh Marines commander and Colonel Murray, the CO of the Fifth Marines standing beside a radio jeep near the center of the column. It was surrounded by a number of vehicles. Curls of smoke wafted from the exhausts, mixing with the snow flurries and then dissipating into the wind. Headquarters people huddled around the vehicles, trying to absorb some of the warmth. The Colonels had placed a map across the hood of the jeep and were staring at it intently. The map was tacked onto a piece of plywood and covered with acetate. When the two operations officers approached, they looked up.

"Gentlemen," Colonel Murray, his sharp features intent, spoke first. "Does the plan still work?" He was direct and to the point.

Colonel Hargraves replied, his eyes sunk deep into their sockets, his unshaven face strained. "Yes, sir, it does. The plan doesn't revolve around how big the enemy force is. It revolves around us being able to maintain our integrity. It's like a giant bubble. We move along all together, all at the same time. If there is a penetration the bubble could burst, unless we react quickly. If there are too many of them and they can exploit a penetration, or they overwhelm our people at some point, then so be it. There is nothing we can do. There is no better plan given what we have."

Colonel Litzenburg smiled, his heavy features, looked solid in the gray light. "I like your confidence, Mike." He turned to Woessner. "You concur, Carl?"

"Yes, sir." His face also showed the pressure of long, sleepless nights and extreme cold. "The enemy may do something unexpected to change the situation, but given what we know, and what we have now, this is the best plan."

Litzenburg looked at Murray. "Do you play bridge Ray?"

"Just enough to be dangerous. My wife and I … with friends … neighborhood stuff. You play seriously though don't you, tournaments and all? Why do you ask?" He had known the old war-horse long enough to know he didn't ask idle questions at times like this.

The colonel brought his coat collar up a little tighter and adjusted his parka hood as a sharp gust of frigid air hit the group. "Yes. I like to play in tournaments sometimes. It is very competitive." He paused, looking around at the troops moving slowly past them, headed for their date with destiny, and then continued. "There is a strategy in bridge that comes into play here."

He thought for a moment, selecting the best way to explain his idea. "When you first look at you hand, after you have won the auction, you develop your plan to make your bid. Normally, you are missing a few key cards, so the play of the hand is not routine. In some situations, you figure out a way so that no matter how the missing key cards are distributed in the other hands, you will still win. There are other times, however, where the only way you can win the hand is if the missing cards are in the proper positions in the defensive hands. For example, your left-hand opponent must have a missing king of hearts and no more than two other hearts. If he has one other heart or the king is in the right opponents' hand, then you lose." He looked at his audience, looking for understanding. They seemed to be tracking with him.

"You have no say in who holds what cards, but, to repeat, the only way you can win is if they are properly placed. Ergo, you have to play the hand as if the cards are where you *want* them to be. If they are not, then you lose. There is nothing you can do about it. If they are where you want them to be, you win."

"Just like the situation we have here," replied Woessner.

"Exactly, Carl. But we do have one other thing going for us."

"Sir?"

"We have our Marines, Carl. Even if the cards are in the wrong places, they won't let us fail. Even if *the plan* fails, they won't. It's a good plan, Carl," he said nodding to Woessner and then to Hargraves. "It's the best we can do with our cards, but if it doesn't work, unlike in bridge, we still have the troops, the best in the world."

The column had stopped again — for the umpteenth time since they had left Yudam-ni that morning. Wind blown snow swirled around the vehicles. It was difficult to see more than forty or fifty yards down the road. In places it looked like the snow was ascending from the ground as opposed to falling from the air.

"What time is it?' asked Corporal Womack. He peered ahead, eyes squinting, looking for a reason for the delay. He saw a line of jeeps, trucks, and tracked vehicles stretched out so far in front of him that it disappeared into the snowy mists. Lines of foot-weary troops were also strung out along the road, some sagging to the ground, sleeping where they fell.

Jacques peeled back his glove and pulled up his sleeve to look at his watch. The crystal was cracked, but the watch still worked. Through the spider-webbed surface he was able to determine that the small hand was on the two and the big hand was on the eleven. "It is one fifty-five my friend. Do you have a date?" he asked playfully.

"Naw. I don't know why I want to know. I guess I just need to keep my mind busy. We been walking for hours. We start, we stop, and we start again. It's just frustrating. And I feel so tired. I don't think I've ever been this tired." He looked up at the hills around him. Earlier, there had been a great deal of shooting on a hill forward of their position. They had to wait for an hour that time. While they waited, Womack had actually fallen asleep on his feet leaning against a truck filled with wounded Marines. The incident had scared him.

Jacques passed a frozen chocolate bar over to him. "Some energy my friend. The K ration candy tastes terrible, but it has sugar. You need the boost. We have been on the go since dawn, coming down off the hill, packing the gear, loading trucks, moving down the road . . . ."

The corporal took the candy gratefully. He popped it into his mouth and let it defrost before he bit into it. "Got any more?" he asked, the words garbled.

"That is the last, mon ami. I have two cans of frozen fruit cocktail inside my shirt and some crackers in my pocket. If we don't get to Hagaru soon, I will be out of food."

Womack thought about that. That was all he had to eat, too. They had left Yudam-ni with their sleeping bags, all the ammunition they could carry, and whatever food could fit in their pockets. The decision had been made to travel light, survival gear only.

"How far did they say Hagaru was?" he asked.

"Fourteen miles," answered Jacques.

"Not real far, is it?" he observed absently.

"No, but we have to move two regiments down a winding slippery road, through narrow canyons, contested by enemy all the way. It will take time."

Womack nodded. He looked up at the hills again. On their right was a string of small crests that climbed up to a larger hill. The larger hill mass was Hill 1542. He could see movement here and there. He couldn't tell if they were Marines or Chinese. On his left, he could see the hill that had held them up earlier. It was Hill 1419, also known as Turkey Hill, named by a battalion from the Seventh Marines who'd had their Thanksgiving dinner at the base of the sharp slope.

Thanksgiving! That had been November 23. It was now December 1. Eight days in real time since they had eaten their turkey back at Hagaru, but to Womack, it had been an eternity.

"Jacques, explain to me again about meters and feet. They call that Hill 1419 but that's in meters, right."

"Yes, my friend. The English and the Americans use feet and yards. The rest of the civilized world uses meters and kilometers," he replied, with a grin, enjoying his gentle needle. "A meter is about 39 inches. A foot is 12 inches. Therefore, there is just a little more than three feet in a meter."

"So," the corporal said thinking, as he spoke, "if I take 1419 and multiply by three and add a little, I can get the height in feet. Let's see that's . . . close to 4300 feet."

"Magnifique! Either you are very smart or my teaching is very superior. I suspect the latter." He grinned at his protégée.

Womack smiled at his big friend. "Now I see why I was having so much difficulty believing the distance I was seeing on the maps. I knew the measurements were in meters, but the hills looked like they're a mile high to me. Fourteen or fifteen hundred meters didn't give my mind the correct picture. Those hills really *are* close to a mile high."

The column started to move again. This time the pace was quicker. Forty-five minutes passed without a stop. When they passed Turkey Hill, they passed a number of trucks loading wounded and dead, the aftermath of the shooting they had heard earlier. The Seventh Marines had fought for the hilltop here and had won. A battalion from the Seventh had ascended the hill and was getting ready to cut across the mountain tops to rescue one of their companies which was cut off at Toktong Pass. Colonel Litzenburg had named them the Toktong Raiders.

They crunched past the trucks mostly in silence. They knew they would see more of the same as they moved along. The road climbed higher and the turns became more narrow and slippery. Behind them, Yudam-ni was around a bend and out of sight. Then they stopped again.

Captain Gruene assembled his officers and NCOs in a ditch behind a truck. The already daylight-deprived valley became darker as the afternoon wore on. The wind whipped around them in sharp gusts, only minimally broken by the wall of the ditch and the body of the truck. Temperature was dropping rapidly again.

"The Third Battalion is taking over the point. Our objective is to keep the train going. We've got to clear resistance in front and on our left, and to protect the regiments. The First Battalion will be in the hills on our right, proving flank security. The Second will be the reserve.

The way that works out is that How Company will be the point company. Item Company will climb the hills on the left and secure Hill 1540. George will stay on the road, in reserve."

The group had mixed emotions. Being in reserve was probably the safest place for now. But when they would actually be needed, the chances were that they would have the toughest job of all.

For themselves, Matt and Mark thought about John. He was back with Item Company. He would be climbing the hill.

"How Company will have a tank to help clear the way, old D-23, which some of you worked with on the other side of the reservoir. It was the only tank that got through a week ago when the Commies shut the road down. The Corsairs have spotted ten or twelve road-blocks along the way. We'll need the tank at every one of them. The trip won't be easy."

Gruene frowned as he glanced at his notes, written on the dog-eared and now wind whipped pages of a pocket notebook. Then he looked up at his grimy leadership core. A platoon sergeants asked "Sir, doesn't it make sense to use our company at point? We've got the most experienced people."

"You're right, gunny," his glove rasped against week-old whiskers when he stroked his chin. "Maybe we should be in the front. But my guess is that the CO wants us for the reserve so he can use us to quench any fires that develop We've only got about a hundred people but we have the best fighting record. Item Company only has two platoons and a bunch of rear echelon "pogues." The flank is the best spot for them right now. How Company has the most people but they have a lot of cannon cockers, who are probably good fighters but lack infantry skills. I could be wrong of course. But, that's the way it looks to me. Who knows what's the best way to use us? We'll have to see . . . ." He trailed off, fatigue evident in his face.

The meeting broke up by itself and the officers and NCOs drifted back to their units to pass the word. Ten minutes later, Item Company started to climb the mountain and How Company moved down the road to join D-23 and continue the assault.

* * *

John wasn't sure what to do next. He was dazed, exhausted, and disoriented. He sat behind a rocky outcrop, trying to get his bearings. He could still hear rifle and automatic weapons firing sporadically around him. Occasional grenade flashes lit up the darkness.

The last few hours had been a nightmare. He had never seen so many Chinese before. They were everywhere. He and his platoon had fought continually as wave after wave of enemy troops swarmed over them. Why he was still alive, he didn't know. He was sure his whole squad was gone, probably his platoon too.

With his gloved hand, he felt around his body. There was a twinge of pain here and there, but nothing seemed serious. Somehow, he had been spared the worst of the holocaust. Must have been knocked out was his thinking, but he couldn't be sure. He didn't remember it happening.

He shinnied himself up so he could see over the top of the rocks. The open area in front of him was littered with bodies, both Chinese and Marine. He didn't see any movement. He slid back down. His mind was oatmeal. He couldn't think clearly.

What the heck is the matter with me? Why can't I clear my thinking? He took off his glove to feel his head, sliding his hand under the wool cap, which was under the helmet, which was under the parka hood. His hand came away with blood on it.

So that was the problem. He might have a concussion. He felt around and touched a sore spot, the source of the blood. He pulled back his hood and took off his helmet and cap. It was only a slight trickle, rapidly freezing. Nothing to worry about. He put his cap on again and as he was putting his helmet back in place, his hand touched a jagged edge inside the dome of the steel pot. It was a hole. He looked at the opening in disbelief. He'd been shot. The helmet had saved his life although he had been knocked unconscious by the blow.

The sight of the jagged opening released the memories. They had climbed that damned hill for an hour, in utter exhaustion, sometimes slipping back on icy surfaces, and sometimes climbing hand over hand. They had driven off a few small bands of Reds along the way. They had nearly reached the top when they underwent a mortar barrage, which scattered them. Hours later, thoroughly exhausted from the climb and the fighting, they assembled most the Company in one place.

A defensive line was established facing an open area in front of them. John remembered assigning the machine guns and BAR's their firing lanes and setting up listening posts. It had to be hastily done.

He remembered the Chinese assault in disjointed images, blaring bugles, whistles blowing, deafening explosions, jagged flashes of light, red tracers stitching lines of fire across the open field. In the eerie light of the swaying illumination flares, John saw hundreds and hundreds of Reds appear at the top of the hill and then sweep across the intervening space.

His memories faded then cleared again. He had fired clip after clip at the attackers. His BAR man was firing. Chinese dropped in waves but there were too many of them. They broke into the Marine lines. He had jumped up and bayoneted a Red soldier. He recalled Lieutenant Boomer, bandages flying, leading a group and counterattacking one of the places where the Chinese had penetrated. He had gathered a few men and attacked a small group of enemy soldiers, himself. How had the lieutenant gotten the bandages? Then he remembered. Earlier, Boomer had pulled him out of a tight spot, driving off three enemy soldiers. The young lieutenant had been hit in the head. He thought Boomer was gone.

His memories faded again, then returned. The battle had been free ranging. There were groups of Marines and Reds along the crest and the up slope, fighting grimly and disparately, neither, asking or giving quarter. There was no way to tell who was winning. The confusion was terrifying.

He remembered no more until he woke up a few moments ago.

As he sat, gathering himself, his brain gradually began to function better. He recognized the cold. He found his body hurt more than he had noticed earlier and he was starting to hear sounds. Someone was moaning to his left. He steeled himself to rise to a kneeling position and looked. A Marine was on his hands and knees trying to get up. John looked around. He didn't see anyone else, friendly or enemy, so he came to a crouching position and called out in a whisper, "Hey Marine." The Marine paused in his efforts to get to his feet and turned toward John. John recognized him as one of the rear echelon replacements assigned to Item Company.

"Can you crawl over here, behind the rock?"

"Yeah. I'll try." He turned and still on hands and knees made his way to John's side. He almost fell twice, but he made it.

"Where you hit?" John looked him over. He didn't see any blood.

"I don't know. My back hurts. I can't stand. I think I was blast-ed by one of those fucking percussion grenades the Chinese use. It just picked me up and dropped me." His face showed his pain, his anxiety, and his fear.

"Okay, take it easy. I just woke up myself. I'll look around a little and see what the situation is. There ain't no shooting going on and we aren't prisoners, so I think we might have won the battle." The Marine smiled weakly at John, glad to have someone to take charge.

An hour later, John had found twenty-seven "mostly" able-bod-ied Marines and ten badly wounded survivors. There was one other corporal, but all the other NCOs and the two officers had been killed. They had won the battle, but the situation was grave. Day was dawn-ing, a benefit mitigated by the start of another snowfall. John sat down to think.

He thought about Lieutenant Boomer. He had been wounded in the same battle where Luke had gone down — John held back a sob — only to die a few days later on another godforsaken hill. Boomer was a good guy. He would have loved to go on liberty with him sometime. He liked cars. He surfed. John's thoughts trailed off. The good died young. The bastards? He thought about his DI, back in boot camp. Somehow they went on

A half-hour later, John was staring across the open area, more asleep than awake when the other corporal, Olin Hayes, slid into a position next to him. After the battle, John had taken charge. At his urging, sometimes backed up by threats, the survivors had arranged themselves into some semblance of a defensive position. They had scrounged around and put together a small arsenal of weapons from the battlefield. Funny part was that many of the Chinese weapons were actually American weapons. There were burp guns, Tommy guns, and even a few M-1 rifles. The "company" still had two working machine guns but their mortars were gone. Perhaps the worst thing of all was that their radios had been destroyed.

A runner for Lieutenant Boomer told John that he had heard the lieutenant calling for help on the radio during the worst of the battle. John prayed that the call got through. He had noticed, a little earlier, before the snow had become too heavy, that someone was watching them with field glasses from the top of the hill. He was sure, they would be attacked again.

"Hey, Flaraty, we don't stand a chance." Hayes was talking to him.

"What? Oh Hayes. Yeah, it could get real sticky." John said, not really catching the meaning.

"No. I mean we can't hold them off. We got to get out of here. We can pull out in the snow."

John looked at him. "I don't think so Hayes. We got to hold the flank. We can't . . . ."

"Flaraty, those orders were for a whole company. We don't even have a platoon. We can't stand up to the Chinese. We got to get out or we'll be cut to pieces."

John looked at him again. "Hayes, you're talking about running, not doing your job. We're the left flank of two whole regiments. We got to stay, and hold!" he said with force.

"Flaraty, we got thirty guys who are dead tired. Half of them have been wounded. We got no food, no water. You and me are the only guys with more than one stripe. There's thousands of Chinese just over that hill . . . ."

"Hayes, keep your shit to yourself. We got a mission to perform. A job to do. Help is coming. We ain't moving. If you keep this up . . . then . . . then." He stopped, his face on fire. He looked right into Hayes' eyes so there would be no question of his meaning.

Hayes backed off a little. He tried another tack. "Look . . . John . . . you said your name was John, right?"

John nodded, glaring at him.

"Look, we ain't going to stop nobody with our little force. We'll just get killed. Then who are we helping? The convoy on the road is still flanked and we're all dead. Let's go back down, tell them what's up here and they can send a real force, maybe a battalion."

"Hayes, you make a good case, but it won't work. If we pull out, we leave the way open to the main body. It's as simple as that. The gooks will swarm down the hill and attack without warning. As long as we're here, they don't know what to do. The Chinese don't know how many we are, which I suspect is why they haven't attacked yet. If they do attack, we'll be able to hold for a while. Besides I'm sure help is on the way. In any event," he turned away from Hayes, stood up, and looked down on him. "We ain't going." He strode over to one of the machine gun positions. Hayes fumed but did nothing.

John wasn't as sure of anything he had said to Hayes as he sounded. He *hoped* help was on the way. He *hoped* the Chinese would wait a while. He *hoped* the troops were up to it. He knew they were all approaching the limit of their endurance. Two weeks of brutal cold, little or no sleep, constant heavy physical effort, a few cans of half-frozen C-rations for food, and the constant threat of violent death was taking its toll. Earlier he had to cuff and kick a few of the men to get them to set up positions properly. There were angry words. John was a new corporal and a young one at that. They had no confidence in him. Luckily, a few still had their wits and stamina. They stood beside him. John was reminded of the problems he had seen substitute teachers have in high school. The students had to put them to the test. The troops were testing him, too.

Tired as he was, he toured the line. He had ordered a fifty per cent alert. One man in two could sleep. He found the alert was more like ten per cent. He went through another round of kicking and poking. A few threats were made by some of the sleepers, but no one stood up to challenge him. They were getting the message. He had just finished his inspection and slid back into his "hole" near the middle of the line when someone shouted, "Here they come."

Instantly, the snow-covered mounds of men, erupted into white plumes of action. Their machine gun on the right flank started to fire in short bursts. A rifleman to the left cranked off a few rounds. But only a few targets could be seen. The snow was churning and swirling, drastically cutting down on visibility. There was a lull.

Suddenly, not fifty yards in front of them, a whole line of Chinese in white padded uniforms emerged from the blizzard. Within seconds, every weapon the Marines had was blazing away. The enemy line disappeared. It was followed by another line, longer this time. They were within ten yards before they all succumbed. The third line was right behind. Most of this line made it into the Marine's position, and once again the fighting was hand-to hand.

John had lost his rifle in the battle the night before, so he had picked up a Tommy gun along with four magazines from a dead Chinese. When the third line hit his position, he mowed down a half dozen of them immediately. Then his gun jammed. He cursed the Red soldier who didn't take care of his weapon. One of the Reds came at him with a bayonet, so he hit him with the butt of the Tommy gun. He heard a clinking sound in the gun as he hit the Red.

Maybe the impact cleared the jam, he thought. He turned the weapon on a clump of padded white figures, squeezed the trigger and, sure enough, six rounds came out and the clump fell.

Temporarily, he was free of targets. He took the time to look around. They seemed to be holding their own. There was no penetration. Then a fourth line of padded figures emerged from the maelstrom. John's heart sank. Hayes was right. There were too many of them.

Resigned to his fate, he decided to sell his life dearly. He knelt down to get out of the flow of bullets whizzing by and changed magazines. He checked his parka pockets. He had two grenades. He took one out and pulled the pin. He held it in his right hand so the spoon wouldn't fly off. He had the Tommy gun in his left hand. He felt his cartridge belt. His combat knife was still there. He stood up looking for a target.

The fourth wave had hit the Marines in a jagged line, clashing with some parts of the defensive front before others. On the right, the enemy had been stopped for the moment, but the fighting was vicious. In front of John six or seven of the white-clad attackers were pouring through a gap. He threw his grenade. Just before he let the grenade go, he heard a large volume of gunfire to the rear of the enemy's position. Before he was able to assess the situation however, his "pineapple" exploded right in the middle of the attackers and he was swinging his Tommy gun into position to finish them off. It wasn't necessary. They were all dead.

Another large group emerged from behind them, and he and a Marine on his left poured automatic weapons fire into them. Some went down, others kept coming. He pulled his last grenades, and launched it into the mass. More enemy went down, but more were coming. John knelt to fire his Tommy gun. The Marine on his left went down. The fighting on the right side of the line had stopped. The Reds had won and were now running over to John's area. Between the two groups, there was at least thirty-five or forty. John lifted his weapon.

His eyes flashed with hatred. His jaw was set, his face a mask of grim determination. He would fight to the end. Many would die before they got him. He would show them what a Marine was made of, what a Flaherty was made of.

Then with an incredible suddenness, the battlefield changed. To his left, he heard a god-awful howl and then a scream, a rebel yell, nightmarish shouts and a series of inhuman roars. The Reds in front of John came to a surprised halt. The screams and roars and howls rapidly increased in volume and then out of the swirling snow emerged twenty-five screaming Marines running at breakneck speed right at the horde of Chinese in front of the Item Company position. A howling black man, twirling an axe over his head and a large blonde man roaring obscenities in French, were in the lead. But the loudest attacker of the all was the man right behind them. He looked like John and he screamed like a banshee. It was Matt — Matt as no one had ever seen him.

Womack, Mark, Wingo, and the Andrews Sisters thundered behind the lead trio, spearheading the rest of the contingent and dramatically adding to the din. John had never seen a more welcome sight.

They crashed into the huddled group in front of John, with a pile driver impact. The white-clad mass stumbled and then fell back, suddenly, completely at the mercy of this pack of screaming madmen. Ivan's axe flew. Heads rolled. Arms were severed, blood splattered. Not to be outdone, Matt swung his rifle and crushed heads, smashed faces and tore bodies with his bayonet. He kicked and drove his body into faces and groins. They were helpless before him

The whole platoon of Marines became entangled with the frightened enemy and the Leathernecks became a blood lusting mob. They cursed and spit at their opponents. They slammed them and threw them to the ground. They smashed their heads with their frozen feet.

Lescoulie shoved enemy soldiers onto the bayonets of their own compatriots as well as onto Marine bayonets. He banged heads together. He kicked and gouged and lay to waste anyone near him. Men died horribly. Decapitated and dismembered bodies surrounded Ivan. The snowy ground at his feet was saturated with frozen puddles of blood. He was covered with red splotches and streaks of gore, none of it his own.

Gradually, the battle waned and then stopped. There was no one left to kill. Their foe was now a quivering pile of red and white lumps at their feet. The Marines looked around warily. In the distance they could hear thudding explosions and automatic weapons chatter, but in their area, the battle was done.

Matt looked at Womack. He had streaks of blood on his Parka. "You okay, Weenie?"
The corporal looked down at his front then at Matt and grinned. That ain't my blood."

Ivan stood quietly, looking at the pile of bodies at his feet. He looked at Jacques. "My shoulder limits me. I can't swing the way I could before."

Lescoulie looked at Ivan then at the bodies. He smiled. "Tell them that"

The whole platoon had participated in the "kill." They were like a feasting pride of lions. They had each slain at least one of the enemy some, many more. And, as horrible as killing was, they could each revel in their success. They had lost two men, both to wounds. One of them was Sergeant Wingo. One of the Reds had run a bayonet through his thigh. The leg had both an entry and an exit wound.

John had been so exhausted and bewildered by the whole thing he had not participated in the last few, wild, screaming minutes of the fight at all. He had just knelt with the Tommy gun and watched.

Mark was the first one to come back to reality. He turned to look at John. "John, you okay?"

"Yeah. Yeah, Mark, I'm okay." Then he thought of something. "Hey Mark. The gooks have been coming at us in waves. He looked over Mark's shoulder into the snowy mist. "There could be more out there."

"I don't think so, Squirt. Hear that shooting?"

He did hear shooting. Then John remembered he had heard some firing just before "The Wild Bunch" had landed.

"That's the rest of George Company attacking the group behind the hill. This fight's over."

25

Greater Love Hath No Man

As glorious as the rescue was, by no means had the ultimate problem been solved. The First Platoon had freed what was left of Item Company, but the other two George Company platoons had run into a viper's nest. They fought for another hour in swirling snow, against unknown numbers of Chinese before the Reds pulled back. As the day brightened and the snow cleared, they could take stock. It wasn't good.

"Matt, you'll have to take the platoon over. Gruene is gone. I've got to handle the company."

Matt was sitting on a rock, spooning half frozen peaches into his mouth. He was feeling depressed. Something dark hung over him. Perhaps it was Luke's death or the killing getting to him, or the cold. There didn't seem to be an end. He had read somewhere that if an infantryman spent enough time in combat, no matter how good he was, eventually he would die. It seemed more than that though. There was something else. It was slippery. He couldn't nail it down.

He looked up at Mark and nodded. "I figured something like this had happened when you didn't come back right away. No problem, Mark. We'll handle it. You'll do a good job, too."

"Thanks, Matt."

Matt looked at his brother with love and a degree of concern. "That battle lasted a long time. Are all the officers gone?"

"Hayden's left, but he's got a round in his leg. He refuses to evacuate, but he can't get around too well."

"Yeah, I read him like that, a little short on maturity, but all heart. How did Gruene get it?"

"I'm not sure. The gunny found him face down with a bullet in his back. There was no other blood. Probably just a stray round."

"Shit, with all he's been through . . . to catch a stray round . . . ." He looked out at the field with the snow-covered bodies and sighed. Then he looked at Mark again. "Do you know what our manpower is?"

"Yeah, I got fifty-seven, I can count on. I'm sending the wounded back down to the road. The gunny is wounded, but he can still walk. He'll lead the group. The first sergeant has taken over the Second Platoon. Hayden will try to lead the third. He's still got his platoon sergeant if he needs help. How many we … uh … you got?"

"Twenty-six. That's twenty-two from our platoon and four from what's left of Item Company. We lost Wingo. He's hurt bad. The corpsman says its going to be touch and go. I took it on myself to send him down with some of the wounded."

"Okay. That's okay. Jesus, what a mess. We got a total of, let's see . . . eighty-seven left out of what had been two Companies with two hundred and twenty plus men each. Over four hundred . . . ."

"Mark, don't get into that." He looked at Mark sternly. "Those men did a hell of a job. They've taken on thousands of Chinese and won. We've stopped the Reds from getting to the main body. That's what we're here for. We're winning. That's what's important."

Mark looked at Matt. He was a little hurt by the comments. But, then he realized he should have been thinking like that, too. Matt was right. Matt was a better leader than he was.

Matt saw his brother's downcast look. "Mark, you look like a chastened puppy. I didn't mean to put you down."

"No, Matt, you're right. We got a job to do. I can't let it get me down. I needed that slap in the face." He stood a little straighter.

"Mark, you were stronger than John or me when Luke . . . uh got it. You've got nothing to be ashamed of."

Mark nodded. It was good to hear Matt say that.

Matt rose and tossed the can. There were still some peaches on the bottom, frozen to the sides. "Show me where you want my platoon. Have you had anyone count the enemy dead yet?"

They walked to the crest of the hill together, stepping around stacks of bodies as they did so. "We had a count of 342 on this little field. This was Item Company's killing zone before we got here. We found another 243 on the other side of the crest where the Second and Third Platoons attacked. Did you get a count in the First Platoon's area?"

"Yeah. John's group and ours accounted for fifty-six. So overall we wasted more than six hundred of them."

"Six hundred and forty-one to be exact." As gruesome as this conversation was, Mark's spirits were lifted.

They neared the crest. The troops were busy trying to dig into the frozen soil. Matt's platoon was moving toward the right half of the line. Matt looked around. This position was a lot better than the one Item Company had tried to defend. "I see we got radios, and a forward air controller and an artillery forward observer and I see lots of machine guns. We should make out just fine." He looked at Mark warmly. He wasn't feeling as confident as he sounded, but he felt Mark, needed support. "I better get with my platoon. Lescoulie has probably taken over and he'll get them all screwed up."

Mark nodded. "Thanks for the consultation, Doctor. You've done wonders for my spirits."

"I'll send you a bill, Chunk." He reached out a clasped his burly sibling to his chest with both arms. "We've probably seen the worst of it." Then he was off to his platoon. Matt was a good Marine, but he was not a good prophet.

Twenty-four horrendous and brutal hours later, a gray dawn showed in the eastern sky. The hundredth straight, fucking day without sun. Matt thought. John had said earlier that when the Japanese occupied Korea, they must have stolen the sun for their flag. He couldn't remember having seen it since he had arrived. Jacques told him it had only been like this the last few weeks. He told him wryly, that it had been very sunny a few months ago back in the mountains in the south.

Matt sat on a small rise. He was smoking a cigarette, something he rarely did. There had been a mini pack of Lucky Strikes, four cigarettes, in his last box of C-rations and he had stuffed them in his pocket for just such an occasion. The events of the prior horrific night had left him shaken. His sense of foreboding had increased.

He blew out a plume of smoke and looked around. He was all-the-way-down-to- the-bone, exhausted. His men were almost senseless in their fatigue. They just lay wherever they had collapsed when the fighting stopped. He left them there. He had decided rest at this point was more important than anything else, including setting up defensive positions.

He looked at John. He was sitting with is back against a rock, dozing. A Tommy gun lay across his lap. God what a fighter that boy – or should he say man – had become. He was one tough cookie.

He looked at Ivan. He was propped against the gnarled stump of a dead tree. He sat upright, rubbing his shoulder and staring straight ahead. Ivan's eyes were not focusing on anything in particular. His axe lay at his side. Matt suspected his shoulder gave him a lot more pain than he was letting on.

Lescoulie was stretched out in the open, sleeping, his arms cradling his rifle and a Tommy gun. The man had the constitution of an elephant. Nothing phased him. He could fight a battle, and then lie down and fall asleep, thirty seconds later.

The Andrews Sisters sat in a group, leaning against each other with their eyes closed. One of them was humming, but he couldn't make out the tune.

He thought about Mark, the latest Flaherty casualty. Mark had been hurt last night in the crazy all night battle, like all the battles that characterized these hilltop clashes. He had been shot and gored with a bayonet. No one knew if he'd make it or not.

Matt flipped the cigarette butt away, the orange glow visible in the half-light, as it tumbled over and over before landing in a small display of sparks. He didn't want to think about the rest of his men or what had taken place during the all night fray, but he had to. It also occurred to him that he might not be able to put up with more nights like that.

Matt heard a noise. He turned his head halfway around, his body protesting. It was Cadway, their last radioman, limping up the slope and holding the handset out. The radio was strapped to his back.

"Matt, I was finally able to get through. It's Colonel Baxter, the battalion commander. He's been trying to reach us. He wants to talk to the CO." Cadway spoke hesitantly, not sure how to handle the situation.

"Thanks, Bart. I'll take it." He grabbed the handset and depressed the send button. "This is Sergeant Farrell here, sir. I'm senior here right now, sir. Over."

There was a pause, then a tinny voice. "This is Baxter, Sergeant. Did you say you were the senior man? Over."

"This is Farrell. Yes, sir. I don't know how much you want me to say on the air colonel, but we're going to need some replacements. Over."

"Don't worry about the radio waves, Sergeant. I think the chances of any Chinese that speak English monitoring this net are pretty slim. I need to get information. I can't worry about someone spying on us." There was a crackle of static as the colonel keyed his mike. Then he came back on. "Also, let's just talk. Don't worry about radio procedure. Now, what happened over the last day? What is your situation, numbers of people, exact location, etc.? Over."

Matt thought for a moment, trying to get his mind to work. Some of his group heard him talking on the radio and they were stirring around, sensing that things were about to change.

"Sir, when George Company came up here to reinforce Item Company, we ran into a large scale attack. The Reds were attacking Item Company just as we got here. We drove them back, but we lost a lot of people. Lieutenant Gruene was killed as well as a number of NCOs. Lieutenant Flaherty had to take over the company." Matt choked when he said Mark's name. "Last night they hit us again, hundreds of them. We fought all night. It just let up and hour or so ago."

The Colonel interrupted Matt's transmission, so there was a little confusion but then Matt heard the colonel asking. "Farrell, what happened to the lieutenant last night? Is he gone, too? Also how many people do you have? What is the enemy situation? Over."

"Sir, Lieutenant Flaherty has been wounded, badly. I sent him down to the road with a number of other wounded troops. He was unconscious. He was being carried down by some of the walking wounded. A Corporal Womack was with him. He also had been wounded, but he could still walk. They should be reaching your area shortly." Matt stifled a sob, then continued. "We lost them all, sir. The CO, the air controller, the forward observer, our mortars, and all but one of our machine-guns. I have thirty men left, sir, and some of them are wounded. We'll hold, but we need some help. It looks to me like we killed a couple of hundred last night. But this morning, I can see there's still a lot of gooks down in the valley on the other side of Hill 1520. We're on the crest of the hill. Over."

There was a sigh, then a long pause, and then the colonel came back on. "Farrell, I'll get back to you in a few minutes. Wait one."

Matt handed the mike back to his radioman and sat down. He hadn't realized he had stood up while he was speaking. The day had become a little brighter but the ever-present pewter gray overhead kept a damper on any emotions.

His conversation with the colonel had awakened his entire contingent and they knew things were going to happen. A number of them looked down the slope into the valley. The communists were still there and appeared like strings of ants moving about. The slope descending to the valley was littered with corpses, the result of last night's battle. Once again, a small force of Marines had held off a much larger force of Reds, but the cost had been high.

The colonel called back. "Farrell, I'm sending up another company to relieve you, a composite company. They're just getting ready to leave. They should be there in a couple of hours. I have a new mission for you if you are up to it. Do you have a map? Over."

"Yes, sir. Wait one" He reached inside his parka, pulled out the folded chart and spread it on the ground. John came over and started to place rocks on it to hold it down. He wanted to get in on whatever was going on.

"Sir, this is Farrell back again. I have the map. Over."

"Good, Sergeant. I want you to look at something on the map." The colonel gave him the coordinates. The numbers intersected on a turn in the road, halfway between Yudam-ni and Hagaru. Matt noted the declension lines on the map were very close at this point, indicating a steep slope on both sides of the road.

"I got it. Over."

"Right at the point where the road turns and the canyon narrows, the Reds have blown the bridge and set up a roadblock. It's been a bitch for us. We can't get through it. The slopes around are too steep to use the Corsairs. Because the slopes are so severe, we can't get infantry up the left. On the right we're still fighting for the crests. Our tank can't get close enough to get a shot because of the way the road turns. The gooks also have rocket launchers and I don't want to risk the tank. That tank is our point weapon in this whole breakout. They could be a sitting duck in this draw." Static filled the air as the colonel adjusted his position before continuing.

"We've been firing artillery at it for hours, but the rounds are bursting too high up on the slopes. It's too narrow for a frontal assault"

Matt was getting the picture. He looked at the map more closely and noted a spur from Hill 1520, where he was, that ran down on a gentle grade all the way to the rear of the roadblock

"Farrell, there's a spur . . . ." Matt flicked his handset to interrupt the colonel.

"Yes, sir I see it. It comes down behind the roadblock. You want us to attack."

The transmission was quiet for a few seconds, then Colonel Baxter said, "You're a quick study Farrell. That's exactly what I want. When I first called, I wasn't aware of your dire straits. I was going to ask the George Company CO to send a platoon. I guess you're all that's left of George. I still need the platoon. I guess you're it. Can you do it? Are your people up to it? Got enough ammunition? Over."

"We'll do it, sir. These guys would rather attack then defend." He looked around at his men. They were stirring, looking at him and nodding. "This bullshit, defending hills against thousands of gooks is getting old. We want to attack someone. We got plenty of ammo, some of it not American, but plenty. Do you want me to wait for our replacements? Over."

"No, get going ASAP." Matt could hear him talking with some other people. Then he was talking to Matt again. "We've been held up and bunched up for hours down here, the whole two regiments. I don't like what's happening on our right. There could be enemy breakthroughs at anytime, then we're sitting ducks, no place to go. Just go as soon as you're set . . . uh, how long do you think it will take? Over."

Matt looked at the map, did a quick estimate of the distance, and then keyed the handset again. "We can be ready to attack in an hour, maybe a little more."

"Perfect, Sergeant. By the way some of the people here in the battalion HQ tell me they know you and we couldn't be in better hands. They tell me you did a real good job at Pusan and Seoul. I feel like we've found the right man. Anything I can do for you at this point? Over."

"Not really . . . ." Tired as he was, the flattery lifted his spirits a little. "Oh, keep putting artillery in there it might keep their heads down a little . . . and also, sir, the wounded . . . have they arrived yet? Over."

"You'll get your artillery. Wait one on the wounded." A minute later "Farrell, there are many wounded coming down from both sides of the road. If you're looking for your lieutenant, there's nothing I can tell you at this point."

"Thank you, sir. We're on our way. I'll call you when we're set. Farrell out."

Matt broke his thirty men into three squads. He put Jacques in charge of one, McAndrew in charge of another, and John in charge of the third. Ivan was content to work in Jacques' squad. When he first thought about how to use his troops it became apparent to him that he had a pretty good bunch of fighting men. Survival of the fittest, he figured. These men had survived because they were good. He watched them preparing. Although they should have been totally exhausted, some sort of a second wind had kicked in and they were all keen to get the job done. In any event, they wanted to get off this fucking hill. As for Matt, even with the new mission, he couldn't shake the personal gloomy feeling, a sense of foreboding.

The way down was easy. After forty-five minutes, Matt called a halt and scanned his map to establish their location. It appeared they were about a thousand yards from the roadblock. He could hear the artillery rounds bursting.

Jacques and Ivan went forward to see if they could pinpoint the exact location. They came back after about ten minutes. They had spotted the enemy!

"We could only see one or two, mon ami, but I think they are an outpost. They were positioned to face up the line of the spur. We had dropped down along the side so they could not see us. I think they are there to guard against surprise attack."

"Did you see any more troops?"

"No, mon ami. We slid down the slope a little further. We could see the road and we could see some boxes and things sticking out from behind a small hill but no more troops. I think the boxes, might be the back of their main position. They looked like ammunition boxes."

Matt chewed on that for a little while. Finally he spoke. "It looks like we have to get by that outpost without tipping off the others. Any suggestions?"

"Let me handle it, Matt. I'll take the 'Sisters,'" said McAndrew. " We're pretty good at snooping and pooping. We work good as a team and there's four of us, in case there's more than just two guys hidden there."

Matt thought a moment. "Okay, Buddy, you got it." The Sisters' plan was to slip off the spur and come up on the outpost from the side. They would try to neutralize it without noise. The rest of the Platoon would work its way alongside the spur to about fifty yards from the outpost. If there was shooting, they would rush the spot in a skirmish line. If Buddy waved to them that he was successful, they would approach the spot quietly and decide what to do from that point on.

When McAndrew and his men took off, Matt called the colonel and told him they were ready to move into an attack position. The colonel told him he'd lift the artillery fire. He also told him that Mark had made it down, but was in serious condition.

A few minutes later, Matt and John were lying side by side watching the outpost. They saw Buddy and Masucci clamber up the slope and dive over a little parapet. Hankins and Anderson were right on their tails. They could see scuffling, an arm raised here, a slash of khaki there, then nothing. Another minute passed and Buddy stood up and waved. Within two minutes the whole "platoon" was in the outpost.

There were three dead Chinese on the ground. Two of them had their throats slit. The other had a crushed skull. Buddy and his men had continued on into the position and turned a little corner so they were out of sight. Jacques and his squad took the point. They moved warily through the position around the base of the hill. They would have to assume that if they saw no Chinese, that Buddy's group had cleared the way.

Moving cautiously around a rocky outcrop, he saw the Sisters bunched together at a small opening in the rocks. Buddy was in front looking through the opening. Hankins was behind. He was holding a strange looking rocket launcher. To Hankin's left, in a small open area, Jacques saw a number of boxes of ammunition including what looked like rocket ammunition.

When Buddy saw Matt, he motioned him forward. As Matt passed him, Hankins held the rocket tube up and grinned. Matt grinned back. "We got a little 'heavy artillery' if we need it need it," said the Marine rocketeer.

When Matt reached the opening, Buddy moved aside and motioned Matt to look. Matt slid into the opening, which was only big enough for one person to pass through at a time.

Matt could see the road. The bridge across a gully had been blown. The sides of the wash were four or five feet high where the bridge had been. From what Matt could see, the canyon opening was very narrow also.

Across the road, Matt saw a squad-sized unit with machine guns and at least one rocket launcher. They were well covered by rocks and pieces of lumber, probably from the bridge. They were facing northeast, along the line of the road before it reached the turn to the south.

There were at least twenty enemy troops on this side of the road. They were facing a more northerly direction, covering the road before it turned toward the west and ran by the other enemy squad.

Stepping back, he looked around. This was not going to be an easy nut to crack. He motioned his men away and he pointed back around the big rock to the outpost area. They moved silently and he followed them. He left one of John's men behind to warn of anyone coming. He gathered Jacques, John and Buddy around him.

"I got an idea. If you guys got anything better, let me know." He looked at their grimy unshaven faces. John and Jacques just nodded. Buddy said, "Hankins says he's got two of the gook rocket launchers and some rounds. He was ransacking the gook's boxes. They're a little smaller than ours are, but we know how to work them. You can include them in your plan."

"Good. I know just where to put them." An idea was formulating.

Picking up a stick, he wiped a small area clear of snow and started to draw the terrain features. First he drew the road which came down from the north. "I saw at least thirty gooks. There's about a dozen across the road, here." He drew a line to the left of the road. "They got machine guns and at least one rocket launcher. They are in a perfect spot to cut down any troops or vehicles that make the turn and come down the road. The bridge is out." He drew the bridge. "Any attacker will get bunched up there. It's a shooting gallery for the gooks. There's about fifteen or twenty on this side that I could see. The way they're set up, there's got to be another ten or fifteen I couldn't see. They're facing up the north part of the road."

Matt looked around to see if they were following him. There were no questions.

"Here's my idea." He looked at John. "John, you take your squad to this gully here." He drew a line to show the runoff gully. "It's high enough, you ought to be able to sneak up to about here, and then snoop and poop out of there across the road to the west to a spot right behind the Chinese squad on that side. There seems to be a little ridge here," he pointed, "which should hide you until your set."

John nodded.

"You got a grenade launcher and Willy Peter?"

"Yeah. I got a launcher." John turned to one of his men. "You got the two white phosphorous grenades still?"

"Yeah I still got 'em. I got a launcher too, and, some rounds." He held up the thin metal tube and two brass cartridges.

Matt smiled. "Good. I'll get back to you in a minute. Buddy?"

"Yo."

"You sneak your men up the gully behind John's men. When he crosses the road you continue in the gully to a spot where you can see both sides. That should be about here." He drew a dot between the two enemy positions. Take the machine gun with you."

He turned to the big Frenchman. "Jacques, you take your men up to the opening in the wall where we looked through and wait. You know where I mean?"

"Yes, mon ami,. I know. What comes next?"

Matt took a deep breath. So much had to fall into place to make this work. "John's squad will have the honors of the first shot." He looked again at his brother, so young but so talented. "When everyone is set, you launch a Willy Peter grenade into the enemy's position." He turned to McAndrew. "As soon as the grenade bursts, Buddy you launch two rockets into the same position. Try to hit someone important, like a machine gun or a rocket man. This has to be fast. You need to reload right away.

Buddy nodded. He was fascinated by the plan thus far.

"John, as soon as the rockets are launched, get up and charge. Hopefully their heads will be down and they'll be confused. The WP and the rockets should mess things up a bit. Also, you're coming in from behind. That should be a surprise. We're counting on you to take that position fast. When you have secured the spot, spread out and start firing into the main position across the road. That means you should be firing at their side, flanking fire."

John was excited. His men had been watching. It was obvious that they liked the plan.

"Buddy, have your riflemen set up, so that as soon as the first WP goes off they start to fire into the position on the *right*. Use the machine gun, too. As soon as the rockets fire their rounds to the left, have them reload and start to fire to the right."

"We're going to be a base of fire for both sides. Interesting," said Anderson as he leaned over Buddy to look at the "map."

"Exactly," said Matt. "Jacques?

"Mon ami?"

"As soon as, John's people start to fire at the main position, you will move your men through the slot in the rocks and assault from the rear. I will be with you."

"I suppose you want us to lift fire at that time?" asked John dryly.

"No, Squirt, just keep firing. Just be sure you have plenty of ammo because I will be attacking you next." He snapped at John with a grin.

"I guess we should lift fire, too," Buddy said turning to Masucci.

"All things considered, I think that would be a good idea," said Masucci.

Matt looked at the two rocketeers angrily at first, and then smiled. Then he laughed. It was all gallows humor at its finest.

They spent the next five minutes organizing. Matt was pleased by the reaction to his plan. He was scared to death it wouldn't work however. He couldn't shake the feeling of gloom that hovered over him, but he also couldn't come up with a better idea.

They moved back to the area in the rocks, behind the ammo boxes. John and his squad were standing in front of the opening checking each other's gear. Matt walked over and grabbed John and hugged him. Then he turned to face all his men.

"No matter what happens next, we've got to win this battle. Both regiments are counting on us." He looked at his crew with pride. "I don't know what you fight for — love, or friendship, or honor, or what — but add necessity to it. We've got to win." He looked at the dirty, shabby group. Their grime was only superficial. He liked what he saw, determination, eagerness, anger and more. They would do the job...and do it well.

Matt turned back to John. "Give the bastards hell, Squirt," he whispered.

John was moved by his brother's short speech. He started to salute! Then he caught himself and smiled. Turning quickly, he led the way through the cut in the rocks and down the slope into the gully. His men followed eagerly. Matt watched them go. His throat ached. First Luke, then Mark. His sense of dread returned.

Buddy came forward with his men. Matt clapped him on the back and said "Good hunting," his eyes tearing. The red-headed corporal smiled and said, "That was a good speech, my friend. I wish I could talk like that. We'll get it done." Matt watched them go down the slope and disappear into the gully too. It never got easy, sending men into combat.

Ivan approached and put his arm around Matt, a rare gesture for the normally stoic warrior. "I too have some troublesome feelings about what we are about to do, what lies before us."

How did he know I was having bad feelings, thought Matt? We were just talking about winning battles and he zeroes in on my subconscious thoughts.

"But I think your plan is good. The men like it. They want to win. It will work."

Matt looked into the black man's eyes. There was so much more there than Ivan ever let on. "I'm not as worried about the plan as I am about John," he said softly. His throat aching again.

"I know. He will be okay. My feelings are . . . I don't know how to say it . . . about more than John or the plan. The plan will work . . . but then?"

"I have those feelings too."

Matt looked up and saw Lescoulie waving at him. He was standing at the one-person slot in the rocks. Matt went to him.

"John's squad is already across the road. They're crawling into position to attack. So far so good. Would you like a look?"

Matt slid into the opening. He saw that John's squad was indeed, almost ready. There was movement in the gully. He saw one rocket tube move past an open spot just below the top of the gully, then another to the left. He thought he saw the barrel of a machine gun a little further over. He looked around at the Chinese. They were all looking the other way. Up the road, he could hear a disturbance. Good old Colonel Baxter, he was doing something to keep the Reds attention forward. The plan was falling into place.

Matt pulled back behind the rock, gave Jacques the high sign, and smiled. Jacques smiled back. Jacques' men were all kneeling, bayonets at the ready, pressed against the rocks, waiting. Ivan was the last one. Matt's emotions stirred. He loved these men. They were real professionals. They knelt quietly, waiting for the word. They would do the job.

A "pop" sounded from across the road. Matt slipped back into the slot in time see the grenade burst in the air. Despite the deadliness of white phosphorous, the explosion was a beautiful thing to behold. The blast was a yellow-white flash followed by a blossom of white smoke and white hot tendrils shooting off in all directions, each carrying a piece of skin scorching white phosphorous.

Phosphorous burns through clothes and into skin in seconds, and it is difficult to extinguish. It must be smothered. It feeds on any form of oxygen, including the oxygen in water. The field expedient is to cover a wound with mud.

The Chinese squad at the barricade, disappeared in the smoke. A moment went by as the Marines waited for the smoke to clear, then from the gully came a "whoosh" followed by a second "whoosh" an instant later. Two explosions, caused by the fiery rockets followed instantly. The Reds in front of Matt began to scramble for position as they shifted to face an unexpected enemy on their left. A machine gun opened up on them, quickly joined by rifle and BAR fire from Buddy's people. A number of the enemy were caught in the open and went down before the sheets of hot lead.

Across the road, Matt could see Marines running and jumping into the rocky trench line behind the barricade. They had their bayonets clipped on and, between the rattle of gunfire, he could hear the rebel yells. They ran in and out of the plumes of smoke from the grenade and rocket explosions. The fighting was hand-to-hand in places. Some of the other Chinese tried to flee and were cut down. One rolled on the ground attempting to extinguish a smoldering piece of metal on his back. A Marine ran a bayonet through him. Within minutes, the position was taken. Matt could see John directing some of his men to fire on the main position. He was using two men to move among the downed Reds, making sure they were dead. Good thinking.

The fire into the main position was murderous. Rockets whooshed, the machine gun and the BARs roared, rifles barked. Matt saw no living Chinese but he also couldn't see the whole position. He stepped back from the opening.

"It's going great, so far. Flaraty took his spot and he and Buddy are pouring it into the main position."

Lescoulie's men were all smiles.

"You ready?"

They all stood, raised their weapons and roared their frustrations.

"Jacques, go get the bastards."

Jacques roared "Vive le Corps," and pushed into the opening

They leaped toward the opening, impatiently waiting for those in front to squeeze through. Ivan was the last in line in front of Matt. Just as he disappeared into the slot, Matt felt a sharp pain in his shoulder. He stumbled forward, stunned A piece of stone chipped off the rock and hit him in the face, drawing blood. He heard a crack go over his head. He fell to a knee and instinctively dove to the ground and rolled to his right. He turned to see where the fire was coming from. Another round hit his left hand, instantly numbing it. His glove flew off. Blood welled up in his palm.

He lay on the ground facing the ammo boxes. Red soldiers were pouring through the opening John and Buddy had used earlier. Chinese reinforcements! He had looked down the road just before they left and had seen no sign of any Communist troops. Now he saw at least a half dozen men and more crowding behind them. He was in a tough spot. Their presence could disrupt the whole attack.

He rolled again, this time to his left and brought his rifle up to a firing position. His left shoulder and bloody hand made it difficult, but he accomplished the feat by sheer determination. He fired two rounds and two Reds went down. He saw another fumbling with a grenade. He rose to a knee and fired one handed from a kneeling position. The soldier fell backwards, the grenade tumbling from his hand. His mates scrambled to get out of the way. Matt fired at one of them and then the grenade went off, killing him and two others. He saw more Chinese moving up to the opening.

Matt now had a moment to gather himself. He ran to his left front so as to place himself against a wall of rock behind an outcrop. The Reds would have to come around the outcrop to get him. One of them did. Matt, his left arm hanging almost useless, shot from the hip. The Communist soldier fell, but three more of his compatriots came around the outcrop and fired at him. Matt raised his weapon, fired two rounds, one missed, the other didn't. One of the Reds fired a round that clipped Matt's right ear. He winced with pain. More important however was that when Mat fired his last shot he heard the ping, as the spent clip ejected from the rifle's chamber. His rifle was empty. It was bayonet time. But he couldn't lift his arm.

Matt stood defiantly waiting for the coup d' grace. Five Red soldiers now stood in front of him. One of them raised his weapon. He never got to fire it.

A dark, roaring, screaming "nightmare" swinging a battle-axe with both hands, smashed into them from behind. They stumbled forward. With one sweep of his mighty arms, he slashed three of the soldiers, decapitating two. A third soldier's head hung by a few tendons. Landing on the remainder, he pinned them with his knees and quickly drove the axe, first into one head, and then the other.

Bouncing up, he looked at Matt and smiled. "You owe me, Matthew. If we were in my country, you would be my slave forever."

Matt smiled weakly. He couldn't speak.

Ivan's expression changed suddenly as he saw the wounds. "I did not realize you were hurt so bad." He looked around. There was a momentary lull in the enemy attack. They could hear that their platoon attack was still in progress.

"Ivan, they're coming in by the opening behind the ammo boxes." Matt's voice was almost a whisper. "You've got to stop them. They could screw up our whole plan. I will try to help." He sagged down to a knee.

"I will stop them, Matthew. You stay here." With that Ivan was off to the opening.

Matt struggled to his feet again. He had to help. It would be more than one man could handle, even Ivan. He stumbled forward. He could see the opening and more Reds were coming through. Ivan was swinging the axe as each one entered. He was a raging demon to those soldiers but they kept coming.

One of them, tucked behind another soldier who was losing his head to the axe, managed to pump a few rounds from a burp gun into Ivan's stomach. Ivan's knees buckled, but then he straightened and slew a few more soldiers, including the one who shot him. He was magnificent. A black avenger, swinging an axe, a throwback to another age. And, he smiled the whole time he fought.

Matt stumbled toward his friend, gaining strength as he moved. He managed to raise his rifle as he went and just as three more Reds emerged he stood beside the Zulu.

The first Red through moved to Matt's right. Matt did a quick stutter step, and then lunged at the man's head. His bayonet sunk into the soldier's face. Matt yanked his blade free and swung to his left. His hand, where he had been shot, was a mass of blood and almost useless but it was frozen to the rifle stock, enabling him to hold the weapon and use it as a deadly tool. The pain was enormous, but Matt fought through it.

Ivan had cut one of the Reds in the shoulder. He was a little late pulling his blade out. Another Red slipped his bayonet into Ivan's side. Ivan winced and them using a backhand stroke, he slashed the Red at the throat. He fell, gushing blood.

The wounded warriors stood back to catch their breath. Two more Reds came out of the gap. Matt banged one in the head with a horizontal butt stoke, the other fell to Ivan's axe.

"We are a team, Matthew. No on can beat us." Ivan roared almost joyously through the pain.

"I don't know Ivan, I think we would be better off with some help."

They were fighting on adrenaline. Later, others would say, the wounds they had would have laid out nine hundred and ninety-nine men out of a thousand. They both had bullets in their bodies. They both had useless arms, which they used anyway. They both were losing blood.

Now they stood, side by side drawing on each other's strength. They had to win. They couldn't let the platoon down. Others would liken this to the pass at Thermopolae. They were the brave Spartans stemming the Persian hordes.

More Chinese came through the opening. The wounded warriors cut them down. They took more hits. They cut down all comers, some by axe some by bayonet. Their strength was ebbing, but they still fought. And then, just as at the pass of Thermopolae, they were out-flanked. A contingent of Chinese had found a way to get behind them.

Before either of them could react, a hail of bullets snapped around them, most missing them, but a few hitting the mark. They each sank to their knees. The bullets also hit some of the Reds coming into the slot in front of the two warriors, but it didn't slow them. One came at Ivan with his bayonet, while Ivan was struggling to stand. Matt lunged at him. Using the force of the man's rush to impale him on the bayonet. His rifle stuck in the Chinese soldier and was jerked from his hand, tearing the frozen flesh. Matt screamed in pain. The man stumbled into Ivan, knocking him over. One of the other Reds jammed his bayonet into the fallen Zulu.

Matt tried to stand. He couldn't. He saw his friend on the ground, and he screamed again, this time in anger. He crawled to him.

One of the enemy soldiers moved to shoot him, but a red spot suddenly appeared on his forehead and he fell over dead. A bullet hole.

There was a crescendo of fire behind the Chinese, then a large number of pissed off leathernecks were running at them. Matt looked up. Jacques was heading directly toward him, cutting a swath through Red soldiers with his rifle and bayonet. It was no contest. The big Frenchman was a madman released. Bodies flew, heads caved, and the enemy piled up at his feet.

At last Jacques was at their side. No one was left standing. The enemy was gone or dead. Marines ran by and headed into the opening. The remainder of the enemy force ran back down the road.

Matt had reached Ivan and he was cradling him in his arms. Tears ran down his cheeks. Jacques knelt down and watched helplessly. Ivan was a mass of wounds. Blood covered his face and spotted his parka in a hundred different places.

The Zulu prince still had a final spark left however. He opened his bullet eyes and with a faint smile, he looked at Matt and said, "I guess we were right about our feeling of doom, Matthew. We just didn't understand who it would be." He stiffened, then his face relaxed and the light disappeared from his magnificent eyes.

Jacques sat back on his heels, slumping as he did. He pulled Matt to him. Matt still clung to Ivan. He hugged them both, rocking and crying. Matt couldn't move. He knew he was going to die, too. He asked about John. Jacques sent for him. He held Matt, while Matt rambled on about honor and family. Perspiration dotted Matt's grimy unshaven face even in the extreme cold. His eyes didn't focus.

He shuddered when spasms of pain ran through his body. He talked about his friends and what they had gone through. He talked about Luke and Mark, his voice now a whisper. He wondered about John. John arrived and slid into position next to the three of them, fear and concern on his face.

"I'm here, Matt. I'm here."

Matt reached out with a trembling hand. He wanted to touch John, but he didn't want to let Ivan go. Finally, his fingers stroked John's face. He looked at his brother, pain wracking his body. Then he looked at Jacques.

"Take care of him Jacques . . . and Mark. . . ." His eyes pleaded.

"Yes, mon ami, Yes. I will take care of them."

He turned back to John. "Take care of Mom and Maggie, John. Talk to Mom about that last night. . . . Help her."

John was crying. He bent over and kissed his brother's cheek. Matt looked at him one last time, shuddered and then relaxed. The marvelous flame in those eyes went out, too. John lay down over both Matt and Ivan and wept.

The way for the two regiments was open. Matt's platoon had devastated the Chinese at the roadblock, killing forty-five at the block itself and another twenty-three at the ammo spot. They took twelve prisoners. When they reviewed the action at the battalion they felt the arrival of additional Chinese troops, while the attack was in progress, was a stroke of bad luck. With it all, the plan was sound. There were only a few Marine casualties and two deaths, Matt and Ivan.

The regiments were on the move again. They ran into a few more roadblocks but they swept those aside with ease. They fought no more big battles in the hills. Other small battles were fought before they reached Hagaru, but nothing of the magnitude of the last few days. It took the head of the column fifty-nine hours to travel the seventeen miles from Yudam-ni to Hagaru. It took the rear of the column seventy-four. The bubble had stretched, but it hadn't broken.

As the exhausted troops marched into the Hagaru perimeter, large numbers of officers and men from the First Regiment lined the road in welcome. Word of their accomplishments preceded them.

Father Canavan, who had made the excursion from Yudam-ni with the Fifth Marines, had stopped and was standing at the side of the road watching his "boys" go by. The rugged priest had been an inspiration to the men all along the "Vale of Tears" as he soothed, cajoled, comforted and nursed them. At one point he had covered some wounded Marines with his body to protect them from mortar blasts. At another, he had picked up a weapon to help. He was sore, hungry and tired but he loved these men and he wanted them to see him and to know that God was with them.

As he stood watching trucks pass with dead Marines strapped to the hood or fenders, he felt a chill. If at all possible, Marines didn't leave their dead behind, but seeing them transported that way was disheartening. The walking wounded, stoically bearing their wounds, shuffled along with them. His heart went out to these brave men. As he watched the grisly parade in a state of reverence, one of the corpsmen ran up to him.

"Padre, we're having a problem. Can you help us out?"

"Certainly, son. What's up?" Shaking himself from his reveries, he grabbed his pack, which he had placed at his feet, and looked at the young corpsman.

"Follow me, sir. One of the Marines is giving us trouble. The doctor thinks you can help."

Puzzled, the priest trailed after the messenger, to a place on the side of the road where a jeep was stopped. There were three dead bodies in the back, a wounded Marine slumped over in the passenger seat, and a filthy looking Marine in the driver's seat, leveling a submachine gun at the doctor. When the doctor saw Father Canavan, he backed away from the jeep and grabbed him.

"Father, thank God you're here. He's gone crazy. We need help," he said in a rush of words. Fatigue plainly showed on the doctor's face. "He says he won't give up his brothers to anyone but God." He glanced back at the jeep, fear showing in his eyes. "He actually stuck that gun in my face and told me to back off or he would shoot."

Canavan looked at the doctor and then back at the jeep. I guess I *am* needed, he thought. "Stay here, let me talk to him." The doctor nodded gratefully.

Father Canavan moved toward the jeep. A practical man, he removed his glove and reached up and pulled his shirt collar out of the bundle of clothing he wore. He wanted the boy in the jeep to be able to see the chaplains' cross.

As the priest approached the jeep, the driver made no overt moves. He watched the approaching figure, the Tommy gun resting on his lap.

Father Canavan stopped by the passenger side. He looked at the wounded Marine. He was sitting, slumped in the seat, breathing laboriously, his head lolled to one side. Father Canavan noticed that he was strapped to the seat

"I'm Father Canavan, son, the Chaplain. Can I help you?"

The driver looked at him but said nothing.

"Son, your buddy here, he needs medical attention. We have a hospital here. He'll be in good hands."

For the first time the driver showed some interest.

"Hospital? A real hospital?"

"Well. It's in a tent, but it's warm in there, and there are plenty of doctors and nobody's shooting at them. They can do a good job for your buddy." Father Canavan sensed the boy needed reassurance.

"Are you a priest, a Catholic priest?" He looked at the gold cross.

"Yes, I am. Are you Catholic?"

A tear appeared at the corner of one of the boy's eyes. "Yes I am." "You helped many men along the way. When I was looking for my brother, the wounded men all talked about you. You fought off some gooks who had slipped through the defenses."

Father Canavan was embarrassed. He wasn't proud of that moment. He had picked up a gun and fired at the Chinese who were shooting wounded Marines. He had killed a few. Priests don't kill people.

"Thank you, son." He hid his pain. "I'm glad I could help." There was a pause, then he asked, "Is this your brother?"

He kept looking at the Priest without any animation. Then he said, "Yes it is. His name is Mark. He was at an aid station, but they had too many wounded. They couldn't get to him, so I took him."

Father Canavan grieved for the boy. "Son, let the doctor here take him. He needs help bad. The doctor and the corpsmen will do their best. I promise you that."

The boy studied the priest for a moment and then nodded his head. There was immense pain in that face. Father Canavan motioned to the doctor and the corpsmen. They removed the wounded Marine. He was surprised when he saw the gold bar on the Marine's collar. The boy's brother was an officer.

The medical people loaded the lieutenant into an ambulance jeep and drove off.

"Before I go to see about your brother, what about you and the rest of these. . . ," he struggled with the word, "Marines . . . in your back seat? What are you going to do about them?"

The boy looked him vacantly for a moment and then said. "They're also my brothers. They were going to leave Luke up at Yudam-ni, but I found him and hid him in a truck. Matt was killed just yesterday . . . and Ivan. . . ."

"All these men are your brothers?" The priest looked into the back of the jeep. One of the bodies was in a bag on the floor. It was frozen into a grotesque shape that could still be seen through the bag. The other two rested on the back seat, one on top of the other. Father Canavan noted that one of the bodies appeared to be a Negro.

"Luke and Matt are my real brothers. Ivan was the same as a brother to me."

Father Canavan studied the boy's face for a moment and then broke into tears. "Son ... I feel so bad for you. You lost two brothers and your best friend and your other brother is hurt." Impulsively he climbed into the jeep and reached out to him. The boy responded and let his head fall into Father Canavan's lap. He sobbed bitterly. The priest told him about his own brother and he said a prayer for all their brothers.

The caravan of trucks and artillery and walking troops shuffled by barely noting the jeep by the side of the road. The overall mood was joy as the division was getting together again. Rest and hot meals and protection would be waiting.

After awhile, the boy raised his head. He looked up at the Priest with hollowed eyes and nodded. "Father, will you take my brothers and make sure God gets them?"

"I'm sure God already has them. " He realized he didn't know the boy's name. "What's your name, son?" Before the boy could answer, something occurred to him. The boy had said his brothers were Matt, Mark, and Luke. He ventured a question, "...It's not John, is it?"

John smiled for an instant. Only a priest would figure that out. "Yes Father" Then he was serious again. "Can I leave them in your hands, Father? I don't want to abandon them. Will you take them and see that they get to God?"

Father Canavan started to cry again. "Yes John. I'll take care of them." He made the sign of the cross over all of them.

26
Requiem

Katie watched from the window as the dark sedan drove down the dusty drive and out onto the highway. Mark was leaving, on his way to Virginia. She turned back to the kitchen and made herself a cup of tea. She then picked up the group of shiny flat boxes that were sitting on the sideboard, and brought them over to the table. After sitting down and sipping at her cup, Katie started fingering one of the small black lacquered cases. She turned it around a few times and then opened the lid. Inside, beautifully displayed against a black felt background, was a gold star suspended from a shiny pale blue ribbon. The ribbon was dotted with white stars. The star was mounted on a circle with the words "Medal of Honor" embossed on the ring. A beautiful engraved scroll, outlining the feats that occasioned the medal lay on the table. The name at the top of the scroll was Sergeant Matthew Flaherty.

Next to the scroll was another black box and another scroll. The name on this scroll said Corporal Ivan Spears. The young officer who had delivered the medals said that as best he could tell no two Marines had ever won Medals of Honor, simultaneously for the same action.

Jacques had actually received Ivan's medal from the Marine Corps. He had volunteered to deliver it to Ivan's family. He had asked Katie to hold it until he could make arrangements to go to Africa.

After Matt's death, the matter of his real identity had emerged. There was no longer any need to keep it quiet, and the records were finally corrected. He was memorialized by the people of Kingmont as a true hero, when they named a new town square after him. Later, there was to be a bronze statue of a charging Marine erected.

There were a number of smaller boxes also on the table. Katie opened each one and studied them. There were four purple hearts. Three were full size medals, the ones for Matt, Luke, and Ivan. Mark's was a miniature, a keepsake for his mother. Mark had to keep his actual medal for his dress uniform. There were two miniature gold crosses, suspended from navy blue and white ribbons for Mark and John. These also were replicas, this time of the Navy Cross, the second highest award for heroism. Mark and John had to keep the actual medals for this award too. There was also a full size Silver Star, on a red, white, and blue ribbon for Luke. The Silver Star was the third highest award for heroism.

Behind the medals was a white box filled with greeting cards. Katie opened the box and took one out.

It was white and showed a drawing of a stick-like figure carrying a Christmas tree through the snow toward a plain boxlike house. Although simple, the card was quite artistic. The design was Maggie's, selected for the Christmas card fundraising drive of the organization that helped Maggie with her handicap.

Katie took another sip of her tea and looked at her treasures. She leaned back in her chair. It had been good to see her boys again, even if it was only the two of them. She forced back a sob. And their big friend Jacques, what a wonderful man he was. He had spent hours telling her all the things he and Matt and Ivan had done over the last few years. He had her alternately, laughing, crying, and laughing again. She had hugged him and told him she was going to adopt him. He turned red, but said he felt honored.

Mark was so much thinner. He was able to walk but had to use a cane. He told her it would be another two months before he would be whole again. He was assigned to the Naval Hospital on Long Island for rehabilitation. He took leave so he could be home with her when the medals arrived. He had just left. He wanted to spend a few days in Norfolk before heading back to the hospital.

John and Jacques left the day before Mark did. John said he wanted to stop in LA to see a friend, before heading back to Camp Pendleton. Jacques had winked at her and rolled his eyes. It seemed John's friend was of the opposite sex.

Her baby, except for Maggie, had changed an enormous amount in the few months he was gone. He looked just like Matt only a little taller and a little more muscular. His body was lean but tough. It seemed to her, he had also developed a hard edge about him. Katie was little concerned about that, but she supposed that he needed some of that in combat.

How quiet the house seemed now. The last week had been like the old days in some ways, with all the activity. Now, she was lonely again.

Maggie would be home from school soon. That would help.

Katie looked out the window. The car was long gone now. She

would always have the pain of the loss of her two sons, but she felt better now that she had talked to Lieutenant McQuinn about that night, so long ago. The young man McQuinn had brought with him — Mister Rollins — yes, that's right, was an Assistant District Attorney. They told her she had nothing to fear. They also told her it was good she had told them about that night, to set the record straight.

There was one more thing to do — tomorrow.

She rose from her chair and roamed through the house, wandering aimlessly. Then she found herself in the living room. A thought occurred to her. She went over to her new record player, one that had an automatic record changer. She switched it on, reached into the cabinet, and took out a record. She placed it on the turntable and pushed the play button. She turned, placed her shawl around her shoulders, and sat in her rocking chair. She heard the changer mechanism whirring, a scratch and then silence. The next sound she heard was a clear female voice singing.

Oh, Danny Boy, the pipes, the pipes are calling,
From glen to glen and down the mountainside.
The summers come and all the roses fallen.
It's you, it's you must go, and I must bide.

Oh, come ye back when summers in the meadow.
Or when the valley's white with snow.
It's I'll be there in sunshine or in shadow.
Oh, Danny Boy, Oh, Danny Boy. I love you so.

But when ye come and all the flowers are dying.
If I am dead, and dead I well may be.
You'll come and find the place where I am lying
And kneel and say an Ave there for me.

And I shall hear your so soft tread above me.
And all my grave warmer, sweeter, it shall be.
For you will bend and tell me that you love me.
And I shall sleep in peace until you come to me.

It was quiet in the church. The late afternoon sun slanted through the stained glass windows and projected elongated shards of multicolored light on the marble walls and tiled floors. Gothic pillars soared to a vaulted ceiling. Votive candles flickered eerily in front of the side altars. One of them honored Saint Joseph, with a large statue of Jesus' earthly father. The candles at this altar were in small red containers. The other was dedicated to Mary, Jesus' mother. The votive lights were blue.

There were also votive candles at the communion railing in front of the main altar. The lights were red, white and blue, a carryover from World War II, when Catholics lit candles for their servicemen, red for Army, blue for Navy, and white for the Marines.

Katie knelt in a pew halfway down the aisle, a full-size marble statue of Jesus Christ on the cross in front of her. The cross was placed so that the crucified Son of God could be seen from anywhere in the church. The feet of the statue were worn from the hands and lips that had stroked them.

Katie looked at the figure above her as tears trickled down her cheeks. The doughty widow had been reviewing and rereviewing her situation. She had done the things she had to do, the honorable things. Now, Katie had to do the hardest thing. She had to reconcile with the Lord.

She had lost two sons. Was this her punishment for her sin? It couldn't be. As a mother, she had done the right thing, hadn't she? Maggie had to be considered, as did the boys. Also, her body was a sanctuary that shouldn't have been violated. Was she wrong about that? Surely God wouldn't punish her for a bad decision. Did he work this way, punishing people for mistakes? Katie didn't think so. That was not the God she believed in. Still, she would feel better if she could talk it out.

Katie looked around at the familiar surroundings. She had asked Father Rafferty to come for confession early so she could to be alone with him. He said he would be there at quarter of four. It was almost that now.

Looking up at the man on the cross again, she sobbed quietly. Christ had suffered too, for mankind's sins. It was really God on the cross, the second person of the Trinity, but it looked like a man. Christ's mother had grieved also. She, too, had lost a son. Katie's doubts flooded back.

A door opened near the main altar. Switches clicked and a few lights went on in the church. A shadow emerged from the sacristy and started down the side aisle. The shadow wore a cassock and a biretta. It was Father Raferty.

Katie watched as he stopped by a door in the wall and opened it. A tiny light went on in the small room. He stepped in and closed the door. A red light over the confessional blinked on.

Katie stood up, blessed herself and moved out of the pew. She walked down the center aisle to the rear of the church, across the back and up the left walkway. She was conscious of her heels clicking on the polished tile. When she reached the confessional, she parted the curtains on one side, slid into the box and knelt on the padded kneeler. The light in the priest's compartment went out and a small door slid open near Katie's face.

"Bless me, Father, for I have sinned. It has been three years since my last confession." She held her breath. By the rules of the church you were supposed to go to communion at least once a year and that usually meant going to confession, too. She waited for the Priest to say something. He surprised her.

"Welcome back, Katherine." He knew it had been a long time.

Katie marshaled her strength and continued. "Father, I have some things to confess. It was three years ago. Can I do it my own way and not use the formal way of confessing?" A hint of the old brogue touched her tongue.

"Certainly Katherine. The formal way is just a guide. Say what you want to say."

Katie breathed easier. "He used to beat me, Father. Wilhelm, not Mike. Mike was a wonderful man. In any case, Van Scooten used to beat me."

Father Rafferty had suspected as much. "Continue, Katherine. I'm still listening."

"He also. . . ." She was a little concerned about how to say this to a priest. "He used to make me do bad things in the bedroom . . . things I didn't want to do."

"I understand, Katherine. You don't have to go into detail. If you didn't want to do them and he made you, there is no sin on your part."

She had thought that to be true, but it was good to hear it from the priest. "I moved out of his bedroom twice, but then later I moved back in. Was I wrong to do that father?"

"I don't think it was sinful, Katherine. But I'm unclear why you would want to do it. If he beat you and made you do things you didn't want to do, why did you go back?"

"I was afraid, Father, afraid of him. Afraid of what he might do to me and to Maggie."

"How awful for you Katherine. It would have been better if you had told someone," he gently chided. "Didn't Matt come home one time when you had trouble and help you out? I mean the time before he came home the last time."

How did he know that? The police of course. Lieutenant McQuinn must have told him. "Yes Father. He was very helpful. After that Will and I had no problems for a long time, but Wilhelm was very spiteful. He did lots of little things to annoy me. He was afraid to do anything real bad but there was lots of . . . of . . . smaller things."

"You don't need to discuss it if it bothers you, Katherine."

"No. No, I need to talk it out, Father. Please bear with me."

"Certainly."

"He would stay out late after he told me he'd be home. He would come home smelling of perfume. He would tell me other women liked his body but I didn't. He told me I was a cold woman. I was dried up." Her voice caught for a moment. "He said Maggie should be put in a home. He said thousands of mean and hurtful things. He would make sure my checking account ran out of money, so I would write bad checks. Then he would pay them and let the merchant feel like I was something . . . somebody . . . without a brain."

"What a horrible life. Did you tell anyone about this, like Matt?"

She was quiet for a moment, then she whispered, "No, Father, I told no one, especially Matt."

"Forgive me Katherine, the answers to these questions help me understand better."

Katie nodded. He couldn't see her in the darkness of the confessional, but he knew that she had nodded. He heard someone enter the church. He looked at his watch. It was almost four. Other people would be arriving soon to go to confession. They could wait. He would stay with Katherine as long as she needed.

"Katherine, why didn't you tell Matt?"

"He would have killed Wilhelm, Father. I didn't want that on either of our souls."

"Oh Katherine. That's such a burden to bear."

"Father, when Matt came home the first time and had his confrontation with Wilhelm, he threatened to kill him if he ever did anything bad to any of us."

Father Rafferty chewed on that for a while, then asked. "Why did Matt threaten to kill him? I have the impression, forgive me, that you had been holding everything in, you hadn't told anyone. What got Matt so mad?"

Katie started to cry. "He broke into our room when Wilhelm was in one of his rages." She had finally gotten it out. "He saw the abuse for himself."

"My Lord, Katherine. How horrible. Did he attack your husband?"

"Yes. He beat him to a pulp." She paused and sobbed softly. " I think if I hadn't stopped him, Matt would have killed Wilhelm that night."

The priest sat back. There were more people in the church, but no one had slid into the other side of the confessional box yet. If someone did, they would have to speak more quietly.

"Before he went back to the Naval Academy," she continued. "He warned Wilhelm that he would kill him if he hurt any of us again. Wilhelm believed him. That's why things were better for a while."

"But, then the finale. You're leading up to the last incident aren't you, the night Wilhelm ... died?"

"Yes," she said quietly.

There was a pause. She didn't seem to want to continue. Then the priest asked, "Did, Matt catch him again . . . uh . . . doing something. . . ?"

"No," she said so softly he almost couldn't hear her, "Maggie did."

"Maggie . . . that sweet. . . ." He fumbled for control of his emotions. The Irish outrage at a child wronged almost overcame his Godly principles. "Maggie saw . . . his goings on?"

"No, Father. She didn't see them. He kept the door locked. She heard them. She tried to get in. John and Luke heard her. They asked what the problem was. She told them what she had heard."

Strong emotions raged within the priest, but he finally got his voice under control. "Did John or Luke do anything?"

"At that point, I didn't know they knew. They discussed it first and decided they needed to call Matt."

"And that's when Matt came home and. . . ."

"Yes," she said softly. "That's when Matt came home. Now he's gone. Is God punishing me for my sins, Father?" She blurted out. "He took Matt and Luke. Is that to be my cross?"

"No, Katherine. God doesn't work that way. Besides, you have no sin Katherine. I'm sure God will understand Matt's state of mind and will forgive or excuse him for what he did, but you have no sin."

Katie looked up sharply. He was getting the wrong message. She could see Father Rafferty's face dimly through the screen. "Father, that's what I have been trying to tell you. Matt didn't kill Wilhelm ... I did."

Father Rafferty was stunned.

"I saw Matt coming across the lawn. I knew Maggie must have told him somehow. I could tell by his stride. I knew why he was at the house. He was coming to kill Wilhelm." Katie was crying again. "Wilhelm had just knocked me into the night stand. I was afraid for Matt. I was angry with Wilhelm. I had put a knife in the night stand months before. I grabbed it and . . . and. . . ."

They both sat in silence for a while. Someone slid into the other side of the confessional. Finally Father Rafferty moved close to the screen and said softly. "There is someone in the other box. Katherine, we need to speak quietly."

She edged closer to the screen.

"Katherine" the priest whispered. "All these years and you let the world think that Matt. . . . Why?"

"It was what Matt wanted. He wanted to protect me and Maggie and the rest of the family. He felt if the word got out that I . . . well . . . there would be a scandal. The Van Scootens could take away all we had. Maggie would have to go into a home. That I might have to go into jail." She started to cry again. "We talked for an hour, about everything, including claiming self-defense. But that might be hard to prove, especially with the high-powered lawyers the Van Scootens could hire. So I agreed. I thought that maybe all Matt would have to do was go away for a few years and then come back and everything would be okay." She cried quietly for a moment, then continued. "I was wrong about that . . . and we have both paid the price."

"Katherine … Katherine …you've had a terrible time."

She lifted her head and moved it close to the screen. "Can the Lord forgive me Father?"

"I'm still not sure there is any sin here, Katherine, but the answer is yes. The only sin God can't forgive is the sin of despair. If you truly believe the sin you committed is so horrible that God can't forgive you, that's despair. Remember Judas? His most grievous sin was not that he betrayed the Lord. It was the fact that he hanged himself. That was despair. God could forgive the betrayal, not the despair. You don't feel that way, do you Katherine?"

"No, I guess not. When I did it, it seemed to be right. I now know it was wrong, but. . . ."

"Katherine, are you sorry you did it?"

"Yes, Father. Truly sorry."

The priest gently flowed into the formal words of the confessional. "Are you sorry for this and all the sins of your past life?"

"Yes, I am."

The Priest leaned forward and whispered, "Ego te absolve . . . a peccatis tuis in nomini, Patri, et Fili, et Spiritu Sancto, Amen." The Latin words of forgiveness. He made the sign of the cross.

Charles R. "Chuck" Dowling

Mr. Dowling spent ten years as a Marine officer serving both on active duty and as a Reserve during the cold war. He has also been a sales manager, marketing executive and a management consultant. He has lived in a number of places in the U.S. and traveled extensively here and abroad. He presently works in the employee benefit field, teaching insurance continuing education classes and writing novels in his free time. The novel *To Keep Our Honor Clean* is one of a planned four book series on the Korean War. He has one other book in the series completed, and a third almost finished.

He presently resides in Florida, in the Orlando area. Happily married, he is the father of two sons and a daughter. He also has four wonderful grandchildren.